"*Godfall* is the genre-mashup novel of my dreams. With breathtaking imagery and razor-sharp prose, Van Jensen gives us a story that is part alien sci-fi, part mystery—with a doomsday cult, a serial killer, and a dash of sandhill cranes—all set against the beautiful backdrop of rural Nebraska."
—ERIN FLANAGAN, Edgar Award–winning author of *Deer Season* and *Blackout*

"*Godfall* blends rural noir with a daring dose of sci-fi to create something wholly new and engaging. Van Jensen comes in hot with his [fiction] debut."
—ALEX SEGURA, author of *Secret Identity* and *Miami Midnight*

"It isn't easy to infuse magical realism with grit, but *Godfall* does it with panache. I was under Van Jensen's spell from the first chapter. A striking debut novel from one of my favorite writers."
—KEVIN MAURER, coauthor of *No Easy Day* and author of *Damn Lucky*

GODFALL

FLYOVER FICTION

SERIES EDITOR: RON HANSEN

GOD FALL

VAN JENSEN

UNIVERSITY OF NEBRASKA PRESS | LINCOLN

The University of Nebraska Press
is part of a land-grant institution
with campuses and programs
on the past, present, and future
homelands of the Pawnee, Ponca,
Otoe-Missouria, Omaha, Dakota,
Lakota, Kaw, Cheyenne, and
Arapaho Peoples, as well as those
of the relocated Ho-Chunk, Sac
and Fox, and Iowa Peoples.

Library of Congress
Cataloging-in-Publication Data
Names: Jensen, Van, author.
Title: Godfall / Van Jensen.
Description: Lincoln: University
of Nebraska Press, [2023] |
Series: Flyover fiction
Identifiers: LCCN 2023005951
ISBN 9781496235213 (paperback)
ISBN 9781496238085 (epub)
ISBN 9781496238092 (pdf)
Subjects: BISAC: FICTION /
Science Fiction / Crime & Mystery |
LCGFT: Science fiction. | Detective
and mystery fiction. | Novels.
Classification: LCC PS3610.E5663
G63 2023 | DDC 813/.6—dc23/
eng/20230421
LC record available at https://
lccn.loc.gov/2023005951

Set and designed in
Adobe Text by N. Putens.

For Doreen.
—V.J.

GODFALL

BEFORE

Under the moonlight, the pool of blood shone black. David squatted and peered into the yard-wide void rent into the dirt and scrub brush. It seemed deep, like he could fall in and tumble through the earth, spit out in China, Australia. Wherever the hell is as far away from Nebraska as a man can get.

"Sheriff. Which way you figure she went?"

David stood on a knee that stiffened when the weather turned frigid, a reminder of a torn meniscus suffered during a high school football game a decade and change earlier. His muscular build made itself known even under his thick, brown coat, which had the words "Sheriff's Department" stenciled in yellow across the back. He stood an inch shy of six feet, though the black Stetson on his head made him seem taller. He wore blue jeans, as he always did. The wind lashed at him, needles against his face. Just his goddamned luck that someone would do this on a night so cold.

He clicked on his flashlight, and the pool of blood burned to life. To the side, Gentry Luwendyke stood with his arms crossed against a sheepskin coat. A puff of exhalation issued from below his unruly mustache, then was whisked away by the punishing February wind.

David carved slow arcs with the flashlight. Some ten yards away, the light caught a smear of red.

"This way, it looks like," David said.

David led the way from one spatter to the next, each splash of blood smaller than the last, moving in a mostly straight line toward the dark rim of trees along the field's western edge. Frost clung to the grass and prairie sage, which crunched like broken glass beneath their boots. By the time they reached a copse of cedars and Russian olives, the trail had diminished to single drops.

A rage was building in David's stomach, combusting until he felt its heat beneath his coat; he was sweating, despite the cold. Someone did this. Someone would have to pay. He clenched the flashlight. No. Not now, he told himself. He could be angry later. Now he needed to focus on the task at hand. Where had she gone?

"There."

David saw her first, lying on her side amid a clearing. She seemed dead, till her chest rose and deflated, and a ghostly plume floated from her nostrils. He leaned over her, careful not to step in the blood running across the ground. David set the flashlight in the grass facing her and pulled off his gloves.

"Sons of bitches," Gentry hissed.

"Rifle shot. Hit her here," David said, tracing his hands along the soft fur of the cow's abdomen.

Into her intestines. Lord knows what organs it hit; she was fading fast.

"Sons of bitches," Gentry repeated, louder.

Suddenly the heifer snorted and spasmed. Her legs thrashed to find a footing. David fell backward and scrambled away as she pounded her hooves, almost righting herself. Then she stumbled and collapsed.

They inched back closer.

"She don't need to suffer no more," Gentry said.

"She doesn't," David agreed.

"I'll do it. My cow."

Gentry's eyes were on the Glock nine-millimeter pistol holstered on David's right hip. David clicked open the leather strap and drew the weapon, cold as hell in his hand.

"No. I can't have anyone else using my firearm. Regulations."

He stepped over the cow's head. She was breathing hard, a froth of mucus and blood bubbling from her nose and mouth. Her obsidian eyes pleaded with him, uncomprehending of the pain inside her, the chaos of the world, the horror of life and the even greater horror of whatever lies beyond it. David had no answers. He rested the barrel against her temple and fired.

|||

The truck rumbled over the rutted dirt road. Under the moon's glow, David could just as well leave his headlights off. The roads ran straight east-west, north-south, a grid carved into the countryside. He'd spent most all of his thirty years here and knew every washout, every curve, every blind lane. And since being elected sheriff three years prior, he knew far too much about what happened inside the farmhouses at the end of each lane.

As he drove, he walked through what he knew. Gentry heard rifle shots. He went out and saw a truck with a spotlight in the pasture. Then he found the blood. Gentry swore someone did it on purpose, a neighbor with an old grudge. Whether there were people in Little Springs who despised Gentry Luwendyke was not in question. That any of those people would gut-shoot a cow was unlikely.

More likely someone had been out with a case of Pabst or Old Milwaukee sliding around the floorboards, trespassing, searching with the spotlight, hoping a doe or buck might spook. David had done it himself when he was young and dumb. Drink enough beers, a distant cow could look like a deer.

There were six trucks in town with a spotlight. Four belonged to people who didn't have the capacity for such shit-headedness. The fifth belonged to the Johnsons, and their boy might have it in him, but the family was off visiting grandparents in the Ozarks. That left one truck, and David knew where he'd find it.

He pulled onto the two-lane highway, which ran east and west parallel to the Platte River. Ahead, the lights of town twinkled. At the foot of towering grain elevators, a green sign declared: "Little Springs Pop. 731." Every decade after the census, there would be a new sign, the population ticking lower and lower.

David turned onto Main Street, a stretch of cracked pavement wide enough for six lanes, made to accommodate the horse-drawn wagons that, a century back, rolled into town each weekend bringing farmers and their crops. On either side, barren brick storefronts had windows covered with plywood. At the far end, a water tower rose up. Years back, the village council had decided to paint it for every season, something to bring a little cheer. But they abandoned the effort soon after, leaving the tower as a massive, leering jack-o'-lantern.

One storefront remained open, its neon sign glowing: Vic's. David scanned the vehicles parked out front. There. A blue Dodge jacked up on oversized tires, a roll bar above the cab with a spotlight attached.

He parked beside it and peered through the truck's window. Crushed beer cans on the floor. A rifle on a rack in the rear window. He tested the door. Open.

David reached below the bench seat and fished out a box of ammunition. A few rounds were missing. He took one, dropped it in his pocket, and headed inside.

Vic's was one room straight back. Bar on the right. A few booths on the left. Two pool tables. Neon beer advertisements and pendant fixtures with mismatched bulbs cast a cacophony of color across the clouds of cigarette smoke. The usual crowd. Overalls and denim, people mostly heavyset, their skin parched and cracked, either from nicotine or the constant wind or both. At the center of the bar, a thickly built man with close-cropped blond hair looked up at the sound of David entering and spun toward him.

"Hey hey! A beer for our sheriff!"

"Hey, cousin," David answered, easing up to the bar beside him.

Vic, the bartender, pushed forward a bottle of Bud Light and a shot glass of whiskey before David could wave him off.

"I'm on duty."

"Fair enough," Jason said, grinning his usual shit-eating grin. "Well, ain't any problems in here, I'm happy to report."

To the other side of Jason was Spady, his black hair poking out from beneath a Nebraska Huskers ball cap, thick stubble dotting his ashen face. Spady wasn't kin, but he'd grown up close enough with David and Jason that he might as well have been. Spady puffed at a Marlboro held in his left hand, then balanced it on an ash tray before using the same hand to lift his bottle of Bud to drink. His right shirt sleeve was pinned at the elbow, where his arm ended. He'd worked railroad crew since high school until the accident, and now nothing but disability pay stretched out before him.

"Big case?" Spady asked.

David realized his hand was still shaking from firing his pistol. He smiled and shook his head.

"Nothing much."

Jason reached for the beer and shot, but David grabbed his wrist.

"Give me a minute. I might just wrap this case up right quick."

Across from the bar, three young men huddled in a booth. He'd seen one of them eyeing him from the moment he stepped inside. David approached them, looming in the way that only those who wear a badge can. They were local kids, kids he'd known since they were in diapers. Two of them—Andy Watkins and Tyrell Taylor—stared, unblinking, into their phones. The third, the one who had been watching David, was Derrick Mews. He looked up smugly. The blue Dodge was his, a fancy truck for a rich kid.

"Sheriff Blunt," Derrick said. "Need to check my license? I'm legal. No more minor-in-possession citations."

"I know how old you all are, Derrick."

The Mews boy was a born asshole who tied firecrackers to cats' tails and spray-painted genitals all over the Old River Bridge. But because he was the only son of Harold and Donna Mews, owners of the feed lot and what passed for wealthy in Little Springs, Derrick always skated.

"How long have you been here?" David asked.

"A while," Derrick shrugged.

With no warning, David pounded his fist on the table hard enough to rattle glasses and earn stares from the bar.

His arms trembled as a wave of rage surged through him. It wasn't just the act itself but what it meant. This town was just barely holding together, and one incident like this could have whole families at war, everyone taking sides, till the whole damn town splintered.

"Jesus," Tyrell said, looking up from his phone. "What?"

"I asked how long you've been here. And 'a while' isn't half specific enough," David warned.

Andy had already fallen back into staring at his phone.

"What does it matter?" he almost whispered. "We're all gonna die anyway."

"The hell is he talking about?"

"Nothing," Derrick said. "This bullshit on the internet. Some weird asteroid is going to hit and kill us all. They think everything on Reddit is real."

"It isn't bullshit," Andy muttered.

David waved them off. "I don't give a shit. The only thing I care about is that some dumb sons of bitches drove onto Luwendyke's land to hunt deer. Except, these dumb sons of bitches were too drunk or too dumb to know better, so instead of a deer, they shot one of Gentry's heifers. It died."

Derrick glanced nervously at his friends, then recovered.

"That is a sad story, sheriff."

David retrieved the rifle cartridge and placed it on the table so that it pointed up, a miniature obelisk.

"See, these dumb sons of bitches don't understand ballistics, which, really, isn't much of a surprise. I can fish the rifle round out of that cow's guts in the morning and compare it to any rifle belonging to anyone in town who happens to own a truck with a spotlight. Now, I find a match and we're looking at trespassing, animal cruelty, poaching . . ."

All at once, Derrick's slick veneer broke, and his eyes turned misty.

"Whoa. Okay. Listen . . ."

Just throw the full weight of justice at the kid. Knock him off the pedestal that his rich folks made for him. Make him suffer. But . . . No. He couldn't go that way. If he brought the hammer down on Derrick, his parents would swing all their influence around town, and Gentry would be on the warpath. His real job wasn't closing cases, meting out punishment. His real job was protecting the town.

David gathered himself, then leaned within an inch of Derrick's face.

"You listen, shithead. Tomorrow morning, I'm going to have Gentry load that cow up and deliver it to your folks' shop. You're going to tell them to pay him the full worth, plus a thousand for his trouble. Should be enough to stop him from pressing charges. And should you ever trespass on his land again, I'm not sure I could be bothered to arrest a man for defending his property. Understood?"

Derrick stared down at the table and nodded.

"Good. Enjoy the year's worth of beef."

David strode back over to the bar.

"Fine work there, sheriff," Spady said.

"You clocked out?" Jason asked.

"Indeed I am."

David downed the shot, set the glass upside-down on the counter, then pounded the beer in a single go.

|||

In the small house at the edge of town, David found Tabby in the living room, curled up on the couch. The TV was tuned to the news. He angled for the bathroom, so that he could have a swig of mouthwash before she smelled alcohol on him and knew the real reason he was so late and another fight started up between them.

"Sorry, honey. It ended up being a hell of a night. You won't believe what that damned Mews kid did . . ."

"David."

He knew that timbre of her voice; his wife was crying. As he came to her, she didn't look up at him, didn't pull her eyes from the screen. He followed her gaze there and saw it. The same image he had seen on the phone in the bar. Gray and grainy amid the black of space.

The news anchor was speaking in an almost reverent tone.

". . . minutes ago came the stunning confirmation from NASA that it is real. This image of the asteroid was first captured by scientists at the Allen Telescope Array."

Not an asteroid, this thing filling the television screen. A head, arms, torso, legs. Not quite human in proportions but unmistakable. A body, hurtling through space.

"We don't know what it is. We don't . . ." the anchor halted, seemingly run out of anything else to say.

David felt Tabby take his hand. He didn't remember moving onto the couch beside her. A pang gripped his intestines. It couldn't be real. But there the image was, a chyron below declaring "UNIDENTIFIED OBJECT ON COLLISION COURSE WITH EARTH." Then all at once the screen cut to black and reappeared inside the Oval Office. The president stepped into view and sat at the desk. He wore none of his usual makeup, and so he looked older, but more human, than he ever had before.

He spoke haltingly, glancing down to his notes and up to someone off-screen, searching. No one knew where the thing came from. What it was. How it remained unseen for so long. Only that it was three miles long, head to toe. If it didn't change course, in six days and twenty-two hours it would make landfall in the United States. Models were forecasting western Nebraska. At the speed it was going, it would strike the earth like a bullet. An extinction-level event, he called it.

The president was saying something about prayer. David looked back to Tabby. Tears ran in waves down her face. They went outside. His feet were bare, but he felt no cold.

There were no streetlights here, at the edge of town. The flat horizon made the heavens feel limitless. Stars and planets shone all around the moon. David searched the sky. Was that it? That bright one, winking in and out?

All that he had done. All that he had fought for, to protect not just these people, his neighbors and friends, but to protect this town. To save it from the inexorable decay of time. And now? Now God was coming down himself to wipe it from the face of the earth. And there was nothing David could do. Nothing but watch. And wait.

ONE

All he wanted was to sleep. He'd been on duty since three o'clock the previous morning—twenty-seven hours straight running from one crisis to the next. A home burglary. An overdose. A domestic dispute that had turned violent. Cars vandalized. A fistfight outside a strip club. Nonstop "shots fired" calls coming into dispatch. Though, thankfully, no bodies. Not yet. He tapped his knuckles against the dashboard, as if it might bring him luck.

David could hardly remember anymore the way it had been before. That easy daily routine of long stops at Pearl's diner for coffee, the hardware store for town gossip, the courthouse to shoot the shit with Jason. Going out to one of his usual spots on the highway and waiting to bust someone from out of state for speeding, or just sitting and staring at the countryside.

Two years ago. Might as well have been another lifetime.

He decided to make one last circle of Old Town, check that everything was peace and quiet, then head back to his apartment for a quick nap. Hope that his dispatcher, Andrea, wouldn't bark into the radio with any new horrors.

From Main Street, Old Little Springs stretched a mile in every direction, small wood-framed homes, sprawling yards of dead grass, broken-down appliances left to rust. It was like the whole community was oxidizing, steadily becoming nothing. A few of the storefronts had reopened, though. None of the houses were empty. The cracked pavement had been repaved—though the water tower remained a jack-o'-lantern. It was comfortable, familiar, this little stretch. Unlike everything around it.

As David rounded a corner, he saw them. A procession of maybe sixty people in black robes that hung low enough to drag the ground, moving with slow, unified steps, as if a monastic order. He drove past, idling close to them, and their faces came into view. Not their actual faces but the plastic masks they wore over them. Tiger masks, eyes wide and ferocious, mouths frozen mid-roar. None glanced at David or made a sound. They never did. "Tonys," the locals called them. Like the tiger from the cereal. Every morning, the Tonys did this. March to the old park. Bow down, pray to the west—to it—then stand and march back to the old theater building, which they'd somehow acquired in the chaos that followed landfall.

"You have a permit?" David hollered through his open window.

No response. He drove on, swearing under his breath.

He eased into the parking lot of Pearl's, a long, rectangular building painted bright pink. Through the windows, he could see the morning crowd already there and a line waiting out the door. It wasn't ever full before, but because the diner sat at the very western edge of town, its windows offered one of the best, unbroken views of it. The thing that looked out of the corner of your eye like a small mountain range rising up a couple of miles outside of town, blocking the horizon.

It was no mountain. It was him. The giant, prostrate on his back. Looming.

Every time David saw it, really looked at it, his guts twisted. The impossible scope—the left side of its beetle-like abdomen rising as straight as a cliff face, maybe a thousand feet. Its arms—two on this side of it, two on the other—were thin relative to the torso but still each a mile and a quarter long and thicker than a house, ending in stubby, four-fingered hands. To the south, its thin legs with oddly spaced joints and a row of barbs along them stretched all the way into the river, which had swelled its bank to carve a new path around the massive four-toed feet. And to the north, its shoulders continued into its head with no neck. Its face lolled to the east, toward town, so that it stared over them. Stared right at David from under a massive brow with clusters of unblinking, lifeless insectoid eyes.

In the hours after landfall, the military had arrived in an endless flock of c-130 cargo planes and transport helicopters, and soldiers had first surrounded the giant, keeping everyone back. Then they built the metal wall that now encircled it. To protect the town, the army claimed. But the giant was dead, and all of the guns pointed out.

David had never been much closer than he was now, but still he could see that the surface of it was scrawled with deep ridges that formed curving patterns that repeated, growing ever smaller. Fractals, David had heard them called. Its skin seemed reflective, though not quite. Like the opalescent mica stones David would find on hiking trips to the Rocky Mountains as a kid, it bent and swirled light. So, it always looked different, changing color through the day along with the sky. Pastel blue and pink in the morning. Blue and white during the day. Gray during storms. Indigo and orange at dusk.

Day after day, it lay there. Right where it landed, settling onto the ground with impossible ease—like an old man easing into a bath. Unmoving. Dead. Killed. At least so it seemed.

Because it wasn't just the giant that arrived that day. There, right where its abdomen met the plate of its chest, a spire emerged and rose up some three thousand feet. A gun-metal black tower jutting into the sky.

A spear. Broken off at the top. Massive beyond comprehension. Stabbed right through the giant. Right in the spot where David was trained to shoot people—center mass.

The spire caught the rising sun and shimmered an effervescent red.

Where did the giant come from? What killed it? How did it land without ripping a hole into the earth? And why, out of a whole universe, did it arrive here, right on David's doorstep? If any of the scientists or government officials had answers to those or a million other questions about the giant, they weren't saying.

"Morning, Gulliver," David said.

A sudden pop of static, and David startled. Just his radio.

"Boss, you awake?"

Andrea's voice.

"Unfortunately."

"I can call Brooke instead . . ."

"What is it, Andrea?"

The tone of her voice already told him: nothing good.

"New Town, boss. Somebody found a body."

David looked away from the giant. To the north and east, where previously Little Springs had disappeared into rolling, barren hills and fields, now a whole new city rose up, New Little Springs. Apartments and strip malls and big box retailers and the new school and the rounded glass tower of the Harold Countryman Federal Building—named after the old hermit who lived right where the giant fell. A god crashing onto earth and only one fatality, like some kind of cosmic joke. And new people to fill all the new buildings. Government workers, soldiers, scientists, lawyers, journalists, retailers, tour guides, restaurateurs, developers, consultants, doctors, teachers, yoga instructors. Them, and criminals, too. Drug dealers. Thieves. Prostitutes. Grifters. Murderers.

David sighed and flipped a switch on the dash. The truck's siren wailed.

|||

He knew he'd found it when he saw the twenty-some people gathered in a clutch outside a strip mall that housed, in order, a Thai restaurant, a vape shop, a tattoo parlor, and a real estate office with sheets of paper showing houses and apartments and parcels of land taped up in the window.

The crowd stood in front of the tattoo parlor, next to posters showing off giant-inspired body art—the same patterns from the giant inked into human skin. Whatever these people had seen, it was bad. Arms clutched to chests. Hands over mouths. Makeup streaked with tears. "He's in there," one said, pointing to the realty office.

David held for just a moment at the door. Since the giant landed and the world had descended on Garden County, the state police had set up an office here. Any serious cases, they said they would take. Leave all the grinding, day-to-day policing to David and his single deputy. He could call them; let them have it. Whoever the dead person was on the other side of this door, he was an outsider. Let another outsider deal with it.

David pulled open the door. To hell with the state police. My jurisdiction, my case.

The overhead lights were off, but the large glass windows let in plenty of light. The room was new, walls painted white. No art or plants. Just a copy machine and a desk with a computer on it. A door at the back that led to a storeroom or a bathroom. No sign of forced entry. No sign of anything. Maybe in the back?

As David stepped forward, a pair of boat shoes became visible behind the desk, toes pointed up. He took another step.

The body lay on its back, a man in khaki pants and a polo shirt that might have once been white. All David could see was blood, thick and dark and almost dry. Coating the torso, which had a gaping hole in its center. A shotgun blast? Blood covered the face, pooled a couple of feet out onto the floor, spattered the arms. No. Arm. One was complete. The other ended at the elbow.

He found the rest of it on the desk, next to a handful of business cards: Sanjay Kapoor Realty. The missing half of the left arm sat on the desk, fingers still resting on the keyboard. It ended all at once, cut through cleanly, as if by a meat slicer, a bisection of muscle and bone and sinew.

Aligned with the wound, a deep notch cut down into the wooden surface of the desk. What the hell could do that? A hatchet? A machete? Some goddamned samurai sword?

He looked back down at the chest. Could that wound have been made with a blade? It was hard to tell through all the blood, but there seemed to be smaller lacerations, almost superficial.

Two years ago, this would've made David sick. Back then, all he knew of death came from the videos and photos he'd seen during his couple of years studying criminal justice at Western Nebraska Community College. Sure, a handful of times after he became a deputy, then sheriff, there would be a traffic accident or an old person dead of natural causes. Nothing like this. Nothing evil.

Even among the horrors David had seen since landfall, this one gnawed at him. It was unnatural. But not just that. It was familiar.

A couple of months earlier, he'd responded to a call at the new airport. An owner of one of the tourist operations—"rent a helicopter for the world's best view of the giant"—had been found outside his hangar, dead, cut all to hell. Jim Holly was his name. David had arrived at the scene just at the same time as the state police. They'd muscled him out; he'd pushed the case out of mind till now. He searched his memory for the scene. How did the body look? Didn't Holly also have a massive wound in his chest?

A siren grew louder outside, and a black Ford sedan—unmarked, windows tinted, Nebraska government plates—parked sharply out front. Two men emerged, both stocky, matching mustaches, khaki pants and white dress shirts beneath blue windbreakers with Nebraska State Police detective badges hanging around their necks. The only difference between them was that one was six and a half feet tall and the other at least a foot shorter. David knew their names were Kirby and Warby, but he could never remember which was which.

"Murder?" the short one asked as they burst inside.

"Bad one," David said, nodding at the desk.

They pulled latex gloves from their pockets, snapped them on, and approached the body.

"Thanks for securing the scene," the tall one said.

Now fuck off, his body language implied.

David didn't move.

"The way the arm was cut. It's still perfectly in place. Like the killer either snuck up on him or they knew each other, and Mister Kapoor there wasn't expecting it. Either way, I don't think it was a crime of passion."

"Uh huh," the short one said.

"It reminded me of the Holly case," David continued. "The wounds . . ."

Neither of the detectives looked up.

"We've had plenty of stabbings," the tall one said.

"Just look at the cut on the arm. Not just any blade can do that. Your forensics turn up anything from the Holly crime scene? I mean, if they're connected . . ."

The short one stood and glowered at David.

"We can't comment on an open investigation."

David grinned, connecting dots that he knew the man hadn't intended to reveal.

"Open? Then you haven't closed it?"

The tall one glared at the short one.

"Not yet."

Now they both stood and moved between David and the body.

"Homicides are ours. You know that," the short one said. "You stick to handing out speeding tickets. Leave the real police work to us."

He could fight them. But he'd tried before and lost. The county didn't have a forensics team, didn't even have a morgue to store a body. Everyone told him to just be thankful for the state's help.

"Good luck," David offered as he left.

Outside, David retrieved a roll of yellow caution tape from his truck and began roping off a perimeter.

A dark sedan pulled into the lot, and David lifted up the tape so that it could park beside the state police sedan. The driver stepped out. An older man with rough and mottled skin, his gray hair cropped close, a dark suit. He was FBI. Agent Erickson. David had crossed paths with him a few times before. He seemed nice enough, though operating one or two planes above David's existence.

Erickson opened the back door, and a woman stepped out. She was young, about David's age, Asian American, in civilian clothes—a T-shirt and jeans, a backpack slung over her shoulder. Around her neck, an olive-hued stone hung from a simple necklace. She was pretty, David thought, then chided himself for instinctively judging her appearance.

"Inside?" Erickson asked in a voice that might once have been gravelly but now was a soft rasp.

David hadn't expected to be addressed.

"Yeah," he managed.

"All right then. Thanks for your help here," Erickson said.

The old man's hand went into his jacket pocket and came out with a burnished metal lighter, which he caressed like a rabbit's foot. David supposed he must've recently quit smoking or was trying.

The woman smiled and nodded at David, then Erickson ushered her into the office.

What the hell was the FBI doing at a murder investigation? And who was the woman with Erickson? David was sure he'd never seen her before.

Kirby and Warby stormed out of the office all at once.

". . . treat us like we don't even rate," the tall one muttered. "It should be our case."

The short one took out a pack of cigarettes, retrieved two, lit both, and handed one up to his partner. They both leaned against the glass and took long, perfectly synchronized drags.

"Takes a real asshole to build castles in another man's sandbox, doesn't it?" David asked.

"Fuck off, Andy Griffith," the short one spat.

"Yeah. Fuck all the way off back to Mayberry," the tall one added.

David started toward his truck, then stopped and turned back.

"The FBI guy—Erickson—did he show up at the Holly murder, too?"

The detectives shared a quick glance, then glared silently at David and resumed smoking. But their eyes had told David all he wanted to know. The FBI was somehow connected to both cases. The only question was, why?

TWO

The first half of the flight, thick clouds enveloped the earth, and Charlotte slept fitfully, her head wedged against the interior wall of the plane. She startled awake some time later, a dream of wading along a sandy creek quickly fading as she remembered where she was. She pulled up the window screen. Sunlight flooded through. The clouds had thinned into cotton balls equally distributed over the land. Below, Nebraska looked like a quilt stretched across a bed, acre-sized squares in shades of brown and gray and green, smoothed as if by God's hand.

It was beautiful. And the sight of it set off a dread that thudded in her chest.

A hand tapped her shoulder.

Charlotte pulled the ear buds from her ears as she looked at her seat mate, a man in pinstriped charcoal pants and a dress shirt with the sleeves rolled up, a purple tie with a paisley pattern. Not unattractive, though with a smile that was the clear product of practice.

"Have you seen him before?" the man asked.

She nodded to the window.

"The giant?"

"Yeah. Gulliver. Hell of a thing, the first time. I should've just watched your face to see your reaction."

"Uh huh."

Be nice, she told herself. You never know who could be a good source. She gave her own practiced smile.

"So, you come here a lot, then?"

"About half my time. Construction contracting. It's the wild west out here. Everyone's fighting for space. Tons of money to be made. How about you?"

"I'm a reporter. Cable news."

He cocked his head and studied her face.

"You know, this whole flight I was thinking you looked familiar. I'm sure I've seen you before."

He hadn't. Or at least the odds were against it. Charlotte had started her career as an on-air reporter at a regional station, but in her six years at the network, she'd been in front of the camera three times, filling in only when there was a desperate need. She was a producer, doing research, writing copy, feeding her work to the anchors, who took all the acclaim and money.

She was good at the job. A well-oiled gear that turned perfectly, smoothly, and silently as the larger machine chugged along. Only, recently, she'd begun to feel that she was unraveling. The only thing keeping her pushing forward was the hope that she would get a shot to be on TV, but that hope was dying. There were always younger faces. Prettier faces. She'd thought about quitting journalism altogether, as so many of her friends had.

Then, a few days ago, the network heads called the producers into a meeting about the giant. Like every other news channel, their ratings had shot up in the wake of landfall. Every day brought new mysteries and revelations and an endless source of guests. Scientists debating how this shifted views of astrophysics. Pastors and rabbis discussing the implications for religion. Politicians evaluating the strategic advantage America had since the giant landed on its soil. Historians wondering if the ancient alien theories were right all along.

But as days turned to weeks and weeks turned to months and still the giant did nothing, coverage grew stale. All that talk about how the giant would change the world forever turned out to be bullshit. Life went on. The sins of that week before landfall—when everyone thought the world would end—were forgiven and forgotten. People went back to work. And still the giant just lay there.

The military held its mile-wide cordon around the perimeter of the giant, allowing no one through the massive, metal-plated wall they'd erected. NASA built up its research operation—Site One—but revealed nothing of the work happening there, in a complex of white buildings in the shadow of the giant's head.

"We need a fresh fucking angle!" shouted Geoff, Charlotte's boss, at the meeting.

Charlotte usually stayed quiet in these meetings. This day, sensing it might be her last and only chance, she spoke up.

"What about the local perspective?" she asked.

Geoff nodded at her to continue. It was too late to stop. She pressed ahead.

"The town where it fell—Little Springs—it had a population of about seven hundred before landfall. Super rural. Farming, ranching. About ninety-five percent white. Everyone drives a truck, everyone listens to country music, everyone owns guns. The prototypical Red State. Then the giant drops out of the sky. And now Little Springs is maybe a hundred thousand people. More coming every day. But the people who are moving there are coming from cities. From Blue States. All over the country, there's this divide between urban America and rural America, and here we have this insane ecosystem where they're being slammed together in the shadow of a giant, dead fucking alien. We've focused on the giant for so long. Maybe it's time we tell the stories of the people around it."

All eyes went to Geoff, awaiting his reaction.

"I like it," he said, finally. "But what's the angle? What's the hook?"

Charlotte supposed that all along she had planned to play the one card up her sleeve. There was no other choice now.

"Well, I grew up there," she said. "Before my family moved away. So, I think I understand these people. I think I could get them to open up to me."

The expected question came. Why hadn't she said this before? And Charlotte offered her usual story, that she didn't much like it there and moved away when she was pretty young and had hoped to never go back. Mostly, the truth.

Geoff gave her the assignment. She'd partner with a cameraman who was already stationed there. She would report on breaking news while working on human interest pieces with a focus on locals. And if she failed, if ratings stayed flat, she would come back to Atlanta, back to the grind, back to anonymity.

The airplane's captain came on the intercom. Descent was imminent. Passengers on both sides would have a good view of the giant. She leaned against the small oval pane.

With a clunk, the landing gear unfurled below them, and the plane banked to the left.

All at once, the giant appeared in full. The photos and footage she'd seen couldn't prepare her for it. Air rushed out of her lungs and hissed through her teeth. Finally, she remembered to inhale.

It was bigger than she expected. Not an entity but a geologic formation. A God-sized man sleeping atop the quilt of the land. The giant's skin glowed under the sun, an ever-shifting blur of yellow and orange and blue traced with geometric patterns that reminded her of the symmetrical innards of a halved cabbage.

And beyond it, the city. Spreading almost out of sight. Buildings like Lego blocks. Squinting, Charlotte tried to make out any familiar landmarks. But she had never seen Little Springs from above, and the sleepy little town had been overrun, as if by an aggressive vine. Below the plane, helicopters buzzed over the giant like carrion flies.

Then the plane banked right, descending rapidly, and impossibly the giant disappeared from view.

She felt a buzz. Her phone had reconnected to service. A text came through from her cameraman.

Call me when you land. Murder. Need you to report.

THREE

The crow had been flying for hours, down from the rocky hills of Wyoming, onto the plains. Though its wings burned with exhaustion, it kept on, pulled forward by a compulsion it didn't understand, a magnetic draw that had led it across a hundred and fifty miles and counting, an urge it only finally comprehended when it came within sight of the narrow, dark thing jutting into the sky. It looked like an impossibly tall tree that had burned, no bark or branches left, just a black trunk. But it was no tree. The bird understood little, but it understood this. This was what called to the crow.

The crow circled clockwise, but seeing nowhere on the smooth sides to find a perch, it flew higher, up to where the wind blew in gusts that felt as if they'd tear the creature's weightless wings from its body. Still it pushed, up and up, fighting the drafts, closer and closer to the top. There, the surface ended, shattered, in a craggy peak some twenty yards across. Eagerly, the crow alit into a nook and gripped tightly. It felt at peace.

Insects. That was what the crow thought as it looked down at its feet, that it had landed atop an anthill, and a swarm had massed to defend the colony. But there was nothing it could see, no source of the tingling. And the sensation came not from outside the crow but inside, racing up its feet, legs, into its chest, its wings, its eyes.

The crow tumbled from the spire. The wind buffeted it, cracked it against the side of the spire as it fell, body limply spinning until it landed in an eruption of blood and black feathers on the giant's chest.

The man in the field watched this through binoculars.

And then he watched as, within the grouping of white, metal buildings near the giant's head that the government called Site One, a massive mechanized crane raised its arm, carrying a compartment, and spun toward the giant, then lowered the compartment onto the giant's chest.

A person wearing what looked like an astronaut's suit stepped out of the compartment, pulling a wheeled cart behind. Slowly, the astronaut meandered around the great field of the giant's chest and used a metal arm to grab the carcasses of birds and deposit them in the cart. It wasn't just the crow. Eagles. Hawks. Owls. Flickers. Barn swallows. What seemed to be hundreds of birds every day, drawn to the spire. Then either dashed against it, or stunned, and falling down like rain onto the giant's torso below.

The man in the field supposed the scientists had some interest in the birds. Or maybe they just didn't want carcasses to pile up like snow drifts. The poor birds. Drawn by instinct but with no ability to comprehend it.

Not like him. Yes, it was instinct that had made him do what he'd done. But the difference was that he had awareness of this compulsion. And more than that, he embraced it.

Something deep and hidden had told him to kill those men. It demanded not just that they die but that they die in the necessary way. That their deaths be made into an image. A revelation.

He was shocked not that he had killed, only by how easy it had been. How naturally it came to him. How satisfying it was, tracing the blade over their skin.

He knew that he would kill again. That instinct deep inside demanded as much. The only question was: who?

Around him, a trill sound kicked up. In the stubble of the harvested corn fields, great clutches of sandhill cranes called out as they lifted off into the sky, becoming gray flecks. The cranes came by the tens of thousands every year, stopping to nest on the Platte River before continuing their migration back north for the summer. It was noon, and as the birds did every day at this time, they soared in flocks, rising on updrafts and warbling in their singsong way.

The flocks began to merge as they approached the giant, and soon they had formed a single cloud, tens of thousands of bodies moving in unison, gliding impossibly close to each other, their song becoming one sound, a wavering call, as the cloud moved clockwise, going around and around the spire, an undulating vortex circling the blade.

FOUR

A shriek sounded above as if the atmosphere was ripping in half. David startled where he stood beside his truck. Overhead, two F-22 Raptors screamed past and out of sight to the north.

"Boy. The birds sure got you that time, didn't they, sheriff?"

David snapped himself back into reality. The truck was parked beside old pumps in front of a metal building with a weathered sign advertising prices for unleaded, regular, and diesel. Beside him, a hunchbacked man worked at the truck's windshield with a squeegee. He wore black pants and a ragged, grease-stained shirt with a sew-on patch that read "Jimmy."

"Suppose so. I think I'm asleep on my feet here," David replied.

He'd been thinking about the case since leaving the scene. The dead man on the ground. That arm still sitting on the desk, as if the fingers might start typing again at any second. Puzzling through the possibilities of who might have committed any given crime was so much simpler before, a matter of thinking through the town's seven hundred residents, their histories and animosities, tumbling all those pieces about inside his head until some started to connect. Now there were too many variables. Too many people. A mountain of puzzle pieces—more than he could possibly hope to hold in his head at once. What he'd learned over the past two years was that most crime traced back to drugs and to look there first. Addicts stealing something to sell in order to get another high. Gun battles between rival dealers. Meth heads turning violent. Maybe . . .

Not his case to solve, he reminded himself. The state police—or the FBI—had it under control. Let it go.

"You doing okay?" David asked.

Jimmy turned from his work and grinned.

"Can't complain. Wouldn't do a bit of good if I did."

Jimmy had been giving that same response since he was a kid, since

22

they all were in school together. Back when Jimmy's dad ran the Pump-and-Go, and it was the only gas station in town. Now there were plenty of other places with cheaper fuel, but David still came here. Habit. Loyalty. Or a combination of the two.

The pump clanged, alerting them that the tank was full. Jimmy retrieved the nozzle.

"Put it on the department tab?" he asked.

"Thanks, Jimmy."

"You get some rest, sheriff," Jimmy said as he limped off.

Just then, a Humvee skidded to a halt on the opposite side of the pumps. The ding ropes barely registered both sets of tires. *Dingding.* Soldiers in camouflage jumped out, and one started pumping gas. None so much as made eye contact.

As a kid, David had been obsessed with the military, memorizing vehicles and weapons. Now the town was crawling with an army presence. Humvees racing up and down the streets. Transport trucks hauling troops or Lord knows what. The massive wall around Gulliver, thirty feet high with sniper turrets every hundred yards. The jets overhead. On the far side of the giant, out of sight to the west, a sprawling army base had grown, holding the tens of thousands of soldiers that kept watch over the massive corpse. Any awe David felt for this had long since diminished. They were an occupying force in his land.

David climbed up into the truck and shook his head to snap himself awake. The sun would start setting behind the giant before long, but that only meant it was late afternoon. He could still make it to his apartment for a nap before the night shift, when the calls always started to pour in from New Town. But he needed fresh batteries for his radio first.

He turned onto Main Street and parked in the shade of a towering blue spruce behind the three-story yellow brick county courthouse, what had for decades been the tallest building in town. A line of people stretched outside—outsiders waiting on driver's licenses and voter registration. Soon enough, the county would belong to them. In the parking lot, he saw his cousin Jason's car, a black Audi.

Instead of going down to the sheriff's department in the basement, David went up to the second floor, to a door labeled: "Jason Blunt, County Assessor." Going back to when their grandpa took over the town's bank, the Blunt family had served as leaders in the community, on the village council and in the county offices. There were good-natured jokes about the "Blunt mafia." David's uncle, Dale, now ran the bank and had bought the local newspaper. While David became sheriff, his cousin Jason—Dale's son—split time between working at the bank and the county assessor job, overseeing any real estate deal.

Inside the office, terrain maps covered the walls, each shaggy with stickie notes. Land marked off to become another strip mall or condo. Above Jason's desk hung a ten-point buck's head and, below that, a rack holding a shotgun. Jason was on the phone, his feet up on his desk, wearing his usual cherry-red Converses.

"Uh huh. Uh huh. Well, you've got to get zoned first. And before that, we need to do an inspection. Soil tests. All that shit. When? Shoot. Looking at two months." Jason looked at David and winked. "Sure, sure. I'll see. Maybe I can sneak you in early."

He rang off and dropped the phone in its cradle.

"Shit, cousin. I'm starting to think it's time to pursue an earlier line of work. What do you think?"

David sat into a wooden chair that was too uncomfortable for there to be any risk he might doze off.

"Bull riders?" David ventured.

"I'd take being a rodeo clown at this point," Jason said.

On the desk was an old framed photo showing four adolescent boys. David had his own copy of it back at his apartment. Standing in front of a rickety tree house were the three cousins—David, Jason, and Ben Junior—and their friend Spady, who might as well have been blood. Since they'd been toddlers, the four of them spent most every waking hour together. At least, they had until senior year of high school, when one day Ben Junior was suddenly gone, run away, his parents said. Then no other news until five years later, when Ben Senior and Bonnie quietly told the family that their only child had died, in circumstances they had no inclination to discuss.

David looked from the photo to the maps on the walls.

"You know a real estate guy named Sanjay Kapoor?" he asked.

Jason pulled his feet off his desk and leaned forward.

"Just that he's dead. Word spread pretty quick. You go to the scene?"

Again, the image of the disembodied arm appeared before David. He nodded.

"Fuck," Jason said with a grimace. "Was it bad?"

David nodded again. He couldn't say any more. Couldn't talk about the gaping wound or the severed arm. If he told Jason, then Jason might tell someone else, and soon the whole county would know. And if everyone knew all the grisly details, the police wouldn't be able to sort good tips from bad ones.

Jason exhaled hard.

"I helped him with a couple of deals, but I wouldn't say I knew him at all. He was a real hard charger. Going around, knocking on every door, offering to buy out locals, then flipping the land to developers. Seemed like maybe a bit of an asshole, but I can't imagine that gets you killed."

David shrugged.

"It doesn't seem like it. But I can't say I understand why any person kills someone else. Anyway, I don't think they have anything to go on."

"State police took it, then? Good. Let it be their problem," Jason said.

Jason searched his memory.

"I'm trying to think. Last time I talked to Kapoor was the Dalton deal. He got them to sell their acreage."

David startled.

"The Dalton farm? No. That land has been in the family for four generations."

"Cash. Enough money to go live in Florida. Sid says he's going to buy a boat, spend every day out hooking marlins. Shit does he know about marlins? Anyway, it's going to be divided up for mixed-use. Retail at ground level, apartments above. Should be real nice."

David was too tired to restrain his reaction.

"And you just signed off on it?"

Jason leaned forward, and the chair groaned beneath his weight.

"I signed off because that's my job, cousin. The Daltons have been living off the food pantry since we were kids. Now they're rich. How is that a tragedy?"

David had no response.

"Listen. I know I shouldn't even say it, but you could take that same road. Your folks' place is just sitting there. I could get you seven figures. Easy. You could give up this bullshit. Ride bulls. Hook marlins. Whatever the hell you want."

David tilted up his hat, so that his cousin could see his eyes.

"It is not for sale. Not now. Not ever."

Jason pushed out his jaw and nodded.

"Yeah. Fine. Just don't come in acting like I'm some villain here. This town was dying. No jobs. No people. And now we have everything. The whole world came right to us, thanks to Gulliver. You want to go back to being a small-town sheriff, you're going to have to find another town."

"I'm not leaving," David said.

Jason leaned back. The fight had gone out of him.

"Yeah, well, you just keep tilting at windmills, then."

David grinned. It was an olive branch, the line about windmills. Their grandma had been the town's librarian and forced all the cousins to read *Don Quixote* one summer, an assignment Jason still complained about.

"Suppose I will," David said.

A knock sounded at the door and it opened almost immediately, before Jason could respond. A woman charged through, and David instinctively stood. Her intense eyes shone brightly amid the olive skin of her face. She wore a floral-patterned scarf as a hijab, black slacks, and a thick sweater; a lanyard around her neck immediately marked her as one of the feds at the Countryman Building. It seemed as if every agency had a presence here. FEMA came in the immediate aftermath of landfall to tend to "survivors"—their term for the locals. Homeland Security. Department of Energy. The Centers for Disease Control. NASA. And for whatever arbitrary bureaucratic reason, the task of wrangling it all fell to the Department of the Interior. The woman's name was Aaliyah Bakhtiari, and because she ran Interior, she was in charge of the giant.

"Ma'am," David said.

He told himself he was being polite, but deep down he knew he was just worried he would butcher the pronunciation of her name. What was she doing here? The feds had never messed with county business before.

Then David remembered. The mosque. It was marked on one of the maps up there on the wall. A parcel of land amid a housing development to the northeast of town. Aaliyah was part of the group that bought the land. But they still needed county approval to build, and the locals were like a colony of bees that had been poked with a stick. Garden County had never had a single Muslim resident, let alone a mosque. All that the locals knew of Islam came from cable news—wars and terrorism and refugees.

"Hey, Aaliyah," Jason said comfortably. "My cousin here was just leaving. Have you met David?"

She extended her hand and he took it.

"Sheriff," she said. "I was hoping I'd see you, too. You'll be at the city council meeting tomorrow night?"

"Village council," he corrected.

"Right," she said, taking back her hand. "We've had some threats. We hear there are people planning to protest. We would appreciate it if there was some security."

David looked to Jason, who nodded.

"I'll be there. Me and my deputy."

He left them to whatever business they had. Downstairs, the sheriff's department consisted of one small room, a closet-sized bathroom, and a single jail cell that they'd taken to using as a supply closet, now that the state had built a lockup outside of town to the east.

There was only one desk, which was actually a folding table that sagged under the weight of an ancient desktop PC, a stack of paperwork, and a bank of phones and radios and black wires that coiled and looped in great piles, as if they were hibernating snakes. The desk belonged to Andrea, as did the whole office, really. She was a monolithic presence, her body a near-perfect sphere. She wore her hair buzzed down to almost nothing, which she said was on account of the phone headset she barked into all day. She had served as dispatcher for the previous sheriff and the one before that. David wasn't sure when or if she ever went home or slept. Each day, she sat there and fielded every call that came in, relaying it all to David and his deputy. She never seemed to eat, instead drinking from two liter-sized thermos cups that she filled daily with diet cherry soda.

"Hey, boss," she said, not looking up from the computer.

David grabbed two batteries from a bank of chargers. He replaced the one in his radio and swapped out the extra in his belt.

"All quiet?" David asked.

"Mostly. Just trying to catch up on forms and reports till the next round of crazy. You handed off the body?"

"Yeah. Let the Staties have it."

"Good. I don't need any more paperwork."

David was halfway out the door, fantasizing about the hour, maybe two, of sleep that lay ahead.

"Only thing," Andrea said, freezing him. "The Tonys marched again yesterday. We had a bunch of calls complaining about it. I know they have a permit for morning marches, but . . ."

She left it at that. David sighed, motionless in the doorway.

"Call Brooke," he said finally. "Tell her to meet me there."

|||

The theater building looked more than anything like a barn, with a sloped metal roof and wood siding. It had shown its last films in the 1970s, so David had never seen a movie there, only grew up hearing stories about it. It sat mostly unused for decades until landfall, and all at once someone had bought it and put up a metal privacy fence around it before the locals had noticed. And by the time they had, it was too late. Some goddamned doomsday cult had taken residence right in the heart of Little Springs.

Brooke stood waiting for him beside the large gate in the fence, tall and athletic in her tan deputy uniform, her blond hair tied up in a loose bun.

"Shit, boss. You look terrible."

"Thanks," David said. "Great to see you, too."

He felt like he barely saw Brooke anymore. The job had grown so big, it was all they could do to divide up the county and the hours and sprint in opposite directions. She was a year younger and, though they weren't related, had always been like a younger sister. Then she had started dating Spady, and so they'd spent most of their lives around each other. Now he mostly felt guilty. It was bad enough that this job was killing him. It didn't need to kill her, too.

"You holding up?" he asked.

"Nothing too crazy. Car crash on ninety-two took a bit to clear. So, what the hell happened with the body?"

"State police have another murder on their hands. Victim is Sanjay Kapoor, some out-of-town realtor, come in to flip land. It reminded me a little of the Jim Holly case."

Brooke looked off, remembering. "The helicopter tour guy. Right. Huh. You think it's a racial motive?"

It hadn't occurred to him. Holly was Black. Kapoor was Indian American.

"God, I hope not," David said. "Things are wound so damn tight already. Anyway, I don't know for sure that they're related. They just had similar wounds. Both cut all to hell. And Kapoor's arm was hacked off. He also had a big wound right here." David tapped his sternum.

"Christ. Sounds almost ritualistic or something."

He nodded.

"I thought as much. Part of why I wanted to rattle their cage a bit."

He looked through the metal bars of the gate, at the theater building, every inch of which had been painted black. Beside the gate was an electronic doorbell. David pressed the button, and it chimed.

"I thought it was a state police show," Brooke said.

David grinned back.

"No harm in poking around. Now, when they come out, I'm going to take lead. But when I nod at you, you ask them about the murder."

"You sure?" she asked.

"Here they come," David said and tilted his hat low over his eyes.

The theater doors opened. It was too dark inside to see anything. Above the doors, the marquee that had once held movie titles and show times now proclaimed, "ANUM HAS FALLEN, ANUM WILL RISE AGAIN." Two tiger masks appeared, seeming to float in the shadows. Then the rest of the bodies emerged trailing black cloaks. Average height. Probably men, David guessed by their shoulders and because the Tonys supposedly had a rule against women speaking.

They made their way to the gate but didn't open it.

"Do you choose to follow the one true path to the heavens?"

The voice hissed through the perforations in the mask. David shook his head.

"All good on the salvation front. Just here to serve you this."

David thrust a sheet of paper through a gap in the gate. With black-gloved hands, one of the robed figures took it.

"Citation," David explained. "Failure to register to demonstrate. You're all square on mornings, but you never cleared it with me to march in the evenings."

The same masked figure spoke again. "We do not march. We prostrate ourselves in the shadow of Anum. We must show him that we offer ourselves. Freely. For Anum's return nears. Even you can feel it, sheriff. He will awaken. Already, he stirs."

Though David could only see the man's eyes through the mask, he was certain it was Quentin Breda. He'd pulled an FBI file on him after the cult settled here. Breda was in his late fifties, born and raised in a Florida swamp, the son of a Pentecostal minister. Had some kind of split with that church, then took to prophesying about the apocalypse. Started a few new churches. Arizona. Utah. He claimed to have special knowledge of a true faith, something that came before Christianity or Judaism, inspiration pulled from the mad British poet William Blake. "Tyger, Tyger, burning bright." That was the reason for the tiger masks, or at least that was the assumption. Twice before, Breda had predicted that a giant being would appear and hasten the end of the world. Twice before, his predicted dates came and went. Then Gulliver fell, and some crackpots found Breda's theories, and his flock grew. And then they showed up here.

David maintained his smile. Of all the outsiders, these were the worst. Some goddamned perversion. And right here. Right in the middle of Old Town. Right on his doorstep. He couldn't force them out—at least not yet—but he'd take any chance he could to spit in their cereal. Technically, he should have given them a warning.

"Flip that paper over, and there's information on the back about paying your fine."

David caught Brooke's eyes and nodded.

"One more thing," she said. "A man was killed today. You wouldn't happen to know anything about that, would you? Maybe some Tony the Tiger got out of the cage and went on the hunt?"

The second man stepped forward, his voice loud and echoing against the mask.

"Don't you talk to him! Women do not speak to him!"

It would've been awful satisfying to punch the man through the gate. Instead, David pointedly rested his hand on his holstered pistol.

"Calm. Down. Should I take that as a 'no'?" David asked.

Quentin exhaled hard against the mask.

"Anum's followers do not stray."

With that, the two men receded into the theater, and the doors closed, swallowing them.

"What do you think?" Brooke asked.

"Hell if I know," David said. "All I know is that anyone who wears a mask is obviously hiding something. There was something else . . . the second guy. His voice sounded almost familiar."

"A local? Mixed up with that bunch? No way."

David shrugged. "Could just be I'm exhausted. I'm going to go stare at my eyelids for an hour, then I'll take evening shift tonight. You go home to Spady."

"You got it, boss," Brooke said.

"And tell that one-armed asshole that we need to grab a beer."

The two of them walked across the dirt street toward their trucks. Behind them, the small blue light on the electronic doorbell blinked steadily, transmitting all that had been said back into the black building.

FIVE

The sky turned black. The air rushed away as the temperature dropped thirty degrees all at once. The clouds sparked, alight with an otherworldly red glow. It was here. Falling. But not like they had said. Not like a bullet fired at the earth. It had slowed. Stopped in the low atmosphere. Hanging there, a body suspended overhead. The clouds came apart, and he could see it in full as it slowly descended. As it did, its skin glowed red again, illuminated along a series of curling patterns. Bits of flaming debris rained down around it.

And . . . no it was not the giant churning through the sky. It was a black mass of spinning air. The tornado. Coming for them. He was a child again, torn from his bed by his father's hands, thrust into the old claw-foot bathtub. The weight of his parents on top of him. The storm screaming outside. Then an explosion, and the weight of his parents gone, and the house around him gone, nothing but empty sky overhead as he stood in the tub, and a pain in his back as he felt the warm wet of blood.

But no, the blood wasn't his at all. And he wasn't in his childhood home. He was in an office. A desk. An arm, crimson gushing out from where it suddenly ended. The hand began to move, fingers striking keys, letters and words appearing on a screen. What was it trying to tell him? He strained to read . . .

David woke all at once from the kaleidoscope of the dream. His clock said he'd slept two hours too long. Hell. He went to the bathroom and caught sight of his shirtless body in the mirror. The always muscular build he'd kept had softened a little. He turned, and he could just see the thick scar that ran from his right buttock up to his shoulder blade. The place where the tornado reached out and touched him. A reminder that he alone had been spared.

He showered quickly and changed into a fresh uniform. The apartment was small, absent of almost any decoration. It was a new build to the southeast, close to where the railroad tracks had been rerouted south of the river, to go around the giant. David hated it, just as he hated every new thing in the town. But he couldn't afford anything else on a county salary, and Tabby had taken the house in the divorce.

He clicked on his radio. "Hey, Andrea. Back in the saddle."

|||

The night passed quietly. David dozed off and on in his truck, though the intermittent sleep only seemed to exhaust him more. Realizing it was Thursday, he went to the little grocery in Old Town just as it opened and came out with two armfuls of plastic shopping bags.

He settled them in the back of his truck and drove a few blocks over, to a single-story cottage amid a large yard. As he carried the bags toward the front door, a survey of the house reminded him of all that he needed to do and hadn't. Leaves piled in every alley of the roof. Paint curled in peels from the siding. Junk filled the yard—generations of broken-down lawnmowers, dishwashers, microwaves, and cars.

Beside the door, mail spilled out of the box. He'd get it on the way out. He knocked with the toe of his boot.

He heard footsteps, and then Bonnie opened the door, peering past him without a word.

"Morning, Bonnie," David said as he shuffled past her with the bags. She closed the door and locked it.

"A car. Black one. Dad saw it earlier, passing by."

"Huh. Well, next time get a license number and I'll run it."

She only then looked down at the groceries.

"Oh, David, you didn't need to!" She turned inside. "Benjamin! Our boy is here."

Bonnie wore a house coat, which stretched against her great folds of skin. She walked with locked knees, scuffling past stacks of newspapers and boxes and bags and piles of clothing that lined the hall. A calico cat ran between David's legs as he deposited the grocery bags on the kitchen counter, pushing dirty plates aside.

"I can take care of putting those away," she offered.

David waved her off.

"No problem. It won't take but a second."

Bonnie went off to join Ben Senior in the den. David finished with the groceries, then quickly washed the dishes. Once he was done, instinct took him to his old bedroom. The floor was piled with the same clutter as the hallway, but the bunkbed was still there. He couldn't remember much of the months after his parents died, only that he ended up here, adopted by Bonnie and Ben, sharing a room with Ben Junior. A room they shared for six years, up until the day that Ben Junior had gone.

It was part of what had pushed him into criminal justice. The idea that he could find out what had really happened to his cousin. There was a time when he thought he'd get his degree and go into the FBI, gain access to all their investigative tools.

But if those two years in college taught him anything, it was that he couldn't survive anywhere else but here. And back then it seemed impossible that anyone from the FBI would ever step foot in Little Springs.

David closed the door and joined his aunt and uncle in the den. The TV was tuned to the news.

"I didn't know you had a cat," David said.

"He came in the old dog door one night," Ben Senior answered from his Barcalounger without looking from the screen. "Keeps coming back. Mom won't stop feeding him all my baloney."

"It's bad for your heart," Bonnie chided. "Better for Nehemiah to eat it."

"You named the cat Nehemiah?"

They shrugged.

The two of them had grown worse. The piles around the house grew taller. They weren't cleaning. He couldn't remember the last time he'd seen them out of the house.

They'd always been strange, Bonnie and Ben. Anxious. Scared of the world. Convinced that evil was at work. The New Year's Eve of the new millennium, they had forced him and Ben Junior to stay up all night praying with them, sure that the world was ending.

They never spoke of the giant, but he knew they felt it. The same thing everyone else felt—across the world, and here especially. What if that thing wakes up? What if it suddenly explodes? What else is out there in the dark of space? What was it that shoved the spear through the giant's chest? And what if it suddenly appears in the sky?

A news report came on the TV. David immediately recognized the strip mall, filmed from just outside the caution tape he had strung up. A reporter gave the shocking details. A realtor killed inside his business in what seemed to be a random attack.

"World is going up in flames, son," Ben Senior said. "All around us. Flames."

He walked out, and neither of them seemed to notice. At the front door, David tugged a ream of envelopes and flyers from the mailbox, some spilling out of his hands. As he knelt to scoop them up, David noticed the car. A black sedan, parked across the street.

He tossed the mail inside the door and closed it. By the time he turned around, the car was gone.

SIX

Within an hour of her plane landing, Charlotte had been live on air, pronouncing the grim details of the realtor murdered in the giant's shadow. Her heart had pounded so hard she was convinced it would show on camera, but her cameraman had convinced her she'd done a great job, jumping in cold. And now here she was again, at the Little Springs Rural High School gymnasium, ready for her second broadcast in two days.

The school building had closed the year before, when the town's growth had forced the construction of a new school complex to hold all the students. The old one had the musty, stale smell of an abandoned space.

The basketball hoops had been raised to the ceiling, and the wooden surface of the court held rows of metal folding chairs. Each seat was taken, mostly filled with locals, she guessed. Almost all of them white, many dressed in Western clothing or jeans and T-shirts. Men with plugs of tobacco in their lips. The bleachers were packed with outsiders. Diverse. Well dressed. Styled hair. Two worlds sharing this space but remaining distinct, a line solidly drawn. Even more people crowded in the doorways and out into the hall.

On the stage, the seven members of the village council had begun to file into their seats behind a folding table, with one microphone at the center. Jason Blunt sat at the microphone, holding a small gavel. His father, Dale, sat beside him. They shared the same bulky build, though Dale's close-cropped hair had gone stark white. At the far right, Henry Smoke eased down his massive frame, wearing a leather vest decorated in Lakota symbols over a blue dress shirt.

The cameraman filmed them from the side of the stage, with Charlotte standing beside him. She was happy to see that none of the other stations had come. None of them knew or cared that the meeting was happening or that it was guaranteed to make for good TV. They were all so focused on the giant. Instead, Charlotte had been looking at the locals. Shadowing them on social media. Hearing what they talked about. And mostly they talked about this. About outsiders building a mosque in their town.

A thrum of voices filled the large room and reverberated from the brick walls, then silenced as Jason banged his gavel. Charlotte smiled. This would be a bloodbath.

| | |

David pushed his way into the school past the crowd. People started to give him ugly looks, then stopped once they saw the badge. He had left Brooke outside to keep an eye on the crowd that filled the parking lot. Ahead, he could hear Jason's voice projected through a loudspeaker. The meeting had begun. Suddenly, a hand grabbed his arm.

"Hey. David."

Tabby. He had begun to force a smile when he saw Brian next to her, then gave up the effort. Brian was taller than David, dressed expensively, his blond hair shaped into a wave. The marijuana business must be treating you well, David thought but didn't say. He told himself that's why he disliked Brian, because he ran a grow house across the state line, where it was legal. Not because Brian had taken Tabby and made her happier than David ever had.

"You sure have your hands full here tonight," Brian said, a forced attempt at humor to thaw things.

"Sure do," David said, not reacting. "I should get inside."

Tabby didn't let go of his arm.

"We were hoping you could stop by some time. Maybe dinner?"

David nodded.

"Sure. You bet. Now, I really should get."

She released him, and he angled into the gym, standing at the back. A bigger crowd than had ever gathered here before. More faces than he could hope to recognize. So many outsiders. An instinct struck—a killer is loose in the town. What if the killer is here? Hiding among the throng like a shark out of sight in the water. Just waiting to strike. The gavel banged.

On the stage, Jason leaned his elbows onto the table. He seemed tired, sapped of the seemingly endless energy he'd always possessed, an entirely different person now from the muscular teenager who had sprinted up and down this court, grabbing rebounds and launching himself improbably toward the rim.

"Okay, now, we have one zoning question on the agenda for tonight," Jason was saying. "This comes with approval from the county zoning committee. Parcel number seven-two-two."

"No mosque!" someone shouted from the rows of chairs, sparking a tremor of angry voices.

Jason hammered his gavel and read from a piece of paper.

"This application comes from the Islamic Cultural Society for Garden County to convert the parcel into a place of worship, as well as a community center."

Jason searched the audience, then landed on a face in the bleachers, near the stage. There, David saw Aaliyah and a group of thirty-some others wearing hijabs or burqas, and men in plain suits and taqiyah caps.

"Imam Bey. Would you please grace us with a few words?" Jason asked.

One of the men, tall and thin with glasses and a white beard, stood and walked to a microphone standing in front of the stage. He had to bend down for it to register his voice.

"As-salāmu 'alaykum," he said in a soft voice. "That means 'peace be with you' in Arabic. And that is my message to you. Our message to you, to our friends in the Abrahamic tradition and those of other faiths or no faith at all. This mosque will be open to all, a place for community and for peace . . ."

"Terrorist."

David scanned the crowd, trying to see who had said it. The imam pursed his lips and continued.

"A place of learning."

"Go back to your own country!"

The imam opened his mouth again, but more shouts came, each of them growing louder. The locals on the floor first, then the outsiders in the stands, yelling out in defense of the imam. Then one man stood, his voice rising above the others, and even though the man faced away from David, he could see the missing arm and knew it was Spady.

"Come to my home? My fucking home? You even try to open that thing, I swear to God . . ." Spady was shouting.

David pushed forward onto the court and through seats and people

38

until he came beside his friend and grabbed his left forearm. On the stage, the TV camera pointed at them.

"Spady," David said, his voice firm but kind.

Spady's arm tensed with a strength that surprised David, almost throwing him off balance. But David's training kicked in, and he twisted the arm back, clutching tighter. Finally, David felt the arm go slack.

The crowd seemed to see this and to understand, quieting just enough to hear Jason banging the gavel.

"Enough! Let's get this over with and hold the vote," Jason said. "All opposed?"

Dale raised his hand, as did the woman beside him.

"I'm abstaining," muttered an old farmer, his arms crossed over his chest.

That left four members of the council yet to vote. "All in favor?" Jason asked.

Henry Smoke raised his hand immediately. Slowly, two more members followed. Then, with a shrug, Jason raised his as well.

"The motion carries," Jason spoke into the microphone. "Now for God's sake let's adjourn."

The room turned to chaos after that. Loud voices. Everyone standing and moving, the locals and outsiders colliding as they squeezed out through the two sets of doors. Spady was gone, and all David could do was yell above the crowd, begging people to move in an orderly fashion, whatever the hell that meant. He glanced for a moment up at the stage, where Jason and Dale seemed locked in argument, but he couldn't hear what was said.

Outside, the crowd moved slowly toward the old football field, where cars were parked in neat rows. The halogen lights were turned on, and David could see Brooke using her flashlight to guide traffic toward the street.

Just as he was about to thank himself that things hadn't turned worse, a yell started up. Aaliyah and her group had just walked out of the gym, and a group of locals had spotted them. Maybe forty people, inching forward, yelling. Faces that David knew. People he bumped into in the grocery store and drank beers with and kneeled next to at the front of the Methodist church to take communion. He didn't see Spady and thought a quick thank you for that.

Aaliyah caught sight of David and opened her eyes wide, imploring. David angled himself between the groups, holding his hands up, palms out.

"Let's all just go home," he started to say.

They kept shouting. Then among the angry crowd an arm swung forward, and something sailed past his head. He turned to see a woman in a burqa reel, holding her hands to her face. She looked up again, shocked but seemingly unhurt.

"God damn it that's enough!" David yelled. "Go home!"

The faces he knew looked at him with anger and disappointment, and then they receded into the night. He went to Aaliyah once he felt sure they were gone.

"How is she?" he asked.

Aaliyah glared at him.

"That was assault. You should arrest them."

David stammered. He tried to play out the possibility. He hadn't seen who it was, couldn't possibly prove anything. But it wasn't just that. He knew that if he charged anyone, it would pit every local against him.

Before he could offer any real response, Aaliyah shook her head as she and the group walked toward the field. David trailed just behind. The field was mostly empty, everyone gone. Brooke stood with her hands on her hips.

"Good work tonight," David said.

"I heard that back there. What a shit show."

She hadn't seen her husband's eruption, so at least there was that. Spady stood, smoking, near Brooke's truck. David and Jason walked over to him, and the three formed a triangle on the field where they'd played football together so many years ago.

"Spady, you're the only smart one out of the three of us," Jason said. "You knew better'n to run for office."

David stifled a yawn.

"If I had just looked at my magic eight ball, it would've told me, 'A giant dead alien is going to drop on your doorstep, and all the world's problems are going to follow it, so you really should not run for sheriff,'" he said.

Spady sucked hard at the cigarette. Then he turned, stood up on his toes, and exhaled into Jason's face.

"You sure managed to sell us out to the fucking heathens," he hissed.

In their lifetime of friendship, Spady had never challenged Jason that directly. A cynical joke here and there, but Jason was the leader of their little group, the id, and the others his wingmen. But Spady seemed changed, absent of any deference. Maybe it was losing his arm. Maybe it was the giant, transforming him as it had transformed everyone and everything else.

Jason pulled back his shoulders, puffing out his chest, looming over Spady.

"The hell was I supposed to do? They bought the land. They crossed every 't' and dotted every 'i.' Squeaky-goddamned-clean. If I voted them down, they could've come back and sued the council for discrimination. Then I have to spend every last tax dollar we have on a legal case we have no hope of winning. I can't pay to have trash picked up. Can't pay his salary." He nodded toward David.

Spady took another drag, the cigarette incinerating itself in his hand.

"Your old man thought different."

Spady sauntered off toward Brooke, and the two of them drove away together.

"Seems like everybody has something to say," Jason sighed to David. "What about you?"

David shrugged.

"Can't say I expected that. That you'd side with them."

"Us and them," Jason muttered. "I remember back when I saw the world that way."

David wished that Ben Junior was there. He'd been the peacemaker of the group, the one who knew instinctively not just when feelings had been hurt but how to make things good again.

"I didn't mean . . ." David started to say.

Jason cut him off. "What would you have done, cousin? If that was you up there?"

There was more resignation in his voice than anger. David didn't answer, and Jason drifted away.

Alone, David looked up into the glare of the halogen lights, and it was possible just for a moment to imagine that he was playing high school football again, that the world wasn't a centrifuge spinning a hundred million miles an hour, that everything wasn't going to fly apart at any second, every last bit of matter colliding and fracturing into infinitesimal pieces barreling into the darkest recesses of space.

SEVEN

The old man stared forward, his eyes wide and caught in an expression midway between wonderment and dread. He sat in an easy chair, gripping the armrests in both hands tightly enough that his knuckles were white.

"Who are you?" he asked, the words tumbling out unevenly.

David didn't answer. He looked up at the clock on the wall, at the second hand that ticked forward, moving steadily past 6:36 p.m. The room was small, just big enough for the easy chair, a bed, and a desk that was covered in newspaper clippings and print outs. The old man wore striped pajamas and a white robe. His face twitched.

If only David could reach out to him, comfort him. But he knew it would end badly, with the old man growing angrier, more confused.

Somewhere, in the distance, a dog barked. And then another, closer. And then more. The high yips of small dogs rising above the guttural whine of a retriever, the ambulance-like wail of a beagle. The clock ticked past 6:37. The old man's eyes tensed, then focused.

"Hi, Grandpa," David said.

The old man's eyes softened. He smiled.

"David. Has the clock just started?" Samuel asked, stretching out his hands.

"Two minutes."

Samuel stood and faced the desk. His spindly legs bowed out, straining to support his thin body. He picked up a sheet of paper.

"Right. We left off with the British research paper on dogs and their sense of smell, that that might have something to do with it. But we felt like we ruled that out, right? They bark at the exact moment that us fogeys wake up, and so the two things must be linked—the barking and the waking up. But since people don't have that same sense of smell . . ."

David listened, trying to keep up. The old man charged into each evening like this, wasting not a single moment. But for David it still took the breath out of him each night, even after two years of this. Two years ago the Alzheimer's patients at the town's nursing home suddenly startled back to life, their memories and personalities returning—for exactly two minutes. Every night since, at 6:37, every dog within five miles of the giant would bark like hell, and at the exact same time those with dementia were themselves again. Each night, David came and sat with his grandpa, waiting, expecting it not to happen again, that the miracle couldn't possibly continue. And then it did. For twenty-three hours and fifty-eight minutes a day, Samuel was catatonic except for fits of paranoia. But ever since the giant fell, for those two minutes, his mind was as sharp as ever.

The rest of the family knew about this, but it was David who came every night. David who helped Samuel in his search to understand what was happening, to see if this awakening could be captured and its effect made permanent.

"So, what do dogs have in common with us?" Samuel was asking.

"With people?"

"With Alzheimer's patients," Samuel said, pointing at himself.

David shook his head and stood.

"Why don't you sit, Grandpa?"

"I sit all damned day." Samuel grabbed another paper from the desk. "Have you read this yet? More than five thousand recorded incidents of pets—dogs and cats, mostly—exhibiting signs of mental telepathy. The animals knew that their owners had been killed or injured, even though they were miles away. Five thousand."

"That's a lot," David said.

"Damn right it is."

"So?"

"Telepathy. Minds connecting invisibly. Some unseen physical force that connects things. That could be it. Something that touches everyone, but the dogs are more sensitive to it. And for whatever reason, it affects us more than it affects everyone else."

David shivered at the vision of some invisible field of energy emanating from the giant and touching him.

"It could be a coincidence," he said. "You remember Sadie? That dog couldn't stop licking herself, not even when her whole body was one giant sore. And you're saying she could, what, read minds?"

Samuel grabbed David's arm, gentle but firm.

"I get it. It's hard, this stuff. Strange. Impossible. But listen to the dogs barking. Look at me." He pointed through the open window, where the outline of the giant was just visible above the skyline. "Look at him. None of it makes any sense. All we can do is try to understand little pieces of it. But to do that, we have to confront the stuff we don't know. Not be scared of it."

Samuel held his gaze, demanding a response. Finally, David nodded.

"Okay. So, possibly a mental connection, some unseen force. But if it's that, how do we know what the force is?"

Samuel released David's arm.

"Now you're asking the right questions. There was a lab at Duke that ran experiments on telepathy for decades. A lot of it for the military and CIA, so some of the work is still confidential. But there might be some reports you can track down."

Samuel jotted notes onto a sheet of paper on the desk, then folded it cleanly and handed it to David. His grandpa had always been the smartest man David knew, though Samuel hadn't even finished grade school. Growing up in the Dust Bowl, he'd had to work the family farm and take on odd jobs to survive. He worked and saved until he could buy out the bank, then kept farming even as he ran it. But at night, he read for hours on end, always nonfiction, any topic, making up for all those years of lost learning. Any question you ever had, you asked him.

He was also a quiet man, speaking only as much as needed, prone to long stretches of staring off into the distance. Whenever anyone found Samuel in a reverie and asked what he was doing, Samuel would smile coyly and say he was playing checkers with God. As a kid, David had envisioned this scene, imagining Samuel sitting at his dining room table and God in his white robes and flowing white beard on the other side, a checkers board between them. More than a few people suggested David had inherited this disposition toward solitude.

Now Samuel had plenty of time to be locked in his thoughts. When he awoke, he trained his voracious hunger for knowledge on the mystery of the giant and this fleeting awareness.

Outside, the dogs quieted. A minute left.

"Okay, your turn," Samuel said. "We left off at the wedding, right?"

David nodded. This was their agreement. Information for information. Samuel jumped back midstream into a story.

"Like I was saying, they wanted to get married at our house. The old place out in the country. Your dad and I built a little wooden arch right next to the creek, between those two old cottonwoods. There was one day that we were working on it, and your dad cut his hand. I'd forgotten that. We were sawing the boards, and he slipped and ran the blade over his knuckles. Nothing too bad, but we were hot and sweaty, so it bled like a son of a bitch. Your mom came out just then, and she saw all that blood and she must've thought I'd killed him."

Samuel paused and swallowed, then continued.

"She was some woman, your mom. She picked up the saw and cut her own hand, and then she squeezed it so that her blood dripped onto the board, on top of his blood. Then she took his hand in hers and said that they were bound together. Forever."

Some of the stories about his parents were old ones, family lore often repeated. Then there were the stories he'd never heard, especially the pieces of their lives that came before he was born. Stories they maybe would've gotten around to telling him if they'd lived, if the tornado hadn't come and sucked them into the sky.

David checked the clock.

"I'll have that research for you, Grandpa."

"Thanks, kiddo. Quick, how is everything? You seem tired."

"Work. All these new people, the town isn't like it was . . . There was this murder the other day. I just couldn't imagine how anyone could do something like that to another person."

"That's a lot of weight to carry," Samuel said, easing back into his chair. "How's Jason doing? I haven't seen him for a while."

"I think he's having a hard time, too. He's working at the bank, running the county assessor office, and running the village council. Just last night they had a big meeting. I had told you about the mosque they want to build. Anyway, Dale voted against it, but Jason voted for it, and it passed. Seems like maybe there's some argument between them."

Samuel stared off for so long it seemed he'd already faded. Then he shook his head.

"I don't know how I failed Dale, but I did. Mom and I tried our best with the boys. I took the belt to them a handful of times. That was just what we did those days. Your dad and Benjamin, they both grew up okay. But Dale, he just had this mean streak in him. Like there was part of him that was a rattlesnake."

Samuel was crying.

"Tell Jason I'm sorry."

The dogs had gone quiet.

"Sorry for what, Grandpa?"

Samuel stared forward. His eyes wide and glassy. He had stopped crying. The clock went tick-tick-tick. Then Samuel's face twisted into a look of fear.

"Who the hell are you?"

Along the hallway of the nursing home, all the doors opened almost at once, family members filing out. Spouses. Grandchildren. Children. Most with eyes red, damp tissues clutched in their hands.

They assembled by the door, where the nursing home's administrator gathered them as she always did, and they recited in unison the pledge they had all long since memorized, a promise that no one outside the building could know about the awakening, that if anyone did learn, the residents here would become test subjects, and things would never be the same. David spoke the pledge robotically, his thoughts elsewhere.

Why was Samuel apologizing? What had happened with Jason? And what did Dale have to do with it? David had never been close to his uncle. He wasn't the kind of man who told jokes or played around with kids. And since David had become an adult, they only had quick exchanges, functional interactions.

He started his nightly patrol. Old Town first. All at once he was at the courthouse, and he wondered if he had gone there by intention. There was Jason's black sedan in the parking lot, and his window showed a light on.

David parked, rehearsing things in his head as he walked toward the building. They could pull out the bottle of bourbon Jason keeps in his desk, shoot the breeze a bit. Then David would mention he had been to see Samuel, and the old man had said something . . .

Above him, the window exploded.

A hailstorm of broken glass fell across David and crashed against the cement around him as his brain struggled to process the roaring sound that echoed in his ears. Thunder? No. The blast of a shotgun.

EIGHT

David took one second to look up, into the empty window. It had gone dark. Then a flash of light and a roar. Another blast of the shotgun.

The sudden illumination revealed two silhouettes inside.

Instinct took over. David was running, right hand pulling his nine-millimeter as he went.

The heavy door came open. He shoved through, into the dark of the building. His feet took him up the stairs.

Another explosion of shotgun fire. He was to the second floor.

A scream. Jason's voice. He had reached the office.

David rammed through the door and leveled his gun.

"Jason!" he yelled.

His eyes swept the dark of the room. The window blasted out. The shotgun missing from its rack. Chairs overturned. A lamp knocked down, bulb broken. The only light coming in was from a streetlight outside, just bright enough to illuminate something on the floor . . .

Not something. Someone. Feet pointed skyward. Feet wearing red Converse sneakers.

David stepped forward into the shadows.

"Jason?"

The legs lay face up, but the torso twisted impossibly, folding over on itself, so that the chest almost touched the floor.

David inched closer, keeping his gun raised. He reached out his hand to shake his cousin, to rouse him. Then he stopped.

The abdomen had been sliced open, a great diagonal wound that went almost entirely through him. Intestines and organs spilled out from beneath sheared-off rib bones that stuck out like teeth.

David followed the body up, to where the neck rose into the lower jaw and then simply ended. He was staring into the bisected tongue and throat cavity, and the white circle of spinal column. It couldn't be his cousin.

Then he saw the rest of the head. It had landed a couple of feet away and sat on the ground, staring forward. It looked as if Jason had poked his head up through a hole cut into the floor. David's stomach seized.

A crackle of static, and David spun, searching the room.

His radio on his belt. "Boss! You there? I heard gunshots. In the building, upstairs. Shots fired in the building!"

David held down the transmit button on the radio. He kept his voice low.

"I'm here. Jason is down. I'm looking for the assailant . . ."

A shadow moved in his periphery, fast. He let go of the radio and swung his gun to the right.

Too late. The shape crashed into him at full speed, and he smashed into a file cabinet, barely keeping hold of his pistol.

The shape went out the door.

"Stop!" David yelled as he pushed himself to his feet and ran out, following.

As he sprinted to the stairwell, he heard the building's front door open below. He ran down, shoved his way out. Gun raised and ready.

David stalked forward into the night. The moon was just a sliver, little help. There were no trees or bushes. Nowhere to hide.

The scrape of shoes on gravel.

David spun to the sound.

There. A shadow moving behind his truck in the parking lot.

"Freeze!"

The shadow charged away, into a neighboring yard. David threw himself after it.

Breath came in gasps. His ribs were bruised, maybe broken. The image of Jason's face, of the fear in his dead eyes, the eviscerated body kept forcing its way to the front of David's thoughts. No. Stay buried. Not now.

David came around a shed, into an expanse of grass leading to a single-story house. Nothing. He stepped forward, into the open, between the open door of the shed and the house.

He started to reach for his flashlight as he stepped toward the cave-like entrance to the shed. It opened wide in front of him, pitch black. His fingers struggled to pull the flashlight free.

Out of the blackness, the form shot out, straight at David.

A man. Face hidden beneath the dark hood of a jacket. Holding something along his right side. A long blade that hissed in the air as it swung forward.

David startled back a step as he fired.

The man ducked to the side, the shot missing high, bullet cracking against something metal inside the shed.

David caught his balance and aimed again, but the man was already in the shadows of the next yard, putting an impossible distance between them. This won't work. Try something else.

David didn't pursue the man directly, instead going out to the street, circling around the block. Maybe he'd be lucky. Maybe the person in the shadows would angle for a way out, rather than keep on sprinting dead ahead through one yard after another.

He eased into an alley, jogging with soft steps, darting from the shadow of one building to the next.

Then the man stepped in front of him, some twenty feet away.

He turned toward David. His face remained hidden beneath the hood of the black jacket. The blade was more than a foot long, its cutting edge running straight, then ending in a slight curve.

"Drop your weapon!"

The man gave no sign of moving. Said nothing.

David steadied his finger over the Glock's trigger and stepped forward. "Last warning!"

In a movement that was as smooth as it was instantaneous, the man turned and vaulted over a six-foot-tall wooden privacy fence into a yard.

Panting, David ran to the spot. He jumped, grabbing onto the top of the fence, and pulled himself up to look over. No sign of anything.

He knew. The man with the knife was gone, disappeared into the black of the night.

David lowered himself down and turned back toward the courthouse. The empty window looked out at him. He stopped resisting and let the vision of his dead cousin come back in full, and he began to scream.

NINE

Time seemed to become elastic. Stretching and slowing then snapping forward in a blur of lights and sirens and shouts and faces. David fought to grab a hold of some piece of it, to seize onto reality and drag himself out of the memory of that office and the body inside it. No. Not *the* body. Jason's body. His cousin—cut apart as if he was a deer that had been shot, gutted and half skinned. David forced his eyes open and saw the wrinkled face of Erickson, the FBI man, leaning into his own. His lips moved slowly, calmly. David centered himself on the words, willing himself to hear.

". . . need to get you away from here. Okay? Can you stand?" Erickson was saying.

David was sitting on the steps of the courthouse. He reached for his hat and discovered it was missing—must've been knocked off when he was slammed into the file cabinet. Around them, dark-suited men and women moved in and out of the building. A forensics team stepped down out of a van, wearing white hazmat suits that made them look like strange spirits wafting past. Caution tape demarcated the whole block. Beyond it, Andrea and Brooke stood. Brooke clutched her face, sobbing. Beside her, David saw Dale. The old man stared ahead blankly. David thought then of Jason's wife. His twin daughters. All the rest of the family.

"I need to go. I have to talk to them," David finally said.

David started to stand, but Erickson held his ground, not letting David past.

"They know already," the old man rasped. "I need you to come with me. Now."

There was no fight left inside David. He let himself be led to a black sedan and settled into the back. Only once the car was moving did David think to ask where they were headed. From his seat behind the wheel, Erickson said nothing.

|||

The man's heart still drummed a frenetic rhythm. The first two times it had been so simple. So clean and perfect. Yes, with each one he had advanced his technique, had taken more time in the artistry of it. But they both had been almost effortless.

Nothing about this had been easy. The last victim had seen it coming and reacted more quickly than expected, grabbing the shotgun down from the rack above his desk and firing. Then the struggle that left the large man in pieces on the floor.

He had only just started into the real work of it, delicately putting blade to flesh, when he'd heard the office's door open and the sheriff yell out. He should have killed the sheriff. He knew that as he waited in the shadows, watching the sheriff enter, seeing the horror in his eyes as he saw the carnage.

But the man had made his choice, and the sheriff lived. Now the sheriff would be after him. The sheriff hadn't seen his face, couldn't recognize him. The man was sure of that. All the same, they were tied to each other now. He could feel it, the inevitability of pursuit with the only uncertainty being how it all concluded.

His heart slowed. He grinned. Good. Let the sheriff come. Because as messy and imperfect as it was, this killing, it was also something new. It was fun.

The man lost himself in thought, imagining the game ahead.

Absentmindedly, he lifted his shirt. The skin of his abdomen was dotted with what looked like large, black goosebumps. With his index finger and thumb, the man squeezed one of the bumps. A tiny metal ball popped free, oily with blood. Shotgun buckshot. He hadn't even felt it, being shot. Couldn't feel any pain now.

He put his fingers to another bump and squeezed.

|||

Erickson guided the black sedan to the north, out of Old Town, heading straight toward the rounded, glass-sided structure of the Countryman

Federal Building. It had always been something like Mount Olympus to David, an inaccessible realm populated by gods whose dictates guided the lives of the mortals below. He supposed that the FBI ran its operations through the building.

David focused on the details of the world flowing past, staying in the present, not letting himself slip back into the reality of what had just happened. Still, as he sat there, his hands refused to stop shaking.

The car ducked suddenly down onto a ramp that led beneath the building and circled around and around, one level after another, until finally they came to a thick metal gate manned by army soldiers carrying machine guns.

Erickson rolled down his window, whispered something to a soldier, and magically the gate opened. The car rolled through, then parked. Erickson stepped out and opened David's door. David looked for an entrance or elevator.

"This way," Erickson said, pointing toward a white van that sat idling nearby.

David recognized the vehicle immediately. It looked like an airport shuttle, though absent any marking beyond the federal government plates. The windows were tinted solid black. Every day, these vans went back and forth between the Countryman Building and Site One, the scientific research base sitting beside the giant's face. David always supposed they ferried people and supplies in and out of the base, ensuring absolute security.

Erickson held out his hands to David.

"Radio and cell phone. And your gun."

"Why?" David started to ask.

"It's the rule," Erickson said. "No outside electronics. And no weapons unless you're army or FBI."

"What's going on? Where are you taking me?"

"Question-and-answer comes later, kid."

David felt himself unbuckling his belt and handing it over, all while he wondered why he was being so obedient.

The van's door slid open automatically. Erickson nodded. David stepped inside, and Erickson followed, each of them taking a separate bench. A man with a crewcut wearing a plain white polo shirt sat behind the wheel. Without a word, he began to drive.

Erickson closed his eyes, as if he was sleeping in place. David began to regain his hold on time, his mind turning again, remembering the murder, locking in the details of the killer. He was a little shorter than David. Five-nine or five-ten. Average build with broad shoulders that marked him as a man. Strong but not muscular. The blade in his right hand, maybe twenty inches long, with the slight curve of a fishing knife. David saw again the man vault so cleanly over the tall fence.

He looked down at his hands, which still trembled. He should have shot the man. He'd had his cousin's killer dead to rights, and he just stood there. He failed.

The van drove up out of the parking deck and onto the street, headed north and then west. Shortly, the buildings stopped at the demarcated no man's land surrounding the giant. Locals gossiped that the stretch was full of land mines. Only one road led through it, a simple blacktop angling directly for Gulliver's face, toward that massive brow and clusters of eyes. They came to the fence circling the giant. Metal plating some twenty feet tall. Twin towers on either side of the road, a solid gate blocking the path. Armed soldiers approached. There was some quick exchange, and the gate opened.

Ahead, the giant grew impossibly as the van moved again, drawing them closer. David had never been this near to it. His hands shook even more. The giant blotted out half of the sky, then more. It would swallow them. Devour them. Not from any overt action but only because it was so big it must have its own gravitational pull.

They came then into Site One itself. From a distance, the buildings seemed small, but now David saw that they were massive—white metal structures the size of airplane hangars arranged in a neat grid, each building connected to the others by tunnels and walkways. It was a trick of perspective, this. Being next to the giant, anything would seem microscopic. All that anyone knew for certain about the compound was that it was run by NASA, and supposedly scientists from around the world gathered there to study the mystery of Gulliver. But beyond that, nothing was said, and the void was filled with rumors and conspiratorial theories.

The road led into an opening on the end of one building, and inside they came to a stop amid a massive area where dozens of the white vans were staged. Beyond that stretched what looked like the security area of an airport. Lanes with scanners, all overseen by more soldiers. Erickson led David into the checkpoint.

A soldier stopped them. Erickson held up a badge, and then the soldier scrutinized David.

"He doesn't have a badge."

"I've already talked with Priest. Call her. Potential contamination."

David read the alarm on the face of the soldier, who inched back from David. The soldier leaned away and spoke into a radio. A few moments later, he waved them on.

"Clear to proceed."

Once they were through the scan and Erickson was leading the way through labyrinthine hallways, David came even with the agent.

"You said potential contamination. What does that mean?"

Erickson held his lighter in his hand, opening and closing it again and again.

"Just code, kid. Bureaucracy-speak. Come on."

They went from that building into another through a covered walkway, and to another and another. At each, Erickson scanned a badge to open the glass doors that blocked the way. The buildings were interconnected so that one could traverse the entire site without ever going outside. Each building was marked with a number. Finally, they stepped into Building Seventeen.

"We're here," Erickson said.

He led the way down a large central hallway, past dozens of unmarked doors. Occasionally, they passed people in civilian clothing and white lab coats who walked without raising their eyes.

Erickson stopped at one door and scanned his badge at a sensor. It clicked, and he opened the door.

"Inside."

David stepped into the dark, and a light came on automatically. Behind him, Erickson shut the door from the outside.

"Hey!" David said.

He tried the door handle, but it wouldn't move.

The room was all white. Three blank walls, then another with a wide mirror—a one-way window, he felt certain. He could feel eyes watching him. The only things in the room were a white plastic chair and a small wheeled cart, the kind nurses move about in a hospital, with wires and monitors. David wondered how late it was; he felt then a tiredness that crested like a wave.

It was silent aside from the scrape of his boots on the tile floor. Why had Erickson brought him here? Why had Erickson taken over the scene?

Then he remembered Erickson appearing suddenly at the site of the realtor's murder. And that the state police detectives had as much as confirmed that the FBI had shown up after Jim Holly was killed. All three victims dead from stab wounds. David saw again the hooded man in his mind's eye. The blade at his side.

"Sheriff Blunt."

The voice seemed to come from above, but there was no one there. A speaker secreted in the ceiling. The voice was robotic, atonal, but with a natural cadence, as if a real person were speaking through some modulator that gave it an artificial inflection. Instinct told him it wasn't Erickson.

"Please remove your uniform. You may leave on your underwear."

He glared at his own reflection in the mirror.

"The hell I will. Who are you? What is this place?"

"Sheriff Blunt. Either remove your clothing or we will send in some-one to do it for you."

For a moment, David thought he would resist. Let them come. Let them try. But what was he going to do? Take on an entire army? He unbuttoned his shirt, tugged it off, folded it, and tossed it to the ground. Then he removed his pants.

"Sit."

He stared at the mirror, seeing only his nearly naked body. His expres-sion betrayed exhaustion, confusion, and a growing spark of anger.

"Sheriff Blunt. Please attach the cuff to your left arm," the voice con-tinued. "And attach the clip to your right index finger."

"Why?"

No answer came. Once again, he found himself suddenly complying, as if exhaustion sapped him of any ability to act on the emotions churn-ing inside him. He grabbed the cuff from the cart and wrapped it around his arm, then clipped the heartrate monitor to his index finger. He sat.

The cuff inflated automatically, the device whirring and clicking and beeping in the cart.

"What is your name?" the voice returned.

"You know my name."

"Please. Oblige us. This won't take long."

"David Blunt."

"Where do you live?"

"Here. Little Springs. You want the address?"

"Where do you work?"

The questions were coming faster, cutting off the end of his responses.

"You just called me the sheriff. You know I'm the sheriff."

Silence. The cuff gripped his arm tightly enough to cut off circulation.

"Fine. I'm the sheriff."

The cuff began to deflate.

"David, what do you dream of, when you dream?"

"Excuse me?"

Silence.

Just as David was about to push for an explanation, the voice returned.

"Thank you, Sheriff Blunt. You may remove the monitors."

"Thank you for what? What the hell kind of question was that?"

He tore the devices away and let them hang from the cart.

"It was a test, sheriff. A test that you passed. Now, please tell us what happened tonight."

David looked again to the door, but he knew it was still locked. His only hope at getting out of this room was to obey.

"I went to the courthouse to see my cousin. Jason."

"Why did you visit him at night?"

With each question, his confusion diminished, replaced by more anger.

"That's my own fucking business. And if you don't stop interrupting me, this is going to take all night."

"It will take as long as it takes," the voice said, showing no reaction. "Continue."

David leaned forward in the chair, putting his head in his hands, and allowed the memories to come forward, taking them through, detail by detail. The window exploding out. Two figures in silhouette. Two more shotgun blasts. Jason on the ground. The form crashing into him.

"You saw it?" the voice interrupted.

It. Not him. They asked if he saw it.

"Him," David corrected. "I saw him."

He continued the story, through the chase into the town, the blade swinging at him, his shot going wide. Then the man disappearing.

"Sheriff. Is there anything you're forgetting?"

He shook his head. The voice remained silent.

David leaned back and forced himself to think. Three killings, somehow connected. The FBI involved in each. Yet they didn't even know the killer was a man. Meaning David was the only person to have seen the killer and live.

There was a click behind him, and the door opened. Erickson returned. Behind him was the woman from the realtor's office. She wore her dark hair in a loose bun and had on sweats. She looked as if she'd been woken from sleep. She carried the same backpack she had had when David saw her before.

David stood.

"What is this?" he asked. "Who is she?"

Erickson held up a hand, signaling him to remain in place.

"This is Dr. Sunny Lee," Erickson offered. "She needs to check one last thing."

The woman pulled on latex gloves, then took a device from her backpack. It was small enough for her to hold in one hand, a simple black box with a few buttons and a meter.

Sunny approached David. She looked into his eyes, sympathetic.

"This will just take a second," she said.

She waved the device over his body, around his face, then moving down to his neck, his chest, along each arm, and finally down his legs. It made steady clicking sounds but didn't react otherwise.

All at once, Sunny was done and put the device away.

"Here. Wear these. We're going to have to keep your clothing to check for any evidence," Erickson said, holding out a gray T-shirt and matching sweatpants.

"My boots and my hat?" David asked as he tugged them on.

"We'll get everything back to you. Your belt and gun, too."

Dressed, David felt his anger return.

"I've been awfully damn patient. I think it's time for you to answer some questions now," David said, then looked at Sunny. "What is that thing you waved at me? What kind of doctor are you? I saw you the other day. At the other murder scene."

Sunny looked to Erickson, who mouthed something imperceptible. Then she looked to David.

"I'm a PhD, not a medical doctor," she said. "I'm a geologist."

David was only more confused.

"Geology? What does that have to do with murders? What the hell is really going on here?"

"There is a serial killer in Little Springs."

A woman's voice came from behind Erickson, by the door. David knew by the rhythm of it that it belonged to the same person who had spoken to him from behind the mirror. He saw a tall Black woman in a dark skirt suit with neon yellow high heels that hammered the floor as she stepped forward. In her hand, she held a manila folder.

"Director Priest," she introduced herself, "Department of Defense Security Service. I manage Site One. And anything of military interest that falls outside of the perimeter."

Beside her stood an overweight man with red hair and small, green eyes set into a wide, unassuming face. He had the stiff posture of a military man but wore the suit of a bureaucrat.

Priest gestured to the man.

"This is Vice Chairman Conover. He runs the military operations here."

Neither Priest nor Conover made any movement to shake David's hand. He looked closely at their faces, committing the names and roles to memory. The old, tired FBI man is Erickson. The big redhead is Conover, the military guy. The Black woman is Priest, with a vague DOD role. And the young Asian American scientist is Sunny.

"A serial killer," David said. "Kapoor and Holly?"

Erickson nodded.

"And now Mr. Blunt."

Conover spoke then for the first time, his voice surprisingly high for such a large man.

"Sheriff, I hope you understand that the situation here is of the highest sensitivity."

All at once, the anger that had been building in David reached a crescendo. He kicked the medical cart, which raced crazily on its small wheels before toppling and crashing to the floor with a loud bang.

"My cousin is dead!" he shouted. "*My* cousin. A murderer is loose in *my* town, and you couldn't even tell me? Now you drag me here. You make me take off my clothes. Answer your questions."

The outburst had burned off the last reservoir of energy he had. David was tired. So goddamned tired.

"We have to protect the sanctity of the investigation," Priest said. "We can't offer any more information than we already have."

"Bullshit," David said. "I'm the only one here who has seen the killer. If I walk out right now, I'll tell the world everything I know, and I'll tell them who you all are, and that you're hiding this thing."

Priest's face hardened.

"Or," David continued, "you let me help solve this case. Give me whatever evidence you have. Everything. I'll help you find the killer, and in return, I will tell the world whatever lies you want told."

The others looked at each other, except for Sunny, who kept her eyes on David. He guessed that Priest, Conover, and Erickson were in charge of things here. And for whatever reason, this geologist had gotten pulled into their orbit.

"Just tell him," Erickson said finally.

Priest looked pained, but then she stepped forward and handed the manila folder to David. He opened it and was greeted with a crime scene photo of Sanjay Kapoor, the body just as he had discovered it.

"I've seen this," David said. "I was there."

"Keep looking," Conover instructed.

David flipped to the next photo. It was Kapoor again, but now the body was stripped naked and washed clean of blood, lying on a metal examining table. The dismembered arm sat beside it. The massive chest wound. Then, as David peered closer, he saw them. Dozens of other cut marks all over the body. Radiating cuts that spiraled out across the skin.

"This looks like . . ." he started to say.

He flipped to the next photo. A closer image. Superficial cuts that were perfectly curved, beginning in the armpit, then going out onto the man's chest and neck. What was that pattern called? A fractal.

He flipped to the next photo. Another body on a table. The tour guide, Jim Holly. The same massive chest wound.

He flipped to the next photo. A closer view of the man's skin, which had been carved with the exact same pattern as Kapoor's. The exact pattern that traced across the body of the giant.

David recognized it then. That large wound in the center of each dead man's chest? It was right where the spire stabbed down through the giant.

"God," he muttered.

"We don't know how or why, but we know the killer has some connection to the giant. Or obsession with it," Erickson said. "The bureau is taking over the investigations so that we can keep this secret. If people learn there's a killer out there, we'll have a panic. And if the details about the patterns leak, we could have copycats, and it would make it impossible to know whether any tips that come in are any good if everyone knows all the details."

"You can be part of this investigation. But you don't speak a word of it to anyone," Priest said.

Priest, Erickson, and Conover all stared at David with stony faces. He glanced to Sunny. She bit her lip, then looked quickly away from him. The others were old professionals. They knew how to lie. But Sunny couldn't hide her reactions. David read it on her face: This story that he'd been given was the truth but only part of it. There was far more that they were hiding.

David looked back to the others.

"I'm in," he said.

TEN

Charlotte found her cameraman, Michael, already waiting for her at the courthouse. Every cameraman she'd ever worked with drove like brakes had never been invented. He stood beside the station's news van, a logo on the side and antenna on the top to broadcast live coverage. It was four in the morning, but the whole town seemed already awake. Beyond the ring of yellow caution tape, dozens of people stood in clutches, wearing coats to guard themselves against the cool spring morning. Their eyes reflected disbelief and sadness. Some were crying, others gaped or gossiped.

It was true, then. Jason Blunt, head of the village council and as much of a beloved son as this town ever had, was dead.

After the village council meeting and the coverage of the mosque, the producers back in Atlanta had asked for more. They'd been the only station to have the news, and it drew big ratings. Charlotte had planned to try to interview Jason, to ask him why he had supported the mosque when so many locals didn't. Now she'd be reporting his death.

She'd known Jason when she lived here; everyone did. He was larger than life itself, physically big but also bursting with energy, someone who seemed to look at existence as a grand game, one he was sure to win.

She pushed the memories away. There was a job to do.

"Do we know what happened?" Charlotte asked.

Michael shook his head. He perpetually looked as if he'd just roused himself from sleep and immediately downed a couple of energy drinks. His coarse brown hair went every direction at once.

"It's strange. Police scanner is dead quiet. Nothing from the sheriff's department or the state police. Sounds like the county dispatcher was in the building and heard shots, then went up and found the body. The sheriff might have been there, too, but I haven't seen him."

Charlotte looked around again, searching for the sheriff. No sign of him. She took out a reporter's notebook to jot down details. Michael grabbed it from her and focused the camera's lens on a page, finding his white balance, then handed it back over. He lifted up the camera and started to shoot the scene—the crowd of mourning people, the people in dark suits standing guard at the courthouse door.

Charlotte stared up at the second-story window with bits of broken glass ringing it, like fangs in a mouth. Michael followed her eyes, then raised the camera and filmed the window as well.

Nearby were parked the vans of other news stations. Their teams were seeing all the same things. Did they know anything that Charlotte didn't? She would have to go on the air within minutes. There was no official confirmation of anything. All she could report on were rumors of a death.

Charlotte took out her phone. She'd only been in town a handful of days, but she'd been busy building up her contacts. She scrolled and landed on the number of a woman who worked in forensics with the state police. They'd met when Charlotte had toured the offices, and then Charlotte bumped into the woman again at a coffee shop and had bought her breakfast. The oldest trick there was in befriending sources. Charlotte tapped out a text.

are you up? sorry to bother you

Three dots appeared. A reply came.

I am. Don't have many details. Got the call about the murder, but then they told us we weren't needed.

Charlotte looked back up at the scene. She recognized the two state police detectives in their matching mustaches and windbreakers standing off to the side. But the people doing things, the ones moving in and out of the building and holding the perimeter, all wore plain dark suits. She tapped another message.

who's working the case then?

Three dots. Then:

FBI

The pieces of it didn't fit. The FBI wasn't supposed to take over cases, only to support the locals when they needed help. And there was something else. The other murder, the one she'd reported on the first day that she arrived. The realtor. Maybe it was all a coincidence . . . She started typing into her phone again.

another murder? do you have the autopsy report on the last one? I can come pick it up later

Three dots. Then:

No. Sorry. There was no autopsy.

Three dots.

I shouldn't say more.

Charlotte let it sink in. There was something here, she felt it. But she would start that digging later. Now it was time to go on air. She inspected her hair and makeup one last time in the van's side mirror, then grabbed the microphone.

"Confirmation from an official source," she said as Michael framed her in front of the courthouse. "Murder."

She glanced across the scene one last time. Where was the sheriff? What did he know?

|||

Erickson drove David to his apartment. A second wind came over him, and his mind raced through the details he'd learned, the gaps in his knowledge.

"Go past the courthouse," he said.

Erickson shook his head.

"No. You need sleep. And there's nothing to see there right now."

The old agent was quiet a while, then spoke again.

"Next few days are going to be the hardest, kid. You're going to want to come at this thing like a charging bull, but you can't. You have to be with your family; there's going to be the funeral. And you're going to want to tell them as much as you can. Because they deserve the truth. But they can't find out. Not about the cuts, the other murders, any of it. So that's your job, from here till the funeral. You go and you mourn with them. You remember your cousin. If anyone asks, you can tell them that you just happened to be at the scene. The neighbors heard the shot you fired into the shed, so you can say that you pursued the assailant but didn't get a good look. The same story that's going in your report."

David nodded, processing.

"I need to write it up."

"It's already written," Erickson said. "Get through the funeral. Then we start the work. I'll give you all the information we have. We'll go to the courthouse, go through the crime scene. Go through all the forensics we have. All of it."

They were both quiet for a few minutes. Then David spoke.

"Do you think we'll catch him?" he asked.

Erickson sighed.

"I've done this a long time, kid. Long enough to know better than to make promises."

ELEVEN

David slipped his hand through the leather loop and gripped it tightly. Across from him, Spady did the same, using his left arm. They pulled, and the coffin glided easily from out of the back of the hearse. The other pallbearers filed in as the coffin emerged from the vehicle, a mix of Jason's friends and some second cousins, all of them stony faced, resolute in purpose. They began the short walk to the grave site.

The coffin felt heavy enough. David wondered what was inside of it, because he was certain it wasn't Jason. The service at the church had been closed casket, and the family had been told they couldn't see the body. That it would be too traumatic. Excuses. The feds had Jason somewhere inside of Site One, doing Lord knows what with him. A spark of anger lit inside him. At the feds for creating the lie, and at himself for perpetrating it.

After Erickson had deposited David back at his apartment, he'd sat and stared and waited for sleep that wouldn't come. Finally, he grabbed a bottle of whiskey from the kitchen and steadily drank it dry, then tottered around the apartment until the world stopped.

In the days since, Erickson's warning had proven out. Most every waking moment was spent with the family, gathering at Jason's house, where his wife, Missy, mostly sat in silence on the living room sofa, an arm wrapped around each of their twin daughters. Extended family and friends filed in and out in a processional of hugs, tears, and casseroles.

Only in the evening would David escape, going to the nursing home to see Samuel. For once, the old man held no interest in the puzzle of the giant. Instead, the two of them sat beside each other on the bed, embracing, as Samuel pulled forward happy memories of Jason as a child. David couldn't bring himself to ask the old man about what he had been saying the night Jason died, the admission of guilt.

The coffin slid into place on the metal structure above the open grave. David stepped back into place amid the family, most of them sitting on folding chairs that had been set up on a thick green carpet. Missy and the girls sat at the front. Missy was as inscrutable as ever, always the antithesis of her ebullient husband. The girls were glassy eyed animals. They were seven—no, eight. Almost the age David had been when his parents died, when the family gathered in this same spot, with two coffins instead of one. David had said nothing to the girls over the past days, despite being the one who knew what they were experiencing more than any other. Truly, it was because of his shared experience. He knew that no matter what he said—what anyone said—it wouldn't help. Nothing can when your world is broken.

Next to them sat Jason's parents, Dale and Debbie. Then Samuel, staring emptily, in a wheelchair. Next to him was Jason's sister, Jenny, who shared her brother's masculine build. Beside them were Ben Senior and Bonnie. A seat was open for David, but he stood just off to the side.

They were near the top of a hill that rose on the south side of the Platte River, just across from town. Ash trees, a few small cedars, and yucca dotted the sandy soil around the rows of tombstones climbing the hillside. Overhead, the sky was unbroken gray.

Beyond the cemetery, they could look down at the river and at the splayed open legs of the giant. Between those legs, three massive forms stretched out. Scientists had said that because the giant was of an unknown species, its biology likely wouldn't exactly match our own. But the three things dangling between its legs sure looked like penises, each the size of a building.

The minister stepped forward, carrying a large Bible. She was a small woman whose upper back was just starting to hunch with age, her gray hair cut short, eyes hidden behind thick glasses. She opened the Bible.

"Dying, Christ destroyed our death. Rising, Christ restored our life. Christ will come again in glory . . ."

Her words faded into the breeze that came over the hill and started the dry grass to whispering. David turned away from the minister as subtly as he could and looked at the crowd that had gathered beyond the family. It seemed as if every resident of Little Springs was there. And beyond them, outsiders. Dozens. A few faces he recognized—Aaliyah and some of the others from the mosque—but most he didn't.

All at once, staring out over that group, the hairs stood up along David's neck. The killer was there. He didn't know how he knew it, but he was certain. Somewhere in that crowd was the man who'd torn his cousin open. A murderer obsessed with the giant. Desperately, he looked from face to face, willing himself to remember them all, to add to his list of suspects. Was it that man, with the bald head and high cheekbones? Or the one with blond hair holding a collapsed umbrella at his side? David wanted to shout out, to tear through the crowd person by person, to demand to know why his cousin had died.

Then he landed on a face he knew. Erickson. The old FBI man gave the slightest of nods. He was there for the same reason. Sunny stood beside him, her face mostly hidden behind large sunglasses.

The minister closed the Bible with a slam, snapping David's attention back to her.

"A new heaven and a new earth," she said. "That is what the Bible promises. Pretty hard to see it, isn't it, if you look at the world around us? Evil invading our town."

Missy clenched the twins closer to her.

"Depravity, all around us," the minister continued. "This world is under siege, brothers and sisters. Just look down there."

She pointed behind her, toward the giant.

"Satan has sent a messenger! A fallen angel, dropped right onto us. We read of this in the book of Enoch. The giants of old came down from the hill and took women; they 'befouled the earth with their deeds, who in all time of their age made lawlessness.' So it is today!"

David's jaw clenched. The minister had been normal enough before. But since the giant fell, it was this same screed Sunday after Sunday. David had stopped going to church, but he knew more and more came to hear her rants. But this day was supposed to be about Jason, not about the giant.

"Is there not lawlessness all around?" she continued. "Is our earth not befouled? That thing is an abomination! It should be destroyed . . ."

Samuel suddenly startled in his wheelchair.

"What the hell is she talking about?" he asked.

Muffled laughter sounded through the crowd. The minister grimaced, then gave up on recapturing the moment. She recited the closing prayer as the funeral director released a lever, the pulleys sprang into action, and the ground swallowed the coffin.

The outsiders moved down the hill to their cars, which leaked out of the gravel parking lot onto the highway and back across the river to the north, toward Little Springs. The locals formed a line, moving past the family, offering hugs and the promise to keep the family in their prayers. All at once, Tabby was hugging David. She looked into his eyes and rubbed the tears from her face. She whispered something about his promise to come over. Behind her, Brian stood and gave a close-lipped nod.

David wandered away from the well-wishers and found Brooke and Spady standing beneath an ash tree. Before them spread out the Blunt family plot. Years back, Samuel had bought up space at the top of the hill so that all the family could be buried there. One stone for Samuel and Mariam. Another for Dale and Debbie. Another for Ben Senior and Bonnie. Another for David's parents. And one for Ben Junior, a headstone that Samuel insisted be placed, though no grave was ever dug.

"Sorry," Spady said, putting his left hand on David's shoulder.

"You, too," David said.

They stood silently a while. Then David spoke again.

"It's funny. I always had this idea in my head, growing up. I thought our family was special. Like we were hand-picked by God for some purpose. Then I grow up, and all this shit happens."

David stopped for a moment. He wouldn't let the memories return, of the funeral for his parents and of how desperately alone and scared he had felt. And then the years of rage that followed.

"There's as many of us dead as alive," he said. "I don't know. I suppose every kid sees their family that way."

Spady lit a cigarette.

"Not every kid."

He puffed intensely at the cigarette. His parents had moved into town when Spady was little, renting a run-down house at the edge of town, living off of donated clothes and the food pantry. As the boys had grown up together, their parents never let them go to Spady's house to play. It wasn't until years later that David understood—Spady's parents were alcoholics. After high school, they'd left town, and if Spady kept in touch with them, he never spoke of it. It was Jason who had befriended Spady, brought him into their group. And now . . .

All at once, Spady turned and locked eyes with David.

"You saw him, didn't you? The guy that killed Jason."

"We aren't going to talk about that. Not now," Brooke said.

She tried gently to pull her husband back, but Spady held where he was.

David nodded.

"I did."

"You know who it was?" Spady asked.

"I don't. Spady, I can't talk about . . ."

Spady leaned closer.

"But you're gonna find the son of a bitch, aren't you? You're gonna find him, and you're gonna kill him."

David nodded again.

"I won't stop till it's done. You have my word."

Spady relented and took a deep drag. "Okay," he muttered as he and Brooke paced away.

Soon enough, all that was left was the family. David had ridden over with Ben Senior and Bonnie. They were all headed to Dale and Debbie's place for dinner, but all David wanted was to be alone. David walked down to Ben and Bonnie's car with them, then waved them along.

"You go on. Think I'll walk," he told them.

The vehicles drove off. All that was left was a backhoe, its scoop still filled with dirt from Jason's grave. David glanced around one last time and saw it. A black sedan. The same make and model as the one he'd seen outside his aunt and uncle's house.

On instinct, David looked up the hill toward Jason's grave and saw the figure, standing facing away from him. A woman in a black dress and coat.

He started up the hill, moving slowly, quietly. As he came closer, even though he couldn't yet see her face, he thought he recognized her. The TV reporter who had broken the news of Jason's murder.

It was noon. The sandhill cranes had begun to flock up from the fields all around them, their warbling call building louder. David came within a few yards of her.

"You didn't bring your cameraman," he called out, not bothering to mask the confrontation in his voice. "My cousin's funeral not big enough news for cable TV?"

She turned but kept her head down. Tears cut through her makeup.

Her body held rigid, almost in panic, as if she'd been caught where she shouldn't be.

"I . . . I thought everyone was gone," she said.

He stepped closer.

"It was you outside my aunt and uncle's house, wasn't it? I saw your car," he challenged her. "What do you want with my family?"

Charlotte choked a gasping sob and wiped a sleeve at her face.

"I'm sorry," she whispered.

When her head lifted, the makeup was mostly gone, leaving her face transformed. As David stared at her, disjointed memories thrust upward through his thoughts, then snapped unexpectedly into place.

"Oh," he mumbled.

Charlotte nodded, then looked back at the ground.

"They buried me," she said.

Another step closer. She wasn't looking at Jason's tombstone but the one beside it.

"Mom and Dad. They buried me. They . . ."

The cranes whorled in their circle above the giant, their song obliterating whatever it was Charlotte said after that.

She stared at the chiseled-out words on the marker: BENJAMIN BLUNT JR.

David understood. He was looking into the face of his cousin.

TWELVE

The morning after Jason's funeral, David woke in darkness to the sound of a knock at his door. He dressed hurriedly and found Erickson at the door, holding a canvas bag.

"Here," Erickson said, pushing the bag into David's arms as he stepped into the apartment.

The FBI man sat on one of the unmatched chairs, then pointed at the couch.

"Sit."

David eased onto the couch. The bag held his uniform, cleaned and pressed. And his black Stetson. He opened his mouth to make a joke about what he would've done if the hat had been missing, then thought better of it. He took the hat out and absently worked the curve of the brim in his hands.

"You are entering a new world, sheriff. A world that has rules. I cannot stress to you enough the importance of these rules. I am going to lay them out for you, then you can ask any questions that you have, and then you will follow these rules."

David nodded his acceptance of the terms.

"The official story is that the FBI is assisting local agencies in your cousin's murder investigation. Anyone asks why, it's because the county and the state police don't have the resources to handle it on their own. As a witness in said murder investigation, you are working directly with the FBI to identify suspects. Granted, some days you're going to need to be out on patrol, doing your regular job. But other days—when I contact you or when you contact me with new information—you will be reporting to FBI offices at the Countryman Federal Building."

Erickson took out his lighter and began to play with it. He continued.

"Except you will not be reporting to the Countryman Building. You will be parking in the bottom level, through the security gate. There, you will leave your phone and radio and gun in your truck. You will wear civilian clothing. You will get into one of the white vans. You will be taken to Site One. There, security will search you and then guide you to Building Seventeen. You will go only where instructed. You will talk to no one outside of myself, Doctor Lee, and Priest and Conover. There, you will have case files from the three murders and any resources that you need."

It seemed as if he was finished.

"Why all the secrecy?" David asked.

Erickson gave him a friendly, pitying look. As if he was talking to a child, one whose capabilities he'd just overestimated.

"Kid, you do understand what that giant is, don't you?"

David didn't answer.

"It's the single most valuable resource on the planet. A gold mine, times infinity. It just happened that it fell here, in our backyard. But the whole world has eyes on it. They all want to know what it really is, what it's made out of, what can be done with it. They want to get their hands on it," Erickson concluded with a knowing look.

"Spies?" David asked.

"Of course," Erickson exclaimed. "What did you think? That the Chinese and Russians and whoever else would just sit on the sidelines and wait to see what we do with the giant? If they find out you have access, then you're a target."

No, he hadn't thought about spies. He'd been too busy cleaning up after the addicts and dealers and hustlers and prostitutes, the carjackers and juvenile delinquents.

"Well," Erickson implored. "Questions?"

David thought. "What happens if I slip up?"

Erickson pocketed the lighter.

"I'll be there to guide you, kid. And you don't have to worry too much about Conover. He's an old navy officer with a whole lot of years behind a desk. But Priest, she is one of the high-ups at the Defense Security Service. Do you know what the Defense Security Service is, kid?"

David shook his head. "No."

"Yeah. Nobody else does, either. Which means whatever she does

is shit that stays in the shadows. Whatever you do, don't piss her off."
Erickson stood. "Good luck."

|||

And so, David found himself in the back of an unmarked white van, headed back to Site One. Erickson's parting gift was an ID badge that was heavy for its size, as if made of metal. It was solid black, the size of a credit card, with a hole punched out so that it could connect to a lanyard.

There were others in the van, a diverse bunch except in that they all kept their eyes down. They must've been given the same rule: talk to no one. He looked out through the window at the apartment towers rising up above the flat horizon. Could there be someone up there, even now, tracking the progress of the white van, trying to learn who was inside?

In the silence, the previous day returned. The encounter at the cemetery. His long-lost cousin, suddenly there, alive and transformed. He hadn't known what to say. All that had come to his lips was the name.

"Ben."

It had been the wrong thing to say. The moment of hopefulness and reconnection vanished as suddenly as it had appeared. It was as if a shield had been lowered, just for an instant, before being raised again.

"It's Charlotte now," she told him.

He tried to recover, insisting that she join him to see the family. Or that they just go somewhere the two of them. To catch up, to remember Jason. It was almost more than he could process, the loss of one cousin and the addition of another happening at once.

She said no, she needed to leave. Work. She hoped she would see him later. She walked down from the hill into the waiting car and was gone. Of course she left. She just saw her own grave. Instead of accepting her, her parents had told the family she was dead. And then what did David say to her? She wouldn't be called Ben anymore. He should've known that. Shouldn't have said it. Should have said anything else.

The van pulled into the massive white hangar, stopping in front of the security checkpoint. David willed the interaction out of his thoughts. He needed to focus. He needed to find Jason's killer. Nothing else mattered.

Walking into the security line, he felt as he had the first day he'd gone off to college. Out of place. Surrounded by people he didn't know. Desperate to be back in the confines of the familiar.

He followed the others, who subjected themselves to full body searches at the hands of soldiers, then walked through multiple scanners. At the end, each tapped a black ID card to a red-lighted kiosk. When it turned green, they proceeded. He tapped his card. The kiosk turned orange. Before he could say anything, a soldier was beside him.

"This way," the soldier said.

It was day, and the halls were busier. People moving to and from offices. A door opened, and he snuck a glance at what seemed to be a laboratory before the door slid shut and chopped off his view. Through another door, he saw what looked like a cafeteria. He hadn't considered it before, but he supposed the bulk of the scientists lived in Site One. There were hundreds, maybe thousands of people here. Far more than the white vans could shuttle in and out each day.

The buildings were laid out on a grid, and windows allowed sunlight through, so that David retained his sense of direction. It seemed that the buildings were numbered in sequence, beginning with the one closest to Gulliver's face, then increasing in a snaking pattern up and down the rows. He memorized the turns they made, in case he ever had to make this journey on his own.

After several minutes of silent walking, they came to Building Seventeen and to an unmarked door. The soldier stood and waited. David wasn't sure what to do, then remembered the ID card in his pocket and tapped it to a screen beside the door. It turned green. He stepped inside.

The room was as large as it was featureless. Maybe the lack of any adornment made it seem even larger than it was. White walls, a white ceiling overhead with recessed LED lights. Around the walls, there were three other doors, each with a security screen. In the middle of the room was a broad table with seats for some thirty people, though only one person sat at it now. Priest. She looked at him with what seemed to be annoyance.

"You're here," she said.

"Is this where I'll be working?"

She stood.

"This is our meeting room. For those of us who know the truth. Conover, Erickson, Doctor Lee, me, now you. That's it. No one else has access to this part of the building."

She walked to one of the doors along the wall.

"Tap your badge here."

He followed her and did as instructed. The second his ID card touched the sensor, the panel flashed red and barked an angry tone. He looked at her, confused.

"Through here is Doctor Lee's lab," she explained. "You are not allowed inside, as you can see."

She pointed to the door at the far end of the room.

"You are not allowed through that door, either."

David wanted to ask what was through that door, but Erickson's warning kept repeating. Don't piss her off.

She led him to the third door and nodded at the security screen. He tapped his ID card. Green. The door clicked as it unlocked.

"This is your office," Priest said, guiding him through.

It was a modest space. Blank white walls. No windows. A desk. A table laden with files. Case files, he could tell. Binders thick with forensic reports, crime scene photos, notes from investigators, transcriptions of witness interviews. The only other door led to a closet-sized bathroom.

"The wall is a white board. There are markers in the desk," Priest said. "Get up to speed. If you have questions, just ask. And none of these files leave this room."

With that, she left, and David had no idea how to contact her, or Erickson, or anyone. He didn't know how to leave or if he could, without permission. So he sat at the table and began to read.

There was a summary briefing on top, something he guessed Erickson had prepared for him, covering the basic sketch of the case. The FBI had initially been alerted to the patterned injuries on Jim Holly, the tour guide, and when Kapoor turned up with matching wounds, they knew it was the same suspect. The case was remarkable mostly for how little evidence there was. No fingerprints or DNA or even fibers. No clear footprints. No witnesses. And no security footage.

That last bit didn't surprise David. Little Springs had been the kind of town where you don't just leave your car unlocked, you leave your keys inside. No one put up security cameras. And New Town had been built so fast, there were plenty of places that didn't have security systems or cameras.

Holly had been killed at the airport, which should be locked down. Except his tourism company was in an old building just outside of the airport proper. There was a mechanic who said he thought he saw a man of average height but couldn't be sure. Nothing that told David anything more than he already knew.

Each of the victims had his own file. David picked up the first, the pilot. Holly had been a commercial helicopter pilot in Texas, most recently running his own operation, flying tourists out over the Gulf of Mexico from Galveston. He'd moved to Little Springs more than a year ago, setting up as soon as the airport was finished. He'd charge a thousand dollars a ticket for a half-hour flight to see Gulliver from above. His wife moved up with him. She was a teacher at the new high school they built to the northeast of Old Town. Holly had no known debts, no prior criminal record. Nothing to suggest that someone would want to stab him to death and desecrate his corpse.

When he first became a deputy, David realized that he approached investigating crimes the way Grandma Mariam had taught him to write poetry. You fill your head with observations and instincts first, she'd said, taking in bite-sized pieces of the world. Then you tumble those fragments about in your mind, letting the rough-hewn edges collide against each other, until one connects perfectly with another, and you discover that they are meant to fit, and gradually more connect, forming the structure they are meant to become.

As a boy, he'd filled notebooks with efforts at poems, bits of lyrics, rhymes. He didn't remember any of it. The tornado had taken the notebooks along with his parents, and he'd never attempted to write again.

He tumbled the pieces he already had. A successful tour guide. A realtor. Jason. Each killed the same way, with the same weapon. But no indication that the three knew each other, aside from Jason and Kapoor maybe meeting over a land deal. No known motive for any of them, let alone a motive that explained all three. And a hundred thousand people out there, the killer hidden among them.

It had been so easy before the giant, before the world flooded into Garden County. Fewer people. Fewer motives. Fewer variables. Simpler patterns. The rough edges of this case refused to fit. Most murders anymore traced back to drugs. A deal gone wrong. Someone trying to rip off a dealer. A junkie getting messed up on PCP and going berserk. But Jason had no connection to drugs. Did he?

The door clicked and opened.

Sunny appeared, carrying a tray with two bowls. An unexpected smell wafted in front of her. David quickly tucked the autopsy photos into a folder before she could see them.

"It's lunch time," she explained. "They told me you were here, so I grabbed an extra serving from the cafeteria. No one has shown you where that is yet, have they?"

"No. Just this room."

She set one of the bowls in front of him. It held a thick, orange stew and rice.

"Curry," she said, reading his face. "You don't like curry?"

She sat beside him.

He sniffed at it.

"I've never had it."

"What? How have you never had curry?"

He shrugged. "There wasn't exactly anywhere around here to get it. We only ever had Pearl's diner, and curry isn't on the menu."

David stared down at the food as Sunny started to eat. She looked back over at him, and a wry smile crossed her face, dotting her cheeks with dimples.

"You're kidding me. The big, tough sheriff is afraid of curry."

"I'm not . . ." He grabbed the spoon. "Fine."

He dipped it into the bowl, then took a bite.

"Well?" she asked.

"Not bad. It isn't a cheeseburger, but not bad."

When they'd finished, she teased him that he sure did eat a lot for a man who didn't like curry. They pushed the tray to the side then, and both surveyed the stack of files.

"So, you're a geologist?" David asked. Rocks. Tectonic plates. What the hell did that have to do with the giant?

Sunny read his look. Her smile faded, and she gave a furtive glance around, as if she thought someone might have snuck inside behind them.

"When NASA created Site One, they reached out to the top researchers in basically every field. Biology, chemistry, biomechanical engineering, astronomy, theoretical physics, you name it," she explained. "This base is sort of the best of the best in science from around the world."

"I get that. But what does geology have to do with an alien?"

"So, the challenge of studying this thing is that we can't see inside of it. If it had any orifices, they've sealed off. And the outside layer is incredibly dense and thick."

"You can't give Gulliver an X-ray," David offered.

"Right. We don't even know if what we're seeing is its skin, or an exoskeleton, or even some kind of armor," Sunny said. "And because all the countries are still fighting over what to do with it and who really owns it, we're not supposed to cut into the giant. So all we can study is the surface. And the surface is made out of crystals."

"Crystals?"

"Right. And that's why they brought me in. On the earth, crystals form when certain types of magma cool, so it falls into geology. I just happened to specialize in crystal structures. I wrote this paper a few years back theorizing about the potential for crystals to be living organisms."

"Living crystals?" David asked.

"They have these really weird properties," she continued, her face lighting up as she described her work. "I ran this experiment where we enclosed hematite in a polymer coat and exposed part of it to blue light, then put it in a hydrogen peroxide bath, and . . ."

"Whoa. Keep in mind I got straight Cs in chemistry in high school."

She laughed, a loud, genuine laugh. It was so strange, talking to her. They'd barely spent any time together, and it was all amid the insanity of a serial killer running loose and a three-mile-long giant dead on the ground. And yet there was an easy rapport. Suddenly this place didn't feel so alien.

Sunny continued. "Basically, we took crystals, put them in a weird environment, and they started to break apart, then come back together in new forms. They moved. On their own."

"So, they were alive?" David asked.

"Well, the real question is, 'What does it mean to be alive?' In science, we've sort of agreed you have to have eight qualities: organized cells, the ability to use energy, reproduction, growth, metabolization, adaptation, movement, and respiration—breathing. The crystals I worked with could do everything except adapt and reproduce. It was all exciting, just wildly theoretical."

"And then Gulliver fell."

"Right. And wildly theoretical became reality. NASA came across my paper, called me in, and set me to work analyzing the giant, to try to figure out what makes it tick."

There was another question. One David had sat on since she first stepped into the room. Something that nagged at him, a rough piece of information that refused to fit.

"How was it that they pulled you into the murder investigation?" he asked, attempting to sound almost disinterested, just continuing the chat.

She tensed all at once. He had stepped over a boundary, into the realm of things he should not know. Which meant there was still more that they were hiding from him.

Sunny reached across him and grabbed a blank sheet of paper and a pen. She sat back down and started sketching. The spiraling patterns of the giant's skin spread across the paper.

"The patterns on the giant's skin seem to be created by the crystal structures. They're fractals. A big pattern that repeats and grows smaller and smaller. I guess they just saw the pattern, and I'm what counts for an expert on it, so they asked for my help," she explained as she drew.

David was about to push more, to tell her the explanation didn't make sense, when she looked over and caught his eyes with hers. Then she looked purposefully back down at the paper. His eyes followed hers. There, amid the circular pattern, she had hidden two small words.

they're listening

David started to look up, to search the room, then caught himself. Don't react. He nodded at her. She seemed almost pleading.

"Got it," he said.

She stood, sliding the piece of paper under the food tray.

"I should get back to work," she said.

She started for the door, and he followed her, opening it. She stopped and looked back at him, her smile reappearing.

"It's nice to have someone else in here," she said.

"It is," David said.

She left then, crossing the big room to the door of her lab, disappearing into an unknown. David saw then that he was inside a labyrinth, one where all the paths were blocked, all truths were hidden behind sensors that would forever flash red. And somewhere out there, roaming free, was the monster.

THIRTEEN

Charlotte sat in her car in the high school's parking lot and waited, eyes shifting from the clock to the front doors of the massive brick building to her phone, killing time by aimlessly drifting through social media and news updates. She found herself coming back again and again to Jason's page. Post after post of people offering condolences and prayers, then older messages of jocular bonhomie between Jason and his friends. Photos that showed him always smiling, big and loud and arrogant, but not in the way of one who thrust that arrogance on others. He seemed arrogantly self-possessed, a man who knew just who he was and how to exist without second consideration.

Jason had changed a great deal over the two decades she spent away. He was taller and fatter—almost every photo showed a beer in his hand. But that confidence had been there from the start. He would always have some plan, some scheme. Something for the four of them to do together—Jason, David, Spady, and her. And then every outing, he would raise the stakes. It wasn't enough that they took Dale's Corvette without asking. They then had to go and see how fast they could drive in reverse, before popping the parking brake and whipping the car around.

Another memory came, unbidden. They'd been about fourteen. Jason had somehow enlisted them in an effort to catch a wild rabbit that they found next to the school during lunch break. Jason had tucked it into a pocket as they went back inside, then set it loose in the hallway. Charlotte could still see the kids shrieking with laughter as the teachers stumbled about, bumping into each other as the animal darted through their legs. That was Jason.

She hadn't admitted to anyone that he was her cousin. With a straight and somber face, she went live on TV and reported that Jason had been murdered, that other details were hazy, that there were no known suspects or motives. Then she had gone back to her hotel room, buried her head in her covers, and sobbed. It felt as though something had been stolen from her, the chance to reconcile with him. But then there was also a degree of relief, that she would never have to face him with the truth. Feeling guilt at the honesty of that relief, she cried even harder.

The truth of her identity had been hers alone. There were those at the station who knew she was transgender. And now some who knew she grew up in Little Springs. But none knew that she had been Benjamin Blunt Jr. That she had created for herself a new gender and a new name and also a new history.

Except, now David knew as well.

He had tried so genuinely to reach out to her. But it had been too much, that day at the cemetery. She hadn't known she was going up to the grave until she saw that all the cars had left. She thought she would be alone. Then, there he was, angry and confused. And she was torn in a million directions at once—grieving Jason, furious at her parents, overwhelmed talking to someone who knew the real her for the first time since she had left. Too much.

Over the years, she'd imagined how various reunions might play out. With David, it was always one extreme or another. Tears and a big hug or screaming and violence. This had been so quiet, so tentative. Maybe it could be the way that it was, finding again the easy connection they'd always held. But a warning inside her also sounded. He knew. And he could reveal her to others.

A bell rang, muffled from inside the building. Within a couple of minutes, the doors burst open and students streamed out in a rush, then a trickle.

She put away her phone and watched them from her car. So many faces. Different faces. Hair dyed in kaleidoscopic colors. Pierced noses and eyebrows and ears. Colorful, edgy clothing. A strange gender fluidity. Boys that dressed effeminately, girls with crew cuts. There were those she recognized as locals—white kids with traditional haircuts in jeans and T-shirts—but they were the minority.

It struck her most how comfortable they seemed in their own skin. An unexpected anger arose within her. If she had dressed like that when she was growing up, someone would've dragged her out onto the lawn and beat the shit out of her. And then she would've been the one in trouble. *What did you expect, wearing that?* How had these kids earned the right to live like this, to dress that way, in this town? In her town?

For seventeen years, she never crossed the boundary of normalcy. Never even approached it. She knew the truth about herself from early on. But show any of that? Mention it to anyone? No. She had boxed her true self up, spent years play-acting through life. Then one day, in her senior year of high school, she had woken up in the room she shared with David, and she knew that she couldn't continue living the lie one minute longer. She made her plan while still lying in bed. She would take the car and the money she'd earned from her job at the grocery store and summers helping on the farm and she would go to Denver. She'd find a job, find a place to stay. Start to unbind her true self.

There had been part of her that wanted to tell David the truth. To explain things to him. She'd been sure that he would understand and support her. Almost sure. But what if he was angry? What if he told her parents? Bonnie and Ben Senior would lock her up, or send her to some kind of camp, or worse. One more morning of play-acting, then she was gone.

The crowd of students thinned out, going off in cars or in buses or on foot. Then teachers began to emerge from the building. Charlotte dredged herself up out of the memories and intently scanned faces. There.

She stepped out of her car and approached an overweight woman in her fifties who had brilliant red hair that had started to gray.

"Mrs. Holly?" Charlotte called out. "I'm sorry to bother you. I wanted to talk to you about your husband."

Charlotte hadn't known how the woman would react, but once she explained that she was a reporter and that she was looking back through unsolved homicide cases, the woman immediately asked if they could sit in her car and talk. She cried a little as she talked about her husband, about their last morning together and how he cooked breakfast as he always did.

Then the woman's face hardened. It wasn't just that her husband had been murdered. The state police wouldn't tell her anything. Nothing about how he was killed. Nothing about any evidence or suspects. There were no reports, not even an autopsy. The only thing she knew was what she'd been told by an airport employee who'd found him. Her husband had been cut all over his body.

Charlotte forced herself to stay calm, to be emotionally attuned to the woman, to share her grief. Inside, she felt an electric hum. She had found it. A void of information with a clear border—something big was being hidden.

Since Jason had died, it had nagged at her that his death didn't make sense. There was too much that wasn't being said. And then the FBI and state police had refused to release any reports. There wasn't even an autopsy, at least according to the official record. Just like Sanjay Kapoor, the victim she'd reported about on her first day back.

So she had set out to digging. Who else had been murdered in Little Springs over the last year? And out of those cases, which ones were missing records?

As her conversation with Holly's widow played out, her thoughts already raced ahead. Was this the work of a serial killer? Was that why the FBI was involved? If so, why were they hiding it?

This would be huge. A big exclusive. Constant coverage. The kind of story that makes a career. But she didn't have enough to go on air. Not yet. She needed official confirmation. She needed someone close to it, someone who could be an anonymous source.

Charlotte thanked Mrs. Holly, stepped out of her car, and walked to her own. She knew what she would do. She needed David.

||||

The sheriff's truck sat in plain view along the highway, window open, speed gun angled out. The truth was, David didn't want to catch any speeders. If he had, there were better places, spots where he could park just out of sight behind a road sign or on the far side of a hill, spots where drivers roared through and didn't see him till it was too late. No, today he just wanted to sit and think in quiet, at least up until dispatch called him with some new horror.

The speed gun beeped to life intermittently as a vehicle went past. Fifty-nine miles per hour. Fifty-seven. Sixty-one.

It felt strangely foreign to him, his old, normal life. The everyday role of sheriff. Responding to calls and tipping his hat to locals. Acting as if there wasn't a killer somewhere hidden in the town, a killer who could strike again at any time. But it wasn't only the investigation and the secrecy around it. The veil had been lifted, if only partially. He had gone to the other side. To Site One.

That first day, when he had finally exhausted himself reading case files and poring over crime scene photos, he had left his new office and hoped that Sunny would be just leaving hers. But there was no sign of the scientist, and so he went to the hall, where he found a soldier waiting for him. Not the same one that had deposited him there. He wondered if they'd taken shifts, watching the door. Or if they had known he was leaving.

He could still see the two words Sunny had scrawled on the piece of paper: "they're listening." Erickson. Priest. Conover. Maybe all of them. Observing him, but why? Did they think he was hiding something? David thought again of Erickson's warning about foreign agents trying to get inside Site One. They couldn't think that David was some kind of Russian spy. Could they?

No. As much as his eyes had been opened, he was still an outsider in that world. They had pulled aside the curtain but only partially. He worked over Sunny's explanation of how she became involved in the case. It didn't make sense. The matching cuts on the victims had nothing to do with crystals. There was something else that they were hiding. The third door appeared in his vision. In Building Seventeen, one door led to David's office, a second led to Sunny's lab. And the third door led . . . Priest hadn't even lied to him. She'd just moved past it, knowing David couldn't get through. He could've asked, but he had better hope of breaking through the door than he did getting Priest to reveal anything.

Okay, he thought. So some of the information is missing. Work off of what is known.

Three men killed. Two outsiders, one local. Two involved in real estate, one a pilot. No useable forensic clues at any of the scenes. No hair. No DNA. No fingerprints that they could connect to the killer. No security camera footage. No witnesses.

The same weapon used each time and mostly the same pattern of wounds. Multiple deep stab wounds to the sternum area. And then the matching superficial cuts replicating the pattern on the giant, inflicted postmortem. But then each also had variations. Holly had been stabbed fatally from behind, as if he had been caught by surprise. Kapoor's arm had been cut off. And then Jason.

David had stared at the folder containing photos of Jason for minutes on end before willing himself to open it. There were photos of the crime scene, which he flipped quickly past. He came to the autopsy photos, which showed Jason's body naked and cleaned, the components reassembled on a metal table.

It helped, seeing it like that. He could imagine it wasn't his cousin but some other corpse. Against the white skin, the damage screamed out in red lacerations and gaping holes. He'd forced himself to think back to that night. The window exploding out. The silhouettes. One more shotgun blast. No, two.

Jason had seen the attack coming. He'd had time to grab the gun—he kept it loaded, despite David always warning him not to—and fight back. Maybe that was why the injuries were so extreme. The killer had broken out of his ordinary method. There was no clear stab wound to the chest, just the diagonal slice that had sheared through Jason's ribs and the clean horizontal cut that took off the top of his head.

Something about this killing had been different. The attack more desperate. He needed to go back to the courthouse. To walk through . . .

Beep-beep-beep

The speed gun shouted at him. Seventy-six miles per hour in a fifty-five zone. David looked up, hoping to see the recognizable vehicle of a local.

It was a maroon conversion van, the paint showing its age. Windows tinted. A Colorado license plate. Something off about it, his gut said. Hell.

David turned the key in the ignition and pulled onto the highway. He gunned it to close in on the van, then flipped the switch to activate his lights and siren.

For a moment, the van accelerated. But David easily kept pace, and it slowed, finally easing onto the side of the road next to a culvert, where there was almost no room on either side of the vehicle between the drop off on the right and the lanes of traffic on the left.

David grabbed the microphone and flipped on the truck's loudspeaker.

"Keep moving. Move your vehicle forward until you can pull completely off of the road."

Nothing from the van. Its engine still ran, though the driver had shifted into park. David could just see hurried movements through the driver's side mirror. Hell.

David waited. That gut instinct flared again, telling him that if he stepped out of the truck, the van's driver would wait until he was close, then drive away. He knew he wasn't supposed to make assumptions, shouldn't stereotype. But oftener than not, what his gut told him rang true.

He switched over to his radio, then spoke into the microphone again.

"Andrea. David here. I've got a speeder pulled over on ninety-two, over by that new Chevy dealership. He's acting squirrely. Is Brooke free that she could come over and . . . Ah, shit."

As he was talking, all at once the driver's side door of the van flew open. A short, stocky Hispanic man flung himself out, right into the four lanes of the highway.

David started to open his door, then pulled it closed as a semi-truck roared by with a blast of its booming horn.

The van's driver ran out into the highway, the truck just missing him.

David checked his mirror, saw an opening. He jumped out, darting to the shoulder in front of his truck just before more cars raced by.

He drew his gun and shouted.

The van's driver was out in the middle of the highway. Vehicles zoomed around him. Horns blaring. The screech of brakes locking.

The man would jump forward, then hop back. Again and again, he was almost annihilated by an oncoming truck or car. Then, impossibly, his stubby legs took him all the way across.

David was still yelling. He lifted his hands to the oncoming traffic. Finally, vehicles saw him and slowed. By the time he made it to the opposite side of the road, the driver was gone, and all David could do was swear into the dirt.

It took an hour to get Jared Lloyd and his tow truck to hook up the van and drag it to the impound lot by the new courthouse. Since Jason's murder, the old building had been shut down, so all county operations had moved to a faceless strip mall. In the first months after Gulliver landed, the federal government had constructed the building to house some of their operations. It had sat mostly empty after the Countryman Building was completed, and the feds offered it for free to the county.

The sheriff's department now had a whole wing. An entry area. A suite of offices. They were going to be constructing some new holding cells. Mostly, it sat empty, except for Andrea, relocated to the largest room, sitting at a new desk. As always, David and Brooke worked out of their trucks, except for when David had to go to Site One.

Out in back of the strip mall was an area ringed with a tall chain-link fence, concertina wire spiraling along the top. They deposited the van there, then David pulled on gloves and went inside.

Some food wrappers and empty soda bottles. No registration in the glove compartment or console. He'd run the license plate and VIN soon enough. In the back, the vehicle had a row of seats that was folded down into a bed. It was only after disassembling the bed and removing it that David found the secret cache. A panel of flooring came up, and beneath lay a trove of packages wrapped in brown paper and plastic.

David had made enough drug busts to know by sight what he'd found. Cocaine. Heroin. Ecstasy. The usual shit.

Underneath the rest, he found a cigar box. He opened it and saw neat rows of clear baggies, each barely bigger than a postage stamp. And inside each bag was what looked as much as anything like bits of sugar. Except, as he held one baggie up to the sky, the contents shimmered unnaturally.

"What the hell are you?" David asked.

FOURTEEN

Every day, it seemed that Little Springs spilled farther over its former boundaries, like a flooding river swelling over its bank. Far up into what was once unbroken farmland, now there stood housing developments and condominiums and little shopping centers, always with more under construction to the north and east. Every day, more people arrived. So, every day, there were more places for them to live and shop and work. It used to be said with a grin that the largest city in Nebraska was Omaha, the second largest was the state capital, Lincoln, and the third largest was Memorial Stadium during a Nebraska Cornhuskers game. Now, Little Springs had more people than Lincoln. Though, until the next census brought more government funding, the county still had to make do with the same resources it had had before. Which was why it fell to David and his one deputy to keep the peace.

Mostly, David avoided this part of town—the suburbs, as he called them. This was where the people with money lived, and they seemed to have few problems. Occasionally there would be a call of someone breaking into a car, or a domestic dispute.

Not that he admitted it, but he also avoided this part of town because it was where Tabby lived.

He wasn't sure what he hated more, the guilt he felt over abandoning Tabby in that week before the giant fell—when they all thought they'd be dead soon, anyway—or that whenever he saw her, she refused to wield that guilt against him. Even their divorce had been calm, silent. Almost perfunctory. He had given her the house, which she then sold. She had given up any claim to his parents' land. And just like that, it was done.

David rolled past one manicured lawn after another. Children playing along the streets. Immaculately dressed people arriving home from work. Some stood and stared as he passed. No one waved to him; but then, he didn't wave to them, either.

The stone-sided townhouse stood atop a slight rise. The lights were on. David parked out front and rang the bell. At the last moment, he remembered to take his hat off.

Tabby answered the door in fitted jeans and a flowing sweater, a necklace of chunky stones, fingers flashing with rings. She looked like a mountain hippie, the kind of person they would've made fun of as kids.

"David. You should've called first. I haven't cooked anything."

"Sorry," he said. "It's been awful busy; I just had a free minute. I don't need anything to eat."

She held the door just long enough to let her annoyance be unmistakable, then opened it wide and gestured him inside. The house opened into a great room with a tall ceiling flowing into the kitchen and dining room.

"Nice place," he offered. "Brian's out?"

He asked quickly, saying nothing more, hoping that Tabby wouldn't realize this visit was more premeditated than he acted.

"Work," she said. "He'll be back from Denver tomorrow. You want to see my studio?"

"Sure."

She led him through the house, to a big room with a window facing west, the spire visible above the outline of the giant, its skin now indigo against the fading red of the sunset. A large easel sat in front of the window, holding a large canvas that revealed the same scene. The land. The sky. The giant. The spire.

The room was filled with more paintings. Hanging on the walls. Stacked on the floor. Stuffed into a large shelf. Each showed the same thing. The only variable was the sky and the coloring. Different times of day, different hues, from deep purples to pastel pinks and blues, harsh reds, garish yellows. Some with the cloud of sandhill cranes circling the spire. Painted in an exacting realism that perfectly captured the otherworldly horror.

Tabby twisted her finger in her hair, watching him.

"Wow," David said. "You've been busy."

She laughed so loud it took him aback.

"Busy. Got it. Thanks."

He waved his hand around the room.

"What? I mean, I'm impressed. You never painted that much. Before. It's a lot of work. I meant it as a compliment."

"That's what every artist wants to hear: 'That looks like a lot of work.'"

"Christ, Tabby. What do I know about art? They look great, okay? Beautiful. It's just . . . It's all the same thing. You don't paint anything else?"

"No, I don't paint anything else," she said, crossing her arms. "That's the idea. Every day, every hour, it looks different. But Gulliver never changes. The world changes around him. I kind of think of it like a mirror, held up to us."

She was quiet a moment, then looked away and continued.

"And it helps. Painting it. It helps me not think about all the terrible stuff going on out there. Or all the stuff we don't know. Or what could happen. It was the only thing that helped me get through, after it fell."

The only thing. Because David was nowhere to be found.

Though he had apologized before, he felt the impulse to do so again whenever he saw her. She gave him a look then that told him that it was done, this moment. That they should move along.

"People buy these, then?" David asked, peering closer at a painting.

"Yes, people buy them. Faster than I can paint them. What do you think paid for this house?"

"Wow. That's great, Tabby. Really."

She wrapped one arm around herself, rubbing at her elbow.

"Brian and I invited you over for a reason, David. I wanted you to hear it from us. We're pregnant."

"Oh," he said.

She laughed, even louder this time, then finally smiled her big smile, the smile that had made him fall in love with her.

"You never did know what to say, did you?" she asked.

He shook his head, grinning back. "No. Sure didn't. Okay, let me try again. Let's see, what am I supposed to ask? When are you due? What are you having?"

"October. We're having a girl."

"A baby girl. What you always wanted. Congratulations, Tabby."

Now that he looked, he could see the forming of a bump in her stomach. A child, growing there. A child that could've been his. Should've been his. No joy came with the thought. Only relief that he wouldn't have to raise flesh and blood, to bring it into the world and watch it suffer. No, things had worked out as they should have.

He wasn't sure if he should hug her, but before he could decide one way or another, she was walking back toward the kitchen asking if he wanted something to drink, and he was turning her down.

At the door, he remembered the reason he'd come.

"You said Brian's back tomorrow?"

She eyed him suspiciously then. As much as David could never read Tabby, she always could see straight through him.

"Why do you keep asking about him?" she insisted.

"It's nothing. I just . . ."

Her eyes hardened.

"Okay," David admitted. "I made a traffic stop. Turned out there was a load of drugs in the vehicle. There was something in there that I didn't recognize."

"And you thought Brian could tell you?" she completed his thought.

David gave a pathetic shrug.

"Brian works in legal agriculture, David," Tabby said. "He isn't some criminal."

"Marijuana might be legal in Colorado, but it isn't here," David argued back.

"You should leave," she said, half turning away. But he'd already seen that she had started to cry.

He held up his hands.

"I'm sorry, Tabby. I really am. I didn't mean anything."

He had started down the stone steps toward his truck when he heard her feet behind him.

"David."

He turned. Her anger was gone, replaced by sadness.

"You're working the investigation. Jason?" she asked.

He nodded.

She stepped closer, lowering her voice.

"There's something you should know. I didn't want to tell you, but you should know."

He stepped closer.

"Missy told me something. A few months ago. Maybe you knew already."

Know what? his eyes demanded.

"Jason was having an affair. I don't know if it has anything to do with it, but . . ."

She said nothing more. Driving home in the dark, David rolled the sentence over and over in his mind. One more detail. One more rough-edged piece. One more jagged edge tumbling through his thoughts, crashing against all the other bits, refusing to fit.

FIFTEEN

It had been balmy that day, but at night a gusting wind launched down from the Rocky Mountains and raced across the plains, and the temperature plunged fifty degrees all at once. After a fitful night of sleep spent chewing over Tabby's secret, David woke early, pulled on his winter parka, and walked out of his apartment into a landscape transformed by a thin layer of snow that raced and swirled in the wind. The gray clouds hung low enough that, to the west, the giant wasn't even visible.

At the new offices, he found Andrea already there, stationed at her desk with her two jugs of soda.

"Quiet night," David said.

"Too fucking cold for crime," she said. "When's the press coming?"

David had scheduled it yesterday. Mardee Overmyer from the *Garden County Gazette* would be coming over to take a photo of the drugs he'd pulled from the van to go along with an article. A nice, big front-page story to show how the sheriff was keeping everyone safe from the outsiders.

He went into his office. He'd locked the drugs in there, inside a safe that someone had moved over from the old courthouse. He saw that a light was blinking on the landline phone on his desk. He supposed he had a message, though he didn't know how to check it. He didn't even know what the number was for the phone.

He took out the packages of drugs and placed them carefully across the desk, staging them to fill as much space as possible. He stared at the cigar box, unsure whether to open it or not.

Brooke came in then with Spady trailing her.

"Miserable fucking day, boss," she muttered, still shaking snow from her coat.

Spady drank steaming coffee from an insulated mug.

"Hey, bud," he said, bumping elbows with David. It was the way they'd started greeting each other once Spady lost his arm. "Meant to say, we're planning a wake, I guess you'd say, for Jason. Nothing fancy. Vic's. Some beers in his honor. Would love if you could help . . ."

"Shit, man. I'm sorry. I can't really, not with everything going on. I barely have time to think," David explained.

Spady pushed up his lower lip and gave a slight shake of his head.

"All good. How's the case coming? You gonna find the fucker that killed him?"

"Trying," David said.

Spady moved past him then, looking at the drugs covering the desk.

"Damn. Look at that haul," he said. "Brooke showed me the dash-cam video last night. It was like Frogger, that fucker running across the highway. He was *this close* to getting creamed."

Spady's hand was occupied with the mug, so he made no gesture to show how close he meant.

When they had been growing up, if you knew the right person, you could score a little weed. Then there had been the sudden growth of methamphetamine, and the Cooke brothers had been busted running a lab out of their shitty little house out in the country. That was while David was at college, and he only heard the stories after he moved back and became a deputy.

In the past couple of years, he and Brooke had grown familiar with most every illegal substance. Opioids, hallucinogens, PCP. Mostly, their busts came through random traffic stops, or they'd find something left behind at the scene of an overdose.

They knew full well where drugs funneled through. There were always deals going on in the parking lot of the Bean Stalk, the strip club out east in the industrial part of town. Then there were a few corners where dealers set up, where users knew to go for a restock.

At first, David had tried to come down on them, only to end up with his ass in his hands when he realized that the dealers didn't hold the drugs themselves. There were intermediaries, go-betweens, hidden links that the dealers and users knew but were invisible to him. David and Brooke had had to finally accept that they were stretched too thin to deal with the drug problem.

It was part of why David had invited the newspaper to come. Maybe it would send a message. He was fighting back. No one needed to know that the bust was pure, dumb luck.

A ding sounded up front, signaling that the front door had opened. Mardee was early.

Then David heard footsteps in the hallway. Lots of footsteps.

The door opened, and Erickson appeared.

"Uh," David stammered, not knowing what to say with Brooke and Spady there.

"Sheriff Blunt," Erickson said. "I understand you've made quite a narcotics seizure. As it turns out, this case relates to an ongoing FBI investigation into cartel activity."

As he said this, he stepped into the room. Behind him, one after another black-suited agents followed. They said nothing, made no eye contact, as they circled the desk. One carried a duffel bag.

"Can we talk in the hallway?" Erickson asked.

Brooke gave David a quizzical look. *Is this okay?* David nodded at her, then led the way out of the office. Behind them, just as the door closed, he saw agents putting on latex gloves and producing large plastic bags.

"Cartel activity?" David asked Erickson as soon as they were all out.

Erickson glanced at Spady, then back to David.

"Cartel activity. We will be taking possession of the seized materials, as well as the vehicle. We so appreciate your department's partnership in the war on drugs."

"But the newspaper . . ." Brooke started to say.

"Whenever we make an arrest, we will be sure to commend your work here," Erickson cut her off.

The door to the office opened. The desk was empty. The agents walked out, each carrying a clear bag. In one, David saw the cigar box. As they walked past, the strong scent of disinfectant wafted out of the office.

"Boss. This okay?" Brooke whispered.

"Fine," David said, hoping he sounded more convinced than he was.

As the agents walked out, he hurried to catch up with Erickson.

"This is my case. This isn't . . ." David left the rest unsaid. "What are you doing?"

Erickson leaned closer, and his voice dropped to a scratchy whisper. "David. What do you dream of, when you dream?"

Not an explanation. That same question. The one he was asked when he was taken to Site One after Jason was killed.

"What the fuck does that mean?" he demanded.

Erickson smiled, inexplicably, and continued on his way. "Excellent work, sheriff."

David, Brooke, and Spady stood there, staring after.

"What the hell was that about?" Spady asked.

David searched for an explanation but found none.

|||

David could tell from the stack of papers on the desk that Samuel had resumed his researching. He wondered if the staff had been helping him, printing off studies and articles, since David hadn't been around.

All at once the dogs began to bark, and then the old man was awake.

"You're back," he said.

"Sorry, Grandpa."

Samuel went to the desk and began looking through papers, eyes scanning.

"No need to apologize, David. I know you have the world on your shoulders out there. How are you holding up?"

David opened his mouth to give what would be his usual answer. *Everything is fine.* The answer he gave to everyone else. To the locals, who needed reassurance that he was protecting them, and to the outsiders, whom he could never allow to see any sign of weakness.

With his grandpa, he couldn't reveal what he knew about Site One or about the killer. And he hadn't yet told the old man about Charlotte— he'd decided it was her choice to reveal her identity to anyone else. But at least with him alone David could be honest about himself.

"I'm in over my head, Grandpa," David said. "There's shit happening that . . . I can't even start to understand it. The thing with Jason. But everything else, too."

Samuel put the papers back down and turned fully to David.

"I'm supposed to be the one in charge, except no one tells me any-thing. No one trusts me," David continued. "And all around me, things are getting worse and worse."

"I'm sorry, kid. It isn't fair, all this landing on you."

David shook his head.

"Ever since that goddamned thing landed here, it's just one disaster after another. I wasn't elected to deal with all these people and their problems. To clean them up when they overdose and try to stop them from killing each other. I'm not their sheriff . . ."

His grandpa's comforting eyes clenched down, hardening. Samuel pulled his hand back from where he'd rested it on David's shoulder.

"Knock that shit off."

The harshness in the voice staggered David. The old man had never talked to him like that.

"You're right. You didn't run for sheriff thinking this was how things would end up," Samuel continued. "Tough shit, kid. I know you weren't raised to think that everything would be perfect and fair. Things happen. You buck up, and you deal with it. Your job is to be sheriff of Garden County."

Only after Samuel remained silent did David realize that his words were intended to elicit a response.

"Yeah," he offered.

"Your job is to be sheriff of Garden County," Samuel repeated, louder. David nodded. "It is."

"Then do your goddamned job."

As he walked across the parking lot to his truck, David clenched and unclenched his fists, trying to think of some retort he could've offered to his grandpa. But as much as he searched, there was nothing he could argue back. The old man was right. David could quit and abandon everyone he'd sworn to serve—and abandon the hope of bringing Jason's killer to justice. Or he could suck it up and try to do the impossible, Sisyphean task that had fallen upon him.

He remembered then the words he'd said, that since Gulliver fell, it had been "one disaster after another." How could he dare say that, when Gulliver's arrival was also what had given him his grandpa back? He wanted to go back inside to apologize, but the dogs had ceased barking. Samuel was gone for another day.

"David."

The voice came from the side. In the dark, it took him a moment to recognize her. It had stopped snowing, but the wind still whipped around them.

"Charlotte," he said, forcing himself to use the correct name.

She walked up beside him, looking stylish in leggings and a thick wool coat.

"Grandpa is in there."

David wasn't sure if it was a question or statement. He didn't know how to explain the awakening or if he should.

"He is," David said. "I try to visit most days. He's pretty out of it just now," he added, hoping it would be enough to forestall her from going inside.

"You always were the closest to him," she said, an undertone of pain in her voice.

"I worked with him a lot on the farm. He loved all of us."

Charlotte inhaled sharply.

"You don't know what it was like."

He glanced away and back.

"I don't. It's just . . . It's hard for me to wrap my head around it. Twenty years ago, we were sleeping in bunkbeds, playing sports together, trying to figure out how to find some beer to drink over the weekend. Then you were just gone."

She looked down.

"It wasn't normal for me. Not ever."

Then she looked back up to him.

"Is there anything you want to know? Anything you want to ask . . . Questions about all of this?"

She drew a circle in the air around her face.

"Questions?" he asked.

"When I tell people, they want to know whether I like guys or girls. Or what the transition was like. What kinds of surgeries I've had."

David grimaced slightly, unable to stop the reaction. He hadn't gotten that far, processing what his cousin had done to transform. David had never seen Ben Junior as effeminate. Charlotte was in every way feminine. He'd seen only past and present and nothing in between.

"The transition. It was hard?" he asked.

"Horrible," she said. "It took me a lot of years to be ready to do it. Then it took years of work. Honestly, the thing that made me finally feel like myself was the surgery on my face."

David studied her brow, her chin, which seemed changed, smoothed, though subtly so.

"Millimeters of bone shaved off," she said, following his eyes, "and it was like I was a totally different person. I still have them. The little pieces of bone. They're beautiful."

"It hurt?" he asked.

"Yeah. But probably the most painful part of all of it was that I had a long-term boyfriend, and he supported me transitioning. But then I did, and I could tell he wasn't attracted to me as a woman."

"Oh. I'm sorry," David offered. "You seem happy now."

"I am who I was always supposed to be," she said. "The person I always felt like on the inside. It's comfortable. Not having to pretend."

They stood in silence for a moment.

"It has to be hard, coming back here," David said. "I haven't told anyone. I won't . . ."

"Thanks. How are you, David? You're tied up with everything with Jason."

He looked off, thinking through what he could say and what he couldn't. Before he could answer, she continued.

"It's terrifying, thinking about a serial killer out there," she said, gesturing around them.

David's eyes widened and his pulse accelerated. He moved closer to her, insistent.

"You know?" he demanded.

She looked worried but certain.

"The three victims. Holly, Kapoor, and Jason. I know it's being kept secret."

He cut her off. "I can't talk about it, Charlotte. Sorry. I can't . . ."

She waved her hand.

"Of course. I'm sorry I brought it up. I . . . It was really good seeing you, David."

"Yeah. You, too," he said.

|||

As soon as she was back inside her car and saw David's truck rumble alive and drive away, Charlotte texted her producers in Atlanta. They'd been waiting on her, she knew.

story confirmed by official source inside investigation. three homicides are linked. FBI investigating. serial killer in Little Springs

The station would tease the news overnight. She would be live on air in the morning, doing a stand up in front of the old courthouse building.

Her heart pumped against her chest. This was it. A huge story. One that no one else had. And hers to break. The whole world would be watching her tomorrow.

A small voice sounded inside. *What about David?* She closed herself to it. She would cite only an anonymous source. No one would know who had revealed the information. David would be fine.

SIXTEEN

The man watched the news as he always did, wondering if today would bring the revelation. It was inevitable that the greater world would become aware of him, of the task he had set himself to. The authorities had to know already. The state police. The FBI. The sheriff. They had seen the three bodies. Seen what he had done to the three bodies. They knew, but they were hiding it. They must be.

And then, all at once, there she was, the female reporter. As soon as he saw that she stood in front of the old courthouse, he knew that this was it. He didn't need to read the chyron beneath her, which proclaimed: "Authorities investigating serial killer in Little Springs."

"Over the past month, the FBI has become involved in three homicide investigations in Little Springs," she was saying. "Last night, we received confirmation from an official inside the investigations that the three cases are linked, each victim believed to have been killed by the same suspect . . ."

Suspect.

She was talking about him. The edges of his mouth crept upward, a grin forming and widening. Now. Now they were paying attention. Now they would begin to see.

But as he listened, the woman said almost nothing else. No other details. Nothing about the message, about the work. The smile disappeared as quickly as it appeared. They were hiding it. Why were they hiding the truth of it?

He turned off the TV and stood. He knew what he needed to do. He would make them see.

|||

The cobalt blue car sat in the parking lot of a small building with a big sign advertising payday loans. The car was a mid-2000s model Ford Mustang, a vehicle that looked like the product of a future that never happened. In the dark of night, the kid sitting in the driver's seat was just a silhouette with the laser-red glow of a lit cigarette at his lips.

The man stood back for a while, watching for the rhythm of traffic, for the frequency of buyers. Where they came from. How they approached. One by one, they would shamble to the car, presumably hand over some cash, then shuffle off toward the back of the building, where someone else presumably waited with the drugs.

They had chosen the spot carefully. It was around the corner from a busier street. Easy to get to, but out of the way. There was also only one streetlight a half block down, so the whole stretch was cloaked in darkness.

The man spasmed suddenly, then clawed his fingers across his chest and shoulders. The pain came on in unexpected waves. Not a pain, exactly. It was a sensation like itching, though magnified exponentially. Needles in his skin. The wave passed. It was time.

He stepped out into the lot, the streetlight behind him. He made no effort to hide beyond the hood pulled up onto his head. If they saw him coming, he was just one more junkie.

He came to the car. The window was up against the cold. He rapped at it with the gloved knuckles of his left hand. His right, he held low.

The window lowered.

"Can I help you?" the kid asked.

He was even younger than expected. Maybe twenty. The sad beginning of a mustache on his upper lip. Tattoos on his fingers. He spoke in Spanish-inflected English.

"I think so," the man said.

He raised his right arm then, and the kid reached forward, expecting cash. Instead, his fingers found the blade, which slid through them so that they dropped, one by one, into the kid's lap.

He screamed for just a moment before the blade pushed back into his throat. Then he gurgled and trembled as the blood erupted out in waves and spurts until his eyes went empty and his body slacked.

The man reached in with his other hand and opened the door. The kid's body slumped out, his torso dangling while his legs sat in place.

The lit cigarette had somehow fallen and balanced perfectly on his knee, where it smoldered.

The man took just a moment to admire the work. It was efficient, but it was also controlled. He'd struggled with that, the first three. He'd been nervous, emotionally charged. This time, he managed to simply slice open the kid's neck without beheading him. Instinct told him that this way was better.

He dragged the kid out onto the pavement and to where the car would block the view of them from the street. Using the knife, he cut free the kid's coat and shirt underneath, pulling them aside to expose the chest. Delicately, he set to work. Blade against skin. Tracing the same, perfectly curving line.

When it was done, he stood above it, taking just a moment to admire. Then with all his force, he plunged the blade down, straight into the chest.

With his left hand, he took the phone from his pocket and tapped the camera icon. Carefully, he positioned it, moving so that enough light could come through, so that he could see the truth of it. He clicked, and the image was preserved.

The man had started to walk away when he turned back. Still, no one was coming. No one had seen. He looked at the building. He knew another of them waited back there. He could feel it. The smile returned to his face.

"The more the merrier," he said to no one in particular.

SEVENTEEN

The call came in the middle of the night, but David was on the night shift and already awake, patrolling the stony, empty town, and so he was the first person at the scene. It was like some kind of still life painting. The empty car sitting in the open lot, lit harshly by the distant streetlight and the neon glare of the sign in the loan shop's window.

As soon as he saw the body and the unmistakable pattern across its skin, he sent a message to the unlisted number that went to Erickson. But the FBI must've been listening in to the dispatch call, because a handful of black sedans arrived all at once within a few minutes.

Erickson stepped out, followed by eight agents, and walked straight past David. David opened his mouth to say something, then thought better of it.

The agents went to work, roping off the scene, poring over the concrete for footprints or any other evidence, photographing the bodies. Erickson stood to one side, surveying, his back to David.

He was being punished. He knew this. He'd been out on rounds in his truck the previous morning when a message came from Erickson: *What the fuck did you do?*

He'd had no clue what the old agent meant. Then Andrea called over the radio. She was getting one call after another. People scared about the serial killer. Or pissed off that the sheriff's department had been hiding it.

On his phone he opened a news app. There it was. A killer stalking the county. An official source. Charlotte's voice, spreading this news.

Their conversation replayed. He could see it now. She'd set him up, all that talk of reconnecting. Then her big bluff, mentioning the serial killer so casually. Obviously, she had done some digging, put together a few pieces. But she hadn't known for certain. It wasn't until he took the bluff that she had her source. Hell.

Then David's phone had begun to buzz, something it had only finally stopped doing a few hours earlier. Dale had called, furious that David had kept details of the investigation from him. One local after another, demanding to know if they were safe, demanding to know why David had lied. *Because they made me!* he wished he could say. But instead he repeated the same thing over and over. *I can't comment on an ongoing investigation.*

It was why David took the night shift. To show the town that he was out on the streets. And because he knew he wouldn't be able to sleep, not with Charlotte's betrayal raging in his mind.

After a couple of hours in the frigid air, Erickson turned from the scene and walked beside David. His hand worked furiously over the lighter in his pocket.

"I fucked up. I know I fucked up," David said. "She came to me already talking about the serial killer, and I didn't . . ."

"I had to convince Priest not to throw you in a big, dark hole," the agent cut him off. "She still might."

He took the lighter out of his pocket, held it up as if to inspect it, then pocketed it again and continued.

"We know the reporter is your cousin. She used you; it's what reporters do. Just don't let it happen again. The leash you're on is real fucking short, kid. And things are about to get real fucking messy. At least she didn't know about the patterned cuts. We aren't completely fucked."

David let his silence serve as an assent.

"All right," Erickson said. "What do you see here?"

It took a moment for David to realize the agent was talking about the crime scene. He surveyed it again, letting thoughts flow freely.

"They've used this corner for a few months now. We knew they were set up here. Everyone did. But we couldn't do anything about it."

They walked forward, to the Mustang.

"It's our guy," David continued. "No question about that. The dealer was sitting in his car. He probably thought it was someone coming to buy. Then the killer was too close."

Erickson pointed into the car.

"Found a pistol in the center console. Poor kid didn't even have time to reach for it."

The four fingers of the victim's right hand rested on the floorboard. Each perfectly bisected. David peered in at them, then leaned over the body on the ground. The head was perfectly in place, so that the only way to tell the neck had been slit open was from the trail of dried blood running down from the straight incision.

"The thing I can't figure out is the murder weapon. It was the same with Kapoor's arm and with Jason's . . ." David couldn't bring himself to finish the sentence. "The cuts are so flawless. But he attacked through the window. There wasn't any room to wind up, to really put any force into the blow. But he still almost cut through the victim's neck. I've never seen a blade that can do that."

David let the image from the night of Jason's death return to his mind's eye. The long blade, curved at the end.

Erickson seemed to be searching his own memories.

"I can't either," the agent said.

They walked on, around the corner of the building. Another young man. This one stripped completely naked. Body splayed out. Chest punched through. Skin laced with spirals drawn in red. His face was frozen in wide-eyed horror.

"No surveillance footage?" David asked.

Erickson shook his head. "Whoever our guy is, he's smart. He's looking for opportunities. I hate to say it, but he's getting better. More refined. You see that sometimes with spree killers. They start out nervous, reckless. Then the more they do it, the more they stay in control."

David looked past the body. A pile of small baggies sat on the ground next to a drainpipe, where they'd presumably been hidden.

"He didn't take the drugs."

"No," Erickson agreed. "Or the money from the car. What do you make of that?"

Why was the old agent suddenly bringing him into the investigation? Asking him questions? Only minutes before, he was sure he'd be taken off the case entirely.

"The past couple of years, I noticed that most people who turned up dead were mixed up in drugs in some way. Deals gone sideways. Or someone ripping off someone else. Nine out of ten homicides, it was something like that. These are drug dealers, so my first instinct is that this has to be about drugs. But because nothing was taken, it feels more like it's symbolic. The killer is making a point."

Erickson rubbed his hands against the cold.

"Pretty weird coincidence, you making that bust the other day, then this right after," he said.

So much had happened in the past day that David had lost hold of his anger over the FBI's seizure of his evidence.

"What the hell was that about?" David asked.

"There are a couple of Mexican cartels with operations in Colorado that we've been investigating for years," Erickson explained. "You just happened to stumble onto one of their drivers. They're both moving in here—they see it as an emerging market. We think there's a war starting up between them. We've had bodies turning up. Mutilated bodies."

"Hell," David muttered. "Then this could be part of a drug war?"

That would mean that all the killings connected to it somehow. Could Kapoor and Holly have been tied into a cartel? It didn't seem likely, but he'd long since given up expecting the best of people.

"Did your cousin use drugs?" Erickson asked, his voice emotionless.

"No," David responded, louder than he'd intended. Then he added, "I would've known."

Even as he said it, he was remembering Tabby's claim. That Jason was cheating on his wife. He'd decided it wasn't true, but still it nagged at him.

"We need to go to the courthouse. Look over the scene. Then start digging through your cousin's records," Erickson said.

David's jaw clenched.

"Sure," he said. "In the morning."

As they walked back out around the building, they saw the four TV news vans that had pulled up around the perimeter of the scene. Erickson looked at David with a hint of warning. David nodded back. Not another word.

|||

Charlotte waited with the other reporters and camera crews, each jostling for position, trying to frame a shot of the blue Mustang to capture just a little of the motionless legs on the ground behind it.

Michael, her cameraman, had heard the news over his police scanner and called Charlotte to wake her. Since she'd been on air, the other stations had scrambled to catch up to the revelation that the killings were connected. The race was on now, she knew. She'd have to work even harder to keep ahead, to make this story hers.

Just then, she saw him. David. Crossing the parking lot, keeping wide of her and the others as he headed toward his truck.

Staying behind the yellow tape, she angled toward him.

"David," she called out.

He kept moving, and so she sped up, finally catching him, standing between him and his truck.

"David!"

He faced her, and the instant that she saw his expression, she regretted approaching him. He knew what she'd done. She could see it. And not just that—it had cost him.

"I . . . I didn't mean . . ." she started to explain.

"I have nothing to say to you," he declared, clearly straining to keep his voice level.

She reached out.

"I'm sorry. Really."

He slapped her hand away.

"I don't know you. Get the hell away from me."

He was gone all at once, and she turned to see Michael there, his camera held in front of him.

"I got it," Michael said. "All of it. That was great stuff."

She forced herself to ignore David's words, the ones that still echoed inside, and turned back toward the crime scene.

"Delete it. We have a murder to cover."

|||

The man knew what to expect this time. He saw the game the sheriff and the FBI were playing. They denied that he existed, denied that the killings were linked. They stood up in front of the cameras and claimed that the two murders overnight had no connection to anything else.

He looked her up, the reporter who had first announced his existence. It was right to choose her. She had seen what all others had been blind to, after all. On the network's website, her profile had a link to an encrypted messaging service. His thoughts returned, as they often did, to the sheriff. The poor, clueless sheriff, who had fallen into something far deeper than he could fathom. It was time he began to understand.

The man clicked the link.

Now the real fun would begin.

EIGHTEEN

The town had changed. David could see it in the eyes watching him as he cruised along the street. Even the locals eyed him uncertainly, warily. They didn't trust him. Not anymore. The town's newspaper ran a front-page story about the killings, saying that David was involved in the investigation but wouldn't comment. It didn't say it outright, but the suggestion was clear—he was hiding things from the people he'd sworn to protect.

There had been a run on groceries. At one store, two customers had gotten into a fistfight over a bag of rice. They were hoarding, stocking up, hiding from the world and the danger lurking through the streets.

He'd also heard that the couple of gun shops in town had been selling through inventory faster than they could bring it in. The tension hummed just below the audible range.

It had stayed bitter cold, and he told himself that the cold always did this. Hardened the people, just as it hardened the soil. As far as stories went, it was a good one. It seemed like only the cultists went outside in Old Town, most days. Morning and night, they marched out to worship and then back into the theater.

David drove to the old courthouse as he always had, though now he had to park beyond a perimeter of orange road barriers. He looked up, where the window to Jason's office was boarded over. Erickson waited at the door. He opened it without offering a greeting. David followed him inside.

In the weeks since Jason's death, already the building had taken on a musty scent. Dust swirled in their wake. For all of David's life, this had been a happy place. A place where his family worked, where he and Jason, Ben Junior, and Spady would run around and play till they were shooed out by one of the clerks. Now he had to force himself to take each step up the stairs, across the hallway, through the doorway marked with Jason's name.

The room had been cleaned, thankfully, the floor scrubbed free of blood. In the light, he could almost keep from seeing the image of his dead cousin. Almost. David swallowed hard. The broken lamp remained, and the chairs and desk were out of place, as they'd been on that night. On the wall, a loose pattern of black dots remained from the impact of the buckshot from Jason's gun.

Erickson had moved to the desk, but David stayed in place, staring up at the wall.

"That's weird," he said to himself.

"What?" Erickson asked, overhearing.

"The shotgun hit up there," David said, pointing. Then he pointed toward the boarded-over window. "And a second one hit there. The window blew out when I was underneath it. I remember the glass falling down around me."

"Right. Two shots."

David shook his head. "I heard three shots. The window. Then two while I was running up the stairs. But there's no other sign of impact."

Erickson looked around.

"Forensics found two spent shells," Erickson said. "Your adrenaline was going. You knew your cousin was in danger. We see it all the time. Witnesses remember things totally different from how they happened."

David eyed the gun rack above Jason's desk.

"You recovered the shotgun, right? How many shells were left?"

Erickson looked off, thinking.

"One," he answered.

"Right. The gun holds four shells. Jason always left it fully loaded, no matter how many times I told him it was too dangerous. One shell left means he fired three times."

Erickson didn't seem to buy this. David turned from him and surveyed the room. *Where?* He paced along the floor. Then he turned toward Jason's desk and squatted down, using his flashlight to illuminate the darkness. A tangle of wires ran down into a messy coil thick with dust bunnies. David reached his hand into the mess, searching. *There.*

He drew out his hand, holding a spent shotgun shell, the plastic end blown open, the buckshot and gunpowder gone.

"Three shots," he said again.

"Son of a bitch," Erickson muttered.

They both scanned the room again, floor and walls and ceiling. No dots.

"What does that mean?" David asked, to himself as much as to the old agent. He was thinking about all the times he went out hunting birds with Jason. How rarely his cousin missed. "Maybe he hit the killer."

Erickson thought hard on it before answering.

"You could survive getting shot with a shotgun easy enough, but there'd be blood. And forensics didn't find any that wasn't Jason's."

"Maybe he was wearing an armored vest?" David mused.

"Maybe," Erickson said.

The agent snapped himself from the reverie and went to Jason's desk.

"I'm going to have a team come and take the computer, copy everything, and go through all the emails, all the files."

David cringed, thinking of these unknown people wandering through Jason's life.

"Then there are all the paper files," Erickson continued. "I'll have copies made of all of these and taken to Building Seventeen."

The agent opened a drawer and fished out a document at random. Then pulled another. And another. He whistled.

"Each of these deals is for millions of dollars. Must be hundreds of millions, all of it going through this office. Jason was the assessor, the head of the village council, and worked at the bank, right?"

"Right. So?"

"Your cousin was the most powerful person in the whole county. He had corporations, developers, government agencies, all coming to him needing a sign off."

The implication was clear enough.

"Jason wasn't crooked," he said, willing himself to believe it.

Erickson raised his hands.

"Just thinking aloud, kid. It's what I have to do. I've been at this shit a long damn time, and what I've learned is it almost always comes back to three things: sex, revenge, or money. When I'm hunting for a motive, that's where I look first."

David exhaled slowly.

"You're right. We look at everything."

"We need his bank records, too," Erickson said. "I'll get a warrant."

"No need," David said. "I'll go see my uncle."

|||

In the lobby of the Little Springs Federal Bank, a glass case displayed items from the building's history. The first key from when it was founded in the early 1900s. The first dollar deposited in its vault. The first check it issued. Photos of the building as it was constructed. And photos of the Blunt family through the years. Samuel and his three sons. A portrait of Dale from before his hair went white, when he took over running the bank. Then, on a small wooden stand, stood a .38 special revolver.

Everyone in the county knew the story by heart. It was 1985. A bank robber was on a spree through Nebraska, working his way west. His run would end in Little Springs. Dale had taken to wearing that .38 in a holster under his suit jacket.

The robber came in and demanded money. Dale stepped out of his office and drew his gun. In the crossfire, a clerk was hit and killed. The robber took a few bullets and bled out on the ground.

For decades, it was the only homicide in the county's history.

David found his uncle sitting in his office, cowboy boots up on his desk, which was empty aside from three matching pens aligned perfectly and a dark ash tray with the remnants of stubbed out cigars. Dale was reading the *Garden County Gazette*, cigar smoke wafting up from behind it.

"I figured you read the paper before it goes to press, since you own it," David said, taking off his hat.

His uncle lowered the newspaper.

"David. Good to see you."

He folded the paper and set it down on the desk, so that the headline about the murders stared at David as he sat down.

"You ready to tell me what the hell is really happening?" Dale asked.

David still felt like a child around his uncle, as if he was forever saying something immature or foolish, and Dale was there to give him a needed course correction.

"I am helping with the investigation. With the FBI," David started to explain. He talked slowly, feeling out words with a delicate care, in the way one walks across a frozen pond. "There are certain details. If people learn those details, then we wouldn't be able to tell good tips from bad ones. I swear, I'm saying as much as I can."

"Then what can I help you with?" Dale asked.

He didn't change his expression or raise his voice, but the anger came through all the same. Dale's son was dead. And David still hadn't found the killer.

"I need all of Jason's records. Work emails and his personal banking history. Every account. Any loans."

"You think my boy was involved in something?"

"No. Of course not. I'm looking everywhere, though. No stone unturned."

Dale drove the stub of his cigar down into the ash tray so hard it unraveled.

"Jason is your blood."

"I know," David answered.

"Fine. I'll pull the files myself. I'll call when they're ready. Anything else?"

David stood and looked out through the door. Across the lobby, a door was marked with Jason's name and title: Vice President.

"Has anyone touched Jason's office?"

Dale shook his head as he pulled a key and slid it across the desk. "You're welcome to take a look."

As David walked across, he felt the eyes of the employees on him. They were wondering if he was there as family or as an investigator. One teller—a young woman—was crying. David didn't know her name; she wasn't a local. She looked up, saw him watching her, and quickly hid her face.

David approached, reading her name from a plate on the desk. "Phoebe, right?"

She nodded, still sniffling.

"Will you help me out?"

He led her to Jason's office and closed the door behind them. She was petite, dressed with the stylish edge of a punk teenager who'd grown up, found some degree of responsibility. She held a tissue, stained with the makeup she'd wiped from her eyes. On her nose and eyebrows were the faint scars of old piercings.

She sat on a corner of the desk, as if by habit.

"You were at the funeral," David said. "I have a good memory for faces. Names, they just come in and go right back out. But you aren't a local."

She nodded. The corner of her mouth twitched.

"My husband is in the army. He was assigned here, right after. Then I got the job here."

"You like it? Working here?"

He could feel her losing her balance, not following the train of questions.

"Um. Yeah. It's just . . . It's been hard, since . . ."

"Since you lost him," David completed her thought.

She opened her mouth as if to protest, then closed it.

"How long?" David asked.

She stared at him for a moment, summoning words that failed to come. Then she collapsed all at once and started to sob, a full-body, shuddering cry. David made no move to comfort her. It was true, then. Jason had had an affair. And it was with one of them—an outsider.

"It was over," Phoebe said, her voice barely audible. "About three months ago. His wife found out. She threatened me. She said she'd go to my husband."

David leaned forward, tensing.

"Missy isn't that kind of woman."

Phoebe's eyes hardened. "She's evil. She doesn't . . . She *didn't* deserve him."

David let the room go quiet as he thought. Missy didn't kill Jason. She was at home with the girls. Besides, he had seen the killer. And it was a man. At least, he thought it was a man. He imagined Phoebe in a hooded coat. Could he mistake her for a man?

"Where were you the night he died?"

"Wait. You can't think that I . . ."

"I don't presume anything," David cut her off. "Where were you?"

"I had a workout class," she answered. Her face had gone white; her hands trembled. "I remember, because then I went home, and I heard . . ."

She'd started crying again.

"You have witnesses who can confirm you were there?"

She nodded.

"I loved him," she said, still crying. "I think he loved me, too. He was just . . . I never met anyone like him."

David allowed himself to glare at her.

"Your husband, you said he's army?"

She nodded. "Security at Site One."

"And where was he, that night?"

She startled, an unimagined possibility revealing itself. Then she shook free of the alarm.

"He was on duty. He works a lot of night shifts. I'm sure you can check."

"I'm sure I can."

Once he was back in his truck, David drove straight to the Countryman Building, then followed the protocols that took him onto the white van and off to Site One. A soldier led him to the room in Building Seventeen, and he passed through, not seeing Sunny, to his office. He looked up to nowhere in particular, then began to speak.

"Conover. We need to talk."

NINETEEN

Once, when Charlotte was a young reporter at a local station in Mississippi, she was out driving between assignments—the kind of stories she would forget by the very next day—when at a stop light, she looked out her window and saw an airplane gliding serenely through the sky toward the airport. All at once, an image came to her fully formed. She saw smoke billow from the engine. That smooth descent became precipitous. An explosion of fire as it collided with the ground. So close, and she would be the first person there. The one to break the news to the world. The one called to go on air on all the national news programs and mournfully recount the tales of loss. And then someone would recognize her talent, and she would be scooped up out of Mississippi, and . . .

Almost as soon as the image appeared, she banished it. She had felt sickened, seeing that hunger within herself. She had wanted the plane to crash.

As sick as it made her feel, she also accepted it. Every famed journalist had some story. They just happened to be in the right place at the right time when something terrible happened. A bombing or a war or a terrorist attack or a riot. They had owned the story, pushed it out into the world, and then been off on a trajectory toward greatness. Terrible things happened all the time, she reminded herself. Why couldn't one of them happen near her?

And now, it had. She lay in bed in her hotel room, laptop open, scrolling through what others were writing about the murders. The network wanted her on TV every day now, which meant every day she needed some update. The thought had struck her of how lucky she was. Not just at the appearance of this story, the attention it brought to her. But also that it gave her bosses something big and shiny. Something that boosted ratings. They'd stopped asking her about her efforts to interview locals, so she'd abandoned that effort. Yes, it was why she'd been sent here in the first place, to be a native daughter talking to her people. But talking to them meant exposing herself, who she really was. And she wasn't ready for that.

The murders were a godsend.

Again, the thought appeared automatically, unfiltered. And as soon as it was out, she felt the throb of guilt. Five men were dead, including her cousin. Her other cousin, she had used and alienated. And here she sat, feeling smugly glad about it all.

Her computer dinged.

More new email. She clicked over and sparked to attention at the sight of the subject line: SECURE SEND—ENCRYPTED MESSAGE ENCLOSED. Only once or twice before had someone contacted her through the anonymous messaging service.

She opened the email and started to read.

"Hello. You have done well. They tried to obscure my work, but you saw through their lies. Did you believe them, about the poor drug dealers? Or did you see through that, too? I think it is time you saw everything . . ."

Her eyes skipped ahead. Below the text were photos. Bodies. Young men, bloodied and . . .

She peered closer. The lines on the skin. The pattern.

It was them, the two who'd been killed. She recognized them from mugshots the FBI had released. As she looked again at the photos, she noticed something. The blood still seemed wet. This was him. It was really him. She realized then that she hadn't taken a breath since she began reading. She glanced down to the bottom of the message, where there was a single button: "Reply."

Charlotte moved the cursor over the button, where it hovered.

|||

A couple of hours after David shouted out for Conover, there was a knock on the door of David's office in Building Seventeen. He'd hoped to see Sunny outside, but instead it was two soldiers. He wondered if there was significance in that, two coming instead of one.

They led him out, and he expected to go to the usual building, where the white vans came in fleets. David had taken to calling it the Terminal. Instead, the soldiers led him to the northernmost building of Site One and then outside, to a field lined with Humvees and armored vehicles, with soldiers in tents doing Lord knows what. They loaded him into one Humvee and then drove to the north, along a gravel road. To their left rose the massive wall that ringed Gulliver, and then beyond that the mountainous giant himself.

This country had been wide-open grazing land before. As a kid, David had come here a few times with his parents. A winding stream called Blue Creek ran down from a spring and cut through here on its way to the river. They would canoe in the creek and hunt for arrowheads along the shore. It had been a Lakota campsite, until the army had massacred the village.

Now, the creek disappeared beneath Gulliver's massive head, as if swallowed again by the ground.

They were above the giant now, and the path arced west, then eventually south. David understood by that point. They were taking him to the military base on the far side of the giant.

In day-to-day life, it almost was possible to forget that Little Springs existed next to the one of the largest military bases in the world. There were reminders. The jets screeching past on their patrols. The occasional convoy of transport trucks. But the base itself was hidden behind the giant, and the tens of thousands of soldiers mostly lived in barracks there and worked either on the base, along the fence ringing the giant, or at Site One. At times, David would see groups of young men with the same high-and-tight haircut out in the town. More than a few times, he'd been called to bar fights where he'd had to break apart drunk soldiers and send them off, back to the base. But mostly it was a separate world.

David had driven past the base before. The border of Garden County wasn't for another twenty miles to the west of the base, so it remained his jurisdiction. But he'd never stepped foot inside. The path came around and joined with a larger road, which then led through a massive metal gate, the name FORT THUNDER stamped across it. He supposed it was some play on the fable of thunder being caused by the stomping of giants, but it struck him as childish.

Inside, the base was a contradiction of order and chaos. It had the obvious pattern of ordered military thinking in that each building was a perfect rectangle, and everything was laid out on a clean grid. But the site had been built in haste, and so there was no greater order. Just row after row of metal buildings, separated by black asphalt roads. A scrambled infrastructure to support the troops that continued to pour in.

The Humvee stopped in front of a large building with a small yard in front of it and a flagpole rising from the center of the yard. The flag hung limp; for once, the wind had stopped.

Conover stood there, waiting. David struggled to get a read on the man. He had soft features, a jowly face, and sleepy eyes, the kind of guy you'd meet at a friend's barbecue and immediately forget.

The soldiers let David out, then drove away.

"Well?" Conover said.

David sensed he was on a ticking clock. He explained what he'd learned about Phoebe and Jason and the claim about her husband being on night duty.

"Did you tell anyone else?" Conover asked. "Erickson?"

"No," David said.

Conover went into the building, and David followed. It was as faceless on the inside as on the outside. A soldier sat at a desk with a computer in front of her. Conover went over and spoke to her, softly enough that David couldn't hear. She began to type. After a minute, she looked up to Conover and shook her head. Conover said something else to her, and she nodded.

The man's expression had shifted just slightly, his eyebrows pinching down harder over his eyes. He didn't want to show it, but he was concerned.

"Come on," Conover said and led the way upstairs.

They went into a large office with a window that looked out on the giant, some two miles away to the east. Being on this side of it was foreign to David, and all at once he felt the destabilizing effect of it, the queasiness that had gripped him for months after it first landed.

The office had no decoration, just some chairs and a folding table used as a desk. Behind it sat a massive man in fatigues with a buzzed head, a massive jaw, and the torso of a bear. His sleeves were rolled up, and the veins and muscles pulsed over each other just beneath the skin.

"The fuck is this?" the man said, seeing David.

"Sheriff Blunt, this is Major Geiger," Conover said, giving the introductions no real effort. "Major Geiger oversees the security of Site One."

Geiger stood, unfolding his six-and-a-half-foot frame, and came around the desk, angling himself between Conover and David.

"Conover. The fuck is this?"

"Your unit includes Austin Chambers."

Geiger thought, then nodded.

"Chambers. Right. Why are you asking about him?"

"Chambers has a wife, Phoebe. She was having an affair with Jason Blunt," Conover explained.

"So?"

"Mister Blunt was murdered. The girl—Phoebe—has an alibi. And she thought that her husband did as well. That he was working late shifts on base."

Geiger's eyes darted. He was piecing together the line of inquiry.

"You pulled his logs."

"I did," Conover said. "He was not working that night. He was not working nights, period. At least not officially."

Geiger growled. "My fucking soldiers only fucking kill motherfuckers when I tell them to."

Conover's face took on an intensity that belied its soft edges. Conover stood to his full height and pushed a finger into Geiger's chest.

"Either the logs are wrong or your soldier is a liar. Or you're running missions off the books. I have zero goddamned patience for uncertainties with this shit. We run it to ground."

Geiger picked up a phone on his desk and barked some orders. They sat and waited a while in silence, then the door opened, and a young woman in camouflage gear ushered in a young man in fatigues. Chambers. She closed the door behind her as she left. Chambers stood, saluting crisply. He had ashen skin and athletic, attractive features, though there was something about his face that unsettled David—something vaguely asymmetric that he couldn't quite pinpoint. Maybe his eyes were set too closely together.

Geiger gave a quick salute, then pointed toward the chair. Chambers sat. He was closest to Conover, but David was close enough to watch the young man. His eyes remained trained on Geiger. There was definitely something off about his eyes. Finally, David realized what it was. He didn't blink.

Conover turned in his chair, facing Chambers.

"Your wife is under the impression that you've been working nights."

Chambers kept his shoulders squared but turned at the neck toward Conover. His eyelids pulled apart, till his irises were surrounded by white.

"Who are you, and why are you talking about my wife?"

"You report to Major Geiger," Conover said, gesturing with his coffee cup. "Major Geiger reports to me. That is the entirety of what you need to know about me. You are the subject of inquiry here."

Almost imperceptibly, Chambers looked to the floor, then back up. He held his hands out, fingers slightly bent, between his legs. They didn't so much shake as vibrate.

"She must be mistaken," he replied. "Sir, why are you talking to my wife?"

His response came fast. Too fast.

"Because she was fucking around."

Geiger and Conover stared at David in disbelief. He'd been silent to this point, but he knew how to play the kid. He could feel it. Before anyone else could speak, David stood and stepped over Chambers, whose eyes showed a mix of fury and confusion.

"Phoebe was fucking around. And that got her into trouble. And now it's spilled onto you."

"No."

"She was. She told me herself."

David glanced quickly to Conover, who gave a quick nod of permission.

"Told me she loved him, too."

Chambers jumped up out of the chair, and for a moment, David thought the young man would take a swing at him. Instead, he pivoted and began to pace, back and forth, as far as the room would allow.

"What the hell is this? Why are you telling me this?"

All the control was gone. Chambers's movements were huge, his body seeming on the cusp of flying apart. He looked about the room, as if searching for something to throw. Chambers wheeled on David and gripped the back of a chair to occupy his furious hands.

"Who is he? Tell me!"

"There's no point with this macho bullshit, kid. He's dead."

Chambers stared, breathing hard, gears turning.

"Did you know Jason Blunt?" David asked.

A pause, eyes bouncing side to side.

"Phoebe worked with him. At the bank. They had an affair, then he was murdered."

"This is real?" Chambers asked, looking again to Geiger.

"Afraid so, kid."

David leaned in, doing his best cop face.

"We know where Phoebe was that night. And I know where she told me you were. But that was bullshit, wasn't it? You weren't at the base. So where were you?"

Chambers collapsed into the chair all at once. His shoulders slumped and his chest heaved.

"Chambers. We need an answer. Now," Conover said.

"With the guys," the young man said, softly.

"What guys?" Geiger prodded.

"My unit. We started a poker game. I'm not so good, I guess. I'm down pretty big. I didn't want Phoebe to know."

"The other men can confirm this?" Conover asked. "I have the list right here. You know we'll pull them all one by one. Check everyone's story. Better be straight."

Chambers nodded.

"As an arrow."

They sent him out, made arrangements for Geiger and Conover to question the others. Conover led David out to a waiting Humvee; he promised to report back on what they learned.

"You believe him?" Conover asked.

"He didn't know about the affair. He was so in control when he came in. Hard to imagine a kid like that not having a good poker face. But the affair hit him hard. Nobody's that good at faking a reaction."

"You read that kid, knew just when to push him, knew how to keep him off balance. Impressive."

"Thanks," David said.

Before he could say more, Conover continued.

"You're also stupid. The shit you pulled with that reporter is making everyone's lives a whole fucking lot harder."

Conover's face had stiffened. It was as if the softness of his features was an act, a mask that he could drop when needed. He continued.

"I've let you in this far not because I trust you, but because you're no threat to me. I know everything you do. Everywhere you go. Everyone you talk to. And no, I can't stop you from talking. But if you speak one more word of any of this to anyone, I will make you disappear. And whomever you talk to, I will make them disappear. I will wipe you from the face of the earth without an ounce of weight on my conscience. Are we clear?"

David steadied himself.

"Crystal."

"Good. Now get the hell off my base."

TWENTY

Every day that passed, David expected another call. Another body found. He couldn't fall asleep anymore, sure that the radio would crackle to life. He didn't want to sleep. When he did, the dreams were unspeakable. Mostly, he patrolled the town endlessly, the same loops again and again, time running past in a way that felt exactly as if it was sand running out of an hourglass. He tried to visit Samuel every evening, but the old man could tell that David's thoughts were elsewhere. Some nights, David just sat there silently while his grandpa read through his research.

There were times, usually at night, while David was driving around the town that he would become convinced that someone was following him. The same headlights—a truck, he thought—would linger behind him, going in and out of traffic, for long stretches. It's just the lack of sleep, he told himself. Don't be paranoid.

When things were quiet and Brooke could handle the patrols, he would go to Site One. The FBI had added copies of Jason's county real estate records, as well as reports and photos of the murdered drug dealers.

Just as there had been nothing to connect Holly, Kapoor, and Jason, now there was nothing to connect the two latest victims. The kid by the car was Enrique Goncalves, twenty-one years old. The one behind the building was Henry Salazar, nineteen. They both had last known addresses in Denver. Each had a couple of drug-related arrests. Nothing major. There were photos of their tattoos in the reports, showing how the iconography marked them as cartel. But they were bottom feeders.

David had asked Erickson for the report from the drug seizure, trying to think through how that might connect. The van he'd pulled over was listed to someone in a Denver suburb, though they said they'd sold it for cash a few months before. Fingerprints didn't hit against any records.

He read through the catalog of seized drugs, types and pounds and ounces of each. But there was something missing. He recognized everything, connected it to the mental tally he had made at the time. There was no mention of whatever had been inside the cigar box, the small baggies full of what looked like sugar crystals.

There was a knock on the door, and this time it was Sunny, tapping with her foot. She held a cup of coffee in each hand. Underneath her white lab coat, she wore a Misfits T-shirt. She set the cups down on the table.

"I didn't know how you take it," she said as she fished out a fistful of sugars and creamer packets from the pocket of her lab coat.

"Don't know what I'd do without you," he said, smiling for the first time in longer than he could remember.

"You'd probably fall asleep on your feet," she teased.

They sat next to each other. David ran a hand through his messy hair.

"I look that bad?" he asked.

"I mean . . . Yeah. Pretty rough," she said with a laugh.

He found himself laughing back. There was something about her that immediately took away the tension he always clenched inside. He mixed a cream and two sugars into the coffee and took a drink.

"Thanks," he said. "For the coffee. Not for telling me I look like shit."

"How's the case coming?" she asked. "I heard about the others."

Right. She was in the loop. He could let his guard down.

"I'm totally lost," he admitted. "It's just one thing after another that doesn't make sense. There's no link between the victims. No pattern in the dates of the murders or the locations. They would all seem completely random if it wasn't for the way they were killed. And all the time I'm in here spinning my wheels, he's out there, just waiting to attack again."

He sighed and took another drink of coffee.

"What about you? Made any breakthroughs?"

She shook her head slowly, her long bangs falling across her face as she did.

"Studying this thing, it's like trying to write literary analysis about a book written in a language I don't know. There are times I can't even describe what I'm looking at, let alone explain it."

"You're actually studying him?" he asked.

"Pieces of him, anyway. The samples are all pieces that broke off on entry. Pieces that the army recovered."

David thought back to that day. Overhead, the giant lit up with energy, as if lightning shot along its skin. Then it began its slow descent through the atmosphere, and flaming arcs rained down from it. Debris, breaking off of the giant, rocketing down toward the earth.

In the days that followed, the army had blanketed the county, searching for any of those lost pieces. There were rumors that some had been missed. That locals had found pieces. It was illegal to possess any, let alone to sell them. But there was talk that a black market existed.

"You have pieces of the giant through there?" David asked, nodding behind them, toward Sunny's lab.

"Just little bits," she said. "And some of the spire, too. They're similar, with the same base structure, but different. Different in color and with slight differences in the shapes of the individual crystal cells. It's not the same thing, but I would say it's sort of like how a human is similar to a fish in a lot of ways, but we're different species."

David shivered. He tried not to imagine the implications of it. That there were things like Gulliver out there in the universe. And that there were other things. Bigger, scarier things. Things that could kill the giant.

"What are you trying to figure out?" he asked. "Sorry, that's probably a stupid way of saying it."

"No, not at all," she said. "It sounds a lot simpler than it is, but I'm working on forming a model of how the giant works."

She looked down at the coffee in front of them, then grabbed a sugar packet and tore it open. She poured the contents down onto the table, forming a small pile of sugar crystals.

"So, life on earth is made up of individual cells. But the giant is made up of individual crystals, when you break the pieces apart. They're each about the same size as a sugar crystal, actually. Right now, the crystals just sit there, inert."

Sunny dragged her hand through the sugar, creating a straight line.

"At some point, when it was alive, there was some force that connected all the individual crystals."

She worked with both hands, shaping.

"Just like our cells form bones and tissue and organs, the crystals formed into the giant. Trillions and trillions of individual crystals, all linked."

She pulled her hands back. On the table, the sugar had been shaped into the rough outline of a man.

"The problem is," she continued, "the giant doesn't emit any electromagnetic energy or radiation or anything. As far as I can tell, there's
nothing that connects the crystals to each other."

"But it's dead, right?" David asked. "Maybe the connection stopped."

"If so, its body should crumble apart basically into a giant pile of sand,"
she said. "The more I study it, the more incomprehensible it becomes."

"Well, it can't be that. There aren't degrees of incomprehensibility."

He looked over at her with a grin, one that she matched.

"And you're the word police now?"

"Grandma was the town librarian," he explained. "You abused the
language, boy, it didn't matter if you were family."

They each took a drink.

"I wouldn't have taken you for a punk," David said, gesturing toward
her shirt.

She grinned, her cheeks flushing just a little.

"Promise you won't make fun of me?" she asked, cryptically.

He nodded.

"My parents were pretty stereotypical high achievers," she said. "We
were in Pasadena, outside of LA, and they wanted to be that perfect family. Which meant I had to get straight As, and I had to either become a
doctor, a scientist, or a lawyer. And I had to do piano and violin and ballet
and all that bullshit. And I hated it. Then in high school, there was this
group of kids at my school that were into skateboarding, and I became
friends with them really just because I knew my parents would hate it."

"Skateboarding?"

"It was ridiculous. I chopped up my hair and dyed it and I'd wear,
like, Clash shirts, even though I'd never listened to them. And we would
skate all over town, and my parents were exactly as pissed as I expected.
I only skated for a few years, but by the end of it, I'd actually started to
listen to punk and got into it."

David drank down the last of his coffee. He looked back to the mountain of case files in front of him. For a few minutes, anyway, he'd forgotten
about them. He'd been looking at the Holly case again earlier, and he
remembered now that something had bothered him about it.

"The first murder. Jim Holly, the pilot. When I was talking to the state
police, they said that the FBI was on the scene."

She tensed. Her hands played with her coffee cup, spinning it slowly.

"Right," she said.

"I was just wondering how they knew," David continued. "There hadn't been any other deaths, so there wasn't a reason to think it was a serial killer. The state police hadn't even figured out what the pattern was before the FBI showed up."

He let it go at that. Her hands trembled just a little. She looked at him, her eyes imploring. Don't ask anything else.

"I don't know," she said then, smiling in a forcibly nonchalant way. "Maybe you should ask Erickson."

She left him alone. Just David and the small sugar man on the table. He stared down at it, and the thought struck him again of the small baggies he'd found in the cigar box, and the iridescent crystals inside, and how they'd looked almost like sugar. But not quite.

|||

David waited on the road that led into Tabby's neighborhood. He left the truck's heat off, using the cold to keep himself awake. He still had almost nodded off when the silver Tesla rolled silently past.

He turned on the engine and pulled out behind the car. He could've just flashed on his brights. Instead, he turned on the lights and siren. The Tesla pulled over. He cruised to a stop just behind it, turning off the siren but leaving the lights running.

Brian rolled down the window, his face showing the strain of maintaining a smile.

"David. I don't think I was speeding. Did I miss a turn signal?"

David leaned down over the window.

"Impeccable driving, Brian. This isn't about that."

Brian let the smile drop.

"You could've just come over."

"I thought this conversation should just be between the two of us."

"Next time, call. So? What is it?"

David tilted up his hat, so Brian could see his eyes.

"I made a drug bust the other day. Pulled over this van for speeding, and the driver ran off. I didn't get him. But inside the van, I found a whole pharmacy of shit."

Brian raised his hands, his eyes pleading.

"How many times have I told you? I don't bring weed across the state line. I have nothing to do with anything illegal."

"I'm not blaming you or saying you're involved. And this isn't about weed."

"Then you know I can't help you," Brian insisted, lowering his hands.

"There was something else," David said, insistent. "Something in with all the other shit, something I'd never seen before. Looked almost like sugar. Tiny doses of it. I don't mean to cause any trouble. You're just the only person I know in that world. So, I'm just asking if you've heard any rumors. Anything that might help me figure out what the hell is going on."

Brian stared forward, revealing nothing.

"People are dying out there, Brian. This might be tied into it."

Brian sighed. His eyes stayed dead ahead as he spoke.

"Our operation is clean, okay? Nothing illegal. But because marijuana used to be illegal, there are still some people in the business from that world. Acquaintances. And they talk. Nothing concrete. But I have heard there's something new. And I don't know anything more than that, but one guy was saying that almost all of it goes to the same buyer."

Brian paused to swallow.

"He said it's the Tigers. The cult."

Of course. Of course, it would be them.

David had taken a step back to his truck when he remembered something and looked back through the window, catching Brian as he'd half rolled it up.

"Oh, Tabby told me the news," David said. "Congratulations."

"Uh huh. Thanks," Brian said as he rolled the window the rest of the way up.

David had only just gotten into the truck and fired up the heater when his phone buzzed. Erickson's number. He read the message.

Get to your office now. Your cousin knows.

TWENTY-ONE

They had all set up in a meeting room that David didn't even know existed, just a couple of doors down from his office in the new courthouse. No one stood as David entered.

At one end of the table was Erickson. At the other was Charlotte, then a man and a woman that David didn't recognize. The woman had a briefcase on the floor beside her.

"Sit," she said.

"What is this?" David asked, his eyes on Charlotte.

Her face showed a twinge that might've been apologetic, but she said nothing. Erickson nodded at the seat beside him. David sat.

"This meeting is for informational purposes only," the woman explained. "Everything said inside this room we are considering off the record."

She introduced herself as a senior counsel at Charlotte's TV network. The man next to her was a producer in the news division. They'd flown in from Atlanta just for this meeting. A meeting they still hadn't explained. Then the lawyer took her briefcase from beside her, opened it, and pulled out two sheets of paper. She held each up for them to see.

David recognized them instantly. The drug dealers, skin cut in the spiraling pattern.

"How . . ." he started to say.

Erickson put a hand on David's arm, stopping him. The lawyer set the photos on the table, facing them.

The producer spoke then, introducing himself as Geoff.

"Our station set up a system to receive anonymous news tips," he explained. "It's an encrypted messaging app. Information comes through, and we have no way of identifying the source. Then we have to verify the information to decide whether it is real and whether it is newsworthy."

But how? Was someone inside the investigation leaking details? Did they think it was David? He'd accidentally confirmed that there was a serial killer, but he didn't do this. He wouldn't.

It was Charlotte's turn to speak.

"I received a message through my encrypted link," she said. "It contained these photos, along with a message. The message claimed to be from the person who killed these men. And the others."

Oh. Hell.

"Based on the photos and the information in the message, we believe this to be true," Charlotte added.

David felt like he was going to be sick. Beside him, Erickson betrayed nothing. No reaction. But David could see that the old agent's hand was in his pocket, presumably working over the lighter he kept there.

"I don't recognize these images," Erickson said coolly. "I do know that broadcasting any such information would imperil our investigations, not to mention cause a panic."

"The public has a right to know," the lawyer said.

"Don't," Erickson said. "Your concerns are ratings and ad revenue. The FBI will be filing an injunction."

"It's too late," the lawyer said. "A piece has already been filmed. It will broadcast tomorrow. We can assure you we have reviewed the matter thoroughly and have redacted any information that we believe would harm your investigation."

Erickson stood.

"Then I guess we're done here."

He strode out.

By the time David got to the hallway, Erickson was gone. David paced, and his stomach churned. The county already felt as if the pressure had grown as high as it could. The second this news was out there . . .

The lawyer and the producer walked past. Charlotte took a step past, then stopped as the others continued.

"I'm sorry," she said.

He didn't respond.

"The others . . . Were the others cut like that, too?" she asked. "Like the giant?"

David wheeled on her.

"I told you not to fucking talk to me."

He expected her to leave then, but she stayed where she was. She looked up at him, and the expression wasn't hurt or remorse, but instead worry.

"David. There's something else. Something in the message. We aren't putting it on the air. But I wanted you to know."

She took a folded-up piece of paper from her pocket and pushed it into his hand.

"I'm sorry," she said again as she left.

He unfolded the paper and started to read.

Why am I doing this? Because the world needs it. This must be done. It's the work that men like Sheriff David Blunt should be doing. Except he is too scared. He chases after me, when he should be thanking me. But his eyes will be opened soon enough.

David found Erickson in the parking lot, next to David's truck. The old agent had the lighter out, his hand flicking it open and sparking it, then snapping it closed, again and again. A movement clearly perfected through years of practice.

"It helped me quit, keeping it in my pocket," Erickson explained. "I couldn't have a cigarette, but I could go through the motions of it."

David handed over the paper. Erickson took it and read. He sighed, then faced west, toward the giant.

"Before that fucking thing dropped out of the sky I had retired. Then all these agents quit, and the bureau needed help. They asked if I'd come back. If I'd known all this shit was coming . . ."

He shook his head.

"Ah, hell. I would've done it anyway."

David took back the piece of paper, folded it, and put it into his pocket.

"We can't stop them? From putting it on the news?" he asked.

"No," Erickson said. "We'd lose even if we fought it. Just got to be ready to contain the damage. I'll see if Priest can pull the NSA in, see if there's any way to crack that encryption."

"There's something else," David said. "Something with the case. There's a source I have in the drug trade. He said that the cult is buying . . . a lot. If we think this is all connected to drugs, maybe we look there. I mean, they're obsessed with the giant. And the wounds are all sort of ritualistic."

He'd strained to relay the information while omitting key pieces. No need to bring Brian into it. And Erickson was obscuring something about the mysterious substance in the cigar box.

Erickson stared off, considering.

"It's thin. We aren't getting a warrant off of that. And I can't just go charging in. After the fuck up at Waco, the bureau is real skittish around anything with a cult. But keep watching."

David spent the rest of the day outside of the compound, parked a block away, where he could see the gate. In the evening, it opened just as all the dogs began to bark across town. David had always been with Samuel at this time. He hadn't realized the Tonys had timed their evening march to the dogs.

They filed out then, one by one, a clean procession of black hooded robes and snarling tiger masks. Keeping the truck in first gear, he crept along behind them, always staying a half block back. If they noticed him, they made no sign of it.

As they walked, they stayed with their heads facing forward, never breaking. The Tonys came to the park, fanned out into lines facing west, and kneeled in unison.

After twenty minutes of this, they stood, gathered back into the long line, and marched back to the theater. The gate clanged shut behind them. No way in. No way to know who was under the masks.

That thought repeated itself. No way to know who was under the masks.

David popped the truck into gear and skidded away over the gravel, to the big box store out east. He'd heard they sold what he was looking for, and he hurried inside, searching. And there, at the edge of the clothing section, he found it. It was a joke, a gag gift. The kind of thing a tourist might pick up as a memento of a trip to see the giant.

The display case held sets of them. Black hooded robes and plastic tiger masks. He inspected the masks. Yeah. They looked just like them. Exactly the same.

David pulled down a robe and mask and headed for the checkout line.

TWENTY-TWO

A couple of blocks away from the theater, the sidewalk came past a small alley that ran between the Gormans' insurance building and the hardware store. In the pre-dawn haze, David felt confident that he couldn't be seen, recessed in the shadows of the alley. And they didn't look anywhere but straight ahead. They wouldn't notice him.

He shook his head. It was crazy. It was stupid. He should walk away. Go back to his truck and think of something else.

Except there wasn't another way. The theater building was a black box. No one in or out except the cultists. None of them ever revealing anything. If there was any chance that they were involved in this—that they had killed Jason—he had to know.

Shoes scraping concrete. They were coming.

All at once, the first of them came past, dark figures passing in front of the oval eyeholes of his mask. He'd counted them the night before when they marched, so that he'd know when to act. He ticked down each that came past, bobbing his body forward and back like a kid timing his leap into a jump rope. Five. Four. Three. Two. One. *Go.*

Smoothly, he stepped out, falling into the back of the line. The person in front of him made no movement, gave no indication of noticing this added presence to the procession, just walked straight ahead. David held the same distance as the others, keeping about two feet between them.

He felt strangely naked, under the robe. He'd worn black sweatpants and a T-shirt and left his belt and gun and badge behind to keep some degree of plausible deniability. This wasn't an official visit. This was just a citizen trying to find religion.

The fence around the theater loomed ahead. The gate was open. They were marching through. One last pang of doubt arose. He could still step out of line. Walk away.

He closed his eyes and marched through. It was only when the gate clanked shut behind him that the realization appeared—while he'd figured out how to get inside the theater, he had no plan to get out.

His fear had been that as soon as the doors to the theater closed, they would all remove their masks at once, and he would be revealed. But he watched through the slits in the mask as the others continued, fully costumed, through the dark of what once had been the theater's lobby and into the theater itself.

It had been a decade or more since David had been inside, and between the darkness and the limited view through the mask, the scene revealed itself only in flashes.

The velvet curtains draping the walls remained in place, as did the wooden seats, with a center aisle running to the front. The only light seemed to come from candelabras along the walls, which, looking closer, had flickering LED bulbs instead of burning wicks.

At the front of the room, a small stage rose up, and then the movie screen, except . . .

It had been painted, the screen. A coat of gray and then lines of electric blue. Lines that looped and curled. Lines that spiraled. Lines that formed the exact pattern that stretched across the surface of the giant. Lines that the killer was carving into people's skin.

The Tonys had begun sitting, and he was standing there, gaping. They were filing into the theater's seats, filling one row after another. Following the person in front of him, David ducked into one of the back rows, sitting on the aisle.

For a long moment they all sat silently. David surveyed them, trying to count heads. Somehow it seemed there were even more inside than had been marching. Maybe some of them stayed here, when the others went out to march. There wasn't any obvious place for people to sleep, no sign of beds or cots. He'd heard from the locals who lived closest to the theater that they sometimes heard the gate opening in the early hours of the morning. Meaning the cult's members could come and go. Meaning he had no idea just how many of them there were, or where they were going, what they were doing, who they were. His hand moved to his hip, for the reassurance of his pistol, and he remembered ruefully that he'd left it behind.

David hadn't noticed it at first, he was so distracted by the pattern on the screen, but on the stage sat what looked like a metal stock tank, an aluminum tub some six feet across and maybe three feet tall. To the side of that stood a small wooden column, the base carved ornately. Atop it was a silver chalice.

The lights went out, and all was black.

Seconds later, they flashed on again, and standing in the center of the stage was one masked figure.

"Brothers and sisters," he spoke.

A hissing sound filled the room. It was all the other Tonys. Exhaling through the perforations in the masks.

Then, as suddenly as it began, the hissing stopped.

"The world was made in perfection. Harmonic, clean. And then we were born into it. We rejected this perfection, because it was not enough."

The more the one on the stage spoke, the more certain David became that it was Quentin Breda, the man who'd founded the cult. He stood perfectly in place as he talked, his head still, arms hidden inside the robes.

"We looked inside ourselves, and we saw a void. Vast, seemingly bottomless. And we decided that this void must be wrong. That we must have been made imperfectly. We decided this void must be filled. We attempt this, still. How? What do we throw into the void?"

Suddenly, he jerked his right hand straight up, pointing a finger dead ahead. A finger that pointed right at him, David thought. No. He was being paranoid.

"Possessions," Quentin said, and the room hissed again.

"Clothes. Cars. Houses. Wealth. Jewelry. All go into the void. But it isn't enough. What else do we try? Sex. Alcohol. Drugs. Food. Violence. Accomplishments. *Trophies.* One thing after another, we push over the edge and into the void. And does the void grow full?"

Hisses from the crowd.

"Never," Quentin continued. "It does not become full. It does not even become less empty. Not one bit. Why? Because this is the nature of a void. A void is all-consuming. Bottomless. Only hunger without end. We spend all our lives feeding it, and it is never sated. All this work, for all our lives, and we do not even lessen its appetite."

Bullshit. All a bunch of incoherent, rambling bullshit. Except . . .

Why did the words cause a vague dread to grip David's chest so tightly?

Quentin lowered his arm.

"Anum shows us another way. Why do you think he arrived pierced through, as he is? Stabbed through his chest. God, arrived on earth, dead. But is he dead? No, brothers and sisters. His first gift to us is the gift of the symbol. The gift of knowledge. He does not have a wound in the center of him. He has a void. Just as we all do. He came to show us our own failure, reflected back. He came to show us that we could, again, be clean."

Hiss.

In the front row, another stood.

"Will you be cleaned?" Quentin asked.

"I will be cleaned," the person answered, then stepped up onto the stage.

Something about the voice struck David. It was familiar. Then the man took off his mask, and David understood why.

It was the same face that David had grown up with, that he'd seen every time he stopped to fuel up his truck. Jimmy. He was clean-shaven for once, his thinning, reddish hair matted down from the mask. No. A local wouldn't be a part of this. He couldn't.

Jimmy dropped his tiger mask to the floor, and then he grabbed at the robe and, struggling a little, pulled it over his head. Beneath it he wore gray sweats that were tight against the hump of his back and asymmetric tilt of his shoulders. He fought off his shoes, then his socks. He pulled off the sweatshirt, revealing a twisted, skeletal torso with tufts of reddish hair. Then he tugged down his pants, until he was naked, one leg jutting at an angle to support his misaligned frame, his penis shriveled in the chill of the room.

David felt some collision of pity and shame. He wanted to yell out, to go and grab the robe and cover Jimmy. His hands gripped at the armrests as he fought down the instinct.

Quentin extended a hand to Jimmy, and Jimmy took it. Together, they stepped into the metal tub, which was filled with water that sloshed around their legs.

"We can be clean again," Quentin said.

And then, with a slow and gentle touch, Quentin scooped water into cupped hands and scrubbed Jimmy's gnarled body, starting at the crown of his head and moving down, caressing every inch of skin as Jimmy stood, expressionless but beatific. It took minutes, this process. Every masked face stared ahead, rapt, as David squirmed in his seat, desperate for it to end. Not because he was embarrassed for Jimmy, or that he worried for him. No, it was out of his own discomfort and Puritanism.

And then it was done. Quentin helped Jimmy out of the tub. Jimmy struggled to dress himself. And Quentin looked once more out at the audience.

"Anum did not come to fill the void inside us, brothers and sisters. Anum came to force us to look at ourselves. To see ourselves as we are. To make peace. We are born broken, and we will never be whole. This is not tragedy but truth."

Quentin moved to the column, standing behind it. From somewhere within his robe, he produced a small leather pouch. He loosened its drawstrings and reached inside.

"Anum will rise again."

His finger and thumb drew out of the pouch, pinched together. He moved his hand over the chalice, and David could just see the light catch against a dusting of tiny, reflective granules that fell into the cup.

It was the same substance. Whatever had been inside the baggies that he'd recovered from the van. That looked like sugar. That Erickson had seen as dangerous enough to take away.

Starting in the front row, the Tonys stood, then moved in order into the aisle and up onto the stage. As they reached the column, they would tilt up their masks and bend down, extending their tongues into the chalice, in the way a cat laps at milk. Then they would continue to the side and back up into the theater.

The Tonys in David's row all stood. He did, too, a second behind them. And then he was walking up the aisle, blocked in by the others now behind him. He would keep his head low. Tilt back the mask just enough. Stick out his tongue and only pretend to touch the water. Whatever the substance was, he sure as hell didn't want it inside of him. Then he could slip out. Tell Erickson everything.

His feet numbly marched him forward and up onto the stage. He reached the column. Inside the chalice was what looked like water. He would just barely tilt back his mask and . . .

"David."

His heart jumped. The words came from beside him. Jimmy stood there, dressed again in the robe but with his mask held in his hand.

"You should've just asked," Jimmy said.

David breathed hard against the inside of the mask. He craned his neck around, struggling to see through the slits. Tiger faces, crowding him. He pulled the mask off. No point in hiding anymore.

David spun, looking from one mask to another.

"Did you kill my cousin?" he yelled.

A voice laughed behind one of the masks. "Hold him."

Hands grabbed David from behind.

"Get the fuck off me!"

He struggled, yanked one arm free, flailed.

The theater's exit was there, just up the aisle. So close. He threw his weight toward it, crashed into bodies, kicked.

Something smashed into the side of his neck. His feet suddenly weren't on the ground. Then he thudded down against the stage.

Hands and arms and bodies piled atop him, tiger masks crowding his vision, breath hissing into his face. A knee drove into his side.

He strained, screamed, but there were too many of them, their grip too tight.

Then some moved back, and through the opening he saw one that he knew was Quentin, the sleeves of his robe still hanging wet from when he had washed Jimmy. His hands held the chalice.

"Just because we're different, you think we're hiding something," Quentin's voice said. "But we are not deceivers. Our business, David, is revelation."

Quentin stepped closer, kneeling over David. Hands pried at his mouth, forcing his jaw down, his lips to open.

Quentin held the chalice over him.

"No!" David tried to scream, though he could only grunt with the hands gripping his face.

Then the chalice tilted, and the water—and whatever was inside it—poured into his mouth. He gagged and spit and thrashed, but still he felt it run down his throat.

|||

He was strapped to a rocket. A rocket that exploded up, out of the theater and through the ceiling and into the sky up and up and up and . . .

No.

He *was* the rocket.

Air roared in his ears, shrieking like the tornado. Like the vortex that had ripped his parents from him, that had almost ripped him in half. And as the rocket . . . as *he* blasted through the atmosphere, he came apart. Skin shedding away, atoms peeling from the heat and friction, dropping away below.

He was being peeled, layer by layer. An onion. Less and less and less and . . .

Desperately, he clawed against it, clenched to himself. Tried to hold the pieces together. And then . . .

Gone.

The thing that he knew that was himself. His body. Was no more.

Still, he was. Out now from the atmosphere, so high above the earth that he could see the full of it, a circle spinning farther and farther away as he blasted now into the emptiness.

Except, it was not empty. The physical of him was gone, and so were his senses. How to describe it? The way he saw . . .

No.

Not saw. The way he *felt*—he felt the things that eyes could not see, that ears could not hear. Bands of energy, a vast matrix of spiraling patterns, all intertwined, a vast fishing net extending into every dimension, radiating from the points at which the lines intersected, all aglow with an emotion that he could not *see* as lilac but that he *felt* as lilac.

The rocket that was the thing that once was him sped along, passing through these bands but not hindered by them, except the rocket that was this non-physical him also was the bands. And as it went, something else eroded: the awareness of self, the identification as a thing that is singular and alone. Just as his flesh and blood and bone had, so too did this awareness drop away.

And then it was not him. It was not David. It was everything. And the thing that had once been David was simply moving through this everything-ness, feeling it, these fluctuations of color or energy or . . .

As his awareness left behind its fixation on self, the scope of the unfurling universe came upon him, of stars and galaxies dancing in grand patterns, alive with a hum. A hum that grew louder. But not a sound that was heard. A sound that was felt. Vibrations. A song. One vast song.

And then, ahead, he saw it. Heard it. Felt it. A towering form amid the cosmos. The giant. Gulliver.

No.

That was not his name. Its name. It was called something that could not be spoken by human lips, that could not be heard by human ears. Something that could only be described as a feeling not unlike the sensation of electricity in the air when a powerful storm is imminent.

The lines that were the net that was all of creation ran into the giant, bonding with it, forming the patterns across its skin.

Then the giant raised its four arms as if to say: Hello. Be calm. It will all be okay.

And there was something else it wanted to say. Something it needed him to know. Except . . .

All at once, the fuel that fed the thing that was the rocket that was him ran out, and he was falling. Falling. And . . .

|||

David was alone. That was all that mattered, not what he had done during the week when the world was coming to an end. Tabby was gone, pushed away. He was freed. Of regrets and expectations and old pains. The apocalypse would come, and he would die, and everything would end, and there would be no more suffering.

He'd always known he would end up here, across the river to the south of town, where the river valley rose gently into limestone hills dotted with ash and yucca, pocked with holes leading down to rattlesnake dens, among haphazard rows of marble headstones.

He stood over the marker that held his parents' names, then sat and leaned his back against the cool stone, didn't talk, just stared at the sky, unbroken by the flat horizon; it had turned to a soft purple, an unnatural shade that reminded him of shampoo.

The sky began to warm overhead. The purple shifted gradually to pink, then orange and red, shifting faster into an intense crimson that made it seem as if the atmosphere itself had ignited.

Then, at once, the shadow fell over everything. The wind gusted like air sucking into a vacuum, yanking David's hat from his head and tossing it among the graves. The temperature dropped to freezing.

His eyes refused to close. He stared up, expectantly, ready. But the shadow didn't fall. It lingered; he could see the outline of the figure itself through scattered clouds. A giant, floating above, blocking the sun. Around its body, the sky shifted to twilight, stars visible in the periphery.

In that moment, when death hung like a fever dream in the atmosphere, he was terrified. He wanted to live. He wanted that damn thing to turn around, to go away, to disappear. To leave his town alone.

Then the figure glowed, a blue-green neon flare emanating from its skin. As David's eyes adjusted, he could make out that the lights formed spiraling patterns. It was descending, though slowly, breaking through the clouds, growing more impossibly large with every second.

Explosions sounded around him. Debris, raining down, carving flaming arcs, then detonating into the ground. David crouched behind the headstone, as if it would offer some cover, as if his parents could shield him from God's hand once more. And all went black.

|||

"David."

His eyelids refused to move. It was as if a heavy blanket lay over the top of him, something perfectly fitted to the contours of his body, weighing him down.

Pain. A throbbing pain appeared all at once in his neck. What had happened to his neck? Oh . . .

Something slamming into him. Hands grabbing him. The theater. The Tonys.

"David."

He forced his eyes open. A hazy human shape appeared. And then a face. The face of someone he had thought he knew.

"Good," Jimmy said, smiling. "You're back."

TWENTY-THREE

Gradually, the weight fell away, and David found himself able once again to move. He strained his aching neck to see that he sat in an easy chair in a small living room, another chair across from him. A TV on one wall, a few small paintings and grainy family photos. He'd seen this place before, he was sure of it. He squinted at one of the photos. A father, mother, and a boy. A little boy with a hunched back. Jimmy. He was at Jimmy's house, the house he'd inherited from his parents.

"What was in the cup?" David asked, words slurring.

Jimmy leaned forward in his chair, hands on his knees. Dressed in a T-shirt and jeans. He was smiling.

No one else was in the room, but still David tensed, testing out how his hands responded as he gripped them into fists. Would he need to fight again? He was wearing the same shirt and sweatpants but no robe.

"You shouldn't have done what you did, David," Jimmy said. "You should've just asked. We would've told you. We aren't hiding . . ."

"What was in the fucking cup?" David asked, his voice firmer.

"We had to show you. So that you could see the truth of Anum," Jimmy continued, as if he hadn't heard David. "You saw him, didn't you? What did he say?"

It was all there, locked in his mind, as clear as it had been when he experienced it. The horrifying explosion into space, the dissolution of everything he knew to be real, including himself. And the giant. Saying . . .

No. It didn't matter what it had said, what he had seen. It was a dream. Just a dream. David glared at Jimmy.

"I thought you were one of us," David said.

Jimmy pulled at one of his ears.

"One of what?"

"Part of this town. Not one of them. Coming in and ruining everything."

Jimmy looked off, then back to David. His smile was gone.

"Ruining our perfect little town. Heh. My folks, they never had enough to keep food on the table. They couldn't afford to send me to the doctor for my back. At school, you all made fun of me every day. You'd all run away from me, call me a monster."

"Jimmy. We were friends."

David remembered. It seemed like fun. Harmless. Now . . .

"You know, Spady grew up right there. Right next to me. If Spady had lost his arm as a kid, you would've just made fun of him, treated him like a freak. But he was good at sports, so you all took him in. But me? I was stuck here, by myself. Alone, until they came. It may sound stupid to you, but they really don't want to hurt anybody. They know that when he awakens, all this pain is going to go away."

They sat silent for a bit.

"I'm just trying to find out who killed my cousin," David said. "If anyone there had anything to do with it . . ."

Jimmy shook his head.

"They didn't. I promise you that. The night Jason was killed, we had a ceremony. Everyone was there."

"You're sure?"

"You know I have nothing to hide," Jimmy said.

Then he grew suddenly defensive.

"We don't make trouble with anyone! Sometimes when we're out, you know people yell at us. Throw shit at us. We never raise a hand. We wouldn't have had to fight you if you hadn't gotten so crazy. Everyone was worried you had a gun. I thought . . . I really thought once you saw, once you experienced it, that you would join us."

"Never," David spat.

For the first time, Jimmy seemed hurt. David exhaled slowly.

"I . . . I'm sorry. I guess I just was desperate. This guy keeps killing people, and the harder I try to solve it, I feel like the less I understand. And he's just out there, waiting. More people are going to die, unless . . ."

No. Not time for that. Focus.

"Jimmy, I need you to tell me. What was in that cup? Some kind of drug?"

There was a sound outside, the deep bleat of a coal train's horn blasting three times in succession. What time was it? What day was it? Jimmy breathed in deep, then exhaled.

"Not a drug. It's him. Anum."

"Bullshit," David said, though already he was stringing together the pieces in his head. Sunny explaining how the giant was made of crystals. Erickson seizing the crystals in the cigar box. That question the agent had asked him. *What do you dream of, when you dream?*

"You know how, in church, you take communion, and they say it's Jesus's body, broken for you, except it's really just bread?" Jimmy was asking. "This is it, brother. His body. Broken for us. It's his gift to us. His way of showing us what is real, the world we will live in when he rises . . ."

And if this was real, then the substance in the cup . . . The substance inside of him . . .

His intestines lurched, and he couldn't quite stifle a gagging sound, but mercifully it seemed there was nothing inside of him to come out.

"There's something else I have to tell you, David. I told them that you wouldn't do anything, that we could trust you. But they don't know you like I do."

David looked up. "What is it?"

For once, Jimmy seemed apologetic.

"They made a video. Nothing gross. But it's you, in the theater, after the communion. And you're . . ."

David could only imagine how he'd looked on the outside as his mind had disassociated. He eyed Jimmy to say, *I get it.*

"They told me to tell you that if you say anything, they'll release the video. So . . . Just please don't say anything, okay?"

It wasn't just their message coming through. This was Jimmy, pleading for the safety of this group, for this place that had welcomed him in when the rest of the world had held him at a distance.

"Okay," David said. "You have my word."

|||

Jimmy had called Brooke to come pick David up, since his truck was still over by the theater, and his feet were still wobbly beneath him.

He'd been out for nine hours. Nine hours that had felt like minutes. Brooke said they figured he was with the FBI. She'd given him a quick look and knew something had happened. He told her part of the truth.

"You did what?" she yelled so loud he jolted in the truck's seat.

He explained the mask and robe, his cockamamie scheme.

"You dumb fuck," she muttered, like an annoyed sibling. "What the fuck happened?"

Though he was technically her boss, they'd known each other far too long to have any sort of power dynamic, and so Brooke's reaction didn't faze him. It was a dumb fuck move. The rest of the story, he made up. He said he was looking for anything that would point to a connection between the cult and the homicides. Then he'd been discovered, and there was a little miscommunication, and some shoving, and he'd hit his head. Then he woke up at Jimmy's house. And after all that, it was one more dead end.

She swore at him a little more, then told him to go to the hospital, which he refused. She in turn refused to take him to his truck, driving instead out of town to the place she shared with Spady, a little yellow house on an acreage right next to the farmstead where David had grown up, until the tornado.

"I can't believe it," Brooke said as she drove. "Jimmy. A Tony."

David stared at the road ahead. As much as he wanted to be angry, he couldn't.

They found Spady inside the house, waiting on the couch with a case of Budweiser cans. He set his own beer down, then held one out for David with his only hand.

"The fuck happened? Bud, you look like you were rode hard and put away wet."

David took the beer.

"A long night," he said.

Brooke shot Spady a look that said, *Don't ask. I'll fill you in later.*

College basketball was on the TV. David stood, drinking, staring at the screen. There was something deep inside him that felt unmoored. He'd seen just how easily he'd gone adrift into . . . whatever that place had been. If he let his focus wander for a moment, how did he know he wouldn't slip away again?

Brooke was saying something to him, he realized.

". . . stay for dinner? I think we have some steaks."

"Sure. Sounds great," David said.

Brooke stepped into the kitchen, separated from the living room by an island, and opened the freezer, rummaging through. She looked back up.

"Steaks it is. And . . . Spady, you had damn well better not light that cigarette in here," Brooke warned.

Spady froze, Marlboro perched in his lips, lighter in his hand.

"Aw, hell, babe. All right. Let's men go have us a beer on the porch." Spady nodded toward the case of beer.

David understood instinctively and grabbed the beers. He grimaced at the weight of them; the muscle running down his neck and into his shoulder burned.

"I don't suppose you'd have a bag of peas in the freezer with all the beef, would you?" David asked.

Brooke peered inside.

"Mixed vegetables okay?"

It had been a warm day, but as the sun disappeared behind the giant, cool air rushed through, trembling the barren branches, buds just beginning to rupture through bark. They sat on a bench on the back deck, David holding the bag of vegetables against his neck.

"You're still on for Saturday, right?" Spady asked as he lit up. "Seven o'clock at Vic's."

Spady read the blank look on David's face.

"Jason's wake. We're all that's left, buddy. You and me. We're going to do him proud and drink that place dry."

No. Not just the two of them. There was Charlotte. But as much as he wanted to believe Ben Junior had returned, he hadn't. Whatever had happened to her over the past two decades, it had changed her into someone he didn't recognize. Not physically but in character. She'd used him. Took advantage of his trust. And worse than all of that was the fact that she didn't seem even to care. So Spady was right. Just the two of them.

"Well?" Spady asked.

"Right, sorry. I'd lost track of my days with everything. Of course, I'll be there."

Out over the pasture, a V of geese glided past, low above the ground. One gave a single, sad honk. Spady pulled deep at the Marlboro. The corners of his lips dipped into a frown. He rubbed absentmindedly at the stump of his arm.

"Brooke says you're helping the FBI out with the investigation."

David nodded.

"I know it's been hard on her, picking up all my slack. You two probably have barely seen each other."

"I mean, she's a little pissed, yeah. But she'll be fine," Spady said. He blew out a plume of smoke and kept his eyes forward. "This serial killer shit. That's for real?"

David said nothing, letting his silence serve as confirmation.

"Fuck," Spady sighed. "You know who did it? You have to have some idea."

David took a drink. Spady was close to Jason, in some ways even closer than David was. He deserved the truth.

"I don't have a clue," David said, shaking his head. "Not yet. But I'll find him."

He hoped he sounded more convinced than he was. Another day had passed, another blind stab at an explanation. Instead, he'd found yet another dead end. All that was left were all those pieces that refused to fit. Victims picked seemingly at random. The possible connection to drugs. He thought then of Sunny. He needed to tell her the truth. What he'd learned. What he'd consumed. He had to keep the FBI from going after the Tonys, but he could tell her.

The two of them drank in silence as the sun waned.

With a squeeze, Spady crushed his can and dropped it to the ground. From the case, he retrieved another beer.

"I just can't figure it," he said.

"Figure what?"

"That whoever killed Jason also killed those Mexican gangbangers." Spady's lip curled in disgust as he said it. He continued.

"I mean, them? Who fucking cares if a couple of *cholos* get themselves killed? But what the fuck does that have to do with Jason?"

Something shot through David, a chill that didn't come from the freezer bag he held at his neck. It wasn't just what Spady said but what he implied. What David knew was in his friend's heart. That some lives were worth more than others. He bristled at it, but even as he did, he wondered—would he have felt that same disdain a few months earlier, before this case had pulled him into the orbit of the giant, before he'd gained a place in the world of the outsiders?

It was the way he'd felt after the tornado, when he'd moved in with his aunt and uncle to share a room with Ben Junior. It would be his home, and yet it wasn't his home, not really. He was a part of two places at once but also belonging fully to neither.

A helicopter wheeled past, the rotor whupping so loud that they didn't bother trying to talk over it until, a minute later, it was over another field, continuing its circuit around the giant.

"Sons of bitches," Spady muttered. "Buzzing the house all day long."

"Yeah," David nodded.

Spady looked away and leaned back, alternating between smoking and drinking. A gulf had opened between them; David could feel it, and he knew nothing he could do to bridge it. They drank in silence, as the sky went from a soft blue to a vibrant pink, deep indigo, and, finally, black.

Brooke came through the back door then.

"Steaks ready?" Spady asked.

She gently shook her head. Her eyes were wide, anxious, and fearful. "You need to come watch the TV," she said.

|||

The hotel room was nicer than any apartment Charlotte had ever had. Modern furniture. Boldly colored art prints on the walls. Massive windows that looked out over the giant, the vista unbroken from fifteen stories up. Yet, after the first couple of days of gaping at the sight, she had closed the blinds and left them that way.

Her pulse raced.

All the other times she'd been on TV, it had been a live broadcast. She had no way of seeing what she looked like, unable to watch herself until on a recording later. Usually, she didn't bother. She told herself it was because she was too busy, always looking forward, never back. It was a good lie, as far as lies went. Even after all these years, all this work to create the identity she'd always wanted, she still hated how she looked. Her ears burned at the sound of her own voice. A hair out of place. A wrinkle across her clothing. A slight verbal tic. Every little flaw, she absorbed and obsessed over.

It was the network that had decided to make this a pre-recorded news report. It was sensitive, so the lawyers had insisted on having time to review. She'd seen it while editing, but this was different. Thrilling and terrifying at once. It was going out to the world.

A commercial for some prescription medication ended, and the live anchors came back, giving one final tease. And then there she was, in an exterior standup, framed with the giant behind her, describing the strange patterns across his skin. Cut to a bird's eye of the giant's body. And then . . .

A match cut to the photo the killer had sent of the drug dealer. Wounds perfectly matching the contours of the giant. And she was explaining the source of the image, that she had revealed the existence of the killer to the world and that then he contacted her, sent her this photo. A hired actor's voice read excerpts of the encrypted message, distorted and haunting.

It was like a movie in miniature, tense and disturbing and unbelievable. And yet it was real. And Charlotte stood in the center of it all. The piece staged her as the hero, the truth-teller who was looking out for residents, alerting them to the danger they faced, seeking justice and truth for the victims' families.

Her phone had started to buzz the second the report started. Congratulatory texts from friends. Notifications from social media. Emails. Dozens of alerts. Then hundreds.

This was what she wanted. The dream she'd always held. One big story.

So why wasn't she enjoying it? Why had her pulse not slowed, even now that the report was over, and the anchors were back on screen? Why was she mostly only thinking about David?

She picked up her phone and started scrolling through messages. Just then, a new email appeared, her eyes catching on the word ENCRYPTED in the subject. Her pulse beat faster. She opened it and began reading.

Well done. Now they are starting to see.

TWENTY-FOUR

The underground garage. The white van. The giant, looming overhead. The security check. David emerged into the labyrinth of Site One. Though he knew his way well enough now, still a soldier accompanied him wherever he went, silent and focused.

Even when he asked where the cafeteria was, the soldier simply pivoted direction rather than answering.

He came into the large conference room in Building Seventeen carrying two coffees. He steeled himself, then knocked at the door that led to Sunny's lab. She would be there. She had to be. Part of him expected Erickson to show up and yell at him, scold that he wasn't allowed anywhere but his own little room. Just as he was about to walk away, the door opened.

Sunny had on a Ramones shirt beneath her lab coat. She seemed tired, but she smiled at seeing him.

"I figured I needed to repay you," David said, holding up the coffee.

"I will gladly take you up on that," she said. "I feel like a zombie in here without any windows to tell what time it is."

He expected her to step out into the room with him, but instead she held the door and gestured for him to follow. He paused, his eyes questioning. She smiled wider, reassuring. He followed.

The lab was one room, about forty feet across and sixty deep. The walls were ringed with cabinets and counters, both piled with glass containers holding crystals, crystals of every color and shape and size. Some looked like blocks of glass, while others were eruptions of spikes. At one side was a tall metal cabinet with signage warning of hazardous chemicals. One row of desks held a variety of equipment—centrifuges, microscopes, and devices David had never seen before.

The center of the room was filled with a floor-to-ceiling glass chamber with a circular base, a sphere with a diameter of maybe ten feet. Along the glass were ports that reached into thick, rubber, arm-length gloves, he supposed to experiment on whatever was inside the glass. At the moment, the interior of the sphere was empty.

Beyond all of this, he noticed how messy it was. Papers everywhere. Test tubes and beakers scattered across surfaces. Books stacked in great piles, some tumbled over.

"Don't judge," Sunny said. "I get kind of laser focused on work. The other stuff . . ."

She waved her hands dismissively. There was a looseness and ease to the way she moved, her mannerisms and expressions. She seemed effortless. He supposed it could be the way Californians were.

She sat and kicked a rogue office chair his way. He handed over one coffee and started to sip at the other.

"You see the news?" he asked.

She shook her head. "We don't have any access to the outside world in here. No internet or cable. There's a TV with a DVD player in my room, though. They have a library that has pretty much everything. You can get music, too."

She jerked a thumb toward a CD player on another table.

"What happened?"

David explained Charlotte's report. Now the world knew about the killer and that he was carving up his victims. And they knew that David and the FBI were conspiring to hide all of this. His phone hadn't stopped ringing since the broadcast. Andrea was flooded with reports, people claiming they knew who the killer was, or claiming they were the killer. A local had called in to say he'd had a cow carved up with those same patterns.

"It's a shit show," David said.

He sipped at the coffee, thinking through his next step. He needed to tell her what had happened inside the theater, but he couldn't say it out loud. They were listening, he'd been warned. If Erickson and Priest learned what had happened, they'd raid the theater, and the video of David would be sent out, and that would be the end of his career as sheriff. But then, if they knew what he'd ingested, they'd probably lock him up in a lab somewhere, study him.

He reached over and pulled a notepad and a pen toward him. He started to sketch, as if he was just doodling. The pattern.

"I've been reading a little about the pattern on the giant," he said as he drew. "Fractals. That they're these perfect, replicating patterns. Except they're also chaotic."

He leaned over the paper, guiding the pen carefully.

"All these little pieces coming together to form a bigger piece."

"Uh huh," she said. "What are you thinking?"

"Just that I assumed the killer was organized, because of the patterns. That he had some compulsion to do this exact thing again and again. But maybe that isn't it. Maybe there's more chaos to it than I thought. Maybe he's targeting people at random."

David had finished the sketch. He passed the notepad to Sunny.

She glanced at it, then stared down, studying. Between the lines, he had written words.

Crystals from giant are on outside. Used as drugs. Tiger cult forced me to take them. Think I'm okay. Don't tell, please.

Her breath turned slow, controlled, intentional. She seemed to survey him, unable to hide her worry. She fidgeted with the coffee.

Then she took the pen from him, as if to sketch.

"I think you're right," she said. "That it's all chaos."

She handed the notepad back over. She'd adjusted the curve of one of the lines, drawing over the top of his. And beside it, tiny words were scrawled.

Need to talk outside of here

A sheepish grin appeared on his face then, despite it all. He hoped she'd think he was acting the part. The truth was, he hadn't asked anyone out since Tabby in eighth grade, so many years ago it might as well never have happened. And in the moments when he could take his mind away from the insanity whirling around him, he found himself again and again thinking of Sunny, wondering what she was doing, trying to understand how she made him feel good, even if only for fleeting stretches.

"So, there's going to be a party. For Jason. It's on Saturday. Just a little thing at the bar in Old Town. I don't know if you'd want to come."

She smiled back, a smile that he told himself had to be genuine. "I'd love that," she said.

|||

As had become routine, when David returned from Site One and got back into his truck and emerged into the familiar world, he radioed Andrea to make sure nothing major had happened. Every time, he worried the answer would come that the killer had found a new victim. But she reported that it had been quiet, or what passed for quiet anymore. Someone had spray-painted slurs onto the driveway and garage door of Imam Bey; Brooke had responded already.

When he checked his phone, David saw a text from Dale. His uncle had Jason's bank statements ready. He headed toward the house.

Jason's parents lived along the bluffs on the south side of the river, in an A-frame cabin that looked like a triangle jutting out of the hillside, with a large cement deck extending out in front of it. The view looked out over the river and the giant's left foot.

Debbie met David at the door, and he bent over to hug her. Old age had started to bend her spine. She kissed the air next to his cheek, and he smelled gin.

Dale sat in the den, waiting with his back toward the door. Cigar smoke swirled around his head. The room had been decked out as a hunter's lodge, with a fireplace built of rock and mounted animal heads lining the walls. Deer. Wild boar. An elk. A bear. Dale made no motion to embrace David, beyond waving his cigar at another chair, a plump leather recliner.

David sank into the chair.

"So, you had a chance to put the records together?"

"I did."

Dale reached into the breast pocket of his shirt, a flannel in green and black stripes. He pulled out a small silvery piece of metal. David struggled against the chair, leaning forward to grab the thumb drive.

"Spreadsheets. I figured you'd want to be able to search them quickly. All of Jason's personal bank accounts, as well as credit card statements and business records."

"Thank you."

"I can get you copies of receipts."

"I don't think we'll need them."

"Anything else?"

"This is plenty. Really. I know it was a lot of work."

"It's nothing."

Dale inhaled deeply at the cigar, which glowed red, illuminating the deep wrinkles of his face. David had the sudden recognition that his uncle was an old man. His close-cropped hair had gone white. His shoulders had started to sag. Even the intensity that always burned in his eyes seemed to have cooled. Had Jason's death done this? Or had time simply done its work while David didn't notice?

Dale flicked the cigar, dropping ash into a triangular ceramic tray perched on the armrest. His eyes seemed to search the room for something.

"That thing on the news. The cuts across the body. Did that happen to Jason? Was he butchered like that?"

The memory of that night returned, as it so often did. The carved-apart body.

"I can't say, Dale. You know I would if I could."

Then Dale was leaning over the armrest, his face red, his hand thrusting the cigar as if stabbing some invisible enemy.

"He was my son. My son! I deserve to know! I deserve . . ."

And then he just sat there, turned awkwardly, cigar smoldering in the air, his face red and eyes wide and lip trembling.

"I'm trying," David said.

Dale stood then, saying nothing, and led David to the door. In the doorway, Dale put a hand on David's shoulder.

"You watch out, David. We can't trust them."

Who did he mean by *them*? The FBI? David had the sensation of being trapped in the midst of warring factions, except there was no way to discern one side from the other.

Driving back to town, as he reached the highway, he heard horns honking, one on top of another. The northbound lane of the highway had slowed to a crawl. A John Deere tractor pulling a tiller chugged along at twenty miles an hour, blocking the whole lane, dozens of vehicles choked up behind it.

Old Gentry Luwendyke. David flipped on his siren and guided his truck next to the tractor, waving at the old man to inch onto the side of the road, clearing room for traffic. Then David drove behind the Deere with his hazard lights on, waving vehicles past with his hand.

As the tractor peeled off of the highway, David continued on, starting his usual nightly patrol. He pulled an energy drink from the glove box, popped the tab, and swigged at it. His crowded thoughts jostled for preeminence. The case. The drugs. The cult.

For the first time in weeks, the volume of all that faded, and something new took prominence. Sunny. She would be coming. To see him. On a date. Was it a date? What if she didn't feel anything about him? What if this really was just a secret meeting? But the way they connected . . .

He glanced into the rearview mirror, and a glare of lights fell over his eyes. Then he checked it again. Headlights behind him. Bright halogen glare. A truck, or maybe a jeep. The same one he'd seen before. The lights he had thought were following him.

No. There were hundreds of vehicles in the county now. Thousands. It was just a coincidence.

Yet, as he guided the truck through the memorized path of his patrol, those headlights remained behind him. One turn. Another. Another. Always hanging back, letting other vehicles come between them. Then reappearing.

His breath held in his lungs. His pulse thrummed.

He sped up, just slightly. Took another turn, this one not part of the routine, whipping to the right. Nothing. Nothing. Then . . .

The headlights, coming easily around the corner, following.

"Hell with this," David said.

He flipped on the lights and siren and pulled over to the side of the road. Let them come, then. He stared at the mirror, unblinking.

The vehicle came closer. Closer. Then it turned off onto a side street, nothing rushed in the movement. He squinted. A jeep, dark in color. Then it was gone, but still David's heart pounded.

|||

Charlotte had come to the house before, parking across the street and watching. Willing herself to go, to be done with it. Rip off the Band-Aid. What a shit metaphor that was. Those were her parents in there. The people who had read the note she left for them and did nothing. Didn't try to find her. Didn't tell her to come home. Didn't tell her they loved her no matter what. They just let her go.

And then, years later, when she had called them at one of the lowest points of her life, in the vain hope that they could make peace, that she could come home to a safe space, that her parents could offer some comfort, they told her she was evil and that she should never contact them again.

All those years went by, and she didn't even know the worst of it. That they had told the rest of the family that she was dead.

So no, Charlotte had not gotten out of her car. She hadn't walked up to the house and knocked on the door. She hadn't ripped off the Band-Aid. But now that was exactly what she was doing.

Because her parents had recognized her on the TV. Somehow, they knew. And they found her contact information and sent her a message telling her she needed to come and see them. Here she was.

Bonnie opened the door. She held it like a shield, crouched behind it. Ben Senior shuffled into view behind her. Charlotte had seen them at a distance at the funeral. Up close, they were all but unrecognizable. Bonnie had nearly doubled in size, her skin pale and waxy, her hair gray. Ben was almost totally bald, except with a few strands combed over and slicked in place. The features of his face seemed inflated; he looked like a Dick Tracy villain.

Charlotte clenched her arms to her side to stop them from shaking. "Hi," she said.

Bonnie sniffed sharply. She looked to Ben, indicating it was his job to speak. The oversize features of his face twisted, as if he held too many emotions and couldn't land on one.

"You asked me to come. I'm here," Charlotte said.

Ben cleared his throat.

"We told you that you aren't welcome here. We didn't want you here then. We don't want you here now. Not after . . ."

He didn't need to complete the thought.

"This town is my home."

"No," Bonnie almost hissed. "You aren't our son. This is not your home."

"I have to be here. For my job," Charlotte pushed back.

Ben took a half step forward, and Charlotte instinctively stepped back. She'd been hit before. It had been years since the last time, but still she knew how to sense it coming. Ben stopped, though, unwilling or unable to follow through on the violence in his eyes.

"You have to leave," he said. "Now."

And then, in that moment, the tension ran out of Charlotte. All the anger and frustration and anguish she'd clenched in the pit of her for two decades just up and turned to vapor. These were not monsters. They were old people. Scared and confused and blind to the world. Blind to themselves. They weren't to be feared. They were to be pitied.

"You were right," Charlotte said. "I'm not your child. But that also means that you aren't my parents. So do not ever think for one god-damned second that you get to tell me what I can and can't do."

She didn't bother to stay and watch their expressions. Instead, she wheeled away and went back to her car, and during the drive back to her hotel she turned the radio to a pop station and cranked the volume and sang along to some inane song with the windows down, despite the chill in the air.

It was only once she was in the hotel lobby that the compulsion to check her phone struck her, and she saw the encrypted message, opened it, and looked at the photo. And then she screamed.

TWENTY-FIVE

There was no lawyer this time. No producer. Just Charlotte, shivering and scared, sitting in David's office at the new courthouse in the chair across from him, the desk he never used now an effective barrier between them.

"I didn't tell anyone," she said. "I didn't know what to do."

Some part of him wanted to comfort her, the part that held onto the memories of the two of them growing up together. But then he remembered that she had made her choice. In the days since she revealed the killer's message, the town had wound itself up even tighter. Parents were refusing to let their children out of the house. Asshole kids had started spray-painting the giant's pattern on any open wall, as if in macabre celebration of the killer. And the case hadn't moved forward one inch. He couldn't hang all of that around her neck, but she sure as hell hadn't helped.

He looked again at her phone, which sat on the desk in front of him. It showed a photo of Charlotte, taken mostly from behind, standing on the sidewalk in front of her hotel. A photo taken by the killer and sent to her. It had no message, but the message was clear. The killer knew where to find Charlotte, and he could sneak up right next to her with no one noticing. Whoever the hell he was, he was ghostlike—or so average and unassuming that he tripped no suspicions, the kind of face that moved past and was instantly forgotten.

"Maybe you should leave town," David suggested, though he couldn't manage to meet her eyes as he said it.

She inhaled hard, sucking in air, and then she started to sob. A loud, messy, choking cry that caught David off guard in its suddenness and intensity. He stood and came half around the desk, but he stopped short of her, caught between his compulsion to put a hand on her shoulder and the anger that refused to fully recede.

After a few seconds, her shoulders stopped shaking, and she wiped a hand across her face.

"I've always felt like I had a target on me," she said. "But this . . ."

She looked up at him, calmed.

"I know what I did to you, David. Using you. It was wrong. I knew it when I did it. I just . . . I've been so long in this other world, and that's just how everyone acts. You do whatever you can to get ahead. And you tell yourself it's okay. But it isn't. I'm sorry."

He sat against the desk.

"I get it. The way the town is anymore, I feel like I'm losing myself."

He glanced back at the photo.

"I'll call the FBI. They'll be able to protect you. If you want to stay, I mean."

She nodded slowly.

He handed her back the phone.

"Maybe we can try to start over again," he said. "Just no talk about the case."

She smiled slightly. As she stood, she looked at the phone, and her brow crinkled.

"What is that?" she asked, mostly to herself.

David moved close to her, so that he could look over her shoulder. And there, on her phone, was a new message from the killer. A photo. As David looked closer, he recognized the door to his own apartment. And beneath it, a line of text:

Tell the sheriff. He isn't chasing me. I'm chasing him.

David ran out of the office and through the hallway, hearing Charlotte's voice echoing.

"What is it?"

He burst out of the front of the courthouse, into the broad, mostly empty parking lot, the farthest bounds of which were lost to the dark of night. His eyes searched, found nothing. Still, he knew it. He could feel.

He was out there. The killer.

Watching. Waiting.

|||

Erickson seemed to take the news in stride. He'd assign agents to keep an eye on Charlotte. They'd be in plain clothes, following at a distance. Maybe they'd be lucky, and the killer would try something. David found the thought far from reassuring.

Then Erickson said it was time to go to Site One.

He offered nothing more, but when they arrived in the meeting room of Building Seventeen, David understood. Conover, Priest, and Sunny already sat around the table, waiting. It was the middle of the night, but they all seemed as if they operated on some other calendar, where day and night didn't matter.

David's head pounded. The adrenaline that had surged through him at the new courthouse hadn't abated, and as his brain coursed with fear and rage, his body burned through what little stores of energy it had left. He was on fumes.

"You got my message?" Erickson asked as they came into the room. He took a seat, so David followed suit.

"We are up to date," Priest answered. "Which means we know that you have failed to come any closer to ending this large-scale fuckup of a case."

Erickson didn't react.

"Any luck on breaking the news network's encrypted communications?" he asked, his eyes on Priest. "He's stalking David now. Him and the reporter. We crack that, this is over."

Priest said nothing but shook her head slightly.

Erickson pivoted toward Conover.

"How about you? You planning on telling me about your rogue soldier that the sheriff here sniffed out?"

Conover's face reddened.

"I ran the lead. It was a dead end. Private Chambers had a hard alibi for all of the murders. He was on duty when the first one was killed and at a poker game with other soldiers during the others. I didn't want to waste your time."

"Yeah, I bet not," Erickson shrugged.

Sitting there, David realized for the first time that he had assumed all along that the government agents—these dark-suited bureaucrats—all stood in one united effort. But he saw it clearly now. Each had their own agendas and secrets, ones that didn't align with the others'. It felt like seeing one skirmish in a vast, unseen conflict.

Sunny said nothing, keeping her eyes down. She and David didn't belong here, among these people. Chance had swept them into this room, but they were nothing more than observers, ignored amid the tectonic collisions.

Priest clenched and unclenched her hand.

"Where does this leave us?"

"We're still empty on forensics," Erickson said. "No good soft information, either. He's smart, our guy. Looking for opportunities with no witnesses—blind spots. He's growing bolder. More performative. The dead drug dealers were staged in a way the others weren't. And it's pretty clear at this point that he's making this personal with the sheriff."

Erickson gestured at David, then back at the others.

"Most likely reason is that David is the only person to see the killer and live. He's a loose string."

A vision appeared of scissors reaching toward a dangling thread. *Snip*.

"You assigned a team to keep eyes on him?" Conover asked.

They talked about David as if he wasn't there.

"We've been following him since the beginning," Erickson said.

The words barely had time to register before the old agent continued in his raspy voice.

"Which is why we knew about his little adventure in the tiger den. Care to fill us in on the particulars of that, sheriff?" Erickson asked, finally looking David in the eye.

The faces all stared at him. Demanding. All except Sunny, whose eyes pleaded with him to stay quiet.

"I . . . I just thought there was something ritualistic about the killings. It was stupid, but . . ."

They all watched him, expressions studious. He shrugged and pushed ahead.

"I had to know. So I dressed like them and followed them inside, and . . . It's strange. What they're doing. It's like they're taking in these broken people and, I guess, comforting them."

If Erickson knew any more, he said nothing.

Conover shook his head.

"Stupid? Yes. Jesus. It was fucking . . ." he searched for a word. "Imbecilic. That's what it was. You could've exposed us. Not to mention, you could've ended up as dead as the rest of them. I'm assuming, since you came out alive, that's another dead end."

All eyes went back to him. David nodded.

Priest glowered.

"So. That's where we are? Nowhere?"

They were all silent an interminable moment. David knew he needed to offer something, to redeem himself to the group.

"I, uh, read something about spree killers once, that they often go back to old crime scenes. I was thinking, I have these wildlife cameras— they're small, motion activated. I could put them at the murder scenes. See if he shows up."

Priest scrutinized him.

"You read something? Where exactly did you study law enforcement, Sheriff Blunt?"

Before he could answer, she continued.

"Don't tell me. I already know. Western Nebraska Community College, where you amassed a GPA of 2.79. Please, sheriff, do share with us what you learned at that esteemed institution about the criminal mind."

His face went hot, and as much as he fought it, he knew they all could see his skin redden, his eyes clench down, his body go rigid. She had pierced straight through him. As he seethed, he opened his mouth to fight back.

"That's good. The cameras. Worth a try."

Erickson spoke, cutting off the conversation. Protecting David from himself.

"I'll go with you," Erickson said. "If the killer is watching you, you need someone to have your back."

David's face still burned. All he could manage was a quick nod.

"I'm going, too," Sunny said then, a bit too loud. Then, catching herself, she added, "I'm going stir crazy in here."

As the others left, she pulled David aside.

"It's Saturday, remember? The wake for Jason. Can I still come?"

Amid everything, he'd forgotten. Most of the time he didn't even know what day it was anymore, all of life playing out as a too-fast scroll of moving images, of patrols and death, of sirens and threats. In spite of it all, he felt himself smile.

"Right," he said. "Of course. Let's go."

|||

Sunny rode with David as they went from one site to the next, Erickson trailing after in his car, watching to make sure no one else followed. If the killer saw them placing the cameras, he'd said, they sure wouldn't do a damn bit of good. David showed her how the cameras worked. They were small, weatherproof, recording in night vision once a motion sensor tripped. People used them around their livestock or out in the open prairie, mostly to see what predators came out in the night.

Once they were done with the other locations, David insisted on a final stop; he guided the truck south of town, across the river, and to the cemetery. There he led the way up the hill and to the family plot, staking down the small camera near the base of an ash tree so that it faced directly toward Jason's grave.

As he worked at it, Sunny stood by the graves. Erickson paced farther down the hill. Once David was done, he joined her and saw that she looked down at his parents' marker.

"The date," she said. "It's the same for both of them."

"Tornado," David explained. "I survived."

That was always how he explained it. Three words. Enough to get the story across and few enough to make clear he didn't want to say anything else. Sunny seemed to grasp this, and she asked nothing more.

She looked up at him, and her face seemed full of worry.

"Erickson said something. That the killer is stalking you. What does that mean?"

David tried to casually shake it off.

"He's sending messages to the reporter."

"Your cousin?"

David looked down at the grave for Benjamin Blunt Jr. *My cousin*.

"Right. A new message came through. It said that he's following me. But the FBI has been keeping tabs on me, so they don't think it's anything more than a threat."

He left out the part about the photo of his apartment door and the vehicle that he kept seeing behind him at night. She seemed to accept it at that.

David lowered his voice.

"You said there was something else. That we could talk outside."

She glanced behind them. Erickson was approaching.

"Later," she whispered.

TWENTY-SIX

So much had changed, but Vic's looked just as it had before the giant fell. Hell, it still looked just as it had the first time David had gone inside as a kid, tagging along with his dad, who would meet up for beers with Dale and Ben Senior every Friday night. The cousins David, Jason, and Ben Junior, and Spady tagging along, would get Cokes and try to play pool, though they were barely tall enough to see up onto the table. He'd felt a vague sense of discomfit: the sour smell of alcohol, the raspy laughter of old farmers . . . But he kept coming, and eventually it felt like a second home.

Brooke had decorated a bit, taping up photos of Jason. Ones from high school. A baby photo. One from just a few years back, a summer fishing trip with Jason proudly holding up his catch: a four-inch trout. Jason's barstool sat empty, his number 33 Little Springs Chiefs jersey draped over it, a beer and a shot of whiskey on the bar, as if waiting for him.

It seemed the whole town crowded inside. Old Town, anyway. No outsiders had been invited. And while Brooke gave a wry smile at David when she saw him arrive with Sunny, she didn't complain. Any guest of David's was welcome.

Spady clapped him on the back and tugged him to the bar, where Vic was waiting.

"We drink this place dry," Spady said. "For Jason."

David accepted a shot. "For Jason."

They drank slowly at first, one beer after another. Locals trickling in and out, cigarette smoke wafting. There weren't any speeches, just old stories traded in small clutches of people. Jason's legendary feats, athletic exploits, embarrassing misadventures. The time he dressed up as an inflatable dinosaur for his twins' birthday party, then came to the bar straight afterward, still in costume.

There were older stories, too, ones that involved the four of them—Jason, David, Spady, and Ben Junior—and David for a moment felt a pang of regret that he hadn't invited Charlotte. But she wouldn't have come. Would she? He didn't know. He didn't want to worry about it. Not tonight.

Listening to the stories, Jason seemed almost mythological. At one point, David found his thoughts meandering out of the bar, away from the revelry, to the printed-out emails the FBI had turned up between Jason and Phoebe, the woman he'd become involved with. Emails that told an entirely different story, of a vulnerable man who felt trapped under life's pressures. He couldn't forget the words of one:

I wish we could run away. I want to leave this place forever. Start new, just you and me. No baggage. Just the road.

David did nothing to puncture the crowd's image of his cousin. Mostly he listened and laughed to the stories, the absurd feats his cousin had managed, the brazen pratfalls. God, it felt good to laugh. He laughed until his abdomen ached.

Sunny sat beside him, listening in, absorbing the stories as she sipped at a vodka and soda. She smiled at him as Clint Black's voice crooned from the jukebox.

"I like you when you're drunk. You actually talk."

David was just about to respond when all at once Spady was beside them.

"You know much about this guy here?" Spady asked, sloshing his drink at David.

His voice slurred heavily, and his eyes twinkled mischievously.

"Honestly, no. He's pretty quiet," Sunny said.

Spady grinned.

"Always has been. I suppose he hasn't told you about skinny-dipping in the river then?"

David's eyes widened with a warning as Sunny giggled.

"Don't," David started to say, but Sunny was already demanding to hear the story.

"No. No he has not," she said, leaning in to Spady conspiratorially. "Do tell."

"Do not dare tell," David warned.

"Oh, no, this one is too good!" Spady crowed.

Spady was happy again, in his element. David pulled his hat as low as it would go over his eyes.

"Well, this one summer, we were what, fourteen?" Spady started.

"Thirteen," David corrected. "You tell the story, at least get it right."

"Thirteen. Anyway, we would ride our bikes down to the Old River Bridge and go swim in the Platte. We were always daring each other. See who could do the most stupid thing. For some reason, that day, we decided to go skinny-dipping."

"No!" Sunny said.

"Oh yes," Spady kept on. "But that wasn't enough for us. Pretty soon we were swimming out into the river. Like always, it becomes a contest. Who can swim the farthest out?"

David took a deep drink and shook his head.

"We're lucky no one drowned," he muttered.

Spady ignored him.

"David, he's the quiet one, but he's always going to push the farthest. This whole county, there's nobody as stubborn as him. We all know it. Jason swims halfway across and back. So, of course, David says he's going all the way over. Mind you, that's damn near a quarter mile. We say fine, let's see it. He takes off, splashing, and it takes him half an hour, but I kid you not, he makes it all the way across the damn river, and he's up there on the far bank, waving at us like he won the Olympics."

"Wow," Sunny said.

"Oh, it was something. But now he's got to get all the way back across, because he's naked, so he can't just streak across the bridge. He starts to swim, his head buried down in the water."

Spady pantomimed the motion as best he could with only one arm. David tilted the brim of his hat even lower, hiding as best he could.

"Did he make it?" Sunny asked.

"Must have. But Jason and Ben and me, we couldn't say for sure, because while he was churning water, we got dressed and hopped on our bikes and took off. With David's clothes in tow."

Sunny squealed as she clapped her hand to her mouth.

"No!"

"We sure did," Spady said, his smile wide. "A while later, he comes riding into town on his bike, one hand on the handlebar, the other one cupping his balls."

"Oh, I made it," David grumbled. "Assholes."

David shook his head again. His cheeks burned.

"Assholes."

Sunny laughed so loud she snorted.

"Oh my God. That's incredible. Poor little David."

"Little David is right," Spady said, elbowing his friend.

"Fuck you all," David said.

He started to wave to Vic for another drink, then gave up and climbed halfway over the bar to grab a bottle of Jack Daniels. He popped the cap and took a long pull.

"Especially you," he said, toasting Jason's picture. "God, I'm gonna miss him."

Spady's smile dissipated.

"You and me both," Spady said.

They drank, told stories, drank more. David's yearning for Sunny to tell him what she knew, whatever the secret was, at some point faded, replaced by a yearning just to be with her, to enjoy the night together, to hear her laughter. The night became an ellipsis of staccato moments.

He was showing her line dancing steps as he drained the whiskey bottle dry, and she gamely followed along.

They were dancing to a slow song. Johnny Cash.

She was wearing his hat. When had she taken it?

He was in the bathroom at the urinal, pissing half on the floor, struggling to stay on his feet.

They were back at the bar, leaning against each other.

There was Erickson, with a hand on David's arm. "Maybe it's time to call it a night?"

And then they were outside, and somehow David was getting into his truck, but on the passenger side. *How?* It was moving. *Who's driving?* Oh. Sunny. They were stopped at a green light.

"Is it a left or a right?" she was asking him.

He summoned as much focus as he could, looking around them. Even drunk, in the dark, he knew this road. They were close to his apartment.

"That way."

Then she was helping him out of the truck and up his stairs.
Then she was easing him down into his bed.
Then, blissfully, nothing.

|||

The old FBI man saw the sheriff and a woman off into a truck, then he headed down the side street along the bar and back into a small, gravel alley that ran behind it, with a clutter of dumpsters, stacked wooden pallets, and empty gas tanks.

The man watched this. And he watched the drunken revelers spill out of the bar, all so casual and unaware, acting as if they thought that this world was safe for them. It was time to remind all of them that they were mistaken.

He came around the edge of the building, clinging to the shadows, stepping carefully so as to not upset the gravel, to keep from making any sound. The FBI man trudged along, moving slow, wearing his exhaustion as if it was a cloak.

This part was always his favorite. The hunt. That electric charge that fired in the base of his skull, that raced down through his whole body.

He felt the solidity of the blade, the way it seemed to cut even the air as he stalked forward from out of the shadows.

The FBI man had reached his car, which he had parked in the alley. He was reaching for the door, his back to the man who moved steadily closer. Closer. The urge screamed inside him for release. He lifted the blade. Just then, gravel crackled beneath his foot.

The FBI agent turned, his reaction shockingly swift given his age and shuffling demeanor.

His hand shot into his pocket—*a gun?* He looked up with an expression that described recognition, confusion, and surprise.

"You?"

The man thrust the blade forward, saying nothing. The FBI agent's hand came out of his pocket, but it was too late.

The blade plunged straight through his chest, splitting the sternum in two, ripping the heart free of its arteries, crackling through bone as it punctured out of his back.

A sort of whimpering sigh came from the agent's mouth, then his eyes darkened as blood erupted from his chest.

The body slid backward, gravity pulling it from the blade and to the ground.

There, the lifeless eyes held open, fixated on the man as he began his work.

The blade seemed to move itself, gliding across skin, scrawling the patterns. Large loops circling into smaller loops, and smaller, never ending.

With each slice, the thrumming in his head lessened, a steam valve releasing pressure.

Someone would be coming. He needed to go.

But it refused to listen, this urge inside him. The work needed to be done. People needed to see. To understand.

Please, his conscious mind shouted. *Stop. Run.*

The blade stopped.

He stood then as the melody of a sad country song echoed out through the back of the bar and reverberated across the cool spring air.

It was only then that he looked at the agent's hand at his side, still clenching whatever he had drawn from his pocket. His hand held not a gun but something small, glinting metal. A cigarette lighter.

The man reached down, pried the lighter free, pocketed it, and walked off into the night.

TWENTY-SEVEN

David's head was spinning, like the inner workings of a washing machine battling an unbalanced load. He propped himself up on his elbows and forced his eyes open. No, it wasn't his head spinning. It was his bedroom around him. Lord, let it stop.

"I gave you some Advil before you passed out. Still, I can imagine you're in rough shape."

Sunny's voice. He scanned the still-rotating room. She sat in a folding chair that she must've retrieved from the kitchen and placed at the foot of the bed. She was wearing one of his Huskers T-shirts and a pair of athletic shorts that hung past her knees. He tried to talk. It didn't work. He swallowed and tried again.

"You're here?"

"I slept on the couch. I borrowed some of your clothes. I hope you don't mind," she said. "Are you going to puke?"

He shook his head.

"No. I'm good. I'll be good. What time is it?"

"Seven thirty. Here. Drink."

She stood, handing him a glass of water. He sipped. Waited. It seemed to take. He drank more. He looked down and saw the same clothes he wore last night.

"I didn't do anything stupid, did I?"

"You didn't go skinny-dipping, if that's what you mean."

"Goddamned Spady."

"No, you were a perfect gentleman. A perfectly drunk gentleman who tried to drive home, like an idiot, so I had to take your keys and drive you here myself."

He rubbed at his pulsing temple.

"Shit. I'm sorry. Thank you. That isn't something I do anymore—drink that much. Not normally. Guess I had some steam to blow off, after everything."

"Everything you've had to deal with, David, I think you're excused."

"I didn't, you know, say anything, did I? Anything about . . . ?"

He didn't have to complete the thought. She sat on the bed beside his legs.

"No. Erickson was keeping a close eye on both of us."

He glanced around, then back to her.

"But they aren't keeping an eye on us here."

"Not an eye," she said, then lifted a hand and pointed to her ear.

Had they bugged his apartment? Of course they had. Here. Maybe his truck. Was someone listening in to him every moment?

Sunny watched him, knowing exactly what he was thinking. She nodded calmly. She'd had months to process her paranoia.

"You know what will really help you feel better?" she asked. "A shower."

"A shower?"

"Hot water. A little steam. Helps the headache, gets the blood moving."

"Oh. Um, okay."

She just sat there. The bathroom was off of his bedroom, the door right beside them. He expected her to step out, to give him privacy. She made no move to leave.

"I guess I'll just . . ."

He nodded toward the bathroom.

"Great," she replied.

She still made no movement.

He took another sip of water and eased himself from bed. Something about her presence helped to steady him. His head still throbbed, but the world's rotations had ceased.

He padded into the bathroom and closed the door. He took a piss, aiming as best he could at the side of the bowl, trying not to make too much noise so as not to be immodest. He started the shower, stripped, and stepped inside through the sliding door. He closed his eyes. It did help. Damned if she wasn't right.

He heard the bathroom door open and close.

He saw her through the warbled glass of the shower door, and his mind searched for a possible explanation.

Through the distorted view, he watched Sunny pull off the shirt and shorts and let them fall onto the floor. Even through the glass, he could tell how beautiful she was, the slender sweep of her body. She pulled open the shower door and stepped inside. She wore only the necklace with the green stone that lay against her skin between her breasts.

"Oh."

She leaned in close and whispered.

"The sound of the water. It's white noise. They can't hear anything we say, as long as we whisper."

"Oh."

"I wanted to tell you. You're right. They're hiding something from you. Erickson, Priest, and Conover."

Just like that, he all but forgot that they were naked, inches from each other.

"What is it?"

"When I first started at Site One, there were already two other scientists working in the lab with crystals. A woman, Megan, and an old British guy, Stuart. Then, one day, Megan went crazy. She took a scalpel and attacked Stuart. She almost killed him. She was out of her mind. Raving. I ran out and waved down a soldier. When he came into the lab, Megan went at him. He shot her and killed her."

He nodded. Miraculously, he found it easy to keep his eyes locked on hers.

"Okay. But what does that have to do with the killings?" he asked.

"The way she cut Stuart—they were patterns. Patterns all across his body. Patterns just like the ones on the giant. Just like the ones that started to show up on all of the victims."

"Jesus. But she's dead. She couldn't be the killer."

"We all thought Megan had just lost her mind. But then, in the autopsy, they found it. Crystals. The kind that come from the spire. They were all along her nervous system. Somehow, she'd exposed herself to one of the samples and . . . I don't know how, but it went into her body."

"What does that mean?"

"The only thing we can figure is that the crystals affected her, somehow. That they made her attack. And then, on all of the victims, around the wounds, I've found traces of the same crystals. They came from the killer, somehow. That's why they have me go to the crime scenes. To look for the crystals. That's how we know the killer is connected to the giant. Not just from the cuts."

Despite the warm water, he shivered.

"God. You're saying the killer . . . has pieces of the spire inside of him?"

She nodded.

"And it's making him kill. This isn't a compulsion. It's an infection."

His intestines churned, not from the hangover but from the dread of that implication.

"You deserve to know the truth."

The truth. Such a simple term, but the revelation came with so many other implications, a whole new web of possibilities and uncertainties that lay between him and the killer.

She shivered just then.

"You're hogging the water."

"Oh. Sorry."

"Don't apologize, David."

She moved closer to him. Her leg grazed his.

"There's something else I need to tell you."

He couldn't imagine anything more alarming than what she'd just said.

"To hide your voice from the bugs, you can also just turn up music really loud."

She smiled and moved closer.

"Oh."

|||

They were lying on the bed, Sunny on her stomach, her torso pulled up on top of his. She traced her finger along his face, up his chin to his ear, then gently stroked it between her finger and thumb. He could barely feel her touch on the knobby, swollen skin.

"What's this from?"

"It's called cauliflower ear. I got it in wrestling. People grab your ears, mash the hell out of them. They swell up with fluid. You can drain it out, but it keeps coming back, no matter what. Eventually it just turns stiff."

"Does it hurt?"

"No. Pretty much numb. They just look stupid."

"They don't."

He ran his fingers through her hair.

"Like I'm going to believe you. You lied to get me naked."

"It worked, didn't it?"

They laughed. David couldn't remember feeling this relaxed, maybe ever. For now, all that existed was this room, this bed, the two of them. The case, the investigation, the giant, whatever this meant for their futures, all of that didn't matter for now.

"What about the scar on your back?" Sunny asked.

"You noticed?"

"Kind of hard not to."

It wasn't just that David never told the story. Ever since the night of the storm, he'd spent every waking second exerting to banish the memory, hide it behind an infinity of doors, locks, gates, and walls. With her, none of that mattered. He was telling her all of it before he thought through what he was doing. And as he talked, he found, strangely, that the act of dredging up the memory didn't hurt so badly as he'd always feared.

"I was twelve. We lived out in the country, Mom and Dad and I. We have bad storms quite a bit. Any time we'd hear the tornado sirens, we knew to go to the storm cellar outside. This one, it came in the middle of the night. There wasn't time to get outside. I don't remember hearing the siren. I just woke up to all this noise. Mom and Dad yelling. The wind screaming. The screen door banging against the house as loud as gunshots. They pulled me into the bathroom and pushed me into the bathtub. This big old claw-foot tub. Then they lay on top of me. Protecting me. Even underneath them, I could still hear it. It was the loudest thing I ever heard—at least, up until the day the giant fell. Just this roar that drowned out everything. I couldn't see. Then this scraping sound. It must have been stuff caught in the wind, hitting against the side of the house. Then all at once, everything exploded. Mom and Dad were there one second. Then they were gone. Part of a wall landed on top of me. That's what did this."

He rolled halfway onto his side, exposing the scar. Twisting his torso, he could just see it if he craned his neck. Sunny ran her hand gently down the length of it.

"God. I'm so sorry."

"It was a long time ago."

"But it still hurts."

"It does. I don't know. It's just one of those things. I've lived with it a lot of years, but it never has made any more sense. Why did it take them and not me? Why did it have to come just like that? Miles of open pasture to either side of us. But it hit the house square, like it was aiming for us."

"It's a miracle. That you lived, I mean."

"I thought you didn't believe in miracles."

She gave him a playful tap to the meat of his chest.

"Anyway, that's my story," David said. "Now, are you going to tell me about your punk skateboard days or what?"

She gave him a mock serious look.

"Oh, those were the crazy years," she said. "I was pretty hard core. Dyed hair. A nose ring. A whole lot of angst."

She reached over the bed for her clothes and came back with her phone. She scrolled through photos and found one of a group of kids holding skateboards. And there, in the middle of them, was Sunny, wearing cut-off shorts and a Ramones T-shirt, nearly unrecognizable except for the mischievous look in her eye. David could tell the kids were all from rich families, with their perfect hair and manicured clothing. They looked less like a group of punks than teenaged models dressed up for a photoshoot.

"Wow," he said.

She put the phone away.

"I know. But skateboarding was the cool thing, and we were all desperate to rebel."

"Did it work?" he asked.

"Oh, my parents were furious at first. I should've been practicing violin or studying. So when I started skipping out on things to skate, we had these huge fights." She saw his confused stare and rolled her eyes conspiratorially. "They're very much the first-generation Asian immigrant parents. They both grew up in South Korea, in Seoul, and immigrated to the States a few years before I was born. My dad never stopped working. He's a bank exec. My mom mostly just drove me around to school and practices."

Sunny looked off, thinking.

"I think I'm a lot like my mom was before she came over. One of my aunts told me that my mom used to be a writer; she had some poetry published back in Korea when she was in her twenties, some kind of edgy, satirical stuff, I guess. I've never read any of it. I don't even know if she still has any. She won't talk about it."

"You're still close to them?" David asked.

"Yeah. I mean, as close as we can be. I can't let them know where I am, and I can't use a phone unless I leave the base. They'd be happy, if they knew. What I'm doing with the giant. Geology paid off after all."

"They didn't want you to study rocks?"

She laughed. "First of all, it is a lot more than just rocks. And no, they thought I should be a doctor. I just figured, if they were going to make me study science, at least I'd pick something where part of the job is traveling around the world, visiting cool places."

He arced an eyebrow.

"Cool places like western Nebraska."

"Exactly."

Delicately, he touched the stone hanging from her neck.

"This something you found on a dig?"

"No. Actually a colleague sent it to me, years back. It's peridot, a piece from Korea. I've never even been, but it's a sort of reminder, I guess. A connection."

A pounding knock sounded at the door. They looked toward the sound, then each other. David sprung up first and searched the floor for clothes. He was halfway to the door when he remembered the photo the killer had sent. He grabbed his pistol from where he kept it beside the door and held it behind his back as he checked the peephole.

Priest's glaring face loomed at him.

He put the gun away, then thought again of Sunny's warning, that there could be bugs anywhere. He was angry and embarrassed all at once, imagining that someone had been listening in. But why was Priest here? Had she heard the conversation in the shower? The revelation about the infection? Was she coming to silence him?

He opened the door just as Sunny stepped into the room behind him. Behind Priest, a cold rain fell.

"What is it?" David asked.

"Finish dressing, you two," Priest said.

He knew it as soon as she said it. Another murder. He could see it in her eyes.

"It's Erickson," Priest said.

TWENTY-EIGHT

They made a stop at the alley behind the bar, but there was no sign of anything. The body was gone. The car, too. No sign of blood on the ground. Another FBI agent had checked on Erickson when he didn't respond to the radio, and soon agents had swarmed the scene. Lucky that they found him, instead of some local, Priest said. They could keep it out of the news.

Standing there, David saw nothing lucky in it, the old FBI man bleeding to death. Dying in the street while David was passed out drunk.

They went then to Site One, where the three of them sat around the broad table in the central room at Building Seventeen. For a long while, they said nothing. There was so little that David knew about Erickson. Where he was from. Whether he had any family. What hobbies he had. Hell, David didn't even know the man's first name.

Still, the death carved at him in a way none of the others had—except for Jason. Erickson had been his protector. Literally following David, watching over him. But in subtler ways, too. In all the madness since David had fallen into the investigation, Erickson had been the steady hand, there to show him the way, to stick up for him to Priest and Conover, to keep him from embarrassing himself. And now, he was gone.

He could tell it had struck Sunny just as deeply, if not more. She had sobbed the whole way to Site One, and even now her eyes were red and puffy, and she said nothing but occasionally sniffed lightly.

The morning between them seemed a lifetime ago. Seemed more a dream than a reality. David wanted to reach out and comfort her, to take her hand. But something told him to hold back. Maybe it was Priest's gaze, or that the murder had so suddenly cut off whatever moment they had shared. Watching her, David puzzled again over this enigmatic woman who had so suddenly become part of his life. What was it that made him open up to her, that put him at ease in a way no one else ever had? He'd never felt that, not even with Tabby.

But this wasn't the time for those thoughts. Erickson was dead. The killer was following David. Maybe David had been the real target. The killer came for him but missed his chance. Then saw Erickson and went after him instead. Could that be the motive?

Or could Erickson have learned something that the killer wanted hidden? Could it be that whatever Erickson knew about those crystals—the drug that people were ingesting—had gotten him too close to the truth?

Subconsciously, David's finger traced a scrawling pattern atop the table as he worked through possibilities.

"We have to keep the investigation moving," Priest said, finally breaking the silence. "The FBI will assign someone new. I'll get that person up to speed. In the meanwhile, the work needs to continue. You did your thing with the cameras?"

David realized she was talking to him.

"Yeah. They're in place. I have the feed linked to my phone."

"Good. What else do we have? Why Erickson? Why last night? How does it all connect? Take me through the night."

Sunny still seemed almost catatonic. David spoke for her, explaining the grand sweep of the night, admitting that he'd gotten good and drunk, that Erickson had been at the bar, that then they'd left.

"You left together," Priest corrected.

"Right."

Sunny looked toward them then. "I talked to Erickson. Outside. He asked if I was okay to drive. I told him I was fine. He said he'd follow us to David's apartment. I didn't realize he wasn't behind us. I didn't . . ."

Priest showed no compassion as Sunny's eyes went wet again.

"First of all, I doubt this needs to be said, but it is a summarily bad idea for any of us to mix our professional and personal lives," Priest said, shifting her gaze between the two of them. "That said, Doctor Lee has been working under a tremendous amount of stress for a long time now. I'm sure you offered a suitable release."

Priest didn't seem embarrassed at all at the conversation. No, she seemed a woman who either saw no need for sex or saw it only as a function, something one could choose to do for practical benefits, like exercise or eating vegetables.

"Now, the investigation. You and Erickson were working an angle that drugs might be the common link," she continued. "Where did that lead you?"

David thought again of the strange substance he'd found in the van that Erickson had confiscated. Then the bitter water poured down his throat by the tiger cult. The propulsive journey into the cosmos. He shook off the vision and began carefully to respond—whatever Erickson knew about that drug, whether it truly was the giant or some other hallucinogen, he had been hiding the truth. And then, there was Sunny's warning.

"Two of the victims were drug dealers, and they were killed right after I made a drug bust. It seemed like it couldn't be a coincidence. But we haven't found any connection to any of the other victims. Obviously, Erickson was investigating all of this, so there's the chance that he found something, and the killer was protecting himself."

Even as he said it, it didn't quite feel right. He couldn't imagine Erickson holding something like that back. If he'd had a line on the killer, he would've rushed to put the case to bed.

"I had thought about going to this club on the east side of town," David continued. "We know a good bit of dealing goes through there. Figured it's worth checking out."

What he didn't say was that he'd learned from Jason's credit card statements that he'd started visiting the strip club over the past several months, once every week or so. Maybe there would be a connection.

"Fine," she said, cutting off further discussion. "Report back exactly what you see."

He looked over to Sunny. She held something in her hands, turning it slowly. It was a black key card, just like the one he'd been given. All at once she gripped it and stood.

"I need to see him," she said.

Sunny moved across the room in purposeful, almost robotic strides. She went not to her own lab but to the door at the far end of the room. The third door. And whatever forbidden things lay inside it. As she reached the door she stopped and turned back, looking at David, her face serious, commanding.

"Come," she said.

Priest stood sharply.

"Doctor Lee. What are you . . . ?"

"He knows already," Sunny said.

Priest made no movement. Hell with it. David stood and went to Sunny. She tapped the card to the sensor. It beeped green. The door opened. They went through.

He followed her down a narrow corridor, lights tinged with blue casting down from above. This opened into a large room, lit in the same unnatural shade. The walls were lined with glass panels, as if to look into another room, but each was opaque. In one corner was a metal cabinet and table. Something about the room felt medical—a faint hint of bleach in the air.

"What is this place?" David asked.

Sunny pushed a button next to one panel. A screen arose, and through the glass the lights sputtered. It was a small room that held only a metal table. And on the metal table was a body. The helicopter pilot. Jim Holly. Naked. Blanched of any color. Skin a map of wounds. Frost formed around the corners of the glass.

She pushed another button at the next panel, then kept moving. Screens rose. Bodies appeared. The drug dealers. Kapoor. And then . . . Jason.

What used to be him. The head cut in half. Torso sliced from hip to shoulder. But this frozen pile of meat and bone was empty of the vibrancy, the energy, the illuminating spark, the thing that had been his cousin.

David bit down. No. He couldn't fall back once again into reliving that night.

She had pressed two more buttons, and two more screens lifted. And there, on the next metal table, was Erickson. He was almost unrecognizable. Not for the litany of wounds but because he seemed so small and shriveled and weak. A faded tattoo of an eagle on one shoulder was the only color to his skin.

Sunny leaned against the glass and cried.

"He died immediately. He didn't suffer much."

It was Priest, standing behind them. She seemed to be trying to comfort Sunny; it didn't work.

"You'll need to inspect the body, Doctor Lee. Confirm that it was him."

Sunny wiped at her eyes and nodded.

David turned then to the last open window. One more body on a slab. He moved closer. It was a woman. Thin. Average height. Shoulder-length brown hair. Where the other bodies were cut and carved, hers bore three simple darkened splotches in a tight pattern around her heart. Gunshot wounds.

"This is the scientist who went crazy?" David asked.

"Dr. Megan Smythe," Priest said. "Sunny told you the rest?"

"Yeah. You're sure? That whatever happened to her is the same thing that happened to the killer?"

"No," Priest said. "We can't be certain until we apprehend the killer and examine him. But it is the exact same pattern of behavior. And we've recovered traces of the crystals from all the victims, so . . ."

She gestured at all the bodies, as if they were anything other than what they were. He fought the impulse to be sick, thinking of all the hours he'd spent here, in his office, reading through case files, only some yards away from Jason's frozen remains.

He hadn't had time to fully process what it all meant, after Sunny had told him. First, they were together, and then Erickson's murder. He thought again of the night that Jason had died. Of the killer shoving him down, the chase through town. The unnatural way in which the man had leapt over the fence. The third shotgun blast that left no trace. So many things that made no sense. Could this be what united them all?

And if the killer was infected with crystals, how could that help him narrow a pool of suspects? If crystals from Gulliver really had been in that water that the Tonys had given him, why didn't it affect him in the same way? Then David looked again at the dead scientist.

"You said you've found crystals on all of the victims and on her," he said, looking at Sunny, not Priest. "Crystals from the spire, though. Not from Gulliver . . . the giant, I mean?"

"Right," she said, her voice still soft.

Then David pointed at Erickson.

"The cuts. The pattern. Then the one wound right through the chest. I'd never thought of it this way, but it's like he's trying to turn each victim into the giant. And then to kill it all over again."

Another piece of information. Another rough shape tumbling through his thoughts, colliding against all the others. But at least now he knew the truth. He had all the pieces, and though there were so many of them, maybe they would start to find a way to fit, one to the next. Maybe this all could make sense.

Eventually, Priest left them, and Sunny moved at once to David and hugged him, throwing her weight into him, and he wrapped her in his arms and held her as tightly as he could, feeling his shirt dampen against his chest with her warm tears.

She looked up at him, and her expression was neither sad nor affectionate. She was scared.

"Be careful," she warned. "There are other areas in this building. Places where I'm not allowed to go. There are things they're hiding, even from me."

|||

David spent the rest of the day in his makeshift office, sitting and staring at the piled-up files and reports and photos. Dark crystals, somehow burrowing through skin, around tissue. Just dust, really, from some alien entity, causing all of the destruction he saw before him.

It made no sense. None of it made any sense.

He opened one of the folders on Jason again. There was a photo of Jason inside of it. Not an autopsy photo but something they'd probably pulled from social media. A photo of him, alive, tight on his broad face, a big grin plastered across it.

Some instinct drove David to tape the photo up on the far wall. Then he sorted through the other files, pulling photos of each victim, and taped those up as well, a few feet between each.

Next he taped up a printout of a satellite map, marked with red circles at the site of each killing. One near the airport. One at the strip mall to the northeast. One at the old courthouse. One in the parking lot to the far east. And one in Old Town, at the bar. No pattern to it. No grand shape described. No focused area.

David took a marker then and began writing on the walls around each of the photos. Whatever details struck him. Small lines going to other relevant details as each single case grew out.

Drug dealers. Killed at night. More precise than others. Took photos to send to media. Happened after drug bust. Related?

Once he was done with this, he stood back, surveying. Four little spider webs on the wall. Each with its own unique pattern but none of them connecting or cohering. No. That wasn't right.

He drew one line, from Jason to Kapoor, the realtor. They had handled a land deal together, but there was nothing else to indicate they knew each other.

Looking again, he realized it wasn't done. He didn't have a photo, so he simply wrote "Erickson" and then circled it. Six victims. Six men who shared nothing in common. Nothing except for the brutal way in which they'd met their end.

TWENTY-NINE

The club's sign was visible from a few blocks off, an elaborate network of neon that moved as different tubes lit and darkened. A nude woman clung to what looked like a vine. Even on a Monday night, the parking lot of the Beanstalk brimmed. Inside, beyond a goateed bouncer, it opened into one massive room. The periphery was dark, surrounding a stage that buzzed with stark, electric light, LEDs fading from one color to the next: magenta, teal, Gatorade yellow.

Around the tables, groups looked up in reverence or glee. They were men, almost all of them, and mostly young, though one table was all gray-haired men in expensive suits. David didn't recognize any locals.

He'd left his cowboy hat in the truck, thinking he'd be less conspicuous without it. He'd brought Spady with him, explaining it as a long-overdue guys' night out, but really Spady was his cover. He couldn't go to a strip club alone and hope to keep a low profile.

Spady eyed the room warily, as if on alert. David wondered if his friend was nervous about the killer, as so many other locals were. Priest had kept her word and made sure that Erickson's death didn't leak out. But everyone still knew that a murderer was loose, that authorities had failed to catch him, and it felt as if anyone could be next.

How would they react if they knew what was really happening? Somehow, the killer had the spire—some part of it—inside of him, and it was making him kill. It was too much. Too insane. Even with all that had happened—a giant, dead alien, his senile grandfather coming to life for two minutes every night—this felt impossible. Because when he considered the possibility of it, he couldn't help but think of the dose that the Tonys gave him. It was the giant, not the spire. But could it affect him just the same?

"What do you think? Table or the stage?" Spady asked.

"Let's take that one," David said, leading the way to a table in a corner of the room.

They sat, and a waitress took their drink order. On the stage, two women danced around metal poles with fake vines attached to them. One woman was a tall, lithe blond, the other a brunette dwarf.

"Is the little one supposed to be Jack?" Spady mused.

"I don't think we're supposed to think too critically about it," David offered.

The waitress returned with beers and an offer of a private room. Spady waved her off.

"Where did you tell Brooke we were going?" David asked.

"Here, of course. Shit, she was just jealous that she had to be on shift and couldn't come with us. Besides, I lie to her, and suppose'n she drives by and sees my truck in the lot. Well, she's got a gun right there on her hip."

"That she does."

Hip-hop blared from the deejay's booth. They watched the dancers, and then David let his attention drift beyond the stage. It was hard making anything out in the shadowy corners of the booths, but as the spinning lights of the stage arced around the room, they illuminated faces. Following the sweep of the lights, he worked his way table by table. He didn't see anyone that he recognized. He didn't know what he hoped to see here. Drugs changing hands openly? Someone parading around with a small baggie of crystalline substance? Whatever went on in this place, it happened out of sight.

Then he saw them. Soldiers, he could tell. They wore casual clothing, but they had the unmistakable tight haircuts and rigid posture of the army. To one side sat Private Chambers, the young man who'd been called in by Conover and Geiger. The man whose wife Jason had fucked. David looked away, hoping he wasn't recognized.

"So, the girl you brought to the bar. What's that about?" Spady asked.

He'd taken out a cigarette and smoothly toggled between that and his beer with his one hand.

"Sunny? I don't know what it is yet. Suppose we enjoy each other's company a bit."

"Anyone at the bar could see that," Spady replied. "I just meant that she isn't one of us. Isn't from the town."

186

There was an undercurrent of judgment in his tone. Just enough to be unmistakable but little enough that he couldn't be accused of it.

"No," David answered. "She isn't. I mean, the town being what it is, there aren't too many gals to choose from."

"Suppose there aren't. I guess I was surprised, seeing you with an Oriental."

"She's Asian," David corrected.

"It isn't the same thing?"

"It isn't."

They drank. The song ended. The dancers left the stage. New ones came out, dancing and steadily shedding what little clothing they wore.

"Brooke knows," Spady said.

David's stomach dropped. She knows. Knows what? About the investigation? About the infection? About the cult and their mystery drug? He'd lost track of the number of truths he was forced to hide.

"We were watching the news and it hit me. That reporter. It's Ben Junior," Spady said. "Or Charlotte. Whatever his name is. Her name."

"Oh."

"You knew already."

Not a question, but David nodded all the same.

"I wanted to tell everyone. But it's her secret to share. And I think it's hard for her."

Spady gesticulated with his beer.

"Hard for her? Shit. Ben was our friend. He was one of us! And then he just disappeared. Just ran away and left us all behind."

"Charlotte. Not Ben. I keep screwing it up, too, but I'm trying."

"Yeah. Whatever."

They fell back to staring at the stage, though neither really watched the dancers. After a few minutes, looking straight ahead, Spady started to speak again.

"It's wrong. This whole goddamned town is broken. When we were kids, the way things were . . . It was the way things had been since our parents were kids. Since our grandparents were kids. And it made sense. You knew who people were, what they were. And now . . . None of it makes a goddamned lick of sense."

Spady took a long drink, then continued as the cigarette traced wisps of smoke in the air above the table.

"All these assholes coming in, thinking they can tell us how to live. We've been getting by just fine without them. We don't need any goddamned help, thank you very much. And then there's all the criminals, that goddamned cult."

Spady finally looked at David, and his eyes were angry.

"You're the one who's supposed to be holding this all together. Protecting us. But goddammit, things are just getting worse and worse. And Brooke is out there nearly every damned night, working herself into the ground, because you're off doing whatever the hell you're doing. You're hiding things. From her. From me. From your people. Why? That's what I want to know. Why are you choosing them over us?"

David looked at his friend. Spady seemed rougher than usual, as if he'd aged years in the past weeks. His five o'clock shadow had grown out into long stubble, which showed flecks of gray at the corners of his mouth. It was so hard to imagine the way things had been—the way people had been. Not just that. It was hard to imagine that they had once been those kids. That the town had been that town.

"You're right," David said. "I have had to hold things back. Even now, there are things I know that I can't tell anybody. It's not because I don't want to. It's because I can't. Jason's killer is still out there, and I'll do whatever it takes to track him down. And if that means pissing you off, or anyone else, that's just the price I'm going to have to pay."

The answer didn't seem to satisfy Spady, but the argument had run its course. Spady turned back toward the stage and muttered something that was lost in the boom of the music.

David stood.

"Need to talk to a man about a horse," he said.

The bathroom had the same harsh lighting of the rest of the club, though the thumping base of the music was thankfully muted. It felt like pissing inside a horror movie.

"You like the short chick?"

David recognized Chambers's voice. He didn't bother to turn around even as he readied himself. He would talk the kid down, if he could. If not, well, a bridge to cross when he came to it.

"Me, I'm not into it," Chambers continued. "It doesn't weird me out or anything. Just not my thing. I like them tall, tight ass, big fake titties. What about you, sheriff?"

Then he heard it. More boots scraping against the tile floor. Too many. David zipped up, flushed the urinal. Behind Chambers, five other soldiers crowded in, one blocking the door. Hell.

David held up his hands.

"Hey, listen, I'm just here to . . ."

The fist cut off whatever else he planned to say. His cheek went numb, then burst with pain.

He was off balance, then a shove and he was on the ground. Cold tile. Boots, coming in a flurry.

He covered his face and curled, protecting as much as he could.

It seemed like it would never end.

Then, mercifully, it did. The boots marched away.

David sat a minute, trying to survey the damage. Bruises. A few bad scrapes. Nothing that wouldn't heal. He pulled himself up onto the sink and washed his hands. In the mirror, he saw an already swollen cheek, a ripped shirt.

When he came back to the table, the soldiers were gone. Spady squinted at him, spotting his cheek.

"What the fuck?" Spady asked.

David waved him off.

"I'm fine. We should leave."

Spady's face curled into a snarl.

"Fuck that. Who was it? I'll fucking kill him."

He was up at once, his face reddening.

"I'll fucking kill him."

"He's gone."

"Who was it?"

David dropped cash on the table and grabbed Spady by the shoulders.

"Some drunk kid, okay? Remember, I'm the sheriff. If I want something done about it, I'll be the one to do it."

They went out into the parking lot, where Spady still seethed. He'd always had a temper, and age hadn't knocked any of the edge from it. The night was dark, clouds blotting out any light from the stars or moon.

The fight gnawed at David. His adrenaline still pumped, and there was a part of him that imagined fighting back. A part of him that was furious and embarrassed. How long had it been since he'd had his ass kicked? High school, he figured.

There was something else. Something that didn't quite fit in this sudden outburst of violence. Chambers was pissed off about his wife; David had no doubt in that. But why come after a man you knew was the sheriff, a man who had nothing to do with that act of adultery?

David opened the passenger-side door of Spady's truck, grabbed his cowboy hat from the seat, and replaced it atop his head. He touched the taut skin of his swollen cheek, which flared anew with pain.

"Hell. Not quite the fun night out we envisioned, was it?" he said.

"Night isn't over yet," Spady answered in a somber voice.

"I don't think I have another club in me," David said, examining his face in the truck's side mirror.

"No. I mean that."

David looked. Spady was pointing north. David's eyes followed, to the horizon beyond the parking lot, where an orange-red glow shone.

All at once, David's phone buzzed.

"Fire."

THIRTY

It was still hours from dawn, but the horizon glowed ahead. A cluster of vehicles blocked the street before they could see the blaze. David had to think through the location, a new development. It was a construction site, he remembered . . . Oh. Hell. The mosque.

A couple of dozen people were there already, black silhouettes against the flames, which rose some thirty feet up into the night sky. Only remnants of the structure remained, bones.

David and Spady came near to it, near enough to feel the heat press against their faces. Then there was someone in front of them, a woman, her eyes wide and intense and angry. It was Aaliyah. She recognized David, but he saw, too, that she recognized Spady, remembered him from the village council meeting, remembered the venomous things he had shouted at her and her people.

She was yelling loud enough to be heard over the roar of the fire.

"Do you see? You let this happen! You let them get away with attacking my people! With threatening us! And now this! We only want to be able to worship God—the same God that you worship—and they attack us with fire!"

David looked past her, at the fire, then scanned the surrounding area. The construction site was in the midst of a residential area, new houses packed tightly on small lots.

"Hell," David said.

Aaliyah circled around David, forcing him to confront her.

"The mosque is gone! It's too late to save it. Don't you understand? Are you just going to ignore me?"

It wasn't that he didn't feel anything for her. That he blamed her for her anger. His training had kicked into gear, and he knew that as bad as things were, they were about to become much, much worse.

"Later. Right now, we need to contain this fire."

"But . . . it's done."

David clapped his hand on her arm. He pointed at the edge of the construction site, where stacks of lumber had begun to combust.

"That wood may as well be gasoline, ma'am."

He turned, pointing to the tufts of decorative grass planted in the yards of neighboring homes, bending and swaying in the gusting wind.

"That grass is going to catch next. The wind will blow embers onto the roofs. The shingles will start to catch, one to the next. The whole goddamned town is going to burn down if we don't stop it."

He could see it in her eyes then. The recognition that there were no fire trucks on the scene. No firefighters. No police. No sirens.

"Where the hell is the fire department?" she demanded.

"You're looking at it," David said.

He turned to Spady.

"We need the water truck. Now! Call Brooke . . . Everyone. We need as much help as we can get."

Spady disappeared into the dark. Aaliyah followed as David strode toward the fire.

"What do you mean, you're the fire department?" she asked.

"We have one truck. And some volunteers."

She was shaking, panic setting in. "Most of these houses, they're my people's."

He nodded but kept his eyes on the fire.

"I know."

Just then the wind gusted. As the towering fire danced and bowed, it spit off a shower of sparks that wafted, a swirl of stars, spiraling through the dark of space, wheeling toward the tall grass. There, a group of neighbors stood, watching.

The embers landed amid the grass. Another gust stoked them, and flames licked up off of the ground.

"Move!" David yelled at the onlookers. "Goddammit, move!"

David sprinted at them, waving his hands. The crowd startled then and ran onto the street, joining the rest who had gathered. He'd seen plenty of bad fires before, but this was different. Before, it wasn't uncommon that a prairie would alight from a stray match, lightning strike, or some old farmer's burn pile going out of control. But those fires raged in mostly wide-open space, where there might only be one house every mile or two. This one could take a whole city if he didn't stop it. This one could kill.

"Who lives in these houses?" David shouted, pointing at the neighboring homes.

A few hands went up.

"You have hoses? Sprinklers? Turn them on. Don't worry about the fire. Spray the yards. Spray the houses. Spray as much water as you can on the roofs."

They all stared.

"Now!"

Several of them darted into action. David turned to the others.

"We need shovels. Axes. Whatever we can get."

He pointed to the ground.

"Here. Dig."

Everyone started to move, Aaliyah's husband leading them toward the neighboring houses and garages. David blocked off some teenagers.

"You. I need you to go into all of these houses. Make sure everyone is outside. Everyone. Take them there, in the street, away from the fire."

They darted off.

Already, the tall grass roiled with flames, a tide surging toward the houses. In the yard of one, an in-ground sprinkler system started up, spritzing water. In several others, men wheeled out hoses and began spraying.

"What are you going to do?" Aaliyah asked David.

He didn't answer. He was already moving toward the construction site. Amid a pile of tools, he found a hammer and stuck the handle through his belt at his back. He picked up a shovel and circled around the burning grass, moving between it and the houses. There was no time to think about how badly his face and his ribs ached, how exhausted he was. He would deal with that later.

Some of the men had emerged with tools of their own. They stood and watched him. David said nothing, just set in to work.

Fifty feet back from the growing fire, David lifted the shovel high up into the air and plunged it down, cracking the arid, brittle ground. He scooped up as much dirt as he could, overturning the grass, flinging dirt forward into the maw of flames.

Again. Blade up. Down. Toss dirt. Again. Again.

It was an impossible task. Each shovel-full of dirt so small.

The flames fed on the fuel of the grass and grew taller. Each burst of wind pushed the wall of fire closer.

Used to be, wind only blew west to east. But the giant changed that. Now it came over and around him in unpredictable swirls and eddies, shifting almost constantly.

Smoke and heat hit David, singed his nostrils, choked his throat, set his eyes to watering.

He stopped only for a moment, to pull off his shirt and tie it around his nose and mouth.

Then he resumed digging.

He recognized the man beside him as Aaliyah's husband. Digging. Throwing dirt.

The other men joined in.

They formed their own wall, men coughing in the smoke, shielding their eyes, some of them still wearing pajamas, turning one blade of dirt after another.

Sweat mixed with soot and soil and ran down David's forehead, stinging his eyes. It was only when he reached up to wipe it away that he realized his hat was gone, blown off in the wind and chaos.

A truck hauling a trailer rumbled over the curb, onto the yard of the nearest house. The trailer held a large plastic tank, the kind used to spray pesticides on fields.

David saw it out of the corner of his eye and hurried toward it as two men hopped out—the McClintock brothers.

"Barney. Sam. You spray the firebreak, okay?"

They didn't say anything, just nodded and set to work, unspooling hoses, firing up a small generator, dousing the upturned dirt with water. In front of it, the men kept shoveling.

More trucks appeared then. More men. Locals. Striding forward with shovels and pickaxes, joining the work without a word. They joined in with the Muslim men, all of them working side by side, deafened by the howl of the wind, the roar of the oncoming flames.

A siren sounded, distant.

That would be Spady with the pump truck, David knew. Once it was here, they'd be fine. As long as the fire didn't leap over them.

He wouldn't complete the thought. Just then, the wind gusted strong enough to rock David back on his heels. A flurry of embers burst up from the tall grass, like snowflakes in a blizzard, and showered down on the roofs of the closest houses.

"Ah, hell," David muttered.

Once sparks hit a house, they could catch in a million ways. Ignite the tar of the roof. Slip into an air vent and ignite the structure from the inside out.

He scanned the houses. Maybe they'd be lucky.

They weren't. A thin plume of smoke leaked up from a vent on one house. Within seconds, fingers of flame emerged.

David dropped his shovel and raced toward the house. His eyes went up to the roof, to the flames.

David came to a gutter and started climbing, awkwardly, using a porch railing to hoist himself up.

The roof was a steep pitch. His knee protested at every delicate step. He was thankful that at least no one had sprayed water on this house yet. The shingles would've been too slick to climb.

Steadily, he inched up to the ridge line; he sat down, straddling it, and pulled himself toward the flames. The fire was in the attic. The heat would build inside with nowhere to escape, turning the whole house into a bomb. There was only one hope of saving it.

David stopped ten feet from the vent and reached back. Thank God the hammer hadn't fallen out as he climbed. It was a sturdy hammer, heavy, with a sharp claw at the back of it. Not as good as a hatchet, but it could work. It would have to.

With the claw side pointing down, David smashed the hammer into the shingles. Barely a dent. Again. Again. Again.

Finally, he broke through the shingles and cast them aside with his off hand.

He hammered down again, into the wood of the roof. Again. Again. Blow by blow, the wood dented, splintered. He didn't allow himself to think. Just one more strike. And one more. One more.

Aaliyah had found her husband, and they stood, staring up.

"Sheriff, what are you doing?" she asked.

David kept hammering. Wham. Wham. His arm and back ached. He could feel the heat of the fire beneath him, through the roof. He was running out of time before the whole structure would combust beneath him.

One more.

With a satisfying crunch, the hammer punched through the wood.

David yanked his face back as a belch of scalding air and fire erupted from the hole. He kept hammering, widening the hole, letting out more heat.

Then it began to rain.

No, not rain. Water, spraying onto the roof. Spady was back with the pump truck. He and another of the volunteers took a second hose and sprinted into the house through the front door.

They'd saved the house. And as David looked back from his high vantage point at the remains of the mosque and the field of grass, he saw that the break had held. The fire was contained.

He eased himself back. A metal extension ladder landed against the side of the house. David skidded over and climbed down, his legs and arms shaking so bad the ladder rattled against the gutter.

The sky had just begun to lighten to the east, from black to a rich, navy blue. It felt like only minutes had passed, but they'd been fighting the fire for hours. Aaliyah stood there with her son and husband. Imam Bey was there, too, though it took David a second to recognize him, dressed informally.

David approached, pulling his shirt from his face and tugging it back onto his torso.

"Missus Bakhtiari, I'm sorry. I'll find out who did this. I promise."

His voice was raspy, almost too faint to hear. Even as he spoke the words, he knew it was impossible. Unless there was a witness, they had no hope. Whatever evidence had existed was consumed. One more case with no resolution. One more way in which he'd failed his town.

Aaliyah held up her hand.

"Later. Not tonight."

As the last remnants of the fire faded, people gathered slowly toward them. Muslims. Locals. Nearly a hundred people. All of them exhausted, eyes watering, hands and clothing stained black with soot.

The wind began to ease up, whistling a somber tune. Imam Bey reached out his hand. David took it.

"Thank you," the imam said.

"I'm sorry we didn't get here in time to save the mosque."

Imam Bey looked around. Somehow, he was smiling.

"We are not hurt, any of us. Because of you, brother Saadiq and his family still have their home. If it is okay with you, I would like to say a blessing."

David nodded.

The others came in closer. The imam raised his hands to the lightening sky. The Muslims began to take each other's hands while the locals watched. Aaliyah held her hand out to David. He took it, then extended his other hand to her husband. Soon, all of them held hands as the imam began to intone in Arabic.

David closed his eyes. He couldn't understand the words, but he felt them. Then the voice was gone, and they released each other's hands.

Did this moment mean everything? Nothing? He supposed only time would tell.

Imam Bey looked past David, at the rest of the locals.

"With this prayer, I offered thanks to God for sparing our lives, for protecting us. I also lowered myself before His power and mystery. He is great, and His will is beyond any man. Somehow, He can take that which seems bad and use it for the purpose of good. Mostly, I thanked Him for you. You are all a blessing, our neighbors."

Several Muslim women appeared carrying boxes of food, bottles of water, urns of coffee. Someone retrieved a folding table from a house, and right there in the street of the cul de sac, they served an impromptu breakfast.

David stepped into line first, and the other locals followed. He took what looked like a large pastry in a napkin and sat on a curb. He sniffed at it, then bit into a soft blend of bread, egg, and meat, spices he didn't recognize. Maybe it was just how hungry he was, but he couldn't imagine that food had ever tasted better.

"Murtabak," Aaliyah said, watching him eat. "It's sort of a cross between an omelet and a pancake."

"Holy shit, it's amazing," David said, crumbs falling from his mouth. "Sorry. Pardon the language. I think I'm too tired to have a filter."

Aaliyah laughed.

"Oh, I barely go ten minutes these days without saying worse than that. Anyway, if you want more, Hassan and his family make them at their diner."

She pointed toward one of the men who had been digging the firebreak alongside David.

"His wife went with some of the others to get food for everyone. You think those are good? Try the sweet kind. I eat too damn many of them."

David looked across his team of volunteer firefighters. He thought back to the night of the village council meeting. Spady had been the loudest in attacking the mosque, but most of the rest of them had been there, too, yelling along with him. Now they sat together, sharing breakfast. And Spady. Where had Spady gone?

"So, you're the sheriff and the fire chief?" Aaliyah asked.

"Sort of. I mean, fire chief isn't really a title. I hear about emergencies as soon as they happen, being the sheriff. It makes sense for me to round everyone up. It's so damn dry here, a fire gets started, the wind can push it out of control in a hurry."

"Why isn't there a fire department?"

"No money for it, for one thing. Plus, it's how we've always had to do things around here. Somebody needs help, everyone comes out to help. There's no 'them' to rely on. Course, town's too big for that now, I guess. I don't know. Maybe that's how it goes. Everything has to change eventually."

He went back to eating. The stinging in his throat and lungs had started to fade. One of the children walked up, carrying David's hat. It was dusty but intact. She held it out.

"Thank you," David said. "I'd be good and lost without this."

Spady was gone, so Brooke gave David a lift back to his truck, where he'd left it at the new courthouse. She'd arrived just after David went up on the roof, she said.

Once he was back at his truck, he pulled out his phone and saw a notification. Something had triggered one of the motion cameras. As exhausted as he was, as much as his body ached, he felt a sudden surge of energy. Maybe it worked. Maybe one thing would go right.

He opened the app, and a green-and-black video appeared. He could just make out the outlines of the tombstones. It was the cemetery. Nothing.

And then . . . a shape moved across the screen.

A coyote, sleek and muscular, moving silently through the night, between tombstones. A predator, stalking.

The coyote turned back, as if in recognition of being watched, and then darted out of view, continuing its hunt.

THIRTY-ONE

Charlotte and her cameraman arrived on the scene of the fire as dawn was breaking, and all that remained was a charred pile filling most of a block, with a few unrecognizable bits of metal poking up out of red-hot coals. It was a good story, she knew. Tragic and ripe with conflict. She would have prime placement on the news, morning and evening. It was the kind of thing that would get national attention.

Yet, she couldn't summon the same excitement that such a story normally gave her. As she stood in front of the wreckage and readied to speak into the camera, her mind was elsewhere, on the unknown face that kept reaching out, kept taunting her, following her. Was he watching her now?

"Let's try that one again," the cameraman suggested after she fumbled a line.

"I got it," she said, as much to herself as to him.

A new message had come through the day before. Not a photo this time, just text.

Ask the sheriff how his FBI friend is doing.

Something had happened. But what? There hadn't been a killing since the drug dealers. Her bosses at the network kept demanding updates. What was the killer's motive? Why weren't the investigators finding anything?

But to learn more, her only good source was David. And he had made it clear how he felt. He wasn't wrong. She had betrayed him, and now there was a wall between them. A wall vaster and taller and stronger than all the years they had been apart.

She needed to go to him, though. Not to use him. Not to learn anything. But to tell him what the killer was saying. To warn him.

|||

Sleep refused to come. There was the sharp pain in his cheek and the aches all across his chest and back, where he'd been kicked. Ibuprofen and whiskey had taken the edge off of it, but it was still there. His muscles in his back and shoulders and arms throbbed from the exertion of breaking through the roof.

It wasn't just that. He stared at the ceiling and thought once again through the details of the case, going through each murder's facts, imagining in his mind's eye the wall he had created, the disparate webs, the parts that refused to compose a whole.

Did Private Austin Chambers fit into it? That was the thought that came again and again. There was something he wasn't seeing. Something about the fight at the club that he knew wasn't random. But if it held meaning—if it fit in some rational way—then how?

David forced his eyes closing, hoping that it would stop his mind from working. Blackness. And then, a vision. The same vision. The old courthouse. A window exploding. The darkened office. The body on the ground. Jason's mutilated body. The killer, escaping right past him. And the deep-rooted feeling that he knew the answer to all of these puzzles already, he just hadn't allowed himself to see it.

Hell with it. He stood up out of bed and got dressed.

|||

David was waiting in the security queue at Site One when an answer came to him. Not an answer. Really, it was more that he realized the question he should've been asking.

The giant and spire were protected inside the massive fence and the army's mile-wide buffer. Every sample of either was housed safely inside Site One. But then, if the killer was leaving traces of the spire on his victims, it begged to be asked: How were these crystals getting outside of Site One and through security? How had the killer become infected?

It was as he worked through this that David looked across the faces of the armed soldiers standing guard along the queue and landed on a face that he recognized. It was a fleeting recognition, but he also knew he could never forget it. It was one of the faces that had loomed over him in the bathroom of the strip club. The face of a man who had stood alongside Chambers and kicked the shit out of David.

Chambers was part of the crew tasked with the security of Site One. Conover and Geiger had said as much, David remembered. He surveyed the vast room. Was Chambers here even now?

Soldiers were stationed throughout the room. They watched over the body scanners. It was soldiers who did the pat downs. They controlled everyone who came in and out of this place. And everything.

David wanted to see Sunny, but he wanted to follow this train of thought before any of its details escaped him.

In his office, he stared at the wall he'd created, which was messy and disconnected, lacking any focus or clarity. All too well, it mirrored his thoughts.

He took a marker and next to Jason's name began writing:

Affair. Phoebe Chambers. Husband Pvt. Austin Chambers. Security over Site One.

He stepped back then. There was something else about Jason's murder. Something different. Something he'd never quite been able to summon as more than a gut instinct.

He forced himself to open the file, and he spread its contents across the table. A chill shot through him as he remembered that Jason's body lay just yards away from him even now, frozen and alone in a darkened room.

He surveyed the crime scene photos. Some showed Jason as he had fallen, his body so destroyed it barely looked human. And then it struck him. That was it. That was the difference.

All the murders had been horrific. But the others were cleaner. Simpler. One killing blow and then the superficial wounds. Kapoor had had his arm cut off, but even that was nothing like the degree of violence inflicted upon Jason.

Jason had had the shotgun. He'd tried to fight back. But still, that didn't account for the scope of brutality. Jason's body had been torn apart, even after he was no longer a threat. It was personal in a way the others weren't, vicious.

He looked again at Chambers's name on the board, the line connecting it to Jason, playing out this possibility. Chambers had discovered his wife's affair with Jason. He'd gone to confront Jason. They struggled, he overpowered Jason, and killed him. He would have access to a bulletproof vest, which could explain the third shotgun blast that seemed to have found its target. And he was a soldier, trained to fight, to kill.

Chambers had an alibi—the poker game—but that could be a cover story from his friends. The same friends that had showed up at the club and tried to kick in David's ribs. So that attack, then, was a warning.

David took the marker and drew a line from Chambers to the two dead drug dealers, continuing to play out this possibility. Somehow, people were buying and selling fragments of the giant and using them as drugs. Chambers had access. If he and his fellow soldiers were smuggling out samples of Gulliver, then selling them into the drug trade, that could be the connection to those two victims. Maybe a deal gone wrong?

He stood back, mulling this, and drew a question mark over the connection.

There was another problem with the theory. There was nothing to connect Chambers to Holly and Kapoor, the first and second victims. Nothing to show that they'd ever crossed paths. No hint of a motive.

He pushed that out of mind. After all his time searching for an explanation, he had the start of one. He would run it down. But how? He'd gone to Conover the last time, only to be told it was a dead end. Did Conover know the truth? Was he involved? David couldn't tell him his theory. Not yet. Which meant he needed to find another way to build a case against Chambers.

The thought of it excited him. Paying Chambers back for the beating in the club. Paying him back for Jason. For Erickson. For all the destruction he'd caused.

As David left, he found Sunny waiting for him in the meeting room between their offices. She seemed more tired than usual, turning to give him a wan smile as he approached. They'd said nothing of the sudden burst of intimacy between them, and it almost felt as if it had never happened.

"How are you doing?" he asked.

She shook her head slowly.

"I was examining Erickson's body. There were traces of it on him. The spire. Just like the others. The whole time, I just kept thinking of him in that last moment. Imagining how scared he must've been when he died," she said.

He wanted to tell her to push it out of her mind. That Erickson died quickly. Probably peacefully. That he was trained for times just like that. But it would be a lie. Erickson had died horribly. All that David and Sunny could do now was to help bring him some justice.

III

It had been almost a week since David had visited Samuel. Somehow the old man had continued to amass new piles of research. David supposed that Samuel had enlisted a nursing home staff member to help in his quest. David sat and listened as his grandfather explained his findings, holding up a hardcover book with dozens of dog-eared pages.

"It's called parapsychology. The study of unexplained mental phenomena. Telepathy. Telekinesis. That's moving objects with your mind. I know, I know. It sounds unbelievable. But there have been hundreds of studies going back decades. Even the military has done research into it. Here's one example. They held up a random assortment of cards and asked people to guess which card they were holding. Again and again, the results came back above chance. Which means there is some connection between people's minds."

The old man handed David the book, the pages open, passages underlined.

"And how does this connect to the giant?" David asked.

It was like he'd missed a week of trigonometry and now had to race to catch up.

"The dogs, remember? They bark at the same time my brain comes online. It's connected. The question is, how? There's this theory within parapsychology that some force exists—psi—that bonds our consciousnesses together. We're all connected, just in a way that's invisible to us. Somehow every night the giant does something. Imagine him giving off this energy, sending a radio signal, except we can't see it or hear it. We can only feel it. And the only effect it has is to make the dogs bark and for me to wake up. It makes no sense only because we can't see it, so we assume it's impossible."

David glanced at the clock. Only half a minute left. Samuel followed his eyes and broke from his lecture.

"You need to be out there, David. I understand. I'm fine in here. I have some help. I have plenty to keep me busy. You don't have to come."

"I want to come, Grandpa."

"I know," the old man said. "But all too often, life has other plans."

As if on cue, David's phone buzzed, and he drew it quickly from his pocket. It could be dispatch. Or Priest.

It was neither. A notification from the app that tracked the motion sensors. He apologized to his grandpa as he opened it, and dark, grainy video feed appeared. The alley behind Vic's. He'd just placed a new camera there, in the spot where they'd found Erickson's body.

Something moved past.

The form of a man. His back to the camera. His head covered with a hood. David knew at once. It was him. The man he'd seen the night that Jason had died. The man he'd let escape once before.

The killer.

Samuel was talking again, his tone angry and confused. Their two minutes were up.

"Who let you in here?" he demanded.

David didn't respond, instead sprinting out of the room and into the dying light. As the barking of the dogs quieted, he climbed into his truck and tore like hell across town.

THIRTY-TWO

The truck's engine roared as he skidded over concrete and swung around turns. David prayed that no one would pull in front of him. The siren was off; he didn't want his prey to know he was coming.

He slowed as he approached the bar, then pulled in along the side street. He drew his pistol as he came to the edge of the alley. He peeked into it. Nothing, just blackness, and he tried to summon in his memory what he had seen here in the light of day, a mental map of the void.

David exhaled and stepped into the darkness. One small step at a time, keeping his left foot forward, the gun raised in perfect position. Another step.

He pivoted slightly as he went. Left to right, then swinging back the other way, scanning the shadows around him. Nothing. Another step.

And then, all at once, he saw it. A shadow that moved, some twenty feet ahead. Then it was still again. Invisible. As if waiting. Some kind of anglerfish poised to devour him. Another step.

"Freeze," David barked, stopping five yards short of the shape in the shadows. Close enough that he wouldn't miss. Far enough to keep well clear of the blade he knew was just out of sight.

The silhouette of a man stood, clinging to the shadows so that nothing was visible beyond the form of him, a hood pulled low over the face. David squinted. Was it Chambers?

"Why did you come here? It wasn't enough to kill him? You had to celebrate it? Dumb fucking mistake," David hissed.

Every fiber of him yelled to just pull the trigger. To be done with it. His hand tightened around the pistol.

And yet, he couldn't. Because if he did that, it would mean he was something other than the man he'd always thought himself to be. He would be as bad as the man standing in the shadows.

He took another step forward.

"Step out. Drop the blade. Then turn around and put your hands on top of your head. Any fast movements and I shoot."

The form in the shadows said nothing. Did nothing.

"Now!" David yelled.

Faster than he could react, the form ducked down, disappearing back into the shadow at the edge of the alley.

David reached down with his left hand, grasping for the flashlight in his belt. He pulled it free, and his eyes glanced away from the shadow just for a second as he lifted the light.

As he clicked it on, the form was already running. Bolting out of the shadow and down the alley, and the light only illuminated the back of him, dark pants and a dark hooded jacket, a blur of movement that was gone, banking right out of view.

"Hell," David spat as he charged after the form.

He came out of the alley just in time to see the man dart down a side street, heading north. He didn't have a clean shot, not that he would've taken it if he did. His training kicked in as he ran ahead. You didn't shoot a fleeing suspect in the back.

The road led to the old railroad tracks, abandoned now. Ahead, the massive forms of grain elevators rose like monoliths. The man sprinted between two of the massive metal silos.

David followed at a controlled run. Between the silos was pitch black. As he flashed his light into the space, it showed emptiness.

He moved forward with careful steps. Ears tuned to any noise, sweeping the area in front of him with the flashlight.

A pile of rusted gears and cogs. A drift of rotten corn.

David came through the space between the structures. Nothing. Just empty tracks and an old grain truck that had sat, unused, in this spot for years.

A scratch. Faint but undeniable.

He stepped forward, training the light on the truck. Moving around the back of it. Another step.

The chain swung down out of the truck, metal clanking as it rushed at him.

David reacted just fast enough to raise his arms in front of his face.

The thick metal links smashed into his forearms and grazed against his head, knocking him backward off of his feet. The flashlight and gun clattered away as he fell onto the cement.

David was on his side, groaning, his mind still racing to process what had just happened. The chain had landed on top of him, and he struggled against the weight of it.

In front of him, the man hopped down from the back of the truck, where he'd been hiding. For a moment, he stood there. Only feet away from David, helpless on the ground.

And then he turned and ran.

As David pushed the chain off, he noted that his forearms weren't broken, though they ached like hell. He grabbed his gun and stood, pointing it out into the night. But there was no one else there. Once again, the killer had slipped away.

|||

He'd expected Priest, but it was Conover who came, and Sunny with him. She was scared, her movements slow and tense as she took her handheld microscope and looked over his hands and arms and face.

"He never touched me," David said.

The encounter replayed once more. The chain swinging down, the killer just standing there. For a second time, he could've killed David. For a second time, he hadn't.

Conover looked at Sunny.

"Finish the scan," he said.

She did as asked, whispering an apology when David winced as her hand grazed his forearm. She finished, and Conover stepped within inches of David, his doughy face twisting in anger.

"You had him. And you fucking lost him."

"I . . ."

"Shut up. You lost him because you are not John-fucking-Rambo or whoever the fuck you think you are. If you'd called me, we'd be done with this shit already. The killer would be in a bag, and we'd all wash our hands of all of this shit."

"I was close. I didn't think there was time," David protested.

Conover put a hand on David's shoulder and gripped, hard. He pulled David away from Sunny, into the shadow of one of the metal silos. Around them, David saw a ring of Humvees, soldiers standing on guard.

More vehicles cruising along the streets, searching. None of it made him feel any more secure.

"I told you it was a dead end with Private Chambers," Conover said, his voice quieter but his expression no softer. "But you're still poking at it, aren't you?"

The wall in his office. They were watching it. Watching him.

"You all brought me in to work the case. I was thinking through possibilities. That's all."

Conover studied him.

"That possibility is cut off. Do you understand?"

If only Erickson was there. He would've backed David up. But Erickson was gone, and David was all out of allies.

"Yeah. Sure. I understand."

Conover paced away. Major Geiger stood nearby, and the two of them huddled, talking in a heated conversation that was just too quiet to make out. Behind them, the outline of the giant was just visible cutting across the darkened sky.

Sunny came over to David.

"You're okay? Really?"

He nodded.

"Just beating myself up for letting him get away. Again."

"You weren't hurt. That's all that matters," she said.

"Only because he held back."

"What?"

"He had me. I was on the ground. I dropped my gun. He could've come at me. But he didn't."

She took his hand, and the suddenness of it surprised him. She didn't care who saw them together, that strange confidence she held that mystified him.

"Can I come over?" she asked.

"Yeah," he answered. "I'd like that."

They made love with an intensity that startled David. He wondered if she felt it as much as he did, the desperate need to escape from the reality around them. And for a while, they did escape.

With her lying there beside him, breathing softly, the warmth of her skin radiating against his own, he slipped blessedly to sleep.

In his dreams, he was deep in some ocean, with no light, the current pushing him this way and that. He could not tell up from down, and though he thrashed about, there was nothing. Nothing except water.

And there was something else. Unseen but looming. Some great being that surged through the depths, something coming toward him, ever closer. A leviathan, its mouth gaping, ready to consume.

THIRTY-THREE

The man checked the burner phone again. Nothing. No response from the reporter. Unacceptable. After all he'd done. All he'd risked. All that he had showed the people of this town. They still didn't seem to see. The sheriff most of all. He was blind, failing to grasp all that had been laid out before him.

The sheriff was part of it, the man had accepted. Part of the effort to hide the truth, to cover it up. They knew what had happened to the FBI agent, but they had hidden it from the world.

No more.

If the reporter and sheriff wouldn't listen, he would go straight to the people themselves. A message. Big and loud and undeniable.

One that everyone would hear.

|||

The neon light shined like a warning in the dark. The building, cracked wood siding like a coffin dragged up out of the earth—Charlotte had dreamed about it for years after moving away, reliving memories of Vic's, of the men inside, harsh and terrifying, the smell of their cigarettes, the threat of their bodies and minds, the confusion it all shot through her.

She stood in the chill of the street. She wore jeans and the thickest sweater she owned, as if it was armor, though she knew how little protection clothing offered from the world.

She thought one last time about turning away. David had reached out to her and let her know that Brooke and Spady had recognized her on the TV. Their long-lost friend Benjamin was back in town, with a new name and face. David had asked what Charlotte wanted to do, and she surprised herself by suggesting they should meet.

They had been such a happy group, when they were teenagers. Looking back, she could admit that they were the popular kids. Jason was the undeniable envy of the school, in a world in which all anyone cared about was athletics. She and David and Spady had been his court. Once Brooke started dating Spady, Charlotte had felt a strange tension. It hadn't been jealousy but instead a surprising kinship. She connected with Brooke in a way she never had with the boys.

More than anything, she needed to talk to David. If this was the price, she was going to have to pay it. Charlotte sighed, then she commanded herself up the three steps and inside.

It even smelled the same. The same locals smoking the same brand of cigarettes, drinking the same domestic beer.

She scanned quickly across the dark recesses of tables and booths and saw David, waving a hand. His face was neutral, and she still didn't know where they stood with each other. Brooke sat across from him, barely changed, aside from her features sharpening a little. She always had been beautiful.

Beside her, Spady barely resembled his old self. He'd been a skinny kid, his hair perpetually buzzed down to a crew cut. He was heavier now, not fat but thick. His skin was pallid, his hair long and unkempt. And the void where his arm had once been . . .

Brooke waved Charlotte into the booth.

"Sorry I'm late," Charlotte said, sitting beside David.

"Oh, don't worry about it," Brooke said. "We had a busy afternoon with a string of B-and-E's."

"Breaking and entering," Spady explained. "These two always fall right into the cop talk."

"Right," Charlotte said. "I know a little of the jargon. I covered the crime beat my first job out of college. Jackson, Mississippi."

"Oh, that's cool. Wow. It seems so weird, seeing you in person after you've been all over our TV. You're famous," Brooke said.

"No. I'm not. Not really," she said.

"So, were you still a dude then? Back in Jackson, Mississippi?" Spady asked, his voice just on the edge of malevolence.

Brooke shot him a look, then smiled at Charlotte.

"Hey, you don't have a drink. I'm just having a Coke, since I've got to go on duty later. You want a beer or something?"

"It's okay," Charlotte said to Brooke. "I don't mind talking about it." Charlotte turned to Spady, biting down her emotions.

"I had transitioned by Jackson. After I left here, I had a few pretty rough years. Denver, then St. Louis. Then I ended up in this program that helped me go back to school. And I kept working, saving up to do all of this."

She gestured with her hands at herself.

"Surgeries. Hormone treatments. Not to mention figuring out how to walk in heels."

Brooke laughed so hard she snorted.

"Oh, shit, you'll have to teach me," she said.

Spady held his scowl.

"You tore yourself apart."

Charlotte tensed her jaw even harder as she stared into the table.

"Yeah."

"Why?"

Charlotte looked up at Spady. She rubbed her hands together. They were large hands, with long fingers. One thing she could never change.

"Spady, I'm going to tell you, the things I've been through, the pain, you understand it as much as anyone."

She pointed at his arm.

"Imagine choosing to do that. Choosing to have your arm amputated. Do you think you would make that choice just for the hell of it? If there was any other way, don't you think you'd avoid it?"

He said nothing but rubbed the nub of his arm against his side, as if it itched him.

"I didn't want any of this," Charlotte continued. "I didn't ask for it. I just had to do it. To survive."

Brooke reached across the table and put her hand on Charlotte's.

"I'm glad you came back," Brooke said. "Are you telling everyone?"

Charlotte nodded.

"I talked to my parents so far."

"They didn't tell me," David said. "How did that go?"

Charlotte laughed. "Oh, about as poorly as it could've. But it's done. That's all that matters—that I gave them a chance."

They talked for an hour, long enough for her to have a drink and mostly to chat with Brooke as Spady sat there, silent, seeming a thousand miles away. They told old stories, remembered old adventures. And then Spady stomped off, with Brooke lingering just long enough to whisper to Charlotte to be patient with Spady, that he would come around.

And then it was just David and her. He moved to the other side of the table, so they weren't sitting beside each other, and she didn't know whether it was so they could talk more easily or so that he could create space between them, to avoid anyone thinking that they could be together.

"That went okay," he said.

"Spady wouldn't even look at me."

"He's in a weird place. What happened to Jason is part of it. But really, ever since his arm . . ."

She leaned over the table, lowering her voice so it was barely audible over the music coming from the jukebox.

"David, did something happen? To the FBI agent? The killer sent me a message."

His eyes told her that he didn't trust her. He thought she was fishing again.

"I'm not reporting. This isn't that. I promise," she said.

"I can't talk to you about this," he said, glancing over his shoulder. "I think I should go."

"Wait," she said, insistent. "There's something else. Since he sent that photo of me, I've been ignoring him. Not responding. Not saying anything on the news. I've been lying to my boss, telling him the killer stopped reaching out. I just . . . I don't want to bring him any more attention. But he sent a new message. Not just to me. To my producers."

"What is it?" David whispered.

"He wants to meet me. To talk. I . . . I don't want to do it. But the station . . . They already messaged him back, saying I would interview him. It's supposed to happen tomorrow night. I . . . David, I need your help."

THIRTY-FOUR

He chose a spot on a walking trail that had been made along some bluffs to the east of town, a stretch of what used to be corn fields but now sat empty, waiting to be transformed into a planned live-work-play community. Only the trail had been built so far, a strip of asphalt that ran a couple of miles, mostly a place where people went to run or walk or bike out of the busyness of the town.

It was dark, the moon half hidden behind thin, impotent clouds. Charlotte sat on a bench, alone, exactly where she'd been instructed. No cameraman. Just her and a pen and a notebook.

"Someone's coming."

Priest's voice whispered beside David.

They crouched in an unmarked black van, parked a half mile away. The innards of the van had been stripped out, replaced with a bank of electronics with several screens showing different angles on the same thing—Charlotte, isolated, unprotected. Low angles from hidden cameras. From the bluff above, where snipers were hidden. A bird's eye view captured by a roving drone.

One of the angles changed, moving down the trail. The figure of a man came, jogging, wearing sweatpants and a sweatshirt, the hood pulled over his head, his face just out of view. Coming ever closer to Charlotte.

"Do you see him?"

Charlotte's voice now, soft and frightened.

Priest grabbed a microphone.

"Quiet, please. We have you covered."

The man came closer still. David's chest pounded. He needed to be out there. To be hidden in the tall grass, ready to rush in. It wasn't just the thrill of the hunt. Of taking down the killer, of being done with all of this madness. He wanted to be there for her. She had betrayed him.

Hurt him. But she was family. Nothing either of them could ever do could change that. He should be there. Protecting her. Not here.

The man moved closer. Closer.

"Hold," Priest said into the microphone.

Conover loomed behind them, silent. Whatever delineation of authority existed between the two of them remained a mystery, but this clearly was Priest's operation.

"Hold," she said again.

The man was within twenty yards of Charlotte. Through the screen, her trembling was visible. *Do something*, David thought. Ten yards. *Now*. Five.

And then the man was past. Jogging off into the night, taking no notice of Charlotte. And as David watched the figure, he saw that the build was wrong, too stocky. It wasn't him. But—David glanced at the clock—the killer was late. It was fifteen minutes past when he'd said he would be here.

"What do you think?" Conover asked.

Priest stared into the screens.

"Let's wait. If he isn't here in half an hour, we wrap it up."

A sound came over the speakers then. A faint buzzing.

On the screen, Charlotte fidgeted, then reached a hand into her pocket. She took out her phone, then hunched over, peering into it.

"Oh," her voice came through.

Priest grabbed the microphone.

"Charlotte. What is it?"

"Oh. Oh, God."

And then she began to scream.

They rushed to her, David jumping out of the van first and outrunning Priest and Conover, pushing his way through the phalanx of soldiers in dark camouflage, making his way to Charlotte, who was standing now.

"Are you okay?" he asked.

She held her phone as if it was infected with some virus. She lifted it toward him, her eyes avoiding the screen. He took it and read.

Sorry to break our date. But I want you all to myself.

Below the text was a photo. At first, David couldn't comprehend what he was seeing amid the jumble of lines and colors. Then his eyes pieced

together the tableau. It was the front of the Pump-and-Go, the gray cor-
rugated siding of the gas station and body shop. And in the center of it
was a man, his face hidden behind the mask of a tiger.

It seemed at first that he wore strange, red-patterned clothing, but
this was part of the illusion. The man was naked, and the thing obscuring his skin wasn't clothing. It was blood that traced across every part
of him and formed a wide pool in the dirt around him.

He was lying on the ground, a metal rod stabbed through the center
of his chest and jutting up into the air.

Priest and Conover caught up to David, who held out the phone for
them to study.

"Who?" Priest asked.

David didn't have to see the face to know. The bloodied body was
twisted, the shoulders uneven, the back hunched. Jimmy.

Jimmy, whom he had grown up with. Jimmy, who he thought was a
friend. Jimmy, who pumped his gas. Jimmy, who secretly was part of
the cult. A secret that David thought only he knew.

Charlotte leaned into David. He could tell from the way that she
breathed that she was crying. Whatever anger he had in him was gone.
He put an arm around her shoulders.

|||

David guided them across town in a convoy to the gas station, engines
roaring. They were too late for Jimmy—and too late to control the scene.
A crowd of locals stood, some crying, some talking in small huddles.
David saw one teenager raise a phone and take a picture.

He rushed past them all and would've gone straight up to the body
if not for Conover, who grabbed him by the arm.

"FBI are on the way. We let them do their job," he said.

And so once again David could do nothing but stand and watch,
knowing they were too late again. And he couldn't lie to himself. This
hurt. Not as bad as Jason. But this was someone he'd grown up with,
one of the town's staples, someone he talked to damn near every day
as he waited for his truck's fuel tank to fill. Jimmy, who would insist
on pumping your gas for you. Every day, David had asked him how he
was. Every day, Jimmy had responded, "Can't complain. Wouldn't do
a bit of good if I did."

Seeing Jimmy's naked body, he thought again of the ceremony inside the theater. Jimmy undressing himself and standing, impossibly confident, in front of all those eyes as another man bathed him.

Now he was dead, lying in his own blood, exposed to the world. The metal bar rammed through his chest was an undeniable symbol of the spire, a perfect recreation. Even the limbs had been positioned in just the right way.

This one was different from the others. Grander. More public. The body was staged, made to be seen.

Conover must've been thinking the same thing.

"He's getting bolder. Fucking with us," he said.

Around them, soldiers pushed back the onlookers and raised barricades, a model of efficiency.

"I got him killed," David said.

"What?" Conover asked.

David shook it off.

"Nothing."

One of the forensic team lifted the mask off of the body. Jimmy's eyes were closed. His face was strangely peaceful.

David looked to the west, where the giant rested, inert. He wanted to scream at it. To rage against it. To find a way to lift it and throw it back into oblivion. *Why are you here? Why are you bringing all this suffering to us? What does any of this mean?*

But he said nothing. He knew all too well that corpses gave no answers.

III

It was early morning by the time he made it back to his apartment. Sunny was still at the scene, investigating the body as the FBI collected evidence and readied to transport the body to Site One, where it would join the others in its own small freezer.

There was just enough time to shower and grab something to eat and change into a fresh uniform. No point in trying to sleep when he knew it wouldn't come.

As he walked up the steps to his door, he saw it. A small, brown box wrapped in a red bow.

He bent over and picked it up. It was just big enough to fit in the palm of his hand. He hadn't thought that Sunny had been over here, but it must've been her. There was no one else that would leave him a gift.

David pulled the ribbon free and opened the box. There was something small and metal and rectangular inside.

And then his eyes realized what it was, just as his outstretched fingers laid ahold of it.

Erickson's lighter.

Stained with dried blood.

THIRTY-FIVE

There were no fingerprints on the lighter. None other than David's. While the FBI forensics team worked, David walked the grounds, looking for anyone who was up, lights on in windows. But no one had seen anything. And there were no surveillance cameras. The killer had walked right up to David's front door, and they had nothing to show for it. Nothing but a dead man's cigarette lighter.

He cleaned up and drove over to Pearl's for coffee, some food. The locals all stared at him, talking in whispered voices. He sat in silence at the counter, his back to the window so that the giant lay out of view, and he could pretend for the duration of his eggs and bacon and toast that the monster didn't exist.

But above him, a TV was on, tuned to the news. Charlotte stood in front of the Pump-and-Go, her face pale even beneath a layer of makeup, as she recounted what had happened. The messages from the killer. Jimmy's murder.

In the past, she had taken a more combative tone in talking about the investigators, but now she spoke of the way they had supported and protected her. Just as they were doing their best to protect the town.

David dropped cash onto the counter and walked out.

He went straight to the Countryman Building, down into the basement, and into a white van. Going through security at Site One, he watched for Chambers but didn't see him. In his office, he already had a new folder waiting for him, the report from the previous night's killing. He never knew who prepared these documents or how they arrived here. In the past, he'd assumed it was Erickson, but now Erickson was gone, and still the files arrived.

He started reading. Jimmy died of blood loss and acute trauma. He'd been struck in the head, but it seemed that that had happened at Jimmy's home. There was some blood found there. He'd been taken to the gas station and killed there. Displayed. The metal rod had been driven more than a foot into the dirt beneath the body.

David added Jimmy's photo to the wall. What else could he add?

Jimmy and Jason had known each other, but Jimmy knew every local in town. He had no connection to any of the other victims.

He'd been left with his mask on. Publicly exposed as a member of the cult. But why? David had seen their operation on the inside. He couldn't imagine them hurting Jimmy, not after what he'd watched them do. So what did that mean? He was killed for some reason related to the cult, but he wasn't killed by the cult.

The killer knew that Jimmy was a part of the cult. Just like David knew. And the other members knew. But who else? It had to be someone connected to them.

He looked again over the board, to where Private Chambers's name was written next to Jason's photo.

If Chambers was involved in the drug trade . . . And the cult was buying up crystals . . .

David could feel the eyes on him. Conover. Priest. Whoever else. He didn't dare draw out the map that he saw inside his mind. All the lines tracing back to Chambers. Conover had warned him to stay away. But how did he know he could trust Conover? Or Priest? Or any of them?

He wrote "cult member" beside Jimmy's photo. The rest he kept to himself.

Sunny answered her door after a few knocks. She'd always been so strangely upbeat, but now there were bags under her eyes, and she seemed almost adrift.

"I was hoping you'd come," she said, leading him into her office.

"You been back from the crime scene for a while?" he asked as he settled into a chair.

"A while," she said. "I don't know how long. I couldn't sleep, so I thought I'd try to get some work done."

In the central glassed-in chamber of the lab, samples of crystals sat amid a variety of mysterious equipment.

"How's it coming?" he asked.

She shook her head.

"I don't know. I . . . There has to be some way that the crystals communicate with each other, you know? Some force. And if that exists, then it's just a matter of stimulating it in the right way to activate it. I keep trying all these different stimuli. Heat. Different types of electromagnetic energy. Radiation. Chemicals. Now I'm trying combinations of everything. I mean, I can get any kind of crystal to grow. But these? They just sit there, dead. They . . ."

She was fighting back tears.

He wheeled over to her and took her hand.

"Did you ever see a dead body, before all of this?" he asked.

She looked up, her eyes quizzical.

"No. I don't think so. No."

"When I went to the old sheriff and told him I wanted to be a deputy, he took me aside, and he told about what it's really like. Not the TV stuff—the real job. That you're mostly dealing with people on their worst days, and that can start to shape the way you view the world. Because if all you see is ugliness, you start to think that's all that exists. But even worse than that, he said you're also the one who deals with people on their last day. And mostly that's going to be natural causes. Old age and heart attacks. But it's also car crashes and suicides. And he said I needed to be damn sure I could handle that. Because if you see too much of death, it can make you fixate on it. Or even worse, it can make you numb."

Sunny looked into his eyes and said nothing. But she smiled and interlaced her fingers into his.

David wished he could stay like this, with her, forever. But the killer was still out there. And for the first time since this nightmare had begun, David had a plan to stop him.

| | |

To the west of the giant, where the highway curved around his head and resumed its straight shot west, a flat stretch of asphalt had been poured to serve as a parking lot for Fort Thunder. A place for visitors or for soldiers to leave a personal vehicle. David chose a parking spot at the far corner, backing in so that he had an unbroken view of the lot. And more specifically of the shuttle that came out of the military base and offloaded all those who were heading to their waiting vehicles and the world beyond.

David had let himself into the county impound lot and borrowed the van from the drug bust. It reeked of cigarettes, and the seats were filthy with crumbs. But it was his one option for something that wasn't his work truck. He needed to go unrecognized by his target. And anyone else who might be watching.

He wore his hat but, in the place of his uniform, had on jeans, a T-shirt, and a dark windbreaker. He'd learned his lesson from the fiasco with the cult. His holster and nine-millimeter were still on his hip. And he wore his backup handgun—a Glock .22—in a shoulder holster, out of sight beneath his jacket.

He leaned back in the seat, the *Garden County Gazette* spread in front of him, though he didn't read it so much as stared through it as he waited.

Hours passed. A shuttle came. Passengers stepped off. He scanned the faces. No sign of Chambers.

Hours more.

He put the newspaper down, unable to sustain the effort of pretending. Out of the side window, he had an unbroken view of the giant. It was strange seeing Gulliver from this perspective, and the size of it struck him anew. Sunny's words ran through his thoughts. The crystals could be activated. They could be alive. He could be alive.

The being rumbled suddenly in his mind's eye, shifted, lifted an arm and pressed a hand into the ground, forced itself up, toppling over the spire, the world trembling as it shuddered and stood.

What if Gulliver woke up?

It was a question he tried so hard to never ask or imagine. And there was Sunny, not just asking the question but working at it, instigating. He remembered again how little he truly knew her. Whatever this was, this fling, had come upon him so suddenly and felt so natural that he had never questioned it. He'd never questioned her.

She was so much smarter than him. So worldly and accomplished. In stepping back from it, he saw that they shared almost nothing. Not their backgrounds or experiences. Only the giant. He was all that brought them together.

And when all of this was over?

The rumble of a diesel engine yanked him up out of his thoughts. Another shuttle approached, lurching to a stop amid the parking lot.

More people disembarked, mostly young soldiers. So many young men with matching close-cropped hair and athletic builds. He searched their faces.

There.

Chambers walked straight to a jeep elevated on large, off-road tires. David thought back to the night he'd been followed in his truck. In his rearview, he'd seen the circular headlights of a jeep. This was it. Chambers was the killer. Why else would he have followed David? And the killer even said as much in his message to Charlotte. He was following David.

The jeep came alive and motored in among a crowd of vehicles pulling out of the lot and turning onto the highway, toward Little Springs. David waited, then turned on the van and followed. There was only one way to go, so he could hang far back and pick up the jeep farther on.

He would follow Chambers. See where he went. What he did. And then what? David hadn't thought through anything beyond the surveillance. Did he really expect to catch Chambers in the act? It wasn't like he was going to walk around with that long knife pulled out, ready to carve up another victim.

But he was also involved in the drug trade. He had to be. If David could catch him in a meeting or making a deal, that would be enough. Arrest him. Pull him off the street. Search all his possessions. Find the knife. End the case.

They came into the northern suburbs, on the gentle rise of land that looked down on Gulliver's head and Site One. Some of the vehicles began pulling off. Others pulled on. The jeep stayed on the highway, driving fast but not aggressively along the four-lane blacktop. David could match the pace without doing anything that might bring too much attention to himself.

Where was he heading?

On the far eastern edge of town, the jeep suddenly changed lanes and turned right without using a turn signal. David slowed and followed, leaving another vehicle between them.

The jeep seemed to meander, moving more steadily as it worked its way back west. It came alongside a large lot, ringed with a chain-link fence. David had been past here before but hadn't paid any attention to it. It was the kind of faceless, industrial space that ringed the edges of every city.

Staying a block away, he pulled the van to the side of the road and sat, idling. There were fewer vehicles here than he would've liked. Less cover.

He peered forward. What was Chambers doing? He seemed just to be sitting there. Or was he on his phone?

The glimmer of headlights appeared in his rearview mirror, the glare blinding him momentarily. The car passed, but then it slowed, pulled to the curb. Just as David started to wonder what the driver was doing, the car's reverse lights came on, and it backed toward him.

As it did, a screech of tires sounded, and a truck was beside him, stopped so close the side mirrors almost touched, and he saw through the window one of the faces of the soldiers who'd attacked him in the club. The car in front was now backed within a few inches of him.

Fuck.

David reached for the gear shift, but even before he could throw the van into reverse, another truck swung into view behind him, coming close enough that its bumper jostled that of the van, and the vehicle shook.

Nowhere to go. No way to move. Except the passenger door . . .

And then the door opened on its own. No. It was Chambers who opened it and climbed into the van beside him. Chambers who held a pistol on David and who grinned a horrible thin-lipped grin.

"I told you to leave us alone, cop," Chambers said. "Only person you got to blame for this is yourself."

As he spoke, Chambers used his left hand to snap open David's hip holster and take out his nine-millimeter. He still had the twenty-two hidden in his shoulder holster, but there was no way he could draw it— let alone fire off a shot—before Chambers killed him.

It had all been so fast, so flawlessly executed. *Military precision.* Hell, what had he thought he was doing? Why had David thought he could somehow outwit and outmaneuver soldiers? This was their life, their training, their entire way of being, forged in war and chaos.

And who was he? Some hick sheriff with a junior college degree. And now he was dead. Just like Jason and Erickson and Jimmy and all the others.

"What now?" David asked, forcing himself to speak.

"Now," Chambers said, "we go for a little drive."

He gestured with the gun toward the gear shift. David steeled himself and shifted into drive.

"Follow the car and the truck. You fuck around, I shoot you. You do anything other than exactly what I say, I shoot you."

Yeah. And then once we reach wherever we're going, and I've done just as I was asked, you shoot me, David thought.

The other vehicles started moving. The car first. Then the truck. Then David, following. And the other truck right behind him. Chambers said nothing as he kept his unblinking eyes on David.

For so long, justice had been all that kept David going through the endless exhaustion and horror. The promise that, if he endured enough, the killer would be found and punished—imprisoned or killed—and all the victims would be avenged.

There would be no justice. At least not for David to claim. He had been right, though. Where Erickson and Priest and Conover and the state police and all the rest of them had failed, he alone had been the one to see the truth. He took no real satisfaction in that knowledge, because he would take it to his grave. Yet, the thought of it stirred him, and he felt himself grow angry. Not at the gun held on him, or at his failure, but at the death and chaos. He couldn't kill Chambers, but at least he could confront him.

"Why?" David asked.

Chambers said nothing but made a vaguely menacing movement with the gun.

"Was it just about money and drugs?" David pressed on.

"Everything is about money," Chambers said.

"How did you figure it out—what the crystals do to you?"

Out of the corner of his eye, David saw Chambers smirk.

"Shit. They haven't shown you shit, have they?"

"I know about the infections," David said.

"You don't know a fucking thing. I bet they didn't tell you about the tests," Chambers chided.

David wanted to ask, *What tests?* But he held himself back. He couldn't give Chambers the satisfaction. But Chambers seemed suddenly to be in a talkative mood, relishing the power he held over David.

"How did we figure it out? They showed us. They gave that shit to us. Tested it on us."

David thought of Sunny. Did she know? Could she have been part of that?

"Bullshit."

"If you think the United States military is too morally superior to test experimental shit on our own soldiers, I'd suggest you study a little more history," Chambers said. "They told us it was some kind of antibiotic at first. Then we all started having visions, and we figured out what it really was. It wasn't too hard to see that it had value. Shit, I mean, people will pay a million bucks just for a gram even without knowing the trip it'll take you on."

David processed it. If they exposed Chambers to the giant, they must have exposed him to some of the spire, too. Those crystals now were inside of him, compelling him to desecrate bodies.

They rode in silence. They were headed out east again, to where the development began thinning out and the land was as it had been before: empty, full of quiet, lonely spaces. He wondered, when the time came, would it be the knife or the gun?

"The dealers I understand," David said. "And I know the cult was a buyer. That was, what, some show of power? And Jason . . . That was personal."

David glanced over and saw something had slightly changed in Chambers's eyes. Some of the intensity had gone out of them, and he studied David without saying anything. David felt the anger flaring back up inside of him, the righteousness.

"What about the others? Were they involved in drugs?"

Chambers was silent. David glanced over, and he saw that the young man seemed to be struggling to process something, his brow furrowed.

"You . . . You think I killed all those people. That I'm the serial killer."

"You or maybe some of them your friends did. My cousin was fucking your wife, so you sliced him open like an animal. You cut off his fucking head. What about Erickson? Why did you kill him? Did he get too close, or was it just for fun?"

"Who the fuck is Erickson?" Chambers asked.

David was boiling. Chambers had killed a man without even knowing who he was.

"The FBI agent you cut to shreds, you piece of shit."

"The fuck are you talking about? You're fucking with me. I've been watching the news. There wasn't any FBI agent killed."

David looked over again. Chambers was confused. He really didn't know. And if he didn't know about Erickson . . .

Chambers seemed to follow this, and his eyes lit up again.

"Fuck. You really thought it was me. That's why you were following me."

Chambers inhaled sharply through his nose, then he suddenly snorted and started to cackle. A loud, high-pitched, gasping laugh that hammered at David as it reverberated around the inside of the van. Finally, it sputtered and stopped, leaving Chambers winded and shaking giddily.

"It was you," David insisted, though his conviction had disappeared.

"Why would I lie to you?" Chambers asked, waving the gun, a reminder that he held all the power.

It was the truth. It wasn't him. Which meant the killer was still out there.

As David rolled that fact through his thoughts, the sense of resignation that had come over him vanished all at once, like a fog cut through by the sun. The killer was out there. And like hell he was just going to march straight into the grave.

They were on a two-lane highway, along an empty stretch with nothing but a gas station up ahead. David glanced at Chambers. He hadn't strapped on his seatbelt. David pushed harder on the gas pedal, and the van responded, closing the gap with the truck in front of it.

Just as they were about to ram into the truck, it accelerated, too, and the car in front of it.

"Whoa. Easy there," Chambers said.

David pushed the pedal even harder. The speedometer crept past fifty, sixty.

The truck again sped up.

"Hey."

David glanced in the rearview mirror. The other vehicle was just behind them.

He pushed the pedal to the floor.

They were coming up on the plaza of the gas station.

Slowly, David took his right hand off of the wheel, holding it beside him, resting it atop the lever for the parking brake.

"Last warning," Chambers said.

With a sudden fury, David grabbed the lever and wrenched it backward, and everything turned to madness.

THIRTY-SIX

The van screamed and jolted as the brakes locked, and the vehicle raged against Newton's first law of motion, as it seemed the body of it would come apart around them. Beside David, Chambers slammed forward into the dash with a groan, his head cracking against the inside of the windshield.

And then an explosion behind them and the van lurched forward, throwing David and Chambers back against their seats. David braced himself; his gambit had worked just as he'd planned. The truck that had been trailing them hadn't stopped in time. It rear-ended them, hard enough that the back of the van launched up into the air, and they hung there in what seemed like zero gravity for a long second, David's body pinned against the seatback, Chambers lolling free in the cab, blood trailing from his head.

Then the van slammed down with a boom like thunder, and the world went blessedly still and silent.

No.

David shook himself into focus. It wasn't over. He forced his shaking hands to unbuckle the seatbelt as Chambers groaned beside him. He was alive.

The door handle came into David's hand and he pulled it. The door opened, and he was stumbling down onto the highway, barely keeping on his feet.

The back of the van sat on the front of the truck, which was smashed almost beyond recognition, the two vehicles merging into each other. As David stepped forward, his boots crunched on broken glass and bits of metal. A hissing noise issued up from the truck's obliterated engine. Inside the cab, the driver slumped over the steering wheel.

David drew the Glock from the shoulder holster under his jacket. But the young man was either dead or so badly injured that he wouldn't be a threat. David started to reach out, to feel for a pulse.

Just then, he heard shouted voices from in front of the van.

"Chambers!"

"What the fuck?"

The fog of the crash still gripped David, but he forced himself to think. Two of them, coming from the lead vehicles. Both would be armed. Highly trained. He had no chance against them. Not out here. Alone. No cover.

They were only some twenty or thirty yards from the gas station, but that was forward, past the two soldiers.

He clung to the driver's side of the van, and then he heard Chambers on the inside, moving.

"Motherfucker pulled the parking brake!"

"Where is he?" one of the voices yelled in response.

Closer. He was almost out of time.

And then David was acting, not thinking. He dropped to the pavement and rolled, sliding underneath the chassis of the van.

He stopped on his belly, facing forward, gun in front of him, clenched in both hands. He stared ahead, holding his breath, waiting for them to appear.

They stopped talking, the three of them. To not reveal their positions, he figured. This wasn't the first time they had stalked a man.

Their feet came into view. On the left, black and gray tennis shoes. On the right, boots. David prayed for them to stay close together, but as they approached the van they separated, the tennis shoes flaring wide to the left, the driver's side, and the boots around to the right.

David's head swiveled back and forth. The second either of them ducked down, saw him, he was dead, a fish in a barrel.

The feet moved methodically, and it seemed from his vantage point almost a dance, choreographed steps and pivots as they scanned the wreckage. He needed them closer. Close enough that he could be sure. He wouldn't be shooting like he was trained—aim at meaty bulk of center mass. He'd have to shoot one in the leg, then pivot and shoot the other. And . . .

Where was Chambers? Why hadn't he stepped down?

Now the two sets of feet were directly beside him, across from each other. They would be figuring it out soon. He had to do it. Had to do it now.

He turned to his left, taking steady aim at the tennis shoes. Maybe eight feet away. Feet close together.

David inhaled and imagined a clean shot. Just the way his dad had taught him with a rifle, staring down a deer.

He exhaled and pulled the trigger.

The gunshot exploded in the tiny space, a roar bouncing between metal and pavement.

He watched only long enough to see an eruption of blood, the feet falter, the legs start to fall.

Then he spun swiftly to the right. To the boots.

"He's under the . . ." a voice started to yell.

David squeezed the trigger twice. The gun recoiled, but his ears were filled with an intense ringing from the first shot, so the only sound it gave was like the crash of a wave.

The man in the boots fell. He landed so that his head was toward the back of the van. David recognized him from the club. Now the face stared at him, confused and hurting.

He still held his gun. David willed him to stop, but the man lifted it forward, toward David.

David squeezed the trigger again, and there was no mistaking that the soldier was dead.

He spun back to his left.

The man in the tennis shoes lay with his feet toward David. He dragged himself away from the van, leaving twin trails of blood. The one shot had pierced both of his feet.

There was still no sign of Chambers, but David couldn't stay where he was. He army-crawled out from under the driver's side, moving slowly, steadily, listening for any sign of Chambers.

David sat with his back against the van. His ears still rang.

In front of him, the man in the tennis shoes had almost reached his destination—his gun, which he had dropped when he fell.

"Don't," David said.

The man looked back. He was little more than a teenager, all anger and intensity. When he saw David, and saw the Glock trained on him, he stopped.

"Good," David said, his voice low. "Where is Chambers?"

The soldier said nothing, but his eyes flitted up, to the van above David, with a look of recognition.

David rolled to his left, toward the back of the van, just as shots rang out from inside, bullets going into and through the van's side panel—*plunk, plunk, plunk, plunk*—and ricocheting against the pavement.

Something burned in David's left hand, and he wanted to scream.

But the kid in the tennis shoes was already at his gun, leveling it at David, using the gunfire as a distraction.

David raised the Glock and fired three quick shots, hitting his target in the shoulder, neck, and temple.

The gun clattered out of the kid's hand as he bled out.

David hunched as low as he could. He stole a quick glance at his left hand, which was red with blood and had a hole clean through the middle of it. He would allow himself to feel pain later. Now . . .

More shots rang out, just over David's shoulder.

He turned, facing the van, and in one motion squeezed off four rounds. Glass exploded as the bullets pierced the window.

Then silence.

Was Chambers dead?

He scanned the windows, keeping low. His hearing started to come back. In the distance, he could hear the wail of sirens. Then . . .

The groan of a door opening on the far side. David held a second, then stood.

Chambers had launched himself out of the passenger side door and was headed at a dead sprint for the gas station. He held a pistol in his right hand and gripped his side with his left. He ran like a wounded animal, desperate and ungainly. One of David's bullets had found a home.

David ran up to the car that had been in front of him. Chambers blindly fired his gun, but the bullet went wide as David ducked behind the vehicle.

He leaned out to look. Gas pumps out in front. Onlookers taking cover, some screaming. He heard the faint cry of sirens coming closer— someone had called it in.

David steeled himself and ran out after Chambers, steady, his gun in front of him, ready to aim and fire. He tacked wide, toward the gas pumps, trying to get an angle, to cut Chambers off.

The soldier seemed to see this and broke off toward a large automated car wash along the side of the building, then disappeared into the dark of it.

As David approached, he saw the trail of blood along the pavement, drops the size of silver dollars. It was a cement garage with twin tracks running through, pulling vehicles by their tires as automated arms brought down brushes, buffers, spurts of water, hot gusts of air.

Holding his pistol in front of him, David stepped steadily into the maw of the structure, past the dryer, which blasted him with a desert wind.

He couldn't hear over the roar of water and churn of mechanized parts.

David hugged to one wall and crouched as low as he could, so that he could see under the spinning arm that hung down from the ceiling.

Foam flicked off of the arm and filled the air, like globs of snow.

It felt as if he'd walked willingly into a creature's maw to be consumed. Any sign of the blood was lost amid the slosh of water and soap.

So many shapes. So many shadows. So many fast movements. His brain screamed at his eyes. *Focus!*

Then, just beyond him, a hatchback appeared on the tracks, being pulled toward him, scrubbers drumming away against the car's exterior, water pelting it.

David froze. He watched. Looking for anything that seemed human. He wouldn't yell a warning. Not like in Jason's office. He would act.

Something moved. A form. Chambers.

David took aim.

Just then, the car lurched forward, pulled between them. Foam showered David.

He wiped it off.

But it was too late. Chambers had come around the front of the car and held his pistol aimed.

The gunshot echoed brilliantly in the enclosed space.

For a moment that seemed never to end, Chambers looked at David with an expression of what struck David as remorse. His gun arm hung limp.

Then Chambers fell over.

He was dead, but the automated car wash kept moving, pulling the car forward, the front left tire catching on the body and dragging it, crunching, lurching as bones gave way with a series of grinding pops, car and body buffeted by brushes and cannons of water.

Two women were inside, mouths agape, screaming with voices drowned out by the roar of the machines.

"Shut it down! Shut the damn thing down!" someone yelled.

David turned, back toward the exit. A shape was there, someone holding a submachine gun. A young man in black tactical gear.

"Who . . . Who are you?" was all David could think to ask.

The man responded, but David could hear nothing over the din of the car wash and the ringing in his ears from all the gunfire. Then the machinery around them froze. The car had stopped a few feet ahead, the whirling arms frozen in place, a streak across the ground behind it, a soupy froth of blood and bubbles.

|||

He came outside to find a phalanx of black SUVs ringing the station, dozens of black-suited soldiers with guns raised. To the back of it, he saw Brooke's truck with lights flashing. She stood outside of it, craning her neck to see. He holstered his pistol and waved to her.

"Thanks," David said to the soldier who'd come into the car wash. "Hadn't been for you . . . Anyway, that was all of them. You can tell your guys to ease up."

The soldier nodded, then signaled to the others, who lowered their weapons; the panic went out of the clutch of people gathered by the gas pumps. Whatever had happened here, it was done.

Conover stepped out of one of the SUVs and stomped toward David.

"Sheriff Blunt. You had specific orders. Those orders were to stand the fuck down."

Whatever capacity David had for punishment had reached its limit. He wasn't going to take more abuse, not after this. Let Conover do what he would.

"You knew," David growled.

It was harsh and sudden enough to throw Conover from his attack. Also, Conover at the same moment looked down and noticed the hole in David's hand. He lost his bluster but kept up an angry tone.

"I was watching them. I suppose you know what they were doing."

David nodded.

"We'd known someone was smuggling out samples. But we didn't just want them. We wanted to bring down the whole operation—the dealers and buyers, too," Conover continued. "Then you go and play hero cop. Now we've got dead suspects and jack shit else to show for it. Fuck. At least this wraps up the serial killer shit with a nice little bow."

"It wasn't them," David said.

Conover's eyes widened, searching for an explanation.

"Of course it was."

"They didn't even know about Erickson. Whoever the killer is, he's still out there."

David held up his left hand, which had begun to throb so badly he felt he might not be able to stay upright.

"Now, if you'll excuse me, I'm going to go find a Band-Aid to put on this," David said.

He walked through the chaos of the scene to Brooke, parked alongside the highway.

"What in the holy hell happened, boss?" she asked, then saw his wound. "Jesus. Your hand."

"Can you drive me to the hospital?" he asked. "Tell you all about it on the way."

THIRTY-SEVEN

The doctors gave David something for the pain, then took X-rays. A miracle shot, the doctor called it. The bullet had fractured when it passed through the side of the van, and only a chunk of it had hit his hand, where it went straight through soft tissue, missing the bones and damaging only a little muscle. They stitched him up and gave him an antibiotic and sent him on his way.

Brooke waited for him in the lobby. He'd told her the truth, albeit only part of it. That there was a larger drug operation going on, and he'd somewhat stumbled into it, and the crew running the operation tried their damnedest to kill him.

He wished so badly to tell her the rest of it. About the infection and people ingesting these crystals and his desperate, dashed hope that this would end the killings. She more than anyone deserved the truth. Brooke was smarter than he was. She didn't take any shit, but she also didn't have that inexplicable male craving for authority—a tendency even David had to fight off, though often enough it overtook him. She was a hell of a cop, and one day she'd be a hell of a sheriff. As it was, she was stuck going out on the job every day playing against a stacked deck.

"You okay, boss?" she asked as she drove him to his apartment.

He'd been staring out, watching dusk fall across the giant.

"Yeah. I don't know. Shit, no. No, I'm not," he answered. "I've had a couple of bullets come my way before, but nothing like today. There's no good reason I'm still alive other than dumb luck. And you know, I never killed anyone before today. A cow, once. Never a person."

He looked down at his right hand, which hadn't stopped trembling.

"And now four men are dead."

"They wanted to kill you, boss. You did what you had to do."

"I suppose. I . . . I didn't hesitate at all."

He was seeing it again. The soldiers bleeding out as bullets tore through them. The one in the truck, his head smashed on the steering wheel. Chambers, stumbling under the car, his body mangled.

"What does that make me, Brooke? That I would do that and not feel a thing?"

She glanced over, then back to the road ahead.

"It makes you a survivor, boss. That's all. A survivor."

|||

Not long after he got to his apartment, there was a knock at the door. Sunny stood there, her face filled with concern. They lay together on the bed, not talking, just holding each other. Priest had told Sunny what happened, and she'd demanded to go and see David.

He went to the window and peered through the blinds. Outside, a couple of dark, unmarked cars sat in front of the apartment. They were watching over him. Conover. Priest. Whoever. He could relax, if only for one night.

She held his heavily bandaged hand and caressed it. His fingertips were bruised and mostly numb. He could barely feel her touch.

"You're a fucking moron, you know," she said.

"I know," he said.

"You can't do that. Going off on your own."

"I know."

She looked into his eyes, unblinking and insistent.

"You can't get yourself killed."

"I'm not trying," he argued back, though without much force.

"No. But you aren't trying to stay alive, either. And . . . You can't do that, okay? I need you."

"Okay," he said, and he pulled her more tightly to him.

Later, he lay in bed and waited for sleep that refused to come. The shootout played through his mind on a loop. The crash. The burst of violence. Adrenaline charging through him, his heart slamming against the inside of his chest. Stop, he told himself, it's over. You survived. Let it go.

Finally, his mind relented, and he stared at the empty expanse of the ceiling. He had survived. But the other part of it was wrong. It wasn't over. Somewhere in the night, a killer watched and waited, readying to strike again.

||||

In the morning, they went back to Site One. Passing through security, David scrutinized the faces of the soldiers. Were all of Chambers's friends dead? Or were some still out there, hidden in plain sight? He hurried along, eager to reach the isolation of Building Seventeen.

Sunny joined him in his office, where he went straight to the far wall and crossed out Chambers's name.

"One more dead end," he said.

They stood back and surveyed the wall, the names and photos and maps. Seven victims, and the only thing that seemed to tie any together—the drugs—had been a mirage. The cases were like bones, with no connective tissue to form them into a body. No tendons or veins or nerves.

"You're looking for connections," Sunny said.

David sat, his body still exhausted from the day before.

"I figure there has to be a motive. It doesn't feel random, like a spree killer. And the messages he's sent to Charlotte show that he's thinking through what he's doing. He's messing with her. Messing with me."

David hadn't told Sunny about Erickson's lighter showing up on his doorstep. He knew how hard his death had been on her already and didn't want to hurt her anew.

She studied the wall.

"So, there's one reason for all the deaths. One motive," she said, thinking out loud. "And if you find the motive, you find the killer."

"That's the idea," he said. "But now there's nothing left connecting any of them."

"It's sort of the same as my work," Sunny said. "I know something is connecting all the crystals that make up the giant, but for the life of me, I can't figure out what it is."

She pointed to the line between Kapoor, the realtor, and Jason.

"What's that?"

"Kapoor was buying and selling properties. Jason had sign-off power on real estate deals. So they at least were connected. I don't know. Maybe some land deal went wrong, and some outsider went after Jason and Kapoor? But that still doesn't connect to any others."

Even as he said it, the idea felt limp, unsupported by anything he'd seen and uncovered. But it was also as good of a theory as he had.

"And you're assuming it's an outsider," Sunny said. "What if it's not?"

"It has to be. The killer is infected by the spire, right? That means it's someone with access. And I'm the only local with a clearance."

Sunny shook her head.

"Not necessarily. Remember when Gulliver fell? Little pieces of the giant and spire fractured off in the atmosphere and rained down all over the county."

David pictured it in his mind. Gulliver looming overhead, glowing. The sky dark. Flaming debris racing through the sky, toward the ground.

"I thought the army came in and found everything," he said.

"They picked up as much as they found, but what if they missed something? We have no idea if some local randomly came across a piece of it."

"No," David said, cutting her off, his defenses raised. "It isn't one of us."

"You can't know for certain. That's all I was trying to say."

"It isn't," he said, more curtly than he wanted.

They sat in silence, and then after a while Sunny stood, put her hand on his shoulder, and whispered in his ear that she was going to her office to work. Then he was alone. Just him and the faces of the dead staring back at him from the wall.

It couldn't be a local. She was wrong.

He stared at the line connecting Kapoor and Jason. Maybe.

He'd already spent hours scanning through Jason's financial records, looking for anything strange. He sorted through the pile of folders on the table, found what he was looking for, and started reading again: Jason's bank statement, a vast scroll of everywhere he'd spent money, everything he'd bought.

David's eyes glazed over amid the tedium of life it reflected. Groceries. Bar tabs. Fuel. Clothing for the twins. A few withdrawals from an ATM that he already had looked up and knew was the one sitting inside the entrance of the strip club. A purchase from a flower shop. Was it for Missy, his wife, or was it for Jason's mistress?

If asked, David would've said he knew everything there was to know about Jason. Yet he was reminded all over again that there was a whole side of his life that Jason had kept hidden. They'd spent all their lives together, he and Jason. Been the best man at each other's weddings. Maybe they hadn't been as inseparable as when they were children, but they still saw each other almost every day at the courthouse. Still got together for every big championship boxing match.

David stopped mid page. Then he flipped backward. One page. Another. Another. Scanning over each line item as he went, searching. No. It wasn't there.

He tossed the sheets aside and picked up another stack, statements from a different account. Again, he flipped one page after another, searching for something—an expense—that had to be there. Except, it wasn't.

David thought back to when he'd requested the records. His uncle Dale had stared at him across his desk. What had he said? *I'll prepare them myself.*

David stood and rushed out. It was time for a family visit.

THIRTY-EIGHT

David made it to the bank just as it was nearing closing time, dusk settling. Inside, the floor was empty of customers and the tellers finished up whatever little tasks they could before clocking out for the day. David had seen his uncle's car parked outside and knew he'd find him here, in his office.

Standing there, David had a sudden memory. The night that seemed now like it was years in the past, though truly it was only weeks—the village council meeting. The schism between Dale and Jason, each voting in opposite ways on the mosque amid the uproar. And Samuel had hinted at a deeper conflict between them. Something old and ugly.

And yet, David had seen the killer. He'd seen him the night Jason died and then again in the alley. It wasn't Dale. Whoever the killer was, he was too athletic, not the right build. Dale didn't kill his son. But that didn't mean he was innocent.

David entered the office without knocking.

Dale sat at his desk, absently smoking a cigar. He turned to David and held an aura of detached imperiousness.

"David," his uncle said.

"Uncle Dale."

"I heard about that madness at the gas station. You okay?"

Dale gestured with his cigar toward David's bandaged left hand.

"I'll be fine," David said.

"Good. That's good. Well, should I hope that you come with some news, finally? We've all been waiting on you to end this case. They're saying on the news that the shooting had nothing to do with Jason's murder. Sit."

Dale pointed the cigar toward a chair.

Normally, whenever David was around his uncle, he took off his hat. He did it reflexively, a gesture of respect. This night, he kept it on. David eased into the chair and leaned back.

"You remember when my dad decided to raise pheasants?"

Dale thought a moment.

"Can't say I do. But that sounds like him. Always with some project. Is this why you're here?"

David met his uncle's hard gaze and held it, ignoring the question.

"I was maybe five or six. He had this idea that he'd start raising them up and releasing them every year. Mom and I never really knew why. Maybe he wanted more around to hunt. Anyway, that's not the point. The point is, Dad put them in the old chicken coop. They were just babies, no more than a couple of inches tall."

David saw the memory as he described it.

"One morning, I went out with Dad to feed them, give them fresh water. I ran out in front, all excited. Every other day, I'd come into the enclosure and they'd run up to me in a pack, chirping and flapping. This day, I didn't see one of them. Didn't hear them either. I looked around. And I saw one, leaning against the fence. Its little head was just small enough to stick out through the opening in the chicken wire. Except its head wasn't there. Not anymore. Just the neck, which ended right at the fence, bitten clean through. The thing is, it wasn't just the one. It was all of them. Each of those pheasant chicks, right in a row up against the fence, heads missing, like it was some kind of mass execution."

Dale sighed, as if this all bored him, then pulled a tumbler and a bottle of Scotch from a drawer.

David studied his uncle's face. The wrinkles. The liver spots. The eyes watery from too many years of late nights with a bottle. He wasn't sure why he had ever feared this man. David leaned forward, elbows on his knees, and continued.

"Those pheasant chicks, you see, they only knew the safety of that pen. They didn't have to run or hide. Dad and I were all they had, and whenever we came, we brought food. Everything was safe. Then whatever it was that came along outside the fence that night—a raccoon or a fox or maybe even one of those stray cats that hung around the property—those chicks had no idea it could be a threat. They were so goddamned innocent that they sat there, looking out, gawking, even as that critter came along and started to bite off their heads. They watched death coming. Stared at it. Waited patiently, curious. Then died. All because they were too dumb to know better."

Dale seemed uncertain, unsteady. He'd never been talked to this way.

"The parable of the pheasants. Okay. Now what's the point?"

"I'm here because of Jason."

"You know who killed my boy?"

There was anger in his voice, and desperation, too.

"What I know is that you used him," David spat back. "I didn't notice it at first, but then I saw it. The title fight back in November. Pay-per-view. Just like always, Jason had Spady and me over to watch it. He paid for the fight. But it wasn't in the records."

"You . . . You must be remembering things wrong. Or . . ."

David had seen all he needed. His uncle's eyes showed him fear, desperation, even as he fought to keep himself calm.

"You doctored the records. You just were a little sloppy. Cut out whole days instead of just a single item."

"I wouldn't . . ."

"I can talk to my friends in the FBI. Have them come and sort through your records. See what kind of discrepancies they find. Or you can tell me right now if you had anything to do with Jason dying."

Dale stood and leaned over the desk, his face burning a deep maroon.

"You son of a bitch! Accuse me of killing my own son? You fail to find his killer. Now you come here and spit this bullshit at me? Goddamn you. He was my son!"

David didn't react.

"Your son that you beat. Yeah, I know about that, too. But this isn't about that, Dale. This is about how you used Jason. Made him run for county assessor so that he could be the one man who said yes or no on any real estate deal. A little extra money on the side, and those deals go through faster, don't they?"

Dale said nothing. He eased back into his chair, the bluster gone out of him.

"So, Jason brings in this extra cash. You run that through the bank. Line your pockets, and you still get to run the county. That's what this is really about—you wanting to feel like you're in charge."

Dale had leaned back, almost crumpling into his chair.

"You can't prove anything," he said, his voice gone soft. "You dig into the accounts, everything will point at Jason. All you'll do is ruin your cousin's name. Is that what you want?"

"What I want? What I want, Dale, is for you to tell me whether all this shit you were pulling is what got Jason killed."

Dale trembled with a quiet rage. When he spoke, it came out with the hiss of a snake.

"You worthless fuck. I'll have that badge off your chest."

David leaned forward from the chair and over the desk, putting his weight on his good hand.

"All your life, you must have hated it here. You were always the smart one. The savvy one. The one who knew how to play politics, how to take a little power and turn it into a lot. Great big fish in a tiny pond. Then Gulliver falls, and no one else sees it for what it really is. But you do. You see the opportunity."

Dale reached for his drink, then stopped, and his hand fell away without grabbing the glass.

"All I've done is save this town. My town. Protect it from the vultures. I would've thought you'd be on our side. My side. But you aren't. You're one of them now."

David laughed, a booming, deep laugh.

"Save this town? Hell, Dale. You and I both know the only thing you care about is yourself, so this town is only as good as whatever value you can suck out of it. You see yourself as that predator, circling the fence."

Dale said nothing.

"But you aren't the fox, uncle. That's the point of the story. You think you're the savvy one, outside of the fence, but that's because you're too stupid to know better. Too stupid to know that you're one more help-less little pheasant, sitting there with your head out in the wild, teeth closing down around your neck."

The old man's eyes lowered.

"Finish your drink. I know you didn't kill your son. But if I find out you had anything to do with it, I'm coming back here and dragging you out by your balls."

David moved to leave.

All at once, Dale came around the desk, his face burning again.

"Jason would be ashamed of you."

David turned back, keeping his hands at his sides.

"Go ahead, Dale. Take a swing. But I guarantee you, I won't just stand here and take a beating the way Jason did."

Dale tensed as if to come at David. Then he stopped, as if a gusting wind had gone slack all at once. David walked out and into the rapidly darkening night.

|||

David's phone call came out of nowhere. Charlotte was in her hotel room when her phone started to buzz, and she tensed up as she always did now when she heard it, thinking it would be another message from him. The killer. A threat. Or a photo of another flayed body. But it was David, and so she hurriedly answered.

"David. Did something happen? Did you find him?"

The killer, she meant. She wouldn't allow herself to hope, to imagine it might be over, that she could go one minute without looking over her shoulder, knowing that eventually he would be there.

David's voice came through.

"No. Nothing. Sorry. I just . . . I wanted to see you."

His voice was even more laconic than usual. He'd always been that way. Somber, even morose. She remembered sitting in their shared room, rattling on to him about something or another—schoolwork, or something about sports, or her annoyance with her parents—and David would be silent, his eyes and his mind elsewhere. She'd thought of him as a turtle, one who retreated into the shell of his own subconscious, poking himself out only fleetingly to sniff at the air before ducking away once more. In her memory, he was always this way. But it could've been that he was different before his parents died. Maybe he hadn't been so somber and detached, and it was the vicissitudes of life that made him this way.

Whatever the reason for his sudden call, after he had trained such rage on her before, he gave no hints.

"Sure," she answered.

Twenty minutes later, she was waiting in the lobby when his truck pulled up in front of the doors. She walked out and joined him. The air was cold, but there was something of spring in it, a slight trace of warmth, or perhaps a chemical signal between the trees, some invisible sign that winter neared its end.

He pulled out onto the street, driving slowly with no apparent aim.

"You were gone by the time I got there. To the shooting," she said. "I heard you'd been hurt."

"Not bad," he said, waggling his left hand, which balanced atop the steering wheel, unable to grip it.

"I don't know if you've seen the news coverage. Everyone's calling you a hero."

He shrugged, clearly uncomfortable with the label.

"I was lucky."

"We make our luck. Isn't that what Grandpa always said?" she asked.

"I think you're right. He always did have some wisdom for every occasion."

"Why did you want to see me, David?"

Outside, the streetlights and quiet houses of Old Town slid past, unchanged from when they'd been teenagers, out cruising at night, feeling as if Little Springs was theirs.

"I wanted to tell you, your folks—Ben Senior and Bonnie—what they did to you was wrong. What they said. The way they acted. I hate that they lied to me. Let me think for all those years that you were dead. But . . ."

David seemed to search for words, then he continued.

"They also took me in when I had nothing. If I'd ended up living with Jason, with his parents . . . They took me in, is what I'm saying. And as mad as I am at them, I still owe them for that. For giving me a place and treating me like their own. They're not well. You saw them. You know what I mean. They're so scared of everything. They aren't really taking care of themselves or the place."

She nodded. She had seen it. Ben Senior and Bonnie had a sickly pallor, and their house had smelled of something spoiled, of mold and decay. It was why she'd found it so impossible to stay angry at them.

"Anyway, I've been going over there, taking them groceries, taking care of the place a little," David continued. "I know you're done with them, and I support that. But I'm going to keep helping them out. And I just . . . I didn't want you to think that I'm choosing them over you."

She looked over at him, and she saw the pain in his face as he struggled over this. He was a good man. A good man in the way men used to be good. Not in the ways of the city, of sleekness and skill and wealth. He was a man who was exactly what he was and knew it. A man who walked with a moral compass held in front of him and imposed those morals not on others but on himself. He cared, even when all so often life punished you for it and showed you how easier the other path was.

Charlotte reached out and put her left hand on his right.

"I'm glad," she said. "Thank you. For taking care of them and for telling me."

David nodded. Just then, he flipped on his turn signal. The truck eased into the parking lot of the nursing home and rolled to a stop. David checked the clock on the dash.

"We need to hurry," he said as he opened his door.

"Why are we here?" Charlotte asked. "I thought you said Grandpa was agitated."

"Just come in."

The administrator stopped them in the hallway and locked eyes with Charlotte. A handful of other visitors filed past, disappearing into rooms.

"David. You know the rule," she said.

"I do," he said. "Charlotte, will you please tell her who you are?"

Charlotte hesitated a moment, but David's expression told her she was safe. The woman was a decade or so older than them, and Charlotte remembered her from when she'd been growing up.

"You remember David's cousin? Ben Junior?" Charlotte asked. "That's me. I go by Charlotte now."

The woman studied Charlotte, and her eyes lit up in recognition.

"Have you told her?" the woman asked.

David shook his head. Charlotte tried to parse the exchange, which seemed loaded with far more secrecy and intensity than the situation warranted.

"Told me what?" Charlotte said.

"What you see here, it stays here. That's the deal. No talking to anyone. Nothing on TV. Can you handle that?" the administrator said.

She realized, despite all the years, all the distance, all of the lies about the murders, she still trusted David. He was the closest friend she'd ever had—a brother. She nodded. They walked down the hallway, and David led her into a room.

Inside, Samuel sat in his recliner, staring ahead. He seemed to track their movements as they entered. David sat on the bed and watched the clock.

Charlotte looked at the pile of notes on the desk.

"What's this stuff?" she asked.

Just then, the chorus of barking dogs rose from outside.

"Hey there, we have a visitor."

Charlotte startled. The voice wasn't David's. It belonged to Samuel. Her grandpa sat there, his eyes suddenly cleared, locked on hers.

Charlotte was crying. Not just weeping but sobbing, all at once. She could barely talk.

"There's something I need to tell you," David started to say, explaining to Samuel.

The old man lifted a hand, palm up, stopping David.

"I know who this is," he said.

With an effort, he stood, and he wrapped his arms around Charlotte.

"This is my grandbaby," Samuel said.

He leaned in till his head pressed against hers. Her eyes wouldn't stop flowing.

"I love you," the old man whispered.

None of them said much more. They sat and stared at each other, marveling at what for each seemed a miracle. A grandfather awoken. A grandchild resurrected. And then, all too fast, it was over, and Samuel disappeared, and they left.

David and Charlotte sat in his truck in the parking lot. She couldn't stop herself from crying for a long time, and David waited, patiently, in silence. Finally, she gathered herself.

"I don't understand," was all she could say.

"No one does," David said. "You just can't put it on TV, Charlotte. Promise me."

She looked over at him, and her eyes filled with tears again. She choked a sob.

"God, David. I'm so sorry."

"Sorry for what?"

"I lied to you, took advantage of you."

Charlotte stared out into the dark of the night.

"This job I do, God, it's terrible sometimes," she said finally. "You sit around and wait for terrible things to happen, then you jump in to cover them. Your best day as a reporter is always someone else's worst day."

"That doesn't make you bad," David offered.

She was quiet then, even longer this time.

"My first job, I ended up covering crime for this local news station. It was a shit city, a dead-end gig. Unless I could cover something that people noticed. But you need big things to happen to make big stories. I remember one day, I was driving around for some assignment, and I saw this airplane, a big airliner, in the sky overhead, coming in toward the airport. And all of a sudden, I was imagining the plane crashing. Everyone dead. And me, so close that I was first on the scene, owning a story that would be national news, a story that could make my career, if only I was so lucky."

She dabbed tears from the corners of her eyes.

"Lucky. I thought it would be lucky for a plane to crash. That's what this job does to you."

He reached across and put his hand on hers.

"You let your mind wander, it'll come up with all sorts of horrible things. Yours. Mine. Anyone's."

"Sure," she said with no conviction.

Suddenly David smiled.

"Hey, you know, the Crane Dance is on Friday," he said. "You should come."

In her years away, she'd somehow forgotten about it. The biggest night of the year in Little Springs. A night when the whole town came together and blocked off Main Street for music and dancing and drinking, all in the name of the sandhill cranes who stopped here on their great, cyclic journey.

"They're still having it?" she asked.

She meant it as surprise that the event still existed at all, a funny tradition persisting in spite of everything the town had experienced since the giant fell, but David misinterpreted.

"We figured the killer won't try anything in the middle of a crowd, so we thought it'd be safe," he said. "I'd really love to have you join us."

"Sure," she said. "I'd like that."

David drove away, headed back to Charlotte's hotel. Neither of them felt the eyes that were on them. Eyes that tracked them as they went, hungry, calculating. The eyes of a predator.

THIRTY-NINE

David grabbed a handbasket from the front of the Old Town grocery store and filled it with canned goods, boxed dinners, milk, bread, a couple of pounds of ground beef. The usual groceries for Ben Senior and Bonnie. His own refrigerator was empty, but all that he picked up for himself was a case of beer.

The store was called The Store—for decades, it had been the only grocery in town. It was four narrow aisles, one checkout counter. The basket was full, but David wandered the aisles. Now there were two other massive grocery stores in town, stocked with everything that grew under the sun, one in the suburbs up north and one out east. But David had never set foot in either of them. All his life, The Store had been where he went for food. He wasn't about to change now.

He was thinking again over his conversation with Charlotte, about all that he had missed, all that he'd overlooked. He had missed the real her, and then he'd missed everything that transpired between her and his aunt and uncle. And then he never questioned their story. Never questioned them. He'd been young, but it was no excuse. He knew he still had that flaw inside of him, taking people at their word.

"Oh, David, I didn't expect I'd see you here."

David turned and at first looked straight over the person who'd spoken to him. It was Bertha Belcher, the owner of The Store. She didn't stand much above four feet anymore, the way her spine hunched over. Her hair was dyed electric red. Back when he was a kid, David would mow her lawn. She always made him lemonade with lemon slices in the cup, floating atop the ice, and it was the fanciest thing he'd ever seen.

"Hi, Bertha. Just picking up some groceries."

Something was off in the way she looked at him. Something that seemed both pitying and judgmental.

"Well, I'm glad to see you're taking it all so well," she said unconvincingly.

He couldn't hide the blankness of his reaction.

"Oh," Bertha said. "You haven't seen yet."

She glanced sideways toward the front counter, where a metal rack held copies of the *Garden County Gazette*. It was a Friday, which meant a new issue was just out.

"I'm sure you're doing your best," Bertha said as David walked over and picked up a copy.

At the top of the page was a big announcement for the Crane Dance, but David's eyes quickly went below it. His heart started beating harder as he recognized a photo of himself. Some old photo of him posing stiffly in uniform. And then the headline: "Residents Lose Faith in Sheriff as Killer Remains at Large."

"Hell," David hissed.

He knew it right away. This was Dale's newspaper; it was his doing. His uncle had some fight left in him after all. He scanned the article quickly. It said he'd lied about the truth. That he had had the killer in his sights and let him get away. That he had blamed locals for the killings. That he should resign or that the county should force a recall vote. His skin prickled as his brain shifted into fight-or-flight mode. It was all bullshit. But it was also all true.

David glanced around him and saw that the few other shoppers all stared his way. Faces he knew. Friends. And now they looked at him with distrust. With fear.

He'd had locals angry at him before. It couldn't be helped, doing the job. You busted someone for drunk driving, they weren't exactly happy about it. This was different. His uncle was turning the town itself against him. He had to end this. Find the killer. Close the case. Things could still be normal again.

David started for the door, forgetting the basket in his hand.

"You have to pay for those, you know."

Bertha's voice behind him, spoken as if he hadn't spent all those years mowing her lawn, as if he hadn't come to The Store to help Bertha out every time there was a shoplifter. She spoke to him like he was a stranger.

"Right. Shoot, sorry, Bertha. Lost my head there."

He put his groceries on the checkout counter. Bertha settled in across from him and started to scan and bag his purchases.

"And the paper?"

He looked down, realizing he still held it in his hand. He dropped it back into the rack.

"No," David said. "Just the food."

|||

All the way to Site One, David felt the anxiety within him growing, metastasizing, until he felt his whole body urging the white van to hurry up in its course. He couldn't just sit here and let himself be thrown out of office. He had to act. To do something.

There was some small voice inside of him that asked if all this wasn't a relief. Being sheriff of Little Springs had been David's dream since he was little. But in the shadow of the giant, it had become a nightmare— even before the murders. These weren't his people anymore. Not his world. If the town wanted to give him an easy out, let them. He could be done with all of it.

But no, he couldn't do that. He'd made a promise to find Jason's killer. Jason, Jimmy, Erickson, all of them needed justice. If David walked away before it was done, he'd carry that with him to the grave.

Also, he alone had seen the killer. And the killer had taunted him, targeting him. Something about it all felt almost personal. While there were people in Little Springs that David had butted heads with, there wasn't anyone he'd call an enemy. He remembered Sunny's words, that it could be a local. He shook his head. It couldn't be a local. Not even Dale.

David was thinking about the newspaper again, about his meeting with Dale. His uncle didn't know anything about Jason's death. And it pained Dale, clearly, despite all his history with his son. The attack in the newspaper wasn't about that. It was because of the bank records. Dale felt threatened, so he needed to threaten David back, find some leverage, try to protect himself.

If Dale wasn't involved, then David was back again to the beginning. No suspects. No motive. No hope of finding the killer before he claimed another victim.

Mercifully, the van came to a stop in Site One, and David was off and through security and on his way to Building Seventeen, where he planned to throw himself into the files. He had no real plan beyond a hope for luck. That some piece of information would leap out at him, or some detail would jog his memory, or that the pieces of the puzzle would suddenly click together in a new way.

He found himself knocking on the door of Sunny's office, instead. He both wanted to tell her about the newspaper and didn't. She was so much smarter than him, she would know what to do. But would it make him seem weak? That he was a failure? Even his own town was turning against him. But then she answered with a welcoming smile, and he was telling her, and she sat and listened, and when she spoke, she didn't try to coach him through a solution, to problem-solve.

"I'm so sorry," she said, taking his hand and leaning her body into his. "That has to be so hard."

David said nothing. He stood there, and all of the anger that had coiled inside of him was suddenly gone.

"You know what you need?" Sunny asked, pulling back from him, a smile on her face.

"What's that?" David asked.

"Some kind of big, weird bird dance. That's what."

"You heard about that, did you?" David asked.

He imagined going now. All the locals would've seen the newspaper. All of them would be looking at him and judging.

But then he looked at Sunny's imploring grin. Hell with it.

"Are you going to ask me or what?" she said.

He couldn't help but smile.

"How about it, Doctor Lee? Will you be my date to the Crane Dance?"

"I'd love to," she said.

For a moment, it was possible to imagine that this was all that existed, that the world wasn't circling around them, faster and faster, threatening at any instant to all fly apart.

|||

The cranes circled about the spire in their massive, shifting circuit, calling out in a voice that sounded alien and godlike. The movement created a glimmered reflection on the surface of the giant, which caught also the blue of the sky and so seemed to be made of water, with waves rippling across it.

The man watched this. Not the cranes but the shifting visual of the giant. His skin prickled at a soft breeze, air that was cool but carried just a hint of warmth and brought with it a message: winter was ending, and spring was coming, and all that had died would live again.

It only reinforced what he already knew to be true—a moment of finality was approaching. He had given himself over to the voice inside him in these weeks, allowed it to subsume him, to make its desires his own. But its appetite never shrank, only grew. And it was hungrier than ever.

So this would be it, he supposed. More blood. More death. And then an end, an end to everything.

Overhead the cranes dispersed, done with their midday ritual.

FORTY

The street and sidewalks of Old Town were packed with people, more spilling out beyond the orange plastic barricades. Hundreds of people. Maybe a thousand. Years past, there had barely been enough people to fill half a block. David and Sunny worked their way through the crowd to make it within sight of the stage, where the band had already begun to play. It was a bluesy country group that had moved into town to play the bars. David could never quite remember their name.

Thick smoke rich with the scent of barbecued beef wafted up from a large black grill, and a line extended back, people with plates waiting their turn. Volunteers from the church put hamburger buns on plates, scooped beef onto the buns, spooned out baked beans and slaw. Under a small tent, Vic struggled to keep pace with everyone demanding a beer.

The previous year, no one had invited any of the outsiders, or even told them about the Crane Dance. A few had happened across it and asked David after the fact. This year, the locals had offered tickets all over town. David hadn't figured many would come, but then he'd been wrong plenty before.

It had started fifty-odd years before, when David's grandma and some of the other women around town came up with the idea to hold an event around the cranes, which gathered here so thickly that even then they drew birdwatchers to town. They settled on a dance, a nod to the mating dance of the cranes. Never mind that the birds actually mated while they were in warmer climates far to the south. More than anything, it was an excuse to gather together and drink and dance and forget about the struggles of life. And so it kept on, a tradition that would not die.

David saw Aaliyah and her family through the crowd and led Sunny over. Behind them, David saw Imam Bey and several Muslim families that he recognized from the night of the fire. David introduced Sunny to them.

"Glad you could made it," David said.

"Of course. Thanks for inviting us," Aaliyah's husband said, then turned to his wife. "Come on. When was the last time we danced?"

He pulled her by the hand toward the open area, where couples twirled arm in arm. Their son made an embarrassed look, then wandered off toward friends.

Sunny held her hand out to David.

"Come on, country boy."

He guided her through the steps, their bodies close, torsos scraping as they circled and side-stepped through upbeat numbers, then locked together when the music slowed into melancholic tunes of love gained and lost, of comfort found in empty spaces and full bottles.

As they danced, they bumped into other couples. Aaliyah and her husband. Andrea, out from behind the dispatch desk with her fiancée. Brooke was in uniform, technically on duty, but David insisted she take the time for a few dances with Spady. Someone kept putting beers in David's hands, and he and Sunny drank as they danced.

He searched the crowd for Charlotte but didn't see her.

"I like this," Sunny said.

"Me, too," he said.

As they carved a slow circle, David's eye wandered above the skyline to the west. It was nearly a new moon. The night was dark enough to shroud the giant. There was only a black space in the sky, where stars could not be seen.

The music stopped then. Dale stepped up out of the crowd, moving slowly to the stage. He looked old, David thought. No longer the imposing force that he had always been but an old, tired man.

Dale leaned into the microphone, which squawked. He tried again.

"Good evening, everyone. Thank you for coming tonight," he said, his voice stiff. "It's time now for the crane dance. Good luck finding a partner."

Men all began moving to one side of the street, women to the other. David let go of Sunny's hand.

"What do I do?" she said.

"Don't worry. I'll find you," he said, retreating.

As David neared the far sidewalk, he saw Charlotte. She stood off the street, to the side, observing the dance, not taking part. They exchanged a quick wave, and then the crowds consumed them.

The men and women gathered in great flocks on opposite sides of the street. As they did, David thought of Charlotte and of the way the very structure of this dance—boys and girls, women and men—pushed her away, reminded her that she didn't belong. He wanted to say something to her, but she'd disappeared. He would seek her out later. Not that he knew what it was like to be her, the pain she'd suffered. But he was trying.

The band started in again, pulling David's attention back to the dance. Slow, steady notes plucked on the banjo. Twang. Twang. Twang. Twang.

Among the men, the drunker or braver ones began to pantomime birds, arms cocked and clutched to their sides like wings, heads moving in swift bobs and nods.

Then the fiddler started in, a peppy melody, and the men began to preen and strut, showing off for the women across the street.

Guitar and drums layered on top, and men and women both fanned out, each forming a single line. As the music built, they marched together, in toward the center of the street. The outsiders lagged just behind, following the movements of the locals, who'd traced these steps since they were teenagers.

They came together, almost touching, then fell back as the tune ebbed. This cycle repeated, stepping in on the rhythm, pivoting, parting ways. A hundred people, all moving as one body, undulating in unison.

Finally, the music built and built and then kept going, the tempo hastening as men and women linked arms at the elbow, partners finding each other, circling around, shifting at the down beat, linking opposite arms, twirling the opposite direction, moving so fast they seemed to fly.

David held Sunny tight. The centrifugal force of their movement tore at them, threatened at any moment to rip them apart, fling them opposite directions. David wouldn't let go of her. He couldn't.

The music shifted to a slow tempo. They held each other, swaying. Sunny pushed back just enough to see his face.

"I'm kind of scared. Of this. Of me and you. It . . . It doesn't make sense. But also, I like it."

"Yeah. Me, too," David answered.

The music picked up again to a faster song, and they let the flow of it carry them.

|||

Charlotte watched, laughing, remembering. She'd only been old enough to take part in the dance once, before she ran away the following year. Growing up, she'd always imagined herself being on the women's side of the street. But then she found herself at the dance, pulled with Jason and David and Spady to the men's side, and she had a girl with her as a date, and that girl went across the street, to the place Charlotte knew she belonged, with the women.

When Charlotte lagged behind in the dancing, Jason and Spady had teased her, showing how much of a rookie she was as they pulled her along. The dance had been fun enough, but then the group of them had stolen away down a dark side street, where Jason had beer in his truck, and they'd started drinking, and suddenly her date—she remembered her name suddenly, Meghan—had kissed her.

Charlotte hadn't thought about that kiss in a long time. Now she scanned the crowd, wondering if Meghan was here, if they would recognize each other. Charlotte wanted to see her, to explain, and she also dreaded it. As she told more people, a tangible weight had lifted. But there was another weight that appeared, a counterbalance. She was vulnerable now. She had begun to reveal herself, and word spread quickly among the locals. A few greeted her, and others eyed her warily from a distance, whispering.

She wasn't ready for more of those revelatory talks that everyone expected. Not tonight. And she'd long since understood that the binary nature of the dance left no room for her. As the music hit a crescendo and the bodies flew around each other in the street, she slipped away, unnoticed.

There were streetlights along Main Street, a few of the larger side roads, and of course throughout most of New Town. But Charlotte quickly found herself on an unlit dirt road. She'd walked this way home from school two decades earlier.

Some of the houses and lots had changed so drastically she couldn't remember them at all. Others looked unchanged, and she found herself flooded with memories of the people who lived there, times she'd visited, exploring on their bikes, sneaking out at night, a childhood that seemed to be limitless, without boundaries or restrictions. They had their imaginations and an infinite canvas on which to paint.

As she walked down an alley, she wondered if that was what had pushed her into storytelling as a career. All those years of playing make believe, of creating adventures, pretending they were superheroes. In all the years she'd been away, why had she never remembered that?

It was then that she became aware of a sound behind her. Footsteps on the sandy road that didn't match her own. She turned.

In the dark, she could only just discern the figure, some twenty yards away. A man with his face hidden beneath a hood.

For a few long seconds they stood, silent, each staring. Then he came toward her. He moved slowly. Patient, calculated steps.

Just as she was about to speak to him, she saw what he held in his hand. A blade, narrow and long and curved.

Charlotte's hand dove into her bag, fingers searching through keys, her phone, tissues, makeup, a cylinder of lip gloss, searching for the tube of pepper spray. *Where?*

In the distance, the music thrummed, a jangly number, all guitar and drums.

Charlotte had no hope that anyone would hear her.

Still, as the dark figure took another step forward, she screamed.

FORTY-ONE

The music slowed. David and Sunny broke from the dance area and made for the picnic tables set out in the open lawn in front of the old courthouse.

Someone finally had taken the police tape down from around the building. Yet Jason's window remained boarded over, as it had since after he was killed. No one had yet begun to talk about what to do with the structure, now that it was empty. As much as the stone up the hill south of town, the brick edifice was Jason's grave marker.

David surveyed the crowd for Charlotte. He was hoping she'd stay. So much of the family was dead to him now. Or just dead. Ben Senior and Bonnie lost in their paranoia. Dale lost in his greed. Samuel lost in dementia. The rest in the ground.

As they stepped onto the lawn, David saw old Henry Smoke sitting atop a table, a cigarette in his hand. They sat beside him.

"Who's your crane?" Henry asked.

"My crane? Oh. This is Sunny," David said. "Sunny, this is Henry."

"Pleasure to meet you," she started to say.

Whatever she said after that was lost in a boom that echoed in the sky.

The music stopped all at once, and the electricity of the crowd dulled to murmuring voices.

"Was that . . . ?" Sunny started to ask.

"Gun shot," David said, already on his feet.

|||

Charlotte had run, and the man had come after her, and—damn her stupid shoes—he was gaining on her when she heard the yelled warning.

"Stop!"

She froze as she looked to her side and saw Brooke, with her shoulders squared and gun drawn, pointed at her. No. Not at her. At him.

The man with the knife stopped, too, but only for a moment. Then he lifted the blade. There was only a foot or two between them.

And then the sky exploded with thunder—*BOOM BOOM*—and the man staggered, and a hiss of air rushed through his lips.

But he didn't drop.

He ran, darting behind a garage, into hard shadow. By the time Brooke reached it, there was no sign of him. She looked at the woman and only then discovered it was Charlotte. She wasn't hurt. Thank Christ, she wasn't hurt.

"Stay with me," Charlotte said, her voice barely audible. "Please."

"I'm here," Brooke said.

Holding close together, they backed into the open space of the street.

Footsteps.

David sprinted toward them.

"Charlotte!" he yelled, seeing her.

"I'm okay," she said.

"Was it . . . ?" he asked.

Brooke nodded.

"That way."

She pointed with her gun at the shed.

David ran ahead. It was only once he'd crossed into the shadows that he remembered he hadn't worn his gun. His hands were empty.

Nobody in Old Town had fences in their yards. One lot spilled into the next. Rickety houses. Clothes lines strung between trees. Piles of firewood. He knew this land. Knew this town like the contours of his skin. The killer wouldn't, he figured. Maybe it was enough to catch him.

He took slow, careful steps. The dance remained quiet, aside from a few faint voices. There was no wind. The night was silent.

David worked his way forward, keeping tight to shadows, along the edges of houses and sheds, along a row of small cedar trees.

He stopped and crouched. Inhaled deeply and held it. Listened.

Nothing. Nothing. Nothing. There.

The crunch of dry leaves. Just ahead. Maybe twenty feet, in the adjoining lot. Beside a motorboat, covered with a tarp, up on a trailer. David leaned out and strained to focus in the gloom. Was that the outline of a man?

It moved, the shape, and there was another sound of feet falling on leaves.

David searched about him for anything he could use as a weapon, but there was nothing. Across the yard he saw firewood, piled almost head high. Good cover.

His knee griped at him. He ignored it as he tensed his legs.

One, he counted in his head. *Two. Three.*

He charged forward out of a football stance toward the boat, fists up. As he came to the logs, the whole pile shifted suddenly, like it was caught in a wave, one that crashed against David, the weight of the wood slamming him back, thrusting him to the ground.

The shadow lingered a moment. The same shadow. The one that had haunted him since that night in the courthouse. It took a half step forward, toward him, the blade ready.

Then it ran away, melting again into other shadows in the night.

David shoved the logs free from his chest, righted himself, and sprinted on, chasing.

The man moved impossibly fast. He curled tight around a house, ducked between it and a shed, vaulted over the hood of a parked car.

David lost more and more ground with every step he took until, after what hadn't even been a minute, the man was gone. In the distance, he heard sirens. He walked back toward Brooke and Charlotte.

They were sitting on a curb behind the old courthouse. Conover and Priest were there, impossibly, with a fleet of black sedans parked at a harsh angle, the doors still open. The sirens grew louder.

There was a crowd by Main Street, but they hung back. David saw Sunny there. He gave a quick wave. *I'm okay. Come over.*

"Anything?" Priest asked.

David shook his head.

"Saw him. He was fast. Too fast."

"You see enough to get a description?" Conover pushed him.

"Too dark. They're okay?" David asked.

He nodded to Charlotte and Brooke, who sat beside each other. Brooke held Charlotte's shaking hands in hers.

"Your deputy did good work. Heard screaming. Saw the attack as it was starting. She hit him, she says. Heck of a shot from that distance, if she did," Priest said.

"Charlotte?" David asked.

"She wasn't able to say anything yet. You might want to try."

David settled onto the curb beside his cousin.

"Charlotte. God. I'm so glad you're okay."

She was crying. Little choking sobs.

"He didn't hurt you?" David asked softly.

She shook her head.

"Cousin, I'm sorry to have to ask you this. I am. But I have to, so we can stop him. Did you see him? Do you think you can describe him?"

Charlotte looked at him. Her eyes were opened so wide the white showed all around.

"Why me, David? Why does he want to kill me?"

She didn't say anything more, just sat there and gently shook her head back and forth, rocking.

Brooke gave David a knowing look. She understood now. Understood the weight of what he'd carried all this time. Understood the extremity of danger facing all of them. The weight of it pulled down at her shoulders, heavier than gravity.

"I hit him," Brooke said. "I know I hit him."

"I know," David said. "He could be wearing a bulletproof vest, or . . ."

He let the sentence die in the air. He didn't know what other explanation there could possibly be.

"God," Charlotte said.

David looked over to Brooke.

"You didn't get a good look at him?" he asked.

She stared emptily back.

"Brooke," he said, snapping her back to attention.

"What?" she asked.

"The killer. You didn't see him?"

"No. I don't know."

Priest was looking around them, at all the eyes peering at them as an ambulance and a state police cruiser raced toward them.

"Okay, this is enough. We need all of you in a secure location," she said, recovering her assertiveness. "Everyone in the car. Now."

|||

They spent the night at the new courthouse. They put Charlotte and Brooke in different holding rooms and asked them to recount their stories again and again. Sunny checked to see if either had any traces of the spire on them, but both were clean.

David watched through one-way glass. Charlotte kept stopping, seizing up in crying fits, then apologizing. David so badly wanted to go and hug her and provide whatever comfort he could. But more than that, his anger boiled over into a rage that surprised him with its intensity. Every bit of his skin felt as if it had been pricked with pins. His heart charged inside his chest. This was it. This was the last time that son of a bitch hurt someone.

"Why would anyone want you dead?" Priest asked Charlotte, as curt as ever.

"I don't know," Charlotte whispered. "I don't know."

In the other room, Brooke looked as if she'd seen a ghost, and it had scared her into a catatonic state. She showed no fear or sadness. She sat there, her face seeming especially pale, and stared straight ahead.

It was nearly dawn by the time they finally let Brooke out of the room. David waited for her as she came out.

"You did good," David said. "You saved her life."

Brooke said nothing.

"I called Spady," he continued. "I told him you're okay. That there was a shooting, you'd have to work late. He was worried, but he knows you're okay."

She nodded.

"Thanks."

"You can't tell him, Brooke," David said. "You understand what's at stake, right? You can't tell anyone."

She nodded again, then she left for home.

Priest said they would take Charlotte back to her hotel and watch over her. David drove behind them, Sunny riding along, then David followed inside, hugging Charlotte as tightly as he could before watching her step into the elevator and disappear.

David drove them toward his apartment but turned at the last moment, pulling onto a dirt road that ran down to the river. Sunny didn't question him. As he stepped out of the truck, she followed.

To the east, where the sky remained open, unbroken by the giant or anything else, the sky exploded in pink and indigo that traced the wispy clouds like watercolor seeping across paper as the sun mounted its first attack against the night.

David led the way through thick brush down close to the river. In the shallow water, cranes stood in great bunches, thousands of them, just beginning to rouse with tentative calls. This was where his parents had brought him when he was little, to this exact spot, a place no one else knew existed.

They stood there, watching, and as Sunny leaned against David, he wrapped her in his arms.

The sun rose, a sliver of fire breaking the plane of the horizon.

The cranes grew louder. In ones and twos, then all at once, they beat their wings and pulled themselves into the sky, flying so close overhead that David and Sunny could hear the soft whap-whap-whap of wing against wind. They moved not as single birds but as one great body, each linked with the other, so that as one dipped or soared or turned, all did the same, effortlessly, etching a grand pattern overhead.

"Oh," Sunny said.

It broke the spell of the long quiet, and David startled, looking down at her. She still studied the birds.

"Oh what?"

"I think I understand."

"Understand what?"

She looked at him. She was smiling. In spite of everything, she was smiling.

"I think I know how Gulliver works."

FORTY-TWO

Sunny didn't say another word after that. She walked hurriedly back to David's truck, climbed inside, took the notebook and pen that he kept in the glove compartment, and began to write.

As he took his place in the driver's seat, David glanced down at the notes that she carved with quick strikes onto the paper, but he could make nothing of the jumble of words and numbers and diagrams that filled one page then spilled onto another and another.

He drove them to the Countryman Building in silence, and she continued in her focused work as they rode in an unmarked van to Site One. David had seen her like this before, when she had an idea in her head that needed working, the way her eyes would focus, her brow furrowing just a little. She could go hours this way, tackling whatever problem sat in front of her, speaking only to herself, muttering as she jogged her memory for names of researchers, journal articles she thought she remembered reading. She would cycle through names. *Henderson? Anderson?* Then go back to scribbling.

A couple of times, David had asked her a question, but she waved him off, as if swatting away an insect. She showed no sign of annoyance, only intense focus. He'd learned to give her the space, to return later once she'd burned out the charge of energy or run headlong into a dead end.

David had no company but his own thoughts as they rode to Site One, unable to see anything through the front windshield of the van except for the giant's massive head, growing ever larger as they neared. The anger that had formed inside of him had abated only slightly, and his mind imagined scenarios in which Brooke hadn't heard Charlotte scream.

David left Sunny at Building Seventeen, then he went to the cafeteria and returned, depositing food and coffee beside her. She took the coffee without a word. She had moved on to other notebooks, and a table of calculations sprawled in front of her. He knew he needed to stay with her, even though she didn't need his help. Perhaps deep down he thought he was protecting her. Not from the killer but from the threat of her own knowledge. Because he knew what it would mean if she had found the thing she said she had found.

The secret to the giant.

David retreated into his office. He looked at the web of victims. Webs, really, disconnected as they were. When he closed his eyes, he imagined a photo of Charlotte up there with the others. Her body, dead and naked, sliced apart. He shook off the vision. It would've happened, if not for Brooke. If she hadn't come upon them, David would have one more relative to mourn, another failure. Another death for the newspaper and the whole town to hang around his neck. And they'd be right.

He took a drink of coffee and clenched his bandaged left hand. A shockwave of pain shot up his arm, snapping him from his pitying. He was still the sheriff. He had a case to work, and now there was something new. One more piece of evidence.

He took a sheet of paper and wrote "Charlotte" on it, taped it to the wall. Then he took the marker and thought.

The first line was obvious. She and Jason were cousins. Maybe the killer had targeted David and ended up killing Erickson instead. Still, then, it didn't explain the others.

He sat and leaned back in his chair. God, he was tired. Maybe it really was just that Charlotte was a public figure, the first reporter to reveal the killer's existence. Maybe her connection to Jason was random.

David closed his eyes. All at once, he was no longer in Building Seventeen but at Grandpa Samuel's dining room table, with his grandpa right there across from him.

"Why her? Why Charlotte?" he asked.

His grandpa opened his mouth and spoke.

"Not everything makes sense, David."

David opened his eyes. He was leaned forward on the table, his head in his arms. He looked up to see Sunny standing beside him. Had she said his name?

He wiped a hand at his mouth, crusty with dried drool. He looked at the clock.

"Is that a.m.?" he asked.

"It's p.m. You were snoring."

"Hnh. Sorry."

"It was cute. You seemed like you were dreaming."

He nodded. "Just talking to an old man."

She asked nothing more as she put her hands on his shoulders, kneading the muscles.

"You're done with your work, then?" he asked.

She looked from side to side, a visual reminder that they were observed.

"Yeah. I'm done."

She went back through the conference room to her office, and he followed. She seemed rested, though he had no idea if she'd slept. At some point, she'd gotten a fresh coffee.

She'd written notes in dry-erase marker all over the glass walls that formed the enclosed chamber at the center of the room. She pointed to them as she began to explain.

"Flocking. That's what made me think of it. The way that the cranes fly. They go into formation, and then as they fly, the wind will hit or they'll change direction. But they always stay in formation, keeping the same relative distances."

She had drawn a formation of dots and then lines denoting movement. David struggled to keep up, shaking loose from sleep.

"Okay. You're doing a good job so far of keeping it at my level."

"Right. So, anyway, birds aren't the only animals that do this. Ants in a colony. Bees in a hive."

"Schools of fish," David offered, uncertain.

"Exactly," she said. "There was this line of thinking by early scientists that it was some kind of hidden force connecting the animals. Telepathy, some said. There was another school of thought called self-organization. Basically, each bird has a sort of master plan imprinted on it from the moment it's born."

"Each bird already knows exactly how every other bird will move?" David asked. "How does that work?"

"Well, it never really went anywhere," she said. "It was tied up in this quasi-religious stuff. Teleology. That whatever message was imprinted onto species, it had been placed there by God. His plan, I guess you'd say."

"And scientists weren't too keen on that, I reckon."

"They weren't. So it went into the dustbin."

David sat. He wasn't quite yet ready to be vertical.

"I can't imagine you're going to tell me you think God is the one pulling Gulliver's strings."

Sunny smiled.

"I'll believe in that, just as soon as I can prove it. Anyway, it struck me, watching the birds, how it's the same problem as the particles of the giant's body. They all seem to be fully independent, and yet they move in sync with each other. Like they're flocking."

"The dogs, too," David said. "Barking in unison."

"Exactly."

"Okay. It isn't God. It isn't telepathy. What is it?" he asked.

"I don't know yet. I haven't even begun to think of how to design the tests, much less run them. I think the most promising thing is this article I found on termites."

"Termites?"

She nodded.

"Individual termites have almost no brain mass at all. And yet as a group, they build these incredible mounds out of dirt and clay. They can be ten, twenty feet tall, with dozens of chambers to regulate air flow and control water. You put a group of termites together, and they just go to work, building, knowing exactly what to do."

David stretched the stiffness from his arms and legs.

"You think something built the giant?" he asked.

"No. I think we've been looking too big. We've assumed all along that the crystals, the pieces of the giant, were communicating with each other some way. That they were giving off energy. But we couldn't detect any energy coming off of it. But what if they don't communicate? What if each crystal contains all of the information it needs to form the giant?"

David stared off, picturing that small pile of sugar crystals that Sunny had formed into the figure of a man.

"If that's the case, they could have some kind of—I'm just white-walling—some kind of internal gravitational force. Just enough to move, to assemble."

She gestured emphatically at calculations she had scribbled on the glass, as if he could begin to comprehend them.

"This is it," she said. "It has to be. Each discrete element has to function on its own. They also have to know the whole plan. They have to contain the vision of the whole. But the only way to understand the whole thing is to first break down one separate component."

She trailed off.

The image kept turning in David's mind—a table covered with sand. A million grains. An infinity. An impossible amount. The grains swirling, rising, taking form, one by one, creating a shape from chaos.

Then David started to remember something, a little phrase, something he hadn't thought of in years.

"The words come first, then the sentence," he said.

Sunny stared at him.

"What's that?"

"The words come first, then the sentence," he repeated, as much for himself as for her. "It was this little thing my grandma would say when she was teaching me to write poetry. She told me I was always too busy thinking about the sentence, about what I wanted to say. I didn't spend enough time on the words, on each one's meaning. Start there, she'd tell me, then the whole will take shape from it."

"Huh," Sunny said. "I suppose it is like that."

But David wasn't looking at her or her notes. He had turned toward the door.

"The words come first," David said, standing.

He walked out, back across to his office. He stood and faced the wall of disparate webs. Sunny followed a couple of steps behind.

"What is it?" she asked.

"This whole time, I've been looking for one motive. One thing that could tie all the murders together. But what if there isn't any one motive? What if it's like the giant?"

Sunny exhaled, thinking.

"You're saying, understand the individual pieces first, then understand the whole?"

David nodded.

"Okay," she said. "What are the basics of each case?"

David started to the far left, at the first picture.

"Jim Holly. Tourist guide and helicopter pilot. He was an outsider who flew over the giant. No enemies, but there are people who hate the helicopters flying around all the time."

He moved to the next.

"Kapoor, the realtor. Another outsider. He was pretty aggressive about trying to push locals to sell property."

He moved to the next photo.

"Jason. Tied up in real estate. He was a local, but he was helping outsiders buy land."

"He was killed right after he voted to approve the mosque," Sunny said.

"You're right," David said. "Amid everything, I forgot that from the meeting he was killed . . ."

He rifled through some documents.

". . . one day later," he finished the thought.

"There were a lot of pissed off people at that meeting," Sunny said.

"My people. Locals." He said it for her.

David replayed it in his head. All the screaming voices. Protesters reaching over the barricades outside.

He moved to the next photos. The two drug dealers.

"The two guys who were tied up with narcotics. It came right after I made that bust."

Next was Erickson.

"Erickson was part of the case. Maybe he was close to the truth . . ."

"That night at the wake, you remember he was in the bar and they got into some kind of argument, right?" Sunny asked.

David searched his scattered memories. He could see glimpses of it.

"Your one-armed friend knew he was an outsider. He was pissed that he was in there for the wake," she continued. "He and some other people started yelling at Erickson."

"Oh, right," he said, trying to summon the memory through his haze of drunkenness from that night. "Then Jimmy, a local but one who was tied up with the cult, with outsiders."

Something was nagging at David. Something he should be seeing on the wall but couldn't. A tangible void. A feeling in the pit of his stomach that he knew the truth but wouldn't allow himself to confront it.

"And then last night," Sunny said, moving in front of the sheet with Charlotte's name. "Another outsider."

"Sort of," David said. "The killer had been communicating with her. Stalking her. All of the murders, the way the killer attacked each victim, it feels so . . ."

"Personal," Sunny finished his thought.

David's mind went back to Jason. That was the key. He'd known this all along. There was something about it. As if he knew already who killed his cousin, as if he had always known. He replayed the night of the village council meeting through his thoughts. The furor of the meeting. Grabbing Spady. The angry crowd outside. And then he and Jason and Spady standing out on the football field, Spady blowing smoke into Jason's face and calling him a traitor.

David saw it then. The thing missing from the wall. The empty space that fit perfectly into each snowflake, binding them as one.

"Oh, Christ," he said.

The panic seized his throat. It was cool in the room, but he was sweating.

"I have to get to my phone."

FORTY-THREE

The small house sat at the end of a dirt lane on the line between acre-ages. It was painted canary yellow, a color Brooke had picked out after she and Spady bought the place.

David's truck fishtailed in the sandy tracks as he sped down the lane. He'd been calling her ever since he got to his phone, but each time, it would ring and ring and ring and then go to voicemail.

The house sat in a ring of cedars, each about ten feet tall, their dark-green branches rusty, laden with reddish pollen. He slowed as he rounded the trees, pulling into the driveway. Both vehicles were there. Spady's old car. Brooke's truck.

He forced himself to breathe, to calm himself. He needed to go inside and act like everything was fine. Just some follow-up with the incident from last night. He needed to take Brooke outside to talk through the shooting—to get her away from the house. Away from him. Still, David hoped it wasn't true. He would do his job, investigate the lead, find a way to clear Spady's name, then keep hunting.

As he walked up the sidewalk, he couldn't stop thinking about it. The shadow. The silhouette. Both times he'd seen it, it had two arms. The killer had two arms.

David knocked and waited.

No answer.

He knocked again. Louder. Then he called out their names.

No answer.

He forced another deep breath, then drew his gun. His bandaged hand ached at the weight of it. He ignored the pain and walked around the house, past the bench seat where he and Spady had sat and drank beers.

The back door was wide open. David stepped through into the silence of the house.

On the tile floor, he saw it. A bare footprint, heading toward the door, out of the house. A footprint stamped in blood.

More footprints, leading from the kitchen. David followed them, scanning the house. At the edge of the kitchen, a ceramic bowl lay shattered on the counter. Around it, spatters and handprints of blood covered the surface.

David almost stepped on her pistol as he came around the counter. It rested on the floor just out of the grasp of her outstretched, motionless hand.

He thought she was dead, but then Brooke's eyes moved. He kneeled beside her, cradling her head. As he lifted her, blood pooled out across the white linoleum.

"Brooke! Stay with me. You're going to be okay."

"David."

Her voice was a halting whisper. Just below her right breast, her shirt was cut cleanly. Beneath it, David saw a deep wound. He set down his gun and put his hands on the cut and leaned, applying as much pressure as he could. She didn't even grimace. Her eyes looked like wet marbles. She was in shock, beyond pain.

"Hold on, Brooke. Hold on."

He lifted a bloody hand and pulled free his phone, then dialed Andrea. He'd already called Priest from the truck. His fingers slipped over the numbers, blood smearing across the screen.

"Andrea! Brooke's house! Send an ambulance! Now!"

He dropped the phone, leaving the line open. Now he used both hands to keep up the pressure while he looked over her body for other wounds. A small cut had started near her left armpit, but it ended only a few inches down.

"He stopped," Brooke whispered.

"Quiet. Save your energy, okay?"

She looked up, and some of her life suddenly reappeared, her eyes wide and blue and beautiful. Then she started to talk, her voice clearer but still faltering.

"He said he had to do it. The thing. It's making him. But he couldn't . . . Not to . . ." she choked.

David kept up the pressure. Blood seeped up, over his fingers. He couldn't feel her lungs rise and fall, could just barely feel her heart as it labored to keep pumping, the pace slackening.

"I'm sorry," she said, her voice weakening. Whatever strength she had summoned was fading.

"No," he whispered. "No."

"I knew. Last night. I saw him. I knew. I think I knew before that." Her voice became a whisper.

"I didn't want . . . I tried to talk to him. I tried."

David willed the ambulance to move faster. Where was it?

Brooke glanced over, at her gun.

"I couldn't shoot him. David, I'm . . ."

She said nothing else.

David held her for a time that felt like days. Finally, he let her go. It wasn't done. He picked up his gun and stood. There, in front of him, were the footprints, leading outside. Now it was time to follow them. To end this.

Outside, the footprints quickly grew fainter, but they led unerringly north, into the row of cedars, where they disappeared among the scrub brush.

David didn't need the tracks; he knew where Spady was going.

David went back to his truck. He tucked the pistol into his waistband, took his shotgun from the rack in the rear window, and loaded eight shells.

He resumed the trail, holding the gun in his right hand, barrel resting across his left forearm. Ready to fire in a flash, just the way his dad had taught him when they'd gone out to walk the fields, to hunt pheasants and quail.

A sudden gust of wind shook the cedars and freed them of their pollen, which came off in ghostlike sheets that held in the air, danced, and disappeared.

Spady never said it, but David knew Spady had wanted to buy this piece of land because of where it sat. Just down from the place where they'd spent so much time playing as children, the place that had been a refuge for the four of them: Jason, David, Ben Junior, and Spady.

It sat right beside David's parents' farm.

He crossed carefully over a half-collapsed barbed wire fence, never taking his eyes from the terrain ahead. He hadn't stepped foot on this land since that day, all those years ago, when the sky opened, and death came for them.

He walked through rows of massive cottonwood trees that had rotted and fallen, lying haphazardly like the ancient columns of some once-great city. The bark had mostly sloughed off, and their trunks were bleached as white as bone.

Somewhere behind him, sirens shrieked.

Too far away to help Brooke. Or anyone else.

David came into a clearing. The years had changed it, but he knew instantly the landmarks. And there was the house. No longer a structure but a pile of broken lumber, grown over with vine and weed. A chill raced along the scar on his back.

"You haven't been back, have you?"

The voice came from beside the house, by a little shed that had somehow gone untouched in the storm, though it now looked rotted enough that a gentle push could topple it.

Spady.

He wore a T-shirt and jeans but no socks or shoes. His clothes were streaked and splotched with blood.

"After we bought the place, I started walking over. I know you don't like it. Me? I find it pretty peaceful. It was actually just over that way," he pointed to the east, "that I found it."

David's hand gripped the shotgun.

"Found what?"

Spady grinned.

"Oh, I think you know."

David lifted the gun just slightly, keeping distance between them.

"She's dead," David said.

Spady's head jerked to the side. Then back.

"Goddammit, David. I didn't mean—I didn't want this. I didn't want to hurt her. It . . . it's this thing. This thing in me."

Beyond Spady, the sun settled over the giant's supine torso, casting the spire in a brilliant red glare.

"What? What made you kill your wife? Kill Jason? Kill all those people?"

David's voice was growing louder.

Spady didn't answer. Not with words.

His arm began to tremble, the one that ended just below the elbow. The stump of it seemed to pulse, like a squid straining to push out eggs.

The skin began to stretch, unfurl. Something black trickled out, like liquid mercury. Only it didn't drip. It grew upon itself, longer and longer.

An arm, emerging from the wound. Only in the place where the hand should have been, the dark, metallic substance thinned and stretched farther, sharpening into a form that David recognized from the night that Jason died.

A blade, long and curved.

FORTY-FOUR

"Don't," David said as he brought the shotgun up with both hands, nestling the stock in his armpit.

This close, he had Spady dead to rights. But Jason had had a shotgun that night at the courthouse, and one shot must've hit Spady. Somehow, Spady survived it unscathed.

Spady held his ground. He seemed to be sweating, his body almost vibrating. His lips curled into a smile.

"It found me," Spady said.

He lifted up the arm, which held solid as it cut the air. Behind him, David saw the spire rising up above the giant.

"This was its gift to me. It gave me my arm back."

The blade straightened then, like a broadsword. Its shape echoed that of the spire. Except where the spire broke off high up in the air, the blade continued to a thin point.

"I can get you help," David said.

It was a line from his training, muscle memory kicking in.

Spady laughed. His skin had paled enough that a map of veins and arteries was visible beneath it.

"You help me? You still don't see it, David. All this time. What I've been doing. I've tried to help you."

He swished the blade through the air, and it curved again, into a cutlass shape, as if by magic. He took a step forward, and David steadied, checking his aim. His finger moved inside the trigger guard. Keep him talking. Keep distance. David took a half step back.

"Help me how, Spady?"

"This is our home. Our land. All those sons of bitches . . ."

He waved the blade out, toward the city that now sprawled around them.

". . . they're invaders. An infection. Trying to take what's ours away from us. You see it, too. I know you do. But you have your hands tied. You have that badge, just like Brooke. It keeps you from doing what needs done."

Spady took another step.

"That fucking pilot, always buzzing his helicopter low right over our house. I didn't know I was going to kill him at first. I just went to tell him to stop. Then . . . The next time I knew what I was doing. The guy who kept calling us, telling us to sell our place, he wouldn't stop pestering. I could feel it. This was what needed done. To fight back. I thought you would see, when you couldn't do anything about those drug dealers, I went and did it for you. I helped you."

David's skin crawled. All along, Spady had been following him. Watching him. Learning from Brooke what they were doing.

"What about Jason? And Jimmy?" David challenged. "They weren't outsiders. And Charlotte, she's basically family."

Spady took another step.

"Jason betrayed us. He sided with those fucking rag heads. Once Brooke told me Jimmy was in the cult, I knew he'd chosen the other side. And Charlotte . . . She's a monster. All of us face a choice, David. Our side or theirs. How about you?"

Another step.

"You cut them to pieces. The FBI agent—his name was Erickson—he was a good man. He was trying to help us."

Spady smirked, proud.

"You don't get it. They're *all* bad. All the outsiders. All this time, I kept hoping you would see the pattern I made for you. The warning to the world, to leave us the fuck alone. I was doing your job for you."

"Don't fucking say that!"

David's finger tightened on the trigger, but he stopped himself from firing. This was his best friend in the world standing across from him.

Spady pointed the blade toward the giant.

"It's that thing. Don't you see it? He's poisoning us. Trying to turn this town into all the other cities out there, dirty and ugly and infested. It's all his goddamned fault!"

Another step.

David held his ground.

"No. You don't get to pass this off. All this blood, it's on you."

Spady's smile vanished.

"That's how you always saw it, David. Everyone makes their own fate. Work hard, keep your nose clean, things will work out. Awful goddammed easy when you grow up with everything."

"My parents died."

"Yeah. Well, my parents did something even worse. They stayed alive."

The sun had lowered behind Spady. David angled to the side, stepping slow, trying to keep a clean line of sight.

"But the spire, David, that will be our savior," Spady said. "It showed me. Oh, David, it showed me things you can't begin to imagine. There's a void out there, calling for us. You can't imagine, the sound of a black hole."

Spady licked at his lips.

"We have a destiny, and that's it. That's what the spire wants to show all of us. Except that goddammed giant went and got in the way. But now it knows, David. It knows all about us."

Spady stepped forward again. Only twenty yards separated them.

"You think it was destiny that made you kill your wife?" David spat.

"I saved her! I saved her from this fucking misery!"

Another step.

David searched for something to say, something to forestall the inevitable. Then he remembered . . .

"Spady, what do you dream about, when you dream?" David asked.

Spady froze. His mouth began to twitch.

"I . . . I dream of cutting. Of piercing through. Everything. You. Everyone. The world. The giant. I need to stab. To pierce. And pierce. And pierce. And pierce. Pierce. Pierce. Pierce. Pierce."

David inched closer. He'd put handcuffs in a side pocket, if Spady would stay still . . .

David took another step. And another. Still, Spady muttered. He was almost to him . . .

All at once, Spady's head snapped back around, and he leapt forward. David fired.

Thunder.

Spady fell.

And then, haltingly, he stood.

Spady's shirt had shredded to almost nothing. Through it, his abdomen was red and peppered with black circles. But no blood. It looked as if he'd been battered, bruises forming. Bruises that moved beneath his skin.

Then David noticed Spady's right arm.

The blade had shrunk, maybe six inches, receded back into his body. As the bruises dissipated, the blade stretched out again, as long as it had been before. On Spady's abdomen, there was no sign of damage.

"Jesus," David muttered.

Spady laughed at that.

Then he lunged forward again.

David squeezed off another round, but his aim went low.

The shot struck Spady in his left leg.

He twisted at the hip but held his footing.

Still Spady came, impossibly fast.

He swung the bladed arm.

The shotgun went light in David's hands. The front half of it sloughed off, sliced cleanly through, just where the barrel met the chamber.

Spady was on top of him, blade raised.

David racked another shell and pulled the trigger, praying for the gun to fire.

It did.

The remainder of the barrel ripped apart as the shell erupted out, into Spady's shoulder, driving him back, pushing the blade sideways.

The blade raked along David's left arm.

David dropped the destroyed gun and ran.

He had hurdled an overgrown hedge and circled the destroyed house when suddenly his arm burned along the cut, so badly he bit his lip to keep from screaming. He turned into a row of cedars, the thick foliage offering some cover.

He stopped once, listening.

Nothing.

He kept moving, dried pine needles crackling underfoot.

The same tree row where the four of them had played army as kids, using sticks for guns. Now, David drew his pistol, steadying it with both hands.

The sleeve on his left arm had been ripped through from his shoulder to his elbow. Blood ran over his forearm onto his left hand, which trembled.

He kept moving.

There was no plan to his action. No thought. No destination. All he had left was instinct, some primordial mix of training and memories.

Tree to tree. Move. Stop. Wait. Listen.

Only the sound of sirens, still far off.

Then, a sound he recognized, though it had been long since he'd heard it.

Water. He was coming up on the creek.

He came out of the cedars into a low stretch of land, the ground spongy beneath him, sucking against his boots with each step.

The stream cut through ahead, some thirty feet across. And right beside it, the tree.

A massive cottonwood that had split ten feet up from the ground into thick branches that held the treehouse. The one the four of them had made.

Some boards had rotted and fallen to the ground, rusty nails jutting up from them. The structure hung crazily to the side, barely clinging to the tree, as if a breeze might blow it down. David stepped beneath it as he spun around, scanning everywhere for a sign of Spady. He brushed against the old rope ladder, frayed but somehow still intact.

Just then, at the edge of the clearing, a rustle, and a tree fell over, cleaved in half.

Through the sudden opening walked Spady, not even attempting to hide. He held the blade in front of him, pointed dead ahead.

"A lot of fun, up there," Spady said, as if all was normal.

Then his face contorted, and it looked as if none of what made him human remained.

David backed up and felt the rope ladder. He coiled his left arm through it, steadying. His skin screamed where the blade had cut him.

"Spady. We don't have to do this."

It was too late. Spady came at him, charging with the blade lowered like a spear.

David jumped, then he pulled down with all his weight on the rope.

The treehouse groaned, then it gave a crack, unmooring from the branch.

The sound startled Spady, just enough for David to step to the side as the weathered boards came free like a calving glacier.

The treehouse rained down onto Spady, driving him into the ground, his yell swallowed by the roar of the impact.

And then silence.

Dust held in the twilit air.

David stepped back, never taking his gunsight from the debris.

The boards shifted. Then they rose. Then they fell away.

Spady stood.

The blade had shortened again. Black splotches covered Spady's skin. Nails stuck out of his shoulder. A broken shard of board had stabbed into his side. He grunted and pulled it free with his human arm.

"David," said Spady. "Don't be scared."

David returned his left hand to the gun. His arms refused to stay steady.

Spady's eyes widened and turned dark. Around his body, the ink swirling beneath his skin congealed and traced its way back to the stump of his right arm. It looked like leeches swimming through his veins.

It massed there at the stump, and the curved blade grew out again.

"You can't stop it," Spady said. "You can't stop death."

Spady charged again.

David backed toward the stream as he aimed and fired.

Bullet after bullet struck Spady's torso.

The blackness inside him raced to each wound. The blade shortened.

Spady staggered with each shot, but still he kept on.

David pulled the trigger again and again, counting. Five. Six. Seven. He was to the creek. There was nowhere else to go.

Spady slashed his right arm at David.

It cut the air and nothing else.

The blade was only a few inches long, so much of the dark matter receding, crystals hurtling through his body, rushing to protect it from damage.

They stood close enough to touch.

David and Spady looked at each other. In that moment, Spady's eyes were clear. He seemed tired, sad, lost. Trapped by tragedy.

"I'm sorry," David said.

"Me, too," Spady said.

Spady lunged with the point of his arm.

David lifted his pistol and fired.

The bullet tore through Spady's left eye and exploded through the back of his head.

The body stood, wobbling but balanced.

Beneath the skin, the dark substance raced into his face, pooling in the wound.

Then, all at once, the black liquid gushed out from his nose and mouth and eyes, pouring down his chest.

Spady fell forward then, his body stiff and ashen, as if already drained of blood. The top half of him landed in the stream with a splash.

The water lapped at the body, and the blackness oozed away. David could see it there, a dark cloud in the stream. And then it was gone.

What was left of Spady's face rested just under water, his right eye staring up as the stream's current nudged against him, too weak to wash him away.

FORTY-FIVE

They came on all at once, Priest and Conover and a fleet of Humvees and soldiers pointing guns and barking commands and an ambulance that was too late to do anything except sit at the end of a dirt lane and wail into the sky.

"It was him," Priest said, looking down into the creek at Spady's body. The words were more a question than a statement. Both seeking a confirmation that this was the killer but also questioning that reality, which seemed impossible. Spady was nobody. Some angry redneck— probably an alcoholic—with only one arm.

It was him.

Ever since that night that Jason died and David went for the first time to Site One, seeing behind the curtain, he imagined this moment. The killer dead or locked away and life progressing again. He'd held that satisfaction and justice in his mind's eye, keeping it in view as motivation for all those times he'd wanted to give up amid the pain and horror. And now . . .

There was no satisfaction. No celebration. It was him. It was David's friend. The person closest to him. A person he should have questioned from the beginning. Instead, they drank beers together, shot the shit, went along as if all was normal. He'd refused to think a local could do something so ugly, and now Brooke was dead, her and all the others.

Conover saw the wound on David's arm, and all at once soldiers were guiding him into a Humvee, where he sat in the back, no one touching him. They drove him to Site One, and Priest and Conover hurried him to Building Seventeen, where Sunny waited, still awake. And as David's eyes met hers, he saw both relief that she was seeing him alive and also recognition that something terrible had happened.

Sunny examined David, and they never told him what she saw—just whisked him off to some new part of the base where he was forced into a shower and stripped and scrubbed, particularly on the wound on his arm, which they attacked with soap and a bristly brush that stung like hell. Then he was dressed in white medical scrubs and put in a room with nothing but a bed and a toilet, with walls and floor and ceiling all in white, so that it felt like a prison cell in heaven.

He sat for unknown hours and watched again and again as his mind played the vision of Spady's head exploding.

If he slept, he didn't remember it. Then a soldier came for him and led him back to the conference room in Building Seventeen, where Priest and Conover and Sunny sat, waiting, and he assumed that whatever bits of the spire might have gotten into his blood, they weren't enough to make him psychotic.

David sat. Conover put his arms on the table and pushed his fingertips together.

"It's over," he said. "I . . . I know you're going through a lot. I just want to discuss . . ."

"We need to know you'll keep your mouth shut," Priest completed the thought. "No loose ends."

David gave her a look that came across clearly enough for him to not need to use any words.

"We appreciate all you've done, sheriff," Conover said. "We've already told the media. The killer is dead. You're the hero. Everyone wants an interview with you. You could be famous . . ."

"I don't want to be famous."

"We don't care if you talk. Just so long as you say the right things," Priest said.

David nodded.

"You have been a valuable asset, truly," Priest offered.

"Have been. Past tense," David noted.

"You know the deal, sheriff," Conover said. "We would allow you to see behind the curtain, to help find the killer. Which you did."

David and Sunny stole a look. Both knew what this meant.

"No more access to the base," David said.

"You get your life back, David," Conover said.

David thought back over the past months. One cousin and two of his oldest friends were dead. One of them a serial killer. Another cousin returned from the grave. The life he'd had before was gone, and there was no bringing it back.

David turned toward the third door, the secret door, behind which they'd hidden the bodies of the victims.

"What about them? Is it over for them, too?"

"What do you mean, sheriff?" Priest asked.

"My cousin. Does he actually get to be buried?"

Priest stared at him and said nothing.

||||

A team in hazmat suits came and took the man—the shell that remained of him—up and out of the creek and into a bag that they zipped snugly over him, so that all was black, and carted it away to somewhere unseen, the body bumping and jostling as the hum of rubber on asphalt sounded beneath.

They unzipped the bag; bright, white artificial light poured across the body, shrouded figures in protective suits moving around, placing it on a table. The air was cold, freezing, not that the body felt it.

There were other bodies around it, those that had died at the man's hand.

Through a glass pane along the wall, Conover and Priest watched, silent. It was done. This chapter, that was. But all about them, the work continued.

They walked down the hallway, a hallway lined with other rooms behind other panes of glass. There were screams ahead, growing louder as they neared. As they came even to his room, they saw him, a young man with his arms shackled, pacing and screaming the same words endlessly.

"It will break. It will break. It will break. It will break."

He rushed to the window, pushing his face against the glass. He was close enough that Priest could see the blackness swirling inside his eyes.

"It will break," he said, watching her.

"Come on," Conover said, leading Priest away.

FORTY-SIX

David's truck rumbled down Main Street in Old Town. Along the far sidewalk, the orange sawhorses still sat, stacked up, from the night of the Crane Dance. He hadn't thought to put them away in the couple weeks that had passed, and Brooke . . .

A blinding pain shot through David, and he gripped the wheel tighter, forcing it away.

Brooke was gone.

Sunny leaned over, pushing her body against his, instinctively knowing he needed her.

They drove past Vic's, past the store, past the bank, where Dale's car sat outside in its usual place.

"What's going on with your uncle?" Sunny asked.

David sighed.

"Every week there's some shit in the newspaper about how terrible I am, a bunch of conspiratorial shit about the murders. Trying to turn the town against me."

"Asshole," she muttered. "If people knew all the shit you've gone through . . ."

She didn't finish the thought. They both knew they could never say any more than the official story about Spady being the serial killer and that he was dead.

The story had been on every channel seemingly nonstop the past days. Charlotte had broken the news and revealed that she'd been attacked, then the other stations picked the story up and ran: the story of a deranged local, attacking the outsiders who'd come to his town. David had turned down the interview requests, and for a few days whenever he came and went, he'd had to scramble past the media trucks that camped out in front of his apartment and at the courthouse.

There were tabloids, too, tracing David and Spady's friendship, claiming some hidden secret: "What Did the Sheriff Know?!"

All of them talked about Spady the same way. A monster. A demon. A psychopath.

But he wasn't any of those things. Not until the spire had infected him.

David steered south, toward the river. Ahead, they saw the single-file line of black robes marching along the sidewalk. As they started to pass the procession, Sunny looked back at the masked tiger faces. There were more of them, maybe a couple of hundred. And they'd begun to go out at all times of the day, instead of only in the morning and evening.

The day of ascension was approaching, they proclaimed. They'd started a website with a countdown clock, ticking the hours until the world's end. Six months. Tourists flew in now just to see them. Stores sold knock-off tiger masks in bulk. No one talked much about Jimmy, though.

David took the two-lane blacktop across the Old River Bridge. He slowed as he approached it.

"This is the famous bridge?" Sunny asked.

She had her window down. The breeze swirled in. Her bangs danced across her forehead.

"Huh?" David asked.

"Skinny-dipping," Sunny clarified.

David smiled sadly.

"Oh, right. Yeah. This is where they left me."

Across the bridge, he followed the bluffs up to the cemetery. A black sedan was already parked there, the driver sitting, waiting. They looked across the stretch of headstones, spotting a figure in a black dress. Charlotte had gone up the hill already.

David took a shovel from the box of his truck, and he and Sunny started up the hill. They joined Charlotte in front of the family plot. Grandma Mariam. David's parents. Jason. David took off his hat and set it on the ground beside his parents' tombstone.

"Well, here's my family," David said to Sunny, as if making introductions.

Charlotte turned toward them and took off her sunglasses. She was crying.

"I had the old stone hauled away," Charlotte said.

Where the grave marker for Benjamin Blunt Jr. had sat, now there was nothing.

"Spady will have a stone. It just wasn't ready in time," she continued.

"What about Brooke?" Sunny asked.

David pointed down the hill.

"Her family has a plot down there. They didn't want her next to him."

No one said anything.

David turned to Charlotte.

"You brought it?"

She nodded as she reached into her purse and pulled out the photo. Jason. David. Ben Junior. Spady. Four boys in the treehouse they'd built, smiling with mischievous innocence.

David took the shovel and stabbed it into the sandy ground. It gave easily, coming up in loose scoops. Within a minute, he'd made a hole a couple of feet deep.

He knelt down, clearing loose dirt with his hands, working methodically, unhurried. Gradually, the hole grew deeper, and each new scoop of soil grew cooler to the touch.

"That should be enough," Charlotte said, finally.

She leaned over beside David and placed the photo in the hole. The four children smiled up at them.

Then David took the shovel and filled the hole.

They stood.

"Do you want to say something?" Charlotte asked.

David stared down.

"Spady told me this story a little back. About the time we built that treehouse, and how he fell out of it, and he landed on this branch. It should've stabbed right through him, but somehow it didn't. He didn't even have a scratch. Not a bruise. I never told him it, but he was the strongest man I ever knew. Life threw everything it had at him, and he took as much as a person ever has before he broke."

David looked off to the side. He could feel the wave of it growing inside, rushing up.

"Spady, you deserved better," he said.

The wave charged up, and David didn't fight it as it crashed. He let himself cry.

He cried for Jason. For Brooke. For Spady. For his parents. For all that he'd lost.

Sunny put a hand on his shoulder, then hugged him tight. He let himself be held. Finally, his eyes ran dry.

They stood there, staring to the north, out across the slow-rolling Platte River, to Little Springs, the jack-o'-lantern water tower and church steeple and grain elevators rising above the treetops, and the gleaming glass spires of New Town jutting up beyond, more going up every day.

And to the west, the giant sprawled, sleeping, refracting the turquoise of the sky, the spire erupting up out of him.

It struck David then that the giant seemed to be holding the spire, containing it, letting no part of it touch the ground, as if the massive being was protecting them still, even in death.

"What are you going to do now?" Charlotte asked.

David realized the question was for him.

He stood a moment, surveying that unimaginable vista, thinking.

Finally, David picked up his hat and placed it back atop his head.

"I have this badge on my chest that says I'm the sheriff," he said. "So, until someone takes it from me, I'm going to go down there and protect my town."

The noon sun beat down. The air around the spire was empty of cranes. They had left in the previous days, there by the thousands, then vanished, moved on to the north, continuing their migration.

David, Sunny, and Charlotte had just started down the hill when a sound stopped them.

A stuttering warble called out from down the river, followed by another: two cranes, flying as one, hugging low to the bluffs as they circled overhead, shadows flickering across the graves, across the three people looking up, watching the birds as their wings clung impossibly to the slight breeze. They pushed on over the water, north, above the city, away, their bodies growing smaller, their tremulous voices fainter, until no sign of them remained.

ACKNOWLEDGMENTS

This book began with a dream, and so I suppose I should thank wherever it is from which dreams emanate. I had many gracious readers of various drafts, and I owe all of them for advice on how to be less bad and encouragement to keep pushing ahead, no matter how foolish it is to think that the world wants—no, *needs*—some of this stuff between my ears. Of those readers, Jean Jensen and Beth Smith were particularly helpful. Any verisimilitude in depicting western Nebraska is thanks to family and friends there. Little Springs is a fiction; my real hometown is Lewellen. My agent, Lucy Cleland, not only shepherded this book to publication but improved it, vastly, with her input. I owe a great debt to the University of Nebraska Press for believing in this book and particularly to Courtney Ochsner for championing it. I thank my sons for giving me faith that a book can make a difference in the world. Lastly, I thank Grandma Doreen, who died years ago yet is omnipresent. She taught me to write and to think, and her dream was for me to achieve my dream, to be an author. Yes, Grandma, I know. You sure as hell aren't content with just one book. Time to get back to writing . . .